VEIL OF DEATH AND SHADOW

ORDER OF REAPERS BOOK ONE

GRAY HOLBORN

Cover Art By: Damoro Design

Edits: Jennifer Murgia and The Blue Couch Edits

ISBN: 978-1-963893-09-0

To "Ralph"
This is the first book I've written without you by my side
I miss you, I miss you, I miss you

PLAYLIST

Please scan for access to the Veil of Death and Shadow Playlist. There are 31 songs for 31 chapters.

CONTENT WARNINGS

This story is a dark fantasy romance and includes the following:

Violence, gore, assault, descriptions of blood and injury, character death, terminally-ill family members, death of a parent, brief mention of a family member's overdose, on-page sex, inebriated sex (alcohol and magical influence), depictions of Anxiety, Depression, PTSD, OCD thought ruminations, suicidal ideation, avoidant attachment, and illness.

Please proceed accordingly and be sure to check in with yourself as you read.

1

MAREENA

SIX YEARS AGO: THE DAY OF THE UNDOING

Death began haunting me long before I took my first breath.

And he's been nothing but enduring ever since.

First, he ripped my father from me when I was nothing more than a bundle of cells nestled deep in my mother's womb. I was told it was a trucking accident, an unexpected snowstorm, that sent him barreling over the curve of a mountain a few hours east of our home.

Then, the day I entered this world, Death took my mother for himself, too.

There'd been others over the years—my mother's sister, who I'd stayed with until just before my first birthday, my father's aunt, who I'd lived with for a decade after that, friends, lovers, neighbors—more than I liked to think about or linger on. Death never let me forget his presence, caging someone else in his dark embrace whenever I got too comfortable, whenever I let my defenses down even a little.

But today, I felt him more acutely than most; his breath trembled deep in my bones, carving anticipation and promise into every twitch of every muscle.

My phone vibrated in my back pocket.

I flinched, then plucked it out and put it to my ear, not even bothering to check the name. I knew who it was. I was late.

"Where are you?" Sora's voice crackled in my ear, deep and whispered, but layered with her barely contained excitement and the soft bustle of a busy room.

I froze, focusing on my surroundings for the first time since I'd left our apartment.

Fuck. Where *was* I?

I'd taken a wrong turn. Several wrong turns, in fact.

This wasn't a totally uncommon occurrence. I often got lost in my thoughts and meandered through the streets, only half paying attention to what I was doing, but this was *particularly* bad timing.

"We said we were getting started at the diner today," she continued, as I quickly searched for an intersection so that I could mentally recalibrate my directions. "Early. You promised. I had a few errands to run this morning, and I *still* somehow beat you here. Frank even agreed to let me spike the coffee. Do you have any idea how much convincing that took? You know he's extra crabby in the morning."

I winced, nodding even though she obviously couldn't see me. "I know, I know. I'm sorry. It's just . . ." I exhaled, relief flooding me as I recognized a burger stop down the road. I wasn't *too* far from where I needed to be at least. "My alarm . . .I was up late and then this morning, I—" I sped up, boosted by the slight chill in the air. This June felt more like a belated January. "Lost track of time. Good work on Frank though, that's impressive. Truly."

Still, as impressive as it was, part of me wished that Frank stood stronger in his resolve. For both of our sakes. If anyone could win a battle of wills with Sora, it was him.

My stomach churned at the thought of starting the party

this early. I had a late shift last night and hadn't been able to turn my brain off until nearly dawn.

Something told me that if I started drinking this early, I wouldn't make it past noon.

Sora was silent for a moment, and I could picture her expression in my head as if she was standing right in front of me, frustration curling into something softer and so much worse—concern.

She sighed. "You mean it's been happening again."

"No," I lied, the word getting half-stuck in my throat, a rock coated in molasses. "Not like before, at least." I winced, pinching the bridge of my nose. "I mean, I have a handle on it."

And I did, more or less.

At the very least, I refused to tell her that I'd spent the last twenty minutes trying to convince myself that the stovetop was off even though I knew damn well that neither of us had cooked something in our stingy apartment in over two weeks.

Or that I'd had a live-action video broadcasting in my mind of Mrs. Odette, our shy, elderly neighbor, being violently burned alive for the last hour.

"We can find someone, another therapist—"

"No."

Therapy helped, but only so much.

It was hard to convince my brain that the intrusive thoughts weren't real.

Not when, occasionally, they were.

A year ago, our apartments *had* in fact burned down because the guy on the floor above us left a paperback on his stove. And while Mrs. Odette was most likely safe and sound in her favorite oversized nightgown right now, a few years ago, my coworker's *real-life* death played out exactly like the version I'd seen churning on repeat in my dreams the whole month leading up to it. He'd choked on an apple, a strange, symbolic visual that had planted a seed of fear in my veins that rooted and bloomed until it actually happened.

No amount of cognitive behavioral therapy or pills could bring him—or the stuff in our old apartment—back.

Superstition? Maybe. Coincidence? Probably. But that lingering "what-if" was far more vicious than any binary explanation could ever be. Death enjoyed his games far too much, and my inability to recognize the difference between one of his bouts and just another Tuesday was one of his cruelest tricks.

"Mars." Her voice was lower now, tender and unguarded—the specific tonal licks she reserved only for me.

She was worried.

Fuck, I didn't want her to be worried. Not today. This was her day as much as mine. Maybe even more. She'd been looking forward to it for weeks.

"With what insurance?" I snorted, ignoring how flat the joke fell, even to my ears.

"We can scrape by. We always do. I can add an extra shift—"

"No," I said, the snap of the word harsher than I'd intended. I took a deep breath, curling the edges of my jacket tight around my chest. The zipper broke last week and I hadn't bothered trying to fix it. "I should be there in twenty minutes," I added, hoping desperately that she'd drop it. Just for today.

"Mars, this is important."

"You know how I get this time of year. My symptoms aren't *back* back. It's just today. It brings stuff up is all."

It wasn't a complete lie. My anxiety had never fully left in the first place; it just sometimes got quieter, my mind bestowing a brief reprieve before splicing my day-to-day activities with visceral scenes of my few-and-far-between loved ones dying. And the compulsions—the checking, the counting, the silent chanting loop I recited in my head—always ramped up to full effect this time of year, like the shifting calendar pages sent a direct signal to my body to get to work fighting me. On everything.

My brain was like a fucked-up Santa Claus—one who only ever brought coal.

You'd never catch me waiting up all night, eager for his arrival.

"Do you want to cancel—"

I shook my head, again, for an audience of no one. "Absolutely not. This is our one day. Anniversary Extraordinaire, remember? We go all out. From dawn until dusk." Though more often than not it ended up being from dawn until dawn the next day. "No matter what's going on in our lives, it all goes on pause for today. Those are the rules. We've written them into the bylaws and everything. Pretty sure I even signed in blood at one point."

She exhaled, long and drawn out, and I could practically see her head tilted against our favorite booth, fingers massaging her temple as she weighed the merits of pushing the discussion further or dropping it. Would I fight her or give in? How far could she push before I shut down altogether? Honestly, she read and understood my moods better than I did. "Mars, we could celebrate tomorrow if you're not into it today. If you want to relax or talk it out?"

She meant it, but that only thickened my resolve.

Today was the most important day of the year.

The day we escaped.

The day we survived.

The day, as Sora dubbed it, my supposed 'curse' was broken.

Today was for Rina and it was for us. We remembered, we forgot, we celebrated. It was the one absolute we lived by. There was no way I was letting my anxiety and baggage break that tradition. Death wasn't allowed to win. Not today.

"No. Just—" I swallowed, scanning the quiet street, stifling my shame from any strangers who might be able to read it—

pluck it from my skin and stare into the bits of myself that I tried like hell not to see, let alone examine. The bits that only Sora seemed able to parse. "Not today. Can we table it? Just until tomorrow. Please?" I felt her warring with herself in the silence. "I promise. Fun today, real talk tomorrow, okay? I won't even fight you on it. If I do, I'll do the dishes for a month without a complaint."

"Liar." There was no malice in the word, just aggressive affection and an eye roll I could sense from over a mile away. Her sigh crackled against my ear, ending in a soft groan that let me know I'd won before any words followed to confirm.

I pinched my eyes tight, waiting for her to give in.

"Twenty minutes? You're farther than our apartment. You got lost again." It wasn't a question, and there was no accusation in her tone. She grunted, then let out a string of curse words, her voice both louder and more distant, like she was holding the phone a few inches back from her face. "Make it ten," she said. "There's a group of feral frat boys here trying to milk their sloppy night out well into the morning. Truly repulsive behavior." Her voice curled with disgust. Never mind that we'd likely be in the same shoes as them twenty-four hours from now. "They don't seem to understand, or care"—her voice grew louder now, her words for them as much as they were for me—"that each cringey attempt to get into my pants is just inching them closer and closer to my fist." I heard a low whistle and Sora groaned. "I can't promise more than ten minutes before I throat punch one of them. Their fates are in your hands. Can you handle that responsibility?"

"Deal." I picked up my pace, knowing that she was only half kidding. Sora was slight and unassuming to the unpracticed observer, a good half-foot shorter than me—absolutely no match for a table of drunk-off-their-ass frat boys—but the girl had a penchant for striking first and asking questions later.

Especially on a day like today, when nostalgia and excitement warred with grief. As cool and calm of a mask as she liked to wear, I knew that today messed with her head too.

Sora's temporary silent frustration was eclipsed by Frank's low rumble threatening to toss the guys out on their asses if they didn't shut up and eat their food.

There was a brief banging sound, like she was clapping her hand on the table, before she added in a half-hushed whisper, "Maybe the old lug doesn't hate me as much as I thought."

"Oh yes, I do." The familiar tenor of his voice trailed over the din and into my ear. "Just hate them more."

I bit back my grin. "I'm hurrying, promise."

"You want your usual? I'll have Frank put the order in now so it's ready when you're here."

"Yeah, usual sounds good."

Sora snorted. Good was perhaps generous.

The over-easy eggs with too-firm yolks and half-frozen hash browns would be tolerable at best. He'd inherited the restaurant from his father, but his father's instinct for cooking apparently wasn't part of the package. Especially not when it came to breakfast foods.

But it didn't matter. We didn't frequent Frank's for the tasty omelets. It was close by, never busy, and, most importantly, cheap as fuck. In Seattle, cheap as fuck was about as rare a find as spotting Sasquatch out in the mountains.

"And Mars?" She sighed, and I could all but see her sinking back into the booth that was more duct-tape and cracked laminate than cushion. "Happy Birthday, my dude."

"Thanks, Sor."

"My girl's finally twenty-one," she said, raising her voice again, this time without threat. The frat boys whooped in the background, followed by a gruff groan that I was certain belonged to Frank. "Hurry up and help me celebrate. This whiskey—" She paused a beat, and I could feel her light buzz melting away any of the lingering tension with its warmth.

"Bourbon?" She chuckled. "I'm going to be so fucking for real, I don't actually know the difference. Whatever it is, it's not going to drink itself."

"Ten minutes." I grinned, ending the call and sliding my phone back into my pocket.

My hurried walk transformed into a light jog, Sora's contagious enthusiasm enough to hush some of my own tension and exhaustion—

Until the breath was pulled from my lungs, and I jolted backward, my arms flailing wildly in an attempt to avoid following the rest of me to the ground.

But a force pulled me back, straightening me before my ass hit the pavement.

I grunted from the whiplash, frozen, as a bus slammed into the crosswalk I should have been standing in.

My heart beat loud and angry in my ears as I processed the close miss.

I tried to take a breath, but my chest still felt tight, my body sizzling with adrenaline. My ears buzzed with the sound of my blood rushing, like I was suddenly acutely aware of every molecule I was composed of.

Close was an understatement. I'd been half a second away from delivering up corpse pancake.

When I looked down, I found a large, pale hand wrapped around my forearm like a vise.

It was, perhaps, strange to describe a hand as beautiful, but that was the immediate thought my just-rescued brain plucked and served up for me to linger on. The fingers were thin and smooth, and I felt their warmth sear my skin through my jacket. The hand's porcelain skin looked soft and velvety, save for the light puckering of veins that appeared unusually dark in comparison.

I glanced up.

The hand was attached to an equally beautiful man.

Messy but stylish silver-white hair, dark brows, pale skin covered in intricate tattoos that snaked up his neck. And the eyes—they were a color I couldn't quite decide on. Dark green, flecks of amber, almost hazel, but unlike any hazel eyes I'd ever seen. If mesmerizing came in a shade, this was it.

Those eyes were also not looking at me but staring down at where the beautiful hand gripped my arm.

Still.

The man's brows were bent in confusion, the corner of his mouth pinched in some expression I couldn't decipher.

I opened my mouth, intending to thank him for the save, but instead loudly barked, "I don't really like being touched."

I felt heat crawl up my neck and bloom across my cheeks.

My brain was so far from being on my side today.

The man blinked a few times, shifting as if he'd just woken from a daydream. With a so-brief-I-might've-imagined-it squeeze, he peeled his perfect fingers away.

"Sorry . . . I . . ." I shook my head, turning to stare at the now very gone bus, feeling absurdly grateful, but still more than a little shocked, that bits of me weren't currently whirring unpleasantly through its wheels like a baseball card in a ten-year-old's bike spokes. A dark, heavy laugh tugged from my throat at the image. "I should be so beyond dead right now. I . . . Thank you."

But when I turned around, I found myself alone.

I scanned the intersection. Tall, tattooed men didn't exactly just blend into their immediate surroundings, impossible to pick out.

Except for this one.

Right.

"Thank you," I yelled, louder this time, hoping the wind might carry my gratitude to wherever he'd disappeared to.

An older man across the street shot me a confused look while he tugged his terrier's leash to hurry away.

"I'm fine," I yelled to him, then again, quietly to myself, "I'm fine."

I took a deep breath, my fingers still shaking with adrenaline and my forearm still tingling with the memory of the man's touch, before I remembered the frat boys and Sora.

The street was quiet and still; the man nowhere in sight.

But for some reason, even as late as I was, I couldn't let it go.

On the left corner, I noticed a small alley carved into a tangle of trees. It was a path that eventually led down to Ravenna Park.

Had he turned down there?

I weighed the possibility. Sora's rule was to never walk through the park alone, but it was daylight and hardly anyone was around.

I turned toward the trees, following the twists and turns. My boots gracelessly snapped twigs and decaying plant matter in my path, until it eventually opened up into a familiar view.

It was a stunning park, and I loved how small I always felt walking down the steep steps to the main loop.

Even with the sun out, the stretch of forest felt dark, the trees tall and twisting in a way that could only be described as enchanting. Down here, it was hard to believe that I was in the middle of a big, bustling city.

A squirrel chittered nearby, winding up a thick trunk, its tiny claws scratching into the bark.

A loud caw reverberated through the air, punctuated by the response of another crow and the soft whir of the creek.

Other than the furry and feathered creatures, it appeared like I was completely alone. The man's silvery hair should be easy enough to pick out of the dark foliage if he'd come through here.

I wasn't sure why I was so intent on finding him, on making him hear and accept my thanks. He'd obviously been in a rush, had thought nothing of it. As if casually saving a stranger was just par for the course.

But it was a big deal.

Not just because I was, you know, alive, but because it was *today*, and I was alive.

Today was my birthday, but it was also the anniversary of my mother's death.

And Amto Amani's.

And Rina's.

And, as of six years ago, it was also the anniversary of the one and only time I'd ever intentionally taken someone's life.

The same day Sora and I escaped to our freedom.

We'd been celebrating a birthday I'd otherwise tried to forget ever since. Her rule, not mine. She'd dubbed six years ago the official breaking of my curse—Anniversary Extraordinaire. Not that she'd ever really believed that I was cursed in the first place.

Her theory was that my fixation with death was just a manifestation of unprocessed trauma and bad luck. It was a theory my old therapist shared as well, and one I tried desperately to believe.

"Their deaths were a coincidence, Mars. They had nothing to do with you. Curses and bad omens aren't real."

Never mind that everyone I'd ever let myself get close to—except for Sora—had kicked the bucket.

But, more or less, she was kind of right.

Not because people I knew stopped dying.

I couldn't seem to get away from death—not entirely.

We were all susceptible to his call, eventually, weren't we?

But no one particularly close to us had died on my birthday since we'd escaped. As absurd as it might have seemed, I clung to that truth with every fiber of my being. A truth that Sora spent the other three-hundred-sixty-four days of the year drilling into me.

This was the one day I let myself think that she was right.

My brain believed things far wilder than broken curses after all, there was no reason I couldn't force it into believing this reality as well.

And, well, I wasn't currently roadkill, so maybe there was something to her half-baked theory.

"Right," I whispered to myself, tugging the collar of my jacket close against my jaw. A dark chill carved along my neck, striking down to my feet.

As beautiful as it was, there was something unsettling about being down here alone, like I was in another world altogether. Sunlight crept through the foliage in iridescent stripes, highlighting dust and particles in the air until they looked almost like fairy dust. The air tasted unusual—metallic and briny—and pulsed with a strange static that had the hair on my arms lifting with anticipation.

And then time seemed to stop.

My fingers grew stiff, my vision slightly blurry, and I felt the familiar current run through my body that preceded most panic attacks. The energy coursing through me was at odds with the general peace of the park—like my body was having a deferred reaction to the bus that nearly ran me over.

I closed my eyes and took a deep breath, waiting for my still-racing heart to realize I was fine and regulate itself back to a normal beat.

"Ground yourself, Mars."

Sora's frequent words echoed through my mind, as if she was here. Normally, I'd roll my eyes and ignore them. But now, I latched on to them as if they were the final thin ledge keeping me from toppling over the cliff.

Pressing the pad of my right thumb against the cool metal of my ring, I focused on the light, minty taste of toothpaste lining my tongue, on the soft, musical bird calls floating around me.

After a few minutes, it worked. My body regulated its way back to functionality.

I gripped my arm, placing my fingers over where the man had held on to me, forcing myself to unbraid the strange feeling that his touch had rooted. I'd never seen him before; there was really no reason for me to be so shaken by the encounter.

It was probably just emotional transfer and gratitude from the rescue.

He didn't just stand there and watch me die.

The bar for men was truly on the ground.

I shook my head. I didn't have time for this.

Frank's.

I was late. Thanks to this distraction, I was definitely way past my ten-minute promise to Sora.

Opening my eyes, I turned back toward the path.

Before I broke out into a run—effectively undoing the whole calm-heart-thing—I froze.

A few feet away, half-hidden next to a pile of leaves, was a small, black, furry lump.

One that had just risen and deflated, as if taking a breath.

I squinted, trying to focus on it as I crept closer.

Not a lump.

A crow.

I crouched down, my fingers hovering a few inches away from the small head, unsure of what to do.

I waited, staring at the bird's chest, hoping for it to take another puff of air.

The feathers of its right wing were ruffled, the appendage bent at a strange angle as if it had recently been injured.

Its eyes were closed, beak scarred and slightly parted so that it looked like it was simply trapped in a peaceful dream.

But I knew it was a dream that it wouldn't wake from again.

The poor little guy was dead.

My chest tightened at the realization, and I fell back on my ass until I was sitting next to the unfortunate thing.

So, Death *had* reared his ugly head again, after all—just when I thought I'd pulled one over on him.

"I'm sorry," I whispered to the bird, feeling only slightly ridiculous. "This—this is probably my fault. Somehow."

The limits of my curse were a little unclear, but something told me the crow got caught in the crosshairs.

I cleared some of the debris away from its body, a sorry attempt at making its resting place a bit nicer, more intentional.

Was this the cost of sparing my own life today?

Would this bird have died if I hadn't followed the strange pull that led me into the park?

It felt wrong to simply leave it here—not when I'd watched it take its last breath, the final witness to its existence.

While I'd grown accustomed to Death's haunting, I was never sure how to handle the aftermath.

It didn't make sense, and hardly seemed fair, that this bird was alive one second ago and now it was just gone—empty—with no one here to properly mourn it. To say goodbye.

I searched around, looking for something, though I wasn't sure what.

I fiddled unconsciously with the silver beads of my ring. I paused, warring with myself for a moment before I tugged it off.

"Crows like shiny things, don't they?" My voice was loud and rough, at odds with the quiet solitude of the woods. I was suddenly hyper aware of the fact that I was an interloper here.

I set the ring on the bird's chest, feeling suddenly absurd and ridiculous.

It was one of those cheap fidget rings. I found it in a resale shop last week.

I wore a much nicer one on my other hand. Someone had given it to me awhile back—an attempt to keep me from picking at my nails and fingers. Now, I felt naked whenever I left the house without it.

It didn't cure my anxiety or anything, but it did give it something to *do*, and sometimes that was all I needed to push through the particularly restless moments.

I didn't have a sentimental attachment to this new one. In fact, I'd half gotten it as a sorry attempt to divorce myself from the sentimentality of the other one. It hadn't worked. I still couldn't leave the house without the original ring.

This one though, I could leave behind with the crow—a final offering of sorts.

With a hesitant finger, I pet the smooth feathers along the crow's neck, marveling at the range of colors reflected against them—black, teal, and blue, like an oil slick. "Rest easy, little gu—"

There was a loud, resounding crack that reverberated through my skull as if it had originated there.

The world went sharp and then hazy, until my vision blurred away altogether.

What felt like a hook curled beneath my ribs, ripping and pulling something from me as a scream pierced the woods.

The sharp, broken sound echoed around me, until I realized it was coming from my throat.

All air rushed from my lungs, and I was jerked up and away from where I'd been seated, the fresh pricks of twigs and thorns scraping against my arms and cheeks wherever I landed.

Pain lacerated through me as I choked on something thick and liquid, tasting of metal.

I couldn't breathe, couldn't speak, couldn't move.

Couldn't even see a goddamn thing.

Panicking, I mentally thrashed at whatever strange power held me in its grasp.

In the emptiness, my mind conjured up images of a man with ink-black hair that curled over amber eyes. It had been eleven years since I'd last seen him in person, but his features were tattooed behind my eyelids with crystal clarity, an ever-enduring promise that we'd meet again.

Death.

He was here.

It was finally time.

Liquid fire coursed through my veins as I suffocated on my own blood. I fought desperately against him, spitting and cursing at the cruel fate that had already stolen so much from me.

It was a futile fight; the strain did nothing but drain me faster.

I didn't care. I fought harder.

Death was relentless, but so was I.

Rage boiled and gurgled in my blood, as I struggled inside a body that disobeyed every order I gave it—until, all at once, everything went silent.

2

MAREENA

SIX YEARS AGO (THE AFTERMATH OF THE UNDOING)

Something hard, dry, and small rained down on my face. With a grunt, I opened my eyes, blinking as I slowly adjusted to the light.

I shifted slightly and winced.

A thin, angry red line appeared on the back of my hand. I pulled the small thorn from where it was embedded in my skin, then flinched when a twig bounced off my forehead.

"What the hell?" I shifted again, trying to better position myself.

I was sitting in a bush, it seemed, only I couldn't exactly recall how I'd gotten here.

I was vaguely aware of a small thud, before an ache bloomed on top of my head.

Sitting in my lap, looking inconspicuous and not at all like it was trying to murder me, was a small, shiny stone.

I glanced up just in time to duck away as another pebble came spiraling toward me.

A crow swooped into sight, its beak stuffed with a small bundle of twigs and rocks.

With a loud caw, the bird opened its mouth, dropping the mess unceremoniously onto my head.

"Ow, what the fuck?" I shifted, ignoring the soft tearing sound as another thorn scraped and tugged at my jacket, the bush reluctant to release me from its grip.

I stood too quickly though and had to grab on to the closest tree as my body fought to bring me back down to a lower center of gravity.

I'd passed out and apparently woken up inside a fucking murder forest.

My head rang and ached with an unrelenting pressure I'd never experienced before.

A wad of grass sprinkled down around me, like I was stuck in a fucked-up snow globe.

A quick glance revealed the culprit—the crow was back, its beak half-full of foliage that it casually peppered over me.

"Stop being a fucking menace." I groaned, dodging his talons when he swooped down low.

What was I doing here? How had I even gotten here in the first place?

My memory was watery and murky, disappearing into a distorted pool each time I tried to grab hold.

I reached for my phone out of habit but found only the black screen of judgment—and my own withered expression—staring back at me.

No charge. Great.

There was a soft whir that grew louder, and I jumped when the crow hopped on my shoulder, its wings flapping chaotically as they tangled in my hair.

I let out an embarrassing squeal and then froze as its beak poked awkwardly through the thick, knotted strands of my hair, not entirely sure what to do.

I tried swatting him away, but that seemed to only further piss him off, burying him deeper into my hair, his beak scratching at the base of my skull with the promise of vengeance.

"Um," I said, straining my neck as I tried to lean away from it. "Nice bird." I cleared my throat, my mouth suddenly impossibly dry at the possibility that this little shit might try giving me a lobotomy at any second. "Please don't eat me. I'm sorry I called you a menace. I'm sure as far as crows go, you're actually very lovely."

The bird tugged, and I winced, preparing for the worst, but he merely pulled out a stray twig and spat it on the ground.

Was this violent little fucker *grooming* me?

My body relaxed slightly, as he found a few more bits of foliage and removed them.

I shrugged awkwardly, hoping that might encourage him to fly away, but he only seemed to plant his feet more firmly, cawing loudly in my ear as if in rebuke.

Right. Totally normal.

I didn't at all feel like some discount fairytale's new gothic princess.

I glanced around, half-expecting someone to jump out of the trees and claim their rabid bird.

As if reading my mind, the bird sprang from my shoulder, its flight path to the ground a little rough and rocky.

Slowly, I took a few steps back, hands held up in surrender. "Good bird. You stay here. I'll get out of your hair"—I grimaced—"er, feathers, I mean."

A twig cracked beneath my boot, and the crow whirled around, something shining in its beak as it squawked again.

Without another warning, it rushed forward in the air, heading straight toward my face—murder gleaming in its beady little eyes.

I spun around, my arms shielding my head, and ran down the path, not looking back until I reached the staircase that led up to the street.

I took the uneven stairs two at a time, tripping a few times. I didn't slow down though, ignoring my pounding headache and the stitch in my side, squinting against the sun as the park opened into the familiar neighborhood.

There was a strange stillness; not a person or car in sight, despite this usually being a heavily trafficked area during the day.

A quick glance behind me proved to be crow free, so I relaxed a little.

Wincing slightly, I peeled off my jacket. Every inch of my body pulsed and ached, like I'd been hit by a truck. I was also in serious need of a glass of water. My mouth felt like it was lined with sandpaper.

Something bounced off my head before dropping to the cement at my feet with a soft, metallic clang.

A ring.

I picked it up, the pad of my finger rolling over the familiar, spinning beads.

My ring.

I slid it on and stood up, before my brain had the wherewithal to process where it had come from.

When I glanced back, I found the satanic crow. It was a few inches away from my feet, standing inconspicuously on the sidewalk as if it hadn't just tried to kill me, its head cocked to the side so one of its eyes could more directly lock on mine.

My thumb slid over the ring, and my memories started to stitch themselves back together.

Anniversary Extraordinaire.

Almost roadkill.

Mysterious man with the pretty hand.

Dead crow—

Taking a deep breath, I glanced down at my feathered friend.

Not so dead.

Was it the crow's friend? Or its mate? Do crows have mates? Or just murders?

Seattle was filled with crows, but as I mentally sorted through everything I knew about the species, it turned out the answer was, embarrassingly, very little.

I ran back down the stairs, back through the forest, until I found the spot of disheveled dirt and foliage where I'd watched the crow take its last breath.

Intuitively, I knew what I'd find but, logically, I couldn't bring myself to believe it.

The patch of dirt was, well, just that—dirt. No dead crow in sight.

I turned around at the sound of soft rustling, to find the stalker crow hopping around awkwardly behind me, keeping more distance than he had before, as if he could sense my impending breakdown.

He was also very much alive.

Maybe he'd taken his friend somewhere?

Or, well, this was a forest. Home to all sorts of critters. Maybe some hungry crow-predator came and grabbed the corpse for a free, low-effort snack.

I shivered, sending a mental thanks that no coyotes had decided to pick at my flesh while I was passed out.

The crow ruffled its feathers, and I noticed that several of them stood out awkwardly on its right wing—like the wing was injured, maybe even broken.

My stomach lurched as I stared at him.

"It *is* you." My tongue was rough and dry as I tried to find the words. "So you didn't die."

The crow just stared at me, still and silent—and with the judgmental air of a cat.

Right.

Not dead. Just playing dead.

A crow who played opossum. I nodded, satisfied. I could live with that reality.

It didn't matter that I'd been truly certain that I had, in fact, watched it die—that I'd witnessed the light fade from its glassy dark eyes.

I was knocked out, maybe I remembered things incorrectly.

The bird let out another caw before awkwardly zooming into the air, clearly bored with my processing speed. Its flight pattern was rough and stilted as it tried to gain air. With no more warning than that, it landed on my right shoulder again, settling down into the crook of my neck as if the spot had been specifically designed as a place for him to rest.

Tentatively, I reached my left hand up and stroked the top of his head.

He nestled gently into my fingers, before burrowing down against my neck and going quite still, as if that was all there was to be said.

"Okay," I sighed. "I guess you're coming with me." I shifted so that I could get a look at him. "But only until we get your wing healed up." I sighed, my chest loosening up a bit, now that I was fairly certain the bird wasn't, in fact, trying to kill me. At least Sora will be happy. She loves animals. Once I convinced myself that I was being stalked by Death, I'd made a very conscious decision to never have a pet. A person could only process so much grief in one lifetime. "No getting comfortable though, understand? You're a wild animal and wild animals belong in the wild." Sora might cave, but I sure as hell wouldn't. "Once your wing is healed, you're back on your—"

The words dissolved on my tongue.

Fuck.

Sora.

Anniversary Extraordinaire.

I was so incredibly late.

My phone was dead.

And I was talking to a fucking zombie crow.

Whispering a quick "Hang on," I took off through the park, my pace uneven and tense at first, as I tried to adjust to the feel of a bird on my shoulder without knocking him off, but evening out by the time I finally got to Frank's.

I burst through the door, my hands on my knees, as I bent over, panting. Running was very much *not* my thing. "I know, I know, I'm late. I'm sorry, I can explain. Sort of. Seriously, you won't bel—"

My gaze shot to our usual booth. It was empty. I glanced around. The entire place was empty actually, the usual bustle of the small diner absent altogether.

The too-bright light above me flickered a few times, illuminating the strangeness of the quiet scene.

How long had I been out for? It couldn't have been *that* long, could it? It was still light out.

Frank's was open every day, from dawn until well after the night rush. The man hardly slept or took a break.

In fact, we usually ended most of our late nights here, ready for a mediocre but greasy cure for whatever future hangover we had brewing. The place wasn't exactly a tourist hotbed, but it was never *this* empty.

"Frank?" I called out, reaching around the counter where I knew he kept a few stray phone chargers. "You here? How long ago did Sora leave?"

I plugged my phone in, but the light illuminating the diner flickered and then went out altogether.

A quick glance at my phone told me the charger wasn't working either.

Maybe there was some electrical issue? Power outage? Did he forget to pay the power company?

Hard to picture Frank closing the diner down even for that.

A door creaked, followed by the familiar hammering beat

of Frank's steps as he rushed down the stairs that led up to his apartment.

He wasn't wearing his usual greasy apron, and when his face emerged below the dip of the staircase, his dark eyes were blown wide, like he'd just seen a ghost. His dark brown complexion was washed of its usual glow, and the soft wrinkles in his forehead turned into trenches as he took me in.

"Mareena?" His body deflated with relief, his grip loosening on a baseball bat that hung limp at his side. "Thank god. Where the hell have you been?"

I eyed the weapon. "Woah now, no need for that," I said, my tone half teasing, half not. "You okay, Frank?" I nodded around the small dining room. "Where is everybody? You try a new recipe again? You know what we've told you about experimenting." I grinned awkwardly. "Don't."

His last attempt at a menu upgrade had included an unidentifiable monstrosity composed, in part, of pickles and peanut butter. A truly egregious combination that I doubted even a pregnant person with unusual cravings would want. Most of his regulars, Sora and I included, had avoided the place for a week in protest.

I thought we'd successfully convinced him to stick with run-of-the-mill sandwiches, salads, and food that could just be tossed into the fryer after that.

His thick salt-and-pepper brows met as he studied me, like he was assessing every inch for injuries. "Where've you been, Mareena? Sora's been looking for you." He shook his head, studying me. "For days."

I opened my mouth to say something, then shut it again. What did he mean *for days*?

"That roommate of yours has been hopping back and forth between this diner and your apartment for three days now, despite the very clear orders to stay inside."

"Three days?" My stomach growled, as if it had just caught

up to the fact that it was, in fact, deeply aware of exactly how many days it had been since I'd last fed it anything. "What orders?"

Frank sighed and ran his hand through his thin hair, scratching lightly at the top, which was just shiny brown scalp. He leaned the baseball bat against the stairwell and walked behind the counter. He grabbed a glass, filled it with water, and set it down, nodding toward the stool across from him.

I sat, my body feeling suddenly exhausted. I held the first sip of water in my mouth for a minute, savoring the cool feeling as it washed over my tongue. Then I finished the rest of the glass in one impatient chug.

He grabbed a bag of bread, a jar of peanut butter, some of those mini plastic jam containers he served with toast in the mornings, and got to work.

"I'd cook you something properly, but the electricity has been faulty since the outage, and I don't trust it right now." He grunted, then nodded at me without looking up from his work. "What's with the bird?"

I stiffened. I'd all but forgotten about the crow that had hitched a ride. "Long story. What's going on?"

He chuckled, but there was no humor to the sound. "Long story."

He slid a plate with the sandwich toward me and grabbed a banana from an overripe bunch on the counter. "Eat this, too. You look like shit."

"I woke up in a bush," I shot back, shoving the sandwich into my mouth, offering some of the crumbs to the crow as an afterthought.

He took a few, only half interested, before Frank opened the small, almost-empty jar of dog treats he kept for the local pups on the counter. Frank may have generally pretended to hate his customers, but he also genuinely loved his customers' dogs. A true Seattleite if ever there was one.

"Break these up and give the pieces to him. Heard crows like dog food."

I did as he said, setting the shattered biscuit chunks on the counter.

The crow wriggled free from my shoulder and hopped onto the counter, his claws clacking tentatively as he walked. He jabbed one of the larger crumbs with his beak a few times, hesitant and curious, before eagerly devouring the crumbled-up treat.

Frank's mouth curved into a half grin as he shook his head. "Crows are fucking menaces—constantly messing up my trash out back. Can't believe I'm allowing one on my counter."

"Trust me, I know." I finished my sandwich, both of us watching the strange bird as he tapped at the treat jar, demanding more. "You said he—how do you know it's a dude?"

Though now that I thought about it, I'd been unconsciously referring to him as a he, too.

He shrugged. "Don't. But he's pretty big, and the boys are usually a bit larger than the gals."

I nodded, moving on to the banana and the glass of water Frank had already refilled twice for me. That was a good enough explanation for me.

"So, three days," I said after my stomach and throat were no longer screaming at me.

The crow was making a dramatic affair of filling its beak with water from a small bowl Frank pushed toward him and tilted his head back awkwardly to swallow.

"Oh thank god, you're fucking here."

I grunted as a familiar soft, floral scent washed over me.

Sora squeezed me so tight that I dropped my partially devoured banana and fought to take a breath. "You didn't bother to come let me know you'd found her? Where the hell was she?"

"She just wandered in here with a bird and her hair full of

twigs, like some feral child of the forest not five minutes ago." Frank's expression dipped into a defensive scowl. "She needed a meal. I fed her. What more do you want from me? I own a diner, not an investigative business."

"I'm okay." I ducked out of Sora's arms and turned toward her. "Really, I'm okay. I think." I studied her and frowned. Her usually bright, teasing expression was nowhere in sight. Instead, there were dark circles under her black eyes and a grayish hue to her pale skin—which had, somehow, grown even paler. Her bloodshot eyes welled with tears, and she didn't even fight the two that escaped down her cheek. I pulled her to me again in a tight hug, applying pressure to her chest like she did for me whenever I felt overwhelmed or on the verge of a panic attack. "Are you?"

She sucked in a ragged breath, sinking her weight against me. "Where the hell have you been, Mars?" Her voice was low, raspy, and I could tell she was fighting back more tears. "You just disappear? For three days? And then you show up here?" She pulled back a few inches and gestured absently behind the counter, her button nose scrunched in disgust. "To see *him* before even bothering to let me know you're alive. I thought you were dead. For three days. Do you have any idea what that's like? With everything going on right now? Do you know what I've been through? Imagining the absolute worst?"

I did know what that was like, actually. My brain provided me with a constant film reel of the worst things I could think of happening to the people in my life. The realization that I'd put her through something like that—even unintentionally—made me want to throw up.

Frank raised his brows, eyes wide, and stepped around the counter. "I'll, er, leave you two girls to it. It's been a day, and I could use a nap. Stay as long as you need." He started toward the stairs, then stopped, removing the lid from the treat jar, before tossing Sora the bat, which she caught effortlessly. "And take that with you when you go, can't be too safe on the streets right now. You're not even supposed to be on them at all. Not that I'm surprised it's you two breaking the rules." He muttered the last sentence more to himself than to us.

The streets? He sounded like a character in a bad eighties B-movie. We were in a pretty safe part of the city, all things considered. There was hardly ever anything more concerning than a few break-ins, and those were almost always nonviolent —just people desperately in need of food and shelter in a city that made both increasingly difficult to access.

What the hell did I miss?

Sora snorted. "Like you haven't also been out on the streets looking for her," she shot back, her dark brow arched in challenge.

Sora was a thin Japanese woman, whose head reached just below my shoulders—in heels. Her smile was sweet, her eyes often shining and kind. But those who knew her, knew her size and soft features were misleading. There was a hidden edge in that smile that flared to a smirk, a dark promise, whenever provoked. She had a face gentle enough to draw somebody in, but a tongue sharp enough to flay. And she was one of the few regulars brave enough to regularly challenge Frank—and charming enough to still be allowed to eat in his restaurant.

Of course, Frank always pretended to find her sometimes abrasive personality obnoxious and annoying, but I could often read through his gruff groans and flared nostrils. She amused him, and he maybe even respected her for not taking any of his shit. Some days, I was convinced that she was actually his favorite customer.

Other than the neighborhood dogs.

With a final grunt and nod in my direction, he climbed back up to his small oasis, the sound of his steps and the creaky wooden door an ominous soundtrack to Sora's lingering anger.

"Dude, where the hell have you been?" She nudged my shoulder, pulling my attention back to her.

Now that the wave of relief had dispersed, I could fully see what a wreck she was.

She was a hairstylist in an edgy studio downtown and her jet-black hair with bright-purple highlights was typically worn in pristine waves that looked like they were pulled straight out of a magazine.

Right now, her hair was a chaotic furl of knots with greasy roots, and there were a few spare brow hairs growing below the always perfectly-plucked arches.

Sora was the kind of girl who wielded her style like a sword: perfect hair, perfect makeup, perfect skin. She took care to mold herself into whichever mask she felt like wearing that day, her precision and skill both a weapon and armor she donned with meticulous attention.

Today, her defenses were down.

My stomach dipped. What the hell had I missed? I hadn't seen her this off-balance in years.

"I'm sorry," I said again. "I literally just woke up in Ravenna Park. Had no idea how long I'd been out until I got here."

"Why were you in Ravenna Park by yourself?" She fell back on the stool next to me and sighed, catching her chin in her hand. "I didn't even think to thoroughly check down there, it's nowhere near the route between here and the apartment. Think I did a quick scan at one point, but I didn't see you. Didn't see anyone."

"I was sort of tucked inside of a bush." I shrugged. "Would've been hard to spot."

She nodded to the crow, his head now shamelessly buried deep inside the jar of treats. "And the bird?"

I studied him, still trying to wrap my head around the strange circumstances of his resurrection.

"Last thing I remember before passing out was touching

him. He was—" I bit my lip, considering. "Well, he was dead. Or I thought he was dead, anyway."

"Your first instinct when encountering a dead bird is to touch it?" she deadpanned. "You get that that's weird behavior, right?"

"I don't know what came over me." I shook my head, gesturing to him as he obnoxiously devoured the crumbs. "Anyway, he's obviously not dead, but I gave him a ring and now he insists on following me around. Sort of absurd, I know."

"Generally, yes, but today, not really." She studied me, her eyes darting between me and the crow. "Or at least, a zombie crow coming back from the dead to stalk you isn't the most absurd thing to happen this week."

"What do you mean?" I snorted. "What the hell beats a crombie?"

She sighed, her expression flattening into something more serious. Something that looked almost like fear. It was just a flash, then gone.

Sora had long mastered the ability to mask anything resembling vulnerability, no matter how disheveled she might look. Where we came from, vulnerability would be used against you. "Something big happened, the day you stood me up."

"I did not stand you up," I argued. "Not my fault I was knocked out."

She shrugged, the corner of her lips tugging into a smirk. "Impact over intent."

I shot her a look, silently demanding something less vague. Jokes aside, fear gathered tight and coiled in the base of my spine, waiting for the shoe to drop.

"I don't know, Mars. I don't want to say you slept through the apocalypse, but I think you sort of did." She ran a hand through her hair, her fingers picking through some of the knots as she fought to find words. "Or maybe not the apocalypse, but some kind of war or attack or . . . something. Something big.

Movie-franchise-finale kind of big. The news stations haven't exactly been providing much information, and the government —as usual—isn't really offering any insight or clarity into the matter. And the little bits of information I've been able to track down seem to contradict each other. They've put shelter-in-place orders out, told people to hunker down and wait, but they're not saying much. Honestly, it feels almost like *they* don't even know what's going on."

The lights flickered again, the hiccupping shadows adding more weight to her words.

She glanced up at the light fixture above us, the shadows it cast dancing ominously over her features. "That's been happening a lot. Electricity everywhere has been fucked. An electromagnetic pulse or something, maybe. I don't know. People are reporting some weird things."

"Weird things like what?"

She didn't speak for a long moment, and I got the sense that she was dreading having to put words to whatever she was about to say, like that might make it more real—like once it was said, it couldn't be unsaid.

After a deep, slow inhale, the words tumbled out of her, as if of their own accord, all in one breath. "At first, I thought maybe it was just some electrical storm or maybe a weird data breach. Like a nerdy anarchist group trying to take out Big Tech, you know? Cell service has been absolute shit, too, completely unreliable. So, I guess I'm not actually mad Frank didn't call. It probably wouldn't have even gone through. Lord knows I've probably rung your number a thousand times in the last twenty-four hours alone. People have been complaining about cars randomly not starting, or sometimes even driving them-selves—like there's some kind of weird power surge going on or something. I don't even know if power surge is the right term for it, to be honest."

She paused; her breath shaky as she absently peeled at the

edge of the counter where the worn plastic overlay was starting to curl. "But then, even stranger shit started to happen. Things no simple power surge or cyber-attack could explain." She bit her lip, then glanced at me, uncharacteristically hesitant as she searched for her next words, these ones pouring out more like molasses than sand. "I've looked on a few message boards during the brief glimpses of internet I've been able to access— and people are reporting some seriously fucked up shit, Mars. Unexplainable shit. I didn't believe it at first, until I saw some of it firsthand."

"Sora, specifics. It's okay, I'll believe you, whatever it is. Just spill, okay? What did you see?" I held my breath as I waited for her to spell it out, my skin tingling like it sensed what was coming before I did.

"This is going to sound like I'm fucking with you, but I swear that I'm not." She pressed her lips together into a tight line, like she was trying to swallow back the words, until they refused to be restrained a moment longer. "I saw a man trans-form yesterday, right in the middle of the street."

"Transform?"

"One minute, he was your average Seattle hipster twenty-something, then his bones started cracking." She glanced at me, her voice quiet and flat. "Mars, he turned into a wolf. Literally."

Silence engulfed us, broken only by the crow's beak as it clacked against the now-empty glass jar.

"You saw a werewolf. Cute." I grinned, expecting her to break into a laugh.

She didn't.

"I'm not fucking with you." There was a raw edge to her voice now, and I felt her desperate plea for me to believe her.

Whatever happened, she believed it. She actually believed she saw a werewolf.

I knew how powerful that kind of conviction in something

could be, especially when you were alone in that truth—sometimes it was more real than anything else.

Intentionally or not, I'd left her alone in that belief, in that fear. For days.

"And that's not all," she continued, the tension in her shoulders easing slightly when I didn't challenge or laugh at her. "People are reporting all kinds of things—supernatural things. Buildings randomly expelling people, folks suddenly appearing and disappearing into thin air, like a damn fantasy portal has swallowed them up and spit them out or something —or like they're some sort of video game spawn. I don't know, it's—" She exhaled through her teeth, and I felt her fear sharpen in that breath. "I know it sounds like I'm on a bad acid trip or something. Trust me, I wish I was, but I'm not. You know me. I've never believed in this kind of shit. I'm usually the one trying to convince *you* that curses and whatnot aren't real, you know? But I'm telling you, either something supernatural is happening, or the whole world's on one powerful-ass acid trip with me. I mean"—she waved her hand frantically between us —"hello, you passed out for three days in a forest, right? What happened to you? You just woke up and that's it? And now you have a zombie bird stalking you? That's extremely weird and not normal, Mars. Something seriously fucked up is going on."

I nodded; my throat suddenly dry again.

She wasn't wrong.

"Look," she said, "all I'm saying is you're not the only one experiencing weird, unexplainable shit. Objectively weird is unfolding everywhere, and no one is giving us any answers."

I grabbed her hand and squeezed it. "I'm sorry."

She stared at our hands, brows furrowed. It was rare for me to be physically affectionate. To initiate touch. Her eyes met mine, dark and shining. "Why are you sorry? I'm not saying any of this is your fault."

"I'm sorry I wasn't there with you. That you've been

processing whatever's going on without me. This sounds"—I shook my head—"fucking terrifying, and I'm sorry you were alone with it."

Her chin dimpled as she swallowed, fighting to keep back tears. With a nod, she squeezed my hand back. "Me too, but I'm glad you're here now."

She dropped her head against my shoulder, resting there as I let everything she said wash over me.

There had to be some kind of explanation for all of this.

The world didn't just go from the real to the unexplainable in one day, did it?

My stomach sank as another reality grew heavy and unavoidable.

Sora was right.

I'd spent my life believing, in part, that I was either cursed or haunted by Death.

On some level, I'd always known that was impossible, ridiculous, even—no matter how real and concrete it often felt.

But if the impossible was suddenly possible, what did that say about my theoretical curse?

I wrapped an arm around Sora's waist, tugging her closer to me, convincing myself that she was real, that she was here, that she was alive. At the end of the day, that was all I needed.

Curse or not, she hadn't been taken from me, and whatever new possibilities this new world opened, I'd fight like hell to make sure she never was.

"Let's go home," I said.

She nodded.

I set my hand out on the counter and waited until the crow climbed up my shoulder.

No idea why I thought he'd understand or respond to the gesture, but he did, quickly nestling himself into the crook of my neck.

The walk back to our apartment was quiet.

We took our usual route, which I was grateful for. I had no desire for detours right now. I wanted whatever semblance of normalcy was left.

The streets were mostly empty, and now that I wasn't frantically running toward Frank's, I noticed things that I hadn't on the way over.

Like the fact that the traffic lights weren't working, or at least not the way that they usually did. Some were completely off, but others shifted through patterns I'd never seen before. Instead of the usual green, yellow, and red, I watched them blink from pink to purple to blue.

A driverless car roamed right by us, missing Sora by only a few inches.

Another car was parked through what looked like someone's otherwise pristine living room.

Most of the houses had their blinds pulled closed, like people were doing their best to keep whatever strangeness had been unleashed on the world out, to shelter in normalcy for as long as they could. Occasionally, I'd see a face poking between crooked blinds, but mostly the typically busy street was a ghost town, except for me and Sora.

And the crow.

I had no idea what to do with him, but I caught Sora's gaze darting to him every minute or so.

Feeling weirdly exposed and vulnerable out here, I tugged my jacket tight around my body. There was a heaviness in the air that made it difficult to fully fill my lungs, and my skin tingled with an electric energy—the awareness of eyes on us that I couldn't see, like an itch I couldn't scratch.

When we got to our block, the bird ruffled his feathers and started shifting with unease.

Sora, catching on a second sooner than I did, reached her arm in front of me, stopping me from rounding the corner.

I froze, the three of us peering awkwardly around the bricked corner store. I started most mornings with a bagel and cup of coffee that Erin, the middle-aged owner, kept on the burner for too long. A quick glance inside and all I saw was a dark, empty store. Like Frank, she'd skipped work today, likely hunkering down in her home up north with her husband and two cats.

I looked around the corner and swallowed back a curse. There were three men I'd never seen before—not in and of itself a strange thing, but there was something odd about them.

Sora's eyes met mine, wide and questioning, both of us too terrified to speak or move.

The air itself was suffocating, like it was drunk on electricity, hungry for power. For blood.

I focused on the tallest of the three men. He looked like your typical tech bro at first glance—white, lean, and dressed in casual clothes—but it was his white shirt that I couldn't peel my eyes away from. It was covered in something dark, something that trailed from his chin and—I did a double take, blinking as if my eyes were simply out of focus, conjuring things up from my imagination—fangs.

The man standing next to him was shorter, but his body was stocky and firm, like he'd been sculpted from muscle and nothing else. Where the other stood casually, expression unreadable, this one's face was contorted in rage, his eyes—an unusual golden-yellow color—were locked on the man covered in what looked suspiciously like blood.

The third man was the most peculiar of the set. He watched the other two with an unreadable, almost bored expression, but I only spared him a passing glance at first.

I couldn't pull my focus from the yellow-eyed one for long, every molecule in my body suddenly acutely attuned to him with an awareness that was almost dizzying.

The other two might as well have not even been there.

My gut churned with an impending sense of doom.

Something was wrong.

I could feel the man standing at a precipice, though I couldn't explain how I knew that or where that precipice would lead once he fell over. But I knew that he would fall, with undeniable certainty.

Without warning, his neck bent back, his strange eyes almost aglow. A loud series of cracks and pops echoed through the otherwise quiet street.

His bones. They were breaking as his body twisted and contorted.

"What the—"

Sora clasped her hand around my mouth and tugged me back behind the building so that we were out of sight. Her fingers trembled against my cheek.

She didn't speak, but her eyes were wide, nostrils flaring, the warning etched across her expression clear as day—*shut the fuck up or they'll kill us.*

We didn't move, didn't breathe for what felt like a full minute.

When I peered around the corner again, there were now two men where there'd once been three.

I blinked, fighting desperately to understand what I was seeing. Where the shortest man had been, there was now a large brown wolf—taller and thicker than any wolf I'd ever seen on TV or in the zoo. A low, deep growl rumbled from the creature, and I swore I could feel the ground shake with the power of it.

My heart raced, its hurried pace beating a frenzied song through my veins. My head rang with the tempo of it, and I was certain they'd be able to hear it from here.

This couldn't be right. This couldn't be real.

Maybe I was dreaming, still passed out in the park, and this was my brain's way of shaking me awake.

Sora told me what she'd seen, and I'd believed her, but it was different seeing this for myself.

It was undeniable.

We were less than twenty feet away from what could only be described as a werewolf.

Sora grabbed my hand, tight and steady, our fingers threaded and nails sinking half-moons into each other's flesh. I focused on the sharp pain, let it ground me as we stood there, both of us too frightened to move, or even breathe. We needed to get out of here, immediately, but I didn't know how to leave without drawing attention to ourselves.

My vision blurred as the man and the wolf brawled, and I focused instead, on the third man watching them.

He was tall, had shoulder-length black hair that was a stark contrast against his pale skin. Now that I let my gaze linger on him, I almost couldn't understand how I'd noticed the other two men at all. He was striking, his hands and arms tattooed in dark patterns that I couldn't see well enough to decipher, but that seemed to almost glisten in the sunlight.

His expression was stoic, his jaw tight as he watched the two men from the sidelines.

Briefly, I wondered if they were fighting over him. Maybe some convoluted lovers' quarrel, but it was only a passing thought. The other two didn't seem to notice him at all.

And as mesmerizing as he was, I almost understood why—there was something almost ephemeral about him, like I had to actively direct my focus to see him, shaping him anew each time I glanced in his direction.

Still, he stood silently—watching, but not passive. The more I studied him, the sharp curve of his brow, the way his almost-black eyes locked onto the wolf, the more it felt like I was watching a hawk, waiting patiently for its next meal.

At one point, he got so close to their fight that I flinched, expecting him to be swept away in their battle, collateral damage. But the men didn't even pause, just continued their gnawing and clawing, their fists and paws swiping at each other as if uninterrupted.

Could they not see him? Or did they just not care, too lost to their own rage?

The wolf kicked out, its paw striking into the third man's chest.

I blinked again, convinced my eyes were deceiving me. Had his foot passed right *through* him? As if he was nothing more than air?

Deep growls echoed around us, the song of their battle punctuated with grunts and loud crashes. The ground beneath them was painted in blood, but I couldn't tell which of them it belonged to.

A sudden bolt of certainty struck through my chest, settling low in my gut. The man—the one who'd turned into a wolf— he was dead. I felt his last breath as if it was my own, felt the cloying touch of death's grip at the base of my throat.

I shook my head, watching the wolf now as he twisted and contorted with the vampire, the two of them locked in a strange, violent dance. The wolf was there, still very much breathing, still very much alive.

In fact, the wolf seemed to be faring better of the two now.

It didn't matter. Whatever truth my eyes saw, I couldn't shake the feeling. The burning conviction I couldn't explain that the wolf's upper hand wouldn't last.

He was alive, but he wouldn't be at the end of this fight. I felt it in my bones, with the same certainty that I felt Sora's hand clutched in mine.

The crow's claws dug into my shoulder, snapping me out of my daze.

"We need to get out of here," I mouthed to her. "Now."

I shivered. Every hair on my body was standing on end, static.

Death.

Death was here.

And he was coming for the wolf.

I didn't want to be here to see it, didn't want to be proven right.

Most importantly, I didn't want Sora anywhere near him.

My chest was tight, my vision dotting in the corners until it became nothing but smears of color and indecipherable dancing blurs.

Sora's arms wrapped around my chest. She squeezed, though I hardly felt the pressure. I understood, in a vague sort of way, that she was trying to calm me down, to help me regulate my panic. But this was no typical panic attack.

My vision swam in and out of focus as my breathing grew shallow and rapid—and I watched as my intuition unfolded into reality.

We were too late.

The man covered in blood buried his hand inside of the wolf's chest, bringing the creature closer, as if dragging him into a violent hug.

The muscles in his arm pulsed and flexed as he twisted and tugged.

With little ceremony or care, he dropped the wolf to the ground.

The wolf didn't get up, didn't lift his head, didn't move.

The man dropped something red and vibrant and fleshy onto the wolf.

His heart.

As the first man took a few steps back from the wolf, the third man moved closer. He knelt next to him, studying him with a removed, clinical expression. His fingers sank into the wolf's flank as if it was made of butter.

Bile crept up my throat, hot and burning. There was something so familiar about the brutality of the gesture, but I couldn't place it.

Suddenly, his eyes latched on to mine, holding my stare for a fraction of a second. I shook my head, as if to dispel him, then tugged Sora back with me.

We ran, as fast as we could, not even stopping to discuss where we were heading.

We didn't slow down, didn't speak, until we were back at Frank's.

I leaned against the familiar gray wall of the diner, my head pressing into it as I fought to catch my breath.

Sora bent over and vomited.

I grabbed her hair, fighting back the urge to do the same.

"Holy shit." She panted, wiping her mouth with the back of her hand. "That was fucking unbelievable." She glanced up at me. "We should call somebody, shouldn't we?"

"Who? And what do we even say? That we just saw a man kill a werewolf?" I shook my head, still not fully believing what we'd just seen myself. "The phones are down anyway, right?"

She stood up. Her face was pale and covered in a sheen of sweat, her eyes sparkling and alive and so at odds with the deathly pallor of her skin. "The other one. Do you think—" A low, humorless chuckle ripped from her mouth as she leaned her head back against Frank's door. "That couldn't have been a vampire, right? I mean, that's absolutely—"

"And the third guy?" I pressed my thumb against my ring, twisting it, fighting to find a word to describe him—cataloging through every sci-fi and fantasy film I'd ever seen. "What was with him? The way the other two literally went through him— like he was just air?"

Sora's brows furrowed.

"I mean, maybe he was a vampire too? Who knows what the hell kind of rules govern them, or—"

"Mars." She studied me, the adrenaline in her eyes fading into concern. "There were just two of them."

"What do you mean?"

"There was no third guy."

3

MAREENA

PRESENT DAY, SIX YEARS AFTER THE
UNDOING

*For as much as things were changed by The Undoing, as the
world had come to call it, they also mostly stayed the same.
Six years ago, the world split into two.*

Or maybe more than two.

*To be honest, the details are still largely unclear. Pundits wasted
their time in a desperate frenzy trying to nail down the specifics that
seemed to be forever out of reach—like a goal post that moved every
time you got too close to it.*

*One thing they all agreed on, though . . . there'd been what could
only be described as a tearing of realms—the world as we knew it
had expanded into . . . well, more.*

*Scientists didn't have answers. Religious leaders and politicians
pretended to.*

*New cults and religious factions started sprouting up every-
where. Some of them practically run the city now.*

And it wasn't just in the United States, it was the entire world.

*A portal to hell (as some conspiracy theorists had dubbed it) had
been opened, and the supernatural world had been unleashed. Some
called it a demon realm, others were convinced it was an alternate
universe, others swore it was the mythical land of Faerie.*

I didn't care much about arguing over the semantics. There hardly seemed a point.

All that mattered was that, overnight, magic seeped into the everyday, sometimes even into people, rewiring life as we knew it entirely.

The few humans affected were changed in small, often meaningless ways. Sora and I knew someone who'd developed an unexplainable inability to walk in a straight line. But only on Tuesdays. Their Tuesday afternoon hikes through the neighborhood became nothing more than a strange, twisted meandering, as if guided by a force they couldn't control. Every other day of the week—no problem.

Occasionally, we'd hear of someone who'd changed more noticeably—they'd turn into a wolf, grow an extra limb, or their hair would change color whenever they had an orgasm.

Those were the exceptions. Most people weren't physically affected by the aftermath. Humans didn't all just suddenly turn into superheroes or mythological monsters overnight.

Sora had a pretty developed theory that any humans who had obtained truly useful powers were scooped up by the various supernatural factions, religious cults, or else held under quarantine by the leftover fragments of human governments that still remained, hunkered down somewhere.

A much less exciting version of the hair thing had happened to me, though I had no control over it, and it never changed.

A few weeks after waking up in that bush, the tips of my hair started to turn to white, like the color and life had simply been . . . sapped. My roots were still their usual inky black, but it was like the universe wanted to give me another useless reminder of Death's ever nearness. As if I didn't have enough of those.

I'd tried dying it back a few times, even shaved my head once, hoping that would fix it. But it eventually always grew back the same anyway—like life bleeding into death.

We didn't tell anyone.

While Sora's theory was kind of out there, there were whispers of people afflicted by The Undoing getting taken or killed by various anti-supernatural coalitions. And since I lived with a hair colorist, it was easy enough to pass the odd shift off as trendy and intentional.

Trivial enough that we were able to skirt under the radar.

When it really came down to it, though, it wasn't humans that seemed most altered by The Undoing.

It was the world itself.

Buildings often buzzed with strange energy, the static in the air occasionally thick with the taste of something no one could name, but everyone felt. Infrastructure was destroyed. Electricity and cars were less reliable, their reaction to magical energy unpredictable and inconsistent. Phones and the internet? Virtually useless.

Of course, when I was desperate, I still took my chances on the bus system—when they were up and running anyway, and occasionally even unmanned altogether.

The first few years were a whirlwind.

We watched governing bodies fracture and fall, and new ones rise in their places. There were wars—too many for me to keep track of, especially with unreliable news sources, and fights for power, literal and figurative, erupting all over the world.

The supernatural creatures—demons as they usually called themselves—mostly stuck together. They were powerful in ways that humans weren't.

And that, more than anything, terrified the humans who'd held all the power in The Before.

No one who had power was ever eager to relinquish it.

In the early days, the United States took to exploring the tears and pockets leading to the new realm. The leaders and 'adventurers,' as they often called themselves, swore the expeditions were for scientific purposes. Eventually, the series of failed missions and the commitment to funding more revealed the truth.

The US empire did what the US empire always did—excited by new lands and all that they promised, it attempted to colonize them. Greed for minerals and resources transformed into greed for magic—

a power that humans and governments couldn't understand, let alone grasp. But they wanted it anyway—more even, because of its refusal to be taken.

Most of the people who went on those early expeditions never returned. Those who did rarely had the capacity to speak about what they'd encountered there in the other realm.

After far too many sacrifices, the desire to survive outweighed the desire for power, and humans finally started to avoid the mysterious tears between worlds, keeping to their own instead.

The first year was terrifying, the second year less so. Strange became normal, and humans did what they did best—they adjusted, adapted, and found ways to keep going.

In a lot of ways, it wasn't all bad.

In fact, some things were a lot better than before.

We focused on the hyper local, tying ourselves to our communities and carving livable paths forward.

Eventually, waking up to a new, infinitely transforming world was just like your average Monday—a bit of a drag, but survivable with strong coffee and the promise of Friday on the horizon.

A SOFT TAPPING above my head ripped me from my journal. I set it down on my comforter and grinned at the beady eyes locked on mine.

"Morning, Menace."

I stood on my bed to unlock the hatch, then shoved the heavy window open a few inches so that he could fit through.

Menace had his own entrance, of course—a doggy-door style flap we'd installed in the kitchen window, there for him to come and go as he pleased—but he'd taken to ignoring it, preferring to interrupt my few minutes of quiet each morning instead.

I didn't mind. I enjoyed his company while I watched dawn lazily creep over the trees.

He dropped a small metal skeleton key on my pillow before busying himself with the treat jar that I kept on my nightstand.

"Hope whoever you stole this from doesn't need it to get home tonight, you little klepto."

I slid the top drawer of my nightstand open and added the new trinket to the rest—stones, dried flowers, broken jewelry, pieces of tinfoil, spare change, twigs.

Menace didn't always deliver gifts with his morning greetings, but when he did, he delivered them with the kind of pride a student used to wear on their graduation day.

I did my best to clear through the collection every few months, but I rarely had the heart to throw any of his gifts away. I redistributed them, of course, when I recognized a stolen item, but I usually held on to the rest like a mother who hoarded her child's decaying baby teeth.

He was quite fond of the collection he'd amassed. I often walked into my bedroom to see his tiny head shoved inside the drawer, adding to and sorting through the hodgepodge of items when I wasn't here, a pirate perusing his precious treasure.

"We're never getting rid of you, are we?" I muttered, biting back a smile when he flew onto my shoulder, nuzzling his head against my cheek. He was a stubborn little dude, but he'd grown quite affectionate in his old age.

Although old might have been an odd way to refer to him. I wasn't exactly sure what a normal lifespan was for an undead crow.

Sora and I watched over him as his wing healed—kept him fed, consulted books on crows when we couldn't get him into a vet, and provided a relatively-comfortable shelter from the strange, changing world.

Truthfully, he'd been a welcome distraction during those

early days. But we'd always expected him to one day get back to being a typical neighborhood crow.

Menace had other ideas though. He'd taken quite eagerly to the partially domesticated life we provided, almost never even interacting with the local murders.

He'd followed us through *two* apartment moves, and while he'd occasionally disappear for a day or two now and then, he'd become a permanent resident in our lives.

In a world where the strange had become conventional, the shock of his undeadness sort of just eventually . . . wore away.

I lifted my hand up to my shoulder, waiting for his thick, black claws to grip my fingers. When they did, I shifted him in front of me, lightly petting the side of his neck with my free hand.

"Did you get up to anything fun this morning?"

He cawed, his eyes flashing briefly from dark as night to a peculiar midnight blue, in the way they often did.

There was a sharp knock, and I jumped.

Menace flew away, feathers ruffled and an indignant shift to his neck at the disruption of his morning attention time.

"Come in," I yelled.

Sora burst in. Her lips curved into a hook, eyes brightening when they landed on the crow. "Hey, you little shit."

He turned away from her, stubborn and unyielding.

With a soft laugh, she tossed him an unsalted peanut—one of his favorite snacks—and his cold shoulder dissolved almost instantly.

He let out a loud caw, picked up the peanut, and started cracking the shell against my dresser.

I swallowed a groan, knowing I'd have to pick up the remnants of his feast later. Hopefully this time, he'd avoid traipsing them all over my sheets. I had no desire to sleep amongst his peanut carcasses tonight.

"Most dramatic bird on the planet." Sora shook her head as

she watched him, her expression both annoyed and bemused. They had a strange, antagonistic but loving relationship that was amusing to watch fester and grow. It made sense in a weird way. They were two of the most stubborn creatures I knew, and they both got great enjoyment out of pushing the other's buttons. "Have you seen my pendant?"

"What pendant?"

"The blue one. Small, pretty, matches my hair." She ran her hand through her shiny, shoulder-length waves, now equal parts blue and black, as if to emphasize her point. "I bartered for it last week at the market. Paid a hefty price, too, but now I can't find it anywhere. I could've sworn I left it hanging on my doorknob." She grimaced. "Anyway, I've clearly misplaced it. I'm sure it'll turn up eventually, but I was hoping to wear it tonight." She snorted before adding, "So much for being a good luck charm."

I bit my tongue. I'd done everything I could to avoid the supernatural world—putting my head down and staying away from all of the new magical shops and attractions that had popped up in the last couple of years. I'd had more than enough brushes with death and the supernatural to last me a lifetime.

It felt like tempting fate, especially when things had been relatively calm and stable lately.

Of course, it also definitely didn't help that being around magic shot my nervous system into overdrive. Any time I was close to an unfamiliar supernatural presence, an electric tingling feeling darted across my skin, impossible to ignore.

Occasionally, it would get bad enough that my vision would start to blur, and strange mirages of buildings or people would emerge transposed on top of whatever setting I was in, as if through a fog.

It was unsettling as fuck, and after watching a vampire rip out the heart of a werewolf with his bare hands, I couldn't wrap my head around why Sora wanted anything to do with the supernatural world.

No thank you.

Menace was the only exception to my rule.

Sora, on the other hand, seemed infatuated with the new world. She often wasted entire paychecks collecting random talismans sold by swindling humans that were more often not duds. She hoarded research on the supernatural and was excited by every demon and magic-afflicted human she encountered.

I still hadn't brought myself to tell her that I was one of them—beyond the weird hair thing, that is.

My visions . . . premonitions? Whatever the hell they were, they hadn't stopped after watching the wolf's murder. It didn't happen often, but every so often, I'd feel death's nearness like a sixth sense—more acutely than any bad omen I'd been plagued with before The Undoing.

I tried desperately to ignore it, as if I could somehow will the unwanted awareness away. But death was a thing that demanded you look.

And sure enough, whoever inspired the feeling—usually a passing stranger—would turn up dead shortly after.

She cleared her throat, brow arched.

"Sorry, what?" I asked.

"My necklace?" she asked, eyes wide.

"Doesn't sound familiar," I said.

Menace let out a caw, then flew into the living room where we kept a small dog bed and cat toys for him. He seemed to prefer the dog bed to the birdcage and perch we'd tried first. Couldn't say I blamed him. I wouldn't want to sleep in a cage either, even if the door was kept open.

"Actually. . ." I snorted, nodding toward my nightstand. "Check the top drawer."

"Fucking bird is a nuisance." Sora cursed as she sifted

through Menace's makeshift treasure chest, holding up a small, sparkly pendant with a triumphant wave. "Is nothing sacred in this apartment anymore?"

"You're just mad he saves the shiniest presents for me."

She shot me a glare. "Well, it's not like you're the only one who feeds him. And I let him stay here too, you know." She raised her voice at the last part, speaking more to the crow than to me. Sora had a theory that Menace understood us when we spoke to him, but I didn't buy it. Mostly because having a wild crow that had been resurrected from the dead as a pet was more than enough strange for me. "Those peanuts he likes so much? I'm the one who bartered for them. Just saying, if he decided to bring me a nice pair of earrings or something, I wouldn't fight him on it."

I nodded to the drawer. "Take what you'd like, I don't think he'll mind."

"Speaking of presents." Sora ran out into the kitchen, returning with a bag that she tossed onto my bed, all faux anger abandoned for a contagious joy that leaked out of her every pore. "Happy Birthday, Mars!"

Right. That was today.

Well, that explained my general grimness and the headache I woke up with.

"Twenty-seven! You know what that means?" At my blank stare, she added, "You officially won't be inaugurated into the twenty-seven club. That's cause for celebration."

"Pretty sure I have to make it to twenty-eight to avoid that, actually."

"Oh. That makes sense, now that I think about it, but that totally ruins what I was going for." She shrugged, then fished a small envelope out of the bag. "I'll just save that card and joke for next year then."

"You didn't need to get me anything." I stared at the bright pink bag, stuffed to the brim with vibrant green tissue paper, as if something might crawl out of it and attack.

"I did." Her body was stiff with barely contained excitement, as if she was the one receiving the present. "You need something to wear tonight."

"What do you mean?" Since The Undoing, our Anniversary Extraordinaire celebrations had taken a bit of a back burner.

Partially because it was now *also* the anniversary of the day the world turned all topsy-turvy, and people went a little wild across the city—some celebrating recklessly, others hoping to usher in whatever impending apocalypse they were touting to their followers as the next big cosmic shift.

House of Gluttony, one of the competing compounds of The Seven Sons of Lucifer, always had a day-long feast that turned into a raging party. Last year I heard five people died from overconsumption. Apparently if the devil did exist, he didn't waste his time rescuing his loyal followers from alcohol poisoning.

And that was one of the tamer celebrations I'd heard about.

The Undoing made today feel less like our day, and more like one we shared with everyone else, however reluctantly.

Last year, we tried to bring the tradition back a bit. We'd gotten our hands on a particularly nice bottle of wine, a true rarity these days, and spent the night passing the bottle back and forth, chugging while we meandered aimlessly through the city. We went for a swim in the lake and then gorged on the perfect mixture of salty and sweet snacks. Perfection all around.

I'd been looking forward to something similar tonight, but judging from the guilty expression painted across Sora's face, I wasn't going to be quite so lucky this year.

As if sensing my hesitation, she fell back on my bed and shoved the bag closer to me. "Don't hate me, okay, but I made some plans for us tonight."

"Sora, we agreed."

"I know the last few years have been a little more low-key than in the past, but this year has been great. Darling"—she tilted her head and put on a drawn-out affected accent—"we've got a beautiful apartment, the restaurant's doing great, and our obnoxious crow-son is a thriving little thief." She gripped my shoulders, shaking me lightly. "Do you know what that is? It's stability, Mars. No curse or bad omen in sight. We're practically a post-apocalyptic white-picket family. We have a lot to celebrate, to be thankful for. So, I was thinking we should go all out tonight. Like we used to. Usher in the next phase of our lives."

I took a deep breath, scrunching my nose. When Sora set her mind to something, it was almost impossible to say no. My exhale turned into a sigh at her victory. "What did you have in mind?"

With a coy grin, she ripped the tissue paper out of the bag, reached inside, and pulled out a short, slinky bunch of fabric. As it unfolded, I realized it was a dress—spaghetti-strapped satiny material up top that flared out with layers of black tulle at the waist. Very punk ballerina.

I loved it.

"A friend of a friend got us on the list for a club tonight," she said, then tossed the dress at me.

I caught it, letting the surprisingly soft fabric roll over my fingers.

There was no denying it, the dress was stunning—the material both liquid and structured. It was nicer than any piece of clothing I'd ever owned. "Sor, this is way too much."

"Shut up." A wide grin split her face as her gaze dipped from me to the dress.

"Sora—"

"Look, I promise I got it for a bargain, okay?" She grabbed it, then leaned forward to hold it up against my chest, closing one eye as she studied the effect. "You know, I think you can even get away with wearing your boots with it. Permission to scrap the heels. So no arguments, okay? It's perfect and you're going to look killer in it, and we've been busy as hell. We deserve to go all out tonight." Her brows slinked up and down a few times. "Maybe you'll even get lucky. It's been, what, three or four months since you've seen Alex? Not that I'm complaining."

Alex was my no-strings-attached hookup. He traveled a lot, we had nothing in common, and he was allergic to emotional attachments.

That made him perfect in my book, and the only one I broke my 'no repeats' sex rule for.

Sora hated him, which only added to the simplicity of our arrangement.

I could never get into something long term or serious with someone my best friend hated.

She was also right.

It had been over three months since I'd had any kind of release with someone other than myself. I may have avoided getting attached to people, but that didn't mean I wasn't into getting laid.

And, well, I was long overdue for a proper fuck.

I glanced down at myself as she held up the dress, trying to picture her vision, but it was hampered by the baggy T-shirt and boxer shorts I was wearing. I let out a loud sigh that transformed into a groan. I already saw my defeat coming from a mile away. So did she. "Which club?"

"Just say you'll go first." Her voice was higher, and she wouldn't meet my eyes.

"Sora..." I narrowed my eyes. "Which club?"

When she didn't say anything, I grabbed the dress and tossed it back so that it draped over her head. "I need details, or it'll be a no from me, babes."

She pulled the dress from her face and walked over to my closet, ruffling through it for a spare hanger. There weren't any, so she reached into the back, tugged an old sweatshirt off its cracked plastic hanger, let it fall to the ground in a crumpled heap, and hung the dress up in its place.

My gaze lingered on the hoodie.

Only when the dress was neatly pressed between my jacket and a significantly less-revealing black dress did she turn back to me, her chin raised, defensive.

My stomach tightened. I knew what was coming before the word even left her mouth.

"Incendiary."

I snorted, followed her to the closet, ripped the dress off the hanger, and pressed it into her chest. Then, I grabbed the discarded sweatshirt—one I refused to wear but still couldn't bring myself to let go of. As I shoved the hanger into its neck hole, I resisted the urge to press my nose to the cotton. His scent was long gone. And even if it wasn't, well, I needed to move the fuck on. It had been years—and if I was honest with myself, I knew it was for the best. For his sake, as much as mine.

Instead, I shoved the sweatshirt carelessly back into its spot, where I could forget about it until the next time I did laundry, or woke up in the middle of the night craving a comfort I was too weak to ignore in that liminal state.

I turned back to her. "Absolutely not."

"Mars," she groaned. Her head tipped back, and she stared at the ceiling like she was arguing with some invisible god. "Do you have any idea how difficult it is to get into that place? The waitlist is, like, six months long. Sometimes more. And tonight is *the* night."

"Then it sounds like someone will be very grateful to get our spot. I'm not kidding, Sora. Pick somewhere else." I leaned against my closet door frame, refusing to back down when her eyes met mine. She was stubborn, but so was I. "Literally anywhere else."

"Tell me why."

"You know why." Incendiary was a popular club in one of

the demon-owned blocks. It was in one of the old warehouses that had been affected by whatever power The Undoing had unleashed. The entire structure flared with it—which meant that it was unpredictable and incredibly dangerous for humans. "Besides, it's like a sex club, isn't it? Owned by what, a lust demon? A succubus, if I remember correctly?"

"Don't get all puritanical on me in your old age." She rolled her eyes. "And it's not a sex club. But even if it was, didn't we just decide you needed to get laid?" She scrunched her nose, studying me. "Which, clearly, you do." She gestured at me vaguely. "You're so uptight."

I clenched my jaw.

It wasn't just the rumors I'd heard about that place.

I avoided that neighborhood entirely. I wanted nothing more than to stay the fuck away from the unpredictable magic that had overtaken the world, and Incendiary was smack dab in the middle of one of the biggest supernatural hotspots in the city.

Occasionally, when I got lost in my thoughts and accidentally wandered within a street or two of that area, I'd get the same feeling I'd had the day we saw the werewolf murdered.

It crept up my spine, sending a wave of ice through my chest—an undeniable conviction that someone was about to die. In those moments, the world would blur, and I'd see strange, unexplainable hallucinations. Visions I couldn't put into words, that I refused to even admit out loud.

Death haunted that neighborhood. I was sure of it.

And I couldn't fight the gnawing feeling in my gut that one of these days, Sora would be the victim of one of those visions.

Sometimes it felt like the more I insisted on keeping us— her—away, the more determined she was to get closer. Like she was a magnet drawn to the supernatural.

Her interest started slowly at first—but more recently, it had grown into an obsession.

"Come on, you used to live for this kind of fun. What happened?"

I shot her a glare. "The world fucking exploded, Sora, what do you think happened?"

"Yes," she said, stretching the word out, "and we survived. Even more reason to enjoy our lives."

"Humans who go there are like fucking feeder fish, asking to be killed," I shot back, though there wasn't any bite to it.

She rolled her eyes. "That's not true. Incendiary has very rigid safety measures in place for humans. And it's owned by a succubus, not a vampire."

"They both feed on humans."

Menace flew back into the room, landing on my shoulder.

I stroked the top of his head absentmindedly. His presence had become like a natural tonic, fighting the tension that built up in my chest.

"Look around, Mars." She gestured absently. "Humans die all the time. And when they're murdered, they're murdered far more often by other humans than they are by demons or stray bits of magic."

She wasn't wrong. Most of the people we'd known who'd died since The Undoing had been killed either by lack of adequate resources or by other humans.

Demons mostly kept to themselves.

"I know, I just—" I massaged my temples, fighting to find the right words, "I can't explain it, okay? I know you don't believe in the curse, but I just—it's just a feeling I get, okay? There's this whole new, inexplicably terrifying world now, and I'm just . . ." I took a breath, my thumb wearing its familiar path over my ring. "You run headfirst into things. And I get why, I really do." Of the three of us, Rina had always been the adventurous one. After she died, it was like Sora had taken up that mantle as a way to honor her. We all processed grief differently. "I'm just so fucking terrified that you're going to end up collateral damage. And if something happens to you, if I lose you too —" My voice cracked, and I shook my head, begging the liquid coating my eyes to evaporate. It was too early for this shit.

"I know that it can be scary." Her features softened. "That doesn't mean it can't be exciting too. This is the world we live in now, Mars. And for better or worse, I'm in it with you. Until the end." She nudged my foot with hers, her eyes latching on to mine when I looked up. "You're twenty-seven today. You've survived some seriously diabolical shit, and we've built a damn impressive life from almost nothing. That's something worth celebrating. I want you to have fun tonight, and I think you would if you gave yourself permission to let loose a little bit. That's the whole point of the Anniversary Extraordinaire. Celebrating. For us and for Rina." Her voice wavered on the name, but she took a deep breath and pushed through. "But if you legitimately want to stay in or go to one of our usual spots, we can do that too. I'm just afraid that you're going to spend the rest of your life holed up on this block, avoiding everything —avoiding connecting with people—just because you don't trust that this life we've built will last. Not everyone leaves, Mars."

I nodded; my throat tight. She rarely brought *him* up, but I heard his name in the silence anyway.

"And, in case you didn't realize it, I'm still here." She nudged her chin toward my shoulder. "The crow is still here, too, right? Not everyone you let yourself love dies, okay?" Her lips curved into a soft grin. "I mean, yeah okay, Menace did die once, and we will all die eventually, so I guess that's not entirely true, but you get what I'm trying to say. And I've got a pretty good track record thus far, yeah?"

I grinned, my shoulders loosening a bit.

"What was that phrase your therapist used again?"

Therapist was perhaps a generous label. Claudine, an old woman who recently started stopping by Frank's every Tuesday afternoon, had taken to dispelling unsolicited advice to whoever would listen while she sat with her mint tea.

But Tuesday afternoons were particularly slow, so, more often than not, I was the sole, unwilling recipient of her shrewd observations—and the worst at ignoring her.

Claudine wasn't a psychologist, but she'd assured me (and anyone who'd listen) that she was an assistant to a very famous one before The Undoing.

For those of us who lived outside of the expensive compounds and districts scattered across the state, licensed professionals were difficult to track down—and meds were beyond expensive.

Not every sector had figured out how to come back from the instability The Undoing created, though the local community groups were working on filling in all the gaps the declining governments had left gaping open.

Until then, Claudine was probably the closest thing to a professional I was realistically going to get for a few more years.

It was at her suggestion that I start journaling in the first place—to help process what we'd all been through when I couldn't shut my brain off.

Sora hadn't even met the woman yet, but she was already a big fan. She'd taken to reciting the bits of wisdom I reported back to her as if she were a kid collecting jokes on popsicle sticks.

"She said"—I cleared my throat, adopting Claudine's easy confidence and soft Boston accent—"'Some ships sink, Mareena. That doesn't mean all ships sink.'"

"Right." Sora's grin widened; her smile contagious. She jabbed her pointer finger against her chest. "I'm the floating ship, okay? I'm not going to sink. I mean, for fuck's sake, you're the one who taught me to swim, remember?"

Bit of a mixed metaphor, but I got the point.

"So, what if we try, just for today, to do something a little bit out of your comfort zone?" she continued. "Open yourself up a bit. And if it ends badly, I promise that I'll join you in staying the fuck away from that neighborhood for the rest of my life. Hell, we can move to. . ." She paused, searching for a spot. "Anywhere. We can make our way all the way to Chicago if you want."

Strange, how big a journey that felt like now. We'd taken for granted so many things.

"Or," I said, voice flat as I swallowed my grin, "we'll just be dead."

"Exactly." She winked. "And in that case, it won't matter either way, will it?" She slid the straps of the dress over my closet handle, a makeshift hanger. "So what do you say, birthday girl? Anniversary Extraordinaire—revived and extravagant as it was always meant to be? Do we have a deal?"

"Deal."

4

———

MAREENA

PRESENT DAY

There was a time when I was younger, that my birthday didn't hold quite so much weight. When it didn't signify pain or survival.

I remembered when I'd rush into the kitchen at the crack of dawn, and Amto Amani would already be started on all my favorites: baked kibbeh in the oven, stuffed grape leaves on the stove, fresh fruit and labneh with pita on the counter.

We'd spend all day grazing on food, walking along the coastline collecting smooth rocks and listening to the waves. I'd swim while she waited on the shore, calling out whenever I let the water pull me out too far, but never rushing me, letting me float until my fingers were pruned raisins and I could barely feel my feet from the cold. Only then would we make our way back to the house, settling in for strawberry pie and ice cream in the late afternoon, because I hated the sponginess of birthday cake and the flakiness of baklawa.

In the evenings, she'd fish through her collection of old keepsakes, and we'd look at the few photographs she had of my father—her nephew—and the one of my mother—their wedding portrait—while she'd tell me whatever stories she remembered about them both. Most of the stories were about him; she'd only met my mother two or three times over the years, but I clung to every word, like she was spinning straw into gold.

I could hear the same story a million times, and I'd still listen enraptured, her soft, melodic voice, its own gift—one I didn't even think to cherish as its own coveted memory, until it was gone.

Now, I hold on to the memory of her telling those stories more tightly than I did the stories themselves. I'd never met my parents, but my aunt was my entire world for the first decade of my life.

The rest of the night would be spent watching comedy films and laughing until we cried while we acted out our favorite parts. She had the kind of laugh that would make the entire room feel full with it, like not even the walls themselves were strong or sturdy enough to contain her joy. We'd cram in as many movies as we could until we couldn't justify staying up a second later.

It had been more than fifteen years since I'd heard that laugh, and the loss of it still carved an ache deep in my bones— one I could never fully shake.

When I lost her, I lost everything that existed in that life— the photographs, the specific scent of our home, the recipes.

I couldn't get the latter back, but when we took over Frank's restaurant a year ago, I'd done my best to recover as many as I could by memory and by taste. It was a work in progress, but one I enjoyed pursuing.

The restaurant was always so quiet after the early morning rush.

It was my favorite part of the day.

As much as I'd grown to love our regular customers and the labor that went into making this place run, there was something about the solitude that soothed me in a way that a busy diner never could.

The light above flickered as I stirred the cooling milk on the stove.

Another electrical surge. Hopefully, it would hold off until I got the rest of this finished.

I turned the light off and opened all the blinds, preferring to work in the natural light that shone through anyway.

Most of the food was already prepped for the lunch rush we'd get in another few hours, which Sora would take over for. We both handled the dinner service most nights, and we also had a few people we could tap in for a shift or two each week, when one of us couldn't cover it.

Like me, Sora had taken quickly to the work, both of us experimenting with new recipes, searching for links to pasts that eluded us.

Sora didn't know her family. We'd met in foster care during middle school, but she and Rina had been hopping from home to home for as long as they could remember.

When she found a Japanese cookbook a few months ago in Frank's surprisingly robust stash, she'd made it her mission to cook her way through every recipe, making substitutes with ingredients we couldn't easily find, just as I did with my attempts at recovering my aunt's dishes.

Food had become an unexpected link to the parts of ourselves that had been taken from us too soon. It was inefficient, up against all that we'd lost, but it was something.

And it was strange that it was this diner that helped us along that journey, the very one that functioned as a refuge when we'd arrived in the city. Almost like it was growing with us.

I didn't grow up wanting to own a restaurant, had never even enjoyed cooking until a year ago, but the daily routine of it had become like a meditation practice, one that I clung to dearly.

And when I had a chance to linger in my memories, trying to replicate Amto Amani's spice ratios—never measured, always eye-balled—and flare, I felt closer to her than I had in years.

"It's smaller than I'd pictured."

A gravelly voice pulled me out of the mindless routine of chopping parsley and mint. When I looked up, I saw Claudine, seated at her usual booth—mine and Sora's old favorite—with another older woman I'd never seen before.

She was a shorter white woman, her back hunched slightly, and she had spiky hair that stood out in every direction. Her face was wrinkled, but in an expressive way that made it clear that she'd had a lifetime of laughing.

"Shit. Sorry." I smiled at them both. "Was so lost in my thoughts I didn't even hear you guys come in." It was Tuesday, but a bit earlier than Claudine's usual time. I searched through the cluttered shelf of mugs until I found two matching ones without chips. "Would you like some tea as well?"

The new woman glanced from me to her friend, her drawn-on brows arched in interest. "No, nothing for me."

"You're sure?" When she nodded, I brought Claudine's usual to her table.

She smiled at me, green eyes wide as she leaned over the cup of tea and breathed in the minty steam floating toward the ceiling.

Claudine never actually drank the tea.

She didn't exactly pay for it either, but that wasn't a big deal. Most things were bartered for when money was difficult to come by, and I supposed she saw her (generally unsolicited) advice as payment enough.

I'd grown so used to her nosy presence that I found myself often looking forward to her visits.

"I'm Mareena," I said to her friend. "Do you live in the area?"

"Greta," she responded, the name almost like a bark in her wispy voice. "I've heard a lot about you, Mareena."

I glanced at Claudine. "Good, I hope."

"Of course, dear," Claudine said, her thin-lipped grin wide and warm.

"You sure I can't get you anything?"

"We're just here for the company if that's all right?" Greta asked. "Good company is hard to come by these days."

"Of course. I'll be behind the counter if you need anything."

I left them to their whispered chatter, glancing over occasionally whenever one woman would lean in and the other would let out a loud, resounding cackle.

There was something so incredibly normal about the interaction—like a window into the past, of what old age was meant to be—that I could almost forget the chaos of the last few years.

I dipped my pinky into the tepid pot of milk, holding it there as I counted, waiting for the moment when the lick of heat would be too much, as Amto Amani had taught me—but after ten seconds, it didn't come.

Perfect.

I spooned in the yogurt starter from last week's batch, before covering the pot and wrapping it in linens. The laban would incubate until tomorrow.

When I reached for the knife, ready to finish chopping the herbs for my tabbouleh, the door flew open.

I froze.

A tall, lean man with dark wavy hair set a bag of things down in the booth nearest the door, his back to me as he shrugged out of his backpack.

My body forgot how to move, as I held my breath, waiting for him to turn around.

It had been years without a word and—

When he did look back, unfamiliar brown eyes met mine, lips that were too thin, skin a shade or two off, a nose too straight.

The knots in my stomach unwound.

Two strangers in one day, that was quite rare for Frank's.

I exhaled, my muscles releasing whatever they'd been holding—anticipation, relief, disappointment. I honestly couldn't be sure.

Mustering a smile as best as I could, I moved toward the man, only to notice the counter was smeared with dark red.

"Shit," I hissed, dropping the knife into the sink.

"Oh dear," the woman, Greta, sat up straighter, studying me.

"Sorry, it's fine." I turned to the man. "I'll be right with you. Just give me a sec."

When I glanced back around, Greta was only a foot or two away from me. She was remarkably quiet and agile for her age.

Her eyes narrowed as she studied the cut, then the knife.

"Blade was sharp," she said, nodding, "that's good. Rinse it off and use some mild soap if you have it. Doesn't look like you'll need stitches. Probably just pressure for a few minutes and a solid Band-Aid."

I did as she said, applying pressure with a clean rag. "Thanks."

"Pardon?" The man was watching me now, brows dipped in concern.

"Can I get you some water?" I asked.

He nodded, and I got to work, setting the glass in front of him as I took his order.

Greta was back in the booth with Claudine.

"Thanks for the help," I whispered to her on my way back behind the counter.

"Once a nurse, always a nurse," she said, though there was a softness—or sadness—to her expression that hadn't been there before. Nostalgia, maybe.

I leaned over the counter, my chin resting in my hands as I studied her. She was undoubtedly retired, and I couldn't imagine her still wanting to work, but someone with a lifetime of nursing skills was beyond useful in these times.

My mind flew to Frank, to the few doctors we had available to us here. "If you're in town for a bit, you should stop by the medical center a few blocks down, they're always looking for help. I mean, if you're interested, of course. No pressure."

The women shared a look, and Greta nodded, her lips pressed into a grim smile. "Thanks, dear. I'm just passing through, but I'll look into it if I change my mind."

"Actually, I think I'm going to head out," the man said, his words hesitant and expression unreadable. He gave me a slippery grin, one that didn't reach his eyes. "Forgot I had somewhere to be."

He collected his things, his gaze shifting from me to the women, confusion etched in the lines between his brows.

"Are you sure? I can get your order to go—" When I reached for a container and turned around, I saw only his back again, as he rushed out the door, his water untouched on the table.

Had the blood made him squeamish?

I'd made sure to wash and sanitize my hands before serving him.

Claudine winced at the sound of the door clanging shut. Her lips pressed into a thin smile as some unreadable conversation passed between the women. She let out a harsh laugh, before turning back to me. "Well, that was rude. But enough about him." She leaned over the table, her chin perched on her hands. "Tell me, how are you today, dear? Any new developments to report? Have you started the journaling practice, like we discussed last week?"

I HAD LESS than an hour before I needed to get back to the diner for the dinner service, which meant that I had just enough time to sneak in a quick visit to Frank.

Sora and I did our best to make the trip every day, trading off when the other had a shift in the diner.

The walk to the medical center—a refurbished hospice with outdated supplies and tech that only occasionally worked—was quiet.

I leaned my head back, soaking in the feel of the sun against my skin. It was hot, and living without air conditioning was becoming more and more difficult each summer, especially now that I spent a good portion of my day in the relentless heat of a kitchen. Maybe one day, I'd get used to my skin feeling constantly sticky, but all I wanted right now was to go for a solid swim.

Maybe I could convince Sora to postpone our night out long enough for a quick dip in the lake before sunset.

"Mareena." A soft voice pulled me from my reverie.

"Hey, Jo. How's your mom today?"

Jo scooped her long, thick braids, holding them off her neck in a makeshift ponytail as the sun drew beads of sweat along her dark skin. She shrugged; her smile full of warmth even as some of it faded from her eyes. "No change, you know how it is."

I did.

Jo spent most of her afternoons working in the med center. That's where I'd met her, though she'd since become a frequent visitor at the diner whenever she could be convinced to get some fresh air and a hot meal, which wasn't as often as Sora and I would have liked.

Like most of us, Jo's plans have radically shifted in the last few years. Before The Undoing, she had an ambitious and rigorous life laid out before her. She'd been admitted to a competitive anthropology program down south and had every intention of seeking a prestigious fellowship after completing her doctoral program.

When her mother and sister got sick, she tossed those plans, abandoned her dissertation, and pivoted to learning as much as she could about medicine. "Research was research," as she often said, and her skillset made the pivot with remarkable ease. It had been too late to save her sister, but she still clung to the possibility that she might find a way to help her mother.

Without money or influence, though, the options most of us had were slim.

The community kept the medical center up and running, and we had volunteers—one former med student, a doula, a seamstress, and Jo. It was more than a lot of the humans living outside of the compounds had, though our access to any state-of-the-art medicine was nothing compared to what it had been in the Before.

Occasionally, if Jo submitted her research to the closest compound specializing in healing—the one run by the Sect of Azrael—along with some patient's blood samples, they'd send back enough to update a piece of equipment or add an extra bed or two. It was their attempt at ensuring our compliance and goodwill, while they benefited from the fruits of Jo and the other volunteers' meticulous labor. Jo did all the work, and their patients would be the ones to survive because of it. Hers were collateral damage, cheap test subjects along the way.

Like I said, some things changed after The Undoing, but a lot of things stayed the same.

"Sora has a plate saved for you when you're ready," I said.

We did our best to make sure no one in the area went hungry—which meant that we were often at the will and kindness of the local farmers to supply us with ingredients at an affordable price, but we made sure during the slimmer seasons

that we at least always had enough for the med center volunteers. It was the least we could do for them after all they'd done
for us—and for Frank.

She yawned, nodded, and thanked me, before heading in
the direction of the diner. Knowing Jo, she probably hadn't had
a full night's sleep in a week. And not just because she was
balancing her research with caring for her mother. She'd taken
to caring for all the patients who showed up at the med center.

Because of Jo and the rest of the volunteers, no one was ever
turned away—no matter how understaffed they were, how few
fumes the volunteers had left to run on, or how unclear or
strange the symptoms often presented.

When my hand closed over the metal handle of the
entrance, my stomach lurched, any ease I'd felt instantly
distorting into a sharp, familiar fear.

A chill settled deep in my chest, making it impossible to
take a full breath. My vision blurred, the building collapsing
and then doubling into a ghost of itself, like a film projected on
top of reality. My skin tingled with an electric surge that made
my stomach twist into knots.

It had been months since I'd felt this so sharply. I'd almost
let myself believe that I'd imagined the other occurrences
entirely.

I blinked, willing the panic to subside—half of my brain
telling me to go back, to leave this place.

Death.

Death was here.

But so was Frank.

My heartbeat thundered in my ears, reverberating through
my skull as I yanked open the door and ran.

The building was quiet, as it often was, though the usual
hum I felt buzzing through the walls was conspicuously lulled
as well.

"No. Please no. Please be alive. Please." I muttered the plea, over and over, a mantra to whatever god existed, as I ran up the staircase to the left, counting the doors until I got to Frank's room.

There were currently fifteen long-term patients in the med center. Frank was one of them.

A little over a year ago, he'd developed a pretty bad cough. It started slow, almost imperceptible at first, but eventually we noticed his dinner service slowing down a bit, and some of the odd jobs around the diner taking a backseat—the corners of the ceilings were covered in cobwebs, the floors were swept every few days instead of being meticulously tidied after each rush, the more time-intensive concoctions replaced by dishes he could whip up in ten minutes or less. Frank had never been a master chef, and the diner may have been in dire need of some upgrades, but he'd always taken the cleanliness of the establishment seriously. He was the sort of guy who welcomed the food inspector twice a year with beaming pride.

At first, we thought it was just the effects of heightened demand. Frank's had become a bit of a community refuge in the early years after The Undoing.

While he was a lot grumpier about it, like Jo, he never turned anyone away, even if they couldn't pay or offer something in return.

When he started slowing down, he hired a couple of teens in the neighborhood to tidy up the place between rushes and agreed to let Sora and I split shifts with him. We helped balance where he was falling short, but it became clear soon after that whatever was going on with him was more than him simply being spread too thin.

Sora and I had done everything we could to convince him to see a doctor.

In all honesty, convince was perhaps too tame a word. Sora had threatened to kidnap him and drop him at a compound if he didn't "buck up and make an appointment at the med center."

Frank, being Frank, brushed off our concerns, even as his health started to decline more visibly. His clothes fit more loosely, his skin turned sallow, and his breathing became labored after every climb up to his apartment. Eventually, he announced that he was taking a break from the diner altogether.

He let Sora and I take over the place until he was back on his feet, which we were happy to do—even if our skills in the kitchen left quite a bit to be desired at first. Some days, he seemed to glow with the excitement of watching us struggle, barking orders from our usual booth while we tripped over ourselves trying to get mediocre brunches served up to his patrons.

Sora often joked that his heckling would be the antidote to whatever ailed him.

For a while, it actually seemed like it was.

The diner grew busier as locals came by every day to spend time with and help Frank. We developed the menu, networked with local suppliers, and remodeled the basement so that Sora could have space to take on hair clients during the afternoons.

Each of us carved out a new purpose, one with meaning in a world that often seemed arbitrary and meaningless.

Before taking over Frank's, I'd spent most of my working hours helping Jo and the others at the med center, teaching swimming lessons to the local kids, and whatever other odd jobs were in need of support. It was fulfilling, but chaotic, and I'd been more than willing to settle down into one line of work I could really sink into—especially if it meant helping out Frank. Grumpy as he was, he was the closest thing Sora and I had to a family besides each other.

The edge of The Undoing was softened as fear bled into purpose, into community.

Until it wasn't.

Eventually, Frank's upward swing shifted focus, moving just as dramatically in the opposite direction. He stopped coming downstairs altogether, handling the bookkeeping and work from his apartment upstairs.

One day, a few months ago, he marched downstairs, announced that he'd be moving into the med center, and told Sora and I to take over his apartment, as he wouldn't be back.

At first, we didn't take him seriously, both of us convinced this was just another of his strange whims.

Two days later, he slipped into the first coma. His vital signs remained steady, and whatever tests we could find and afford came back fine, but he still didn't wake up. For weeks, we had no idea what was wrong with him.

Until one day, two weeks into it, he opened his eyes.

Only then did he see fit to offer any explanation.

Apparently, just before The Undoing, he'd been diagnosed with a rare cancer. One that he'd stubbornly told no one about, and one that had been transformed by whatever magic lived in the world now, fueling him somehow. He was fine for a few days, got some of his affairs in order, and then fell into a coma again.

After that, every few weeks, the timing impossible to predict, he'd simply wake up. As if nothing had happened. He would remain lucid and like the old Frank for a few hours— once, an entire day—with enough energy to hang out in the diner, visit with his friends, critique our new dishes, and remi- nisce about the Before. And then, just as suddenly, he'd fall back into a sleep, even deeper than the one before.

When he was first diagnosed, his doctor had given him less than six months to live, but whatever power had been unleashed in the world had sustained him far longer. He thought of every day beyond that prognosis as a gift, but I couldn't help feeling like his illness was a ticking time bomb.

No one fully understood the effects this new world had on the human body, especially since it seemed to affect everyone so differently. Would we have Frank for another month or another decade? Would he get better—these deep sleeps his body's way of healing? Or would he simply fall asleep so deeply one day that he would never wake up? There was no way of knowing.

I stopped outside of his door, my fingers trembling as I fought for the strength to open it and see him for myself. The memory of every patient I knew who'd occupied this room before him filtered to the top. They were all long gone now.

Years before Frank took up residence here, before Jo and the other volunteers even, back when this was just a run-of-the-mill hospice, I volunteered a few times a week. For a while, it had seemed the obvious place for me.

If I was going to be haunted by Death, why not spend my time in the place where Death was most welcomed—desired, even?

It was difficult, at first—getting attached to people, knowing my time with them would always be cut short.

Sometimes, I swore I could feel it, would know within a day or two when someone would surrender to Death's grip, their breath a rattle in the shape of his name.

Eventually, the more time I spent here, the more I started to understand that in some cases, death could be a form of grace. That sometimes there was peace in the quiet of it, in the absence of a pain that couldn't be otherwise silenced.

But I had never known the people in the hospice—who they were before they stepped into this building, before they desired that specific kind of peace. They didn't take shape in my life outside of these walls, I didn't cling to them in the way that I did to people like Sora.

And as much as I desperately tried to keep everyone but her

at a distance, Frank had long ago weaseled his way in. Become family.

People had a way of doing that, no matter how hard I fought against it. One moment, they were acquaintances—sometimes, like in Frank's case, one I didn't even particularly like much— then, one day I'd wake up to find they'd become an essential figure in my life.

It was infuriating and heartbreaking all at once—and each time it happened, it was like the protective walls I'd built had all been for nothing. They'd have to be restructured and rein- forced to account for the new liability just waiting to rip my heart out all over again.

Other than Sora and Amto Amani, Frank was the longest fixture in my life. And while this place was no longer one meant to house people as they waited for death to deliver them to whatever came next, I still struggled to shake the feeling each time I walked inside.

Like I carried the stench of decay in my skin.

My world had become inseparable from Frank's, even more so since The Undoing. I worked in his restaurant, I lived in his apartment, I fed his community.

Like I said, he'd weaseled his way in. And that meant that every day, I woke up petrified that whatever had been holding death back would let go, that whatever strange gift Frank had been given in the form of added time would be stolen— permanently.

It may have been greedy to demand more, to want Frank to have more time, but I couldn't help it.

I didn't want to lose him. I didn't want to lose anyone else.

Closing my eyes, I took a deep breath. I waited until I was steady, and then I opened his door, silently praying that what- ever strange sense I had was wrong. Distorted. Just this once.

The room was white, as plain as it had always been. Frank

didn't have much taste for knick-knacks or decor. His apartment had been equally plain before Sora and I moved in—nothing but the essentials, though many of those were missing, too.

The familiar, gentle whir of beeps permeated the room, the machines scattered around the bed blinking their usual lines and numbers. We had a few generators, but the med center hadn't experienced power issues in the last year or two—almost like the building itself protected the people here.

I exhaled sharply, the sound of it as desperate as I felt.

There, in the bed, lay Frank.

His feeding tube and catheter were still hooked up, his pajamas clean and newly changed.

I leaned back against the wall and watched him breathe, swearing that I felt the walls breathe along with him, that his breath flowed through me, too.

My vision blurred, this time from tears that I failed to keep back.

I slid down the wall, burying my head between my knees, and took slow, painful breaths.

He was okay. He was alive.

It was just in my head.

Not real.

Silently, I echoed the sentiment over and over, sliding the beads on my ring with each repetition of the promise.

I wasn't sure how long I stayed like that, how long I sat with him in that room, how many times I watched the oxygen fill and empty from his lungs before I could convince myself that he wasn't gone—that he was here—but the feeling had long gone from my legs.

Sora was right.

I couldn't live like this forever—locked in fear, constantly waiting for the worst to happen.

That was no life, and it helped no one.

I stood on tingling feet, pressed a quick kiss to his forehead, before closing the door behind me, quietly as I could, even though most of the patients up here were deep in a sleep that I could never shake so easily.

"Shit." The word was low, deep—an echo.

When I turned to search for it, I found Menace flying through the hall—a ball of wings and feathers and chaos. He let out a sharp caw, the gentle thrust of his wings weaving wind through my hair as he landed on my shoulder.

A tall figure was hunched over near the top of the stairwell, just outside of Mrs. Pederson's room. They stood slowly, their eyes locked on mine.

Or at least, I assumed that they were.

They wore a dark jacket with a thick hood pulled up so far that I could only see the briefest glimpse of pale pink lips and a sharp, smooth jawline.

"Sorry," I called out, embarrassed by the waver in my voice. "He's a bit obnoxious, but he won't hurt you."

My breath hitched when I glanced at the figure's hands, the only other part of them not covered by shadow or cloth. Long fingers, banded by silver rings, wrists covered in ink.

A flare of recognition hit me like a bullet to the chest.

The memory of the man on the day of The Undoing. His hand on my arm, the feel of his grip forever tattooed against my skin.

When I blinked, he was gone.

I ran back down the hall, took the staircase two at a time, but he was nowhere to be seen. Disappeared, just as he had before.

Menace, annoyed by the rocky movement of my chase, flew above me and back out the open window.

"Mareena, you okay?"

I tensed, then let out a shaky breath when I turned around and found Aidan studying me, his blue eyes shining with concern.

Aidan was what he called a 'forever student' working his way through a never-ending internship. Like most med students around the world, he dropped out of school after The Undoing. Now, he spent most of his time here, trying to help where and when he could, never able to quite shake the itch to help people who needed it.

"Fine." I offered a small smile as I tried to calm my racing heart. "Do you—who was that guy?"

His brows bent in question.

I gestured back in the direction I'd just come vaulting, as if that offered something helpful. "Upstairs, just now." I gestured awkwardly above my head. "Had a hood on."

Aidan shook his head, lips pursed as he studied me. "I haven't seen a man. Mary just left to get help with the body, but there's no way they're back already." He took a step toward me, his hand lifted as if poised to touch my forehead, before he took a step back. He cleared his throat, his gaze dropping from mine. "Mareena, are you—are you sure you're feeling okay?"

Aidan asked me to dinner a few weeks ago—an invitation I politely rejected, but things had been a bit stiff between us since. I'd turned him down as kindly as I could, told him that I wasn't in a place to get serious with anyone.

Which was true. I just didn't fully explain to him why.

It wasn't like I could explain that I said no for his sake, not mine.

I actually really liked Aidan. He was smart, cute, kind—genuinely just a good guy all around.

But he also made it clear that he wasn't interested in something casual—a one-off fling.

This community needed him. Frank needed him.

Which meant that he was off-limits, as far as I was concerned.

In another world, things might have been different. But until we lived in that other world, they couldn't be. Aidan and I could be casual friends, friendly acquaintances, nothing deeper than that.

I nodded, then tensed as my brain caught up with the rest of what he'd just said. "The body?"

"Yeah." Aidan took a deep breath and ran his hand through his golden waves. "Mrs. Pederson died a few minutes ago. She's been circling the drain for days. It's sad, but I guess—I don't know, at least she's at peace now, you know?"

My stomach sank as I realized that I'd felt her death coming, that it was *her* death I'd sensed. Not Frank's. And then it sank further with guilt when I thought of how grateful I was that Frank was still alive, that we hadn't lost him yet.

He winced, misinterpreting my expression. "I'm sorry, I hope that's not too crass. I didn't realize you were upstairs all this time, or I would have told you. You two weren't close, were you?"

I shook my head.

I'd only known Mrs. Pederson for the month or so that she'd been admitted here, and she'd been unconscious for most of that time.

"Did she have a family? Did they know—" I let the question trail off.

Was it possible that man had been her grandson or some distant relative?

Aidan shook his head, his eyes softening. Like Jo, he was in dire need of a few nights off. The skin beneath his eyes was practically bruised from lack of sleep. "No. She was brought in by a few folks who found her sleeping down by the canal. We haven't been able to track anyone down since. From the bits we did get out of her, it sounds like most of her family has long passed on."

I nodded, both of us quiet in the heaviness of the moment, unsure what to say.

"Do you—" My voice cracked as I met Aidan's crystal stare.

"You mentioned that she's at peace. You don't think that Frank —" I cleared my throat, pausing as I calculated how long it had been since he'd last been awake. Almost four weeks. The longest he'd been under yet. "You don't think he's in pain, do you?"

Aidan set his hand on my shoulder, and I tried not to flinch under the weight of it.

I knew, on a practical level, that whatever bad omen I carried wasn't contagious by touch, but that didn't stop the rumination from cycling through my thoughts relentlessly.

That something bad would happen.

That I was wrong. A contaminant.

"I can't say for certain whether or not he's in pain, but I don't think that he is, if that helps at all." He squeezed my shoulder, and I took a step back, wishing immediately that I could ease the flash of hurt in his expression as he let his hand fall back to his side. "He's lucky to have you, Mareena." He cleared his throat. "We all are, actually."

I swallowed the sudden urge to laugh.

Lucky.

If only Aidan knew the kind of luck I brought to the people that I cared about.

It would instantly sour whatever crush he still harbored— and far more swiftly than any rejection ever could.

5

MAREENA

PRESENT DAY

The line to Incendiary was wrapped fully around the block.

"This is wild." My jaw slacked at the impeccably dressed clusters of beautiful people, all impatiently waiting for their chance to get in. I hadn't seen this many people together since before The Undoing.

"The wild thing is that only a handful of them will make it inside tonight." Sora's eyes were bright, her body trembling with contagious excitement. "From what Rex said, most of them come here on the off chance that one of the demons inside will grab someone on their way out to help dispel some of the, uh . . . energy."

"Rex?"

My stomach clenched at the thought. Humans were largely split when the demon world was revealed. Some hated them instantly, others feared them, and then there were just as many bound up in utter fascination—a desire to become one of them. Or die trying to get close.

Other than the humans who were hit with backlash from The Undoing, I hadn't heard of any being straight up turned into a demon by another demon. That didn't mean it wasn't possible—and that didn't stop the cult-like obsession many harbored. They gave up everything they had for the small chance of becoming a vampire or some other mythical creature. Most of them just settled for living on the outskirts of the supernatural world, becoming blood donors for vampires, or offering whatever other services they could think of.

The thought of their idol fascination always confused me, but for the first time, I could almost understand it. The energy out here was palpable, the people looking more alive and eager than I'd felt in years.

"He's the one who got us in. Met him recently."

"And he is . . ." I pressed.

My skin tingled with waves of energy, like there was an electrical current buzzing in the air. Even from outside, I could feel the thrum of power emanating from Incendiary. The building felt like it was alive—just as, if not more, than the people flocking to it.

Instinct told me to run, but when I caught sight of the smile carving across Sora's face, I swallowed it back. She was right. I needed to fucking relax.

I refused to live in fear for the rest of my life, not after everything we'd done to ensure we'd have a life at all to live. Anything less would be just as tragic as death.

My body relaxed into the energy pulsing around us.

One night of fun, I could do this.

"A friend," she said, ending the discussion there. She grabbed my hand and tugged. She was surprisingly strong for someone so small.

I let her guide me to the front, where a bulky man stood with a clipboard, his beady eyes like lasers as they shifted from us to the cluster of girl's staring daggers at Sora for cutting the line.

"Sora and Mareena," she said, her voice clear and confident.

"Rex had us on the list for tonight. He told me not to wait in line."

A girl behind us snorted, and I shifted closer to Sora, as if I could shield her from the woman's glare, her anger like a blade against my back.

"We can wait," I whispered to her.

"We can't." Her stare was locked on the man's, her brow arched in challenge.

He grunted, the trace of amusement a singular crack in his mask—there and then sealed back up again—as he studied his clipboard, flipped the top sheet over and scanned down the back. He paused, his eyes lingering on words I couldn't see.

I fidgeted with my ring, sending up a silent prayer that he'd just turn us away or send us to the back of the line where we could wait for hours, pretending like there was a chance we'd get in, only to pack it up for a quiet night at home. Now that we were here, the heat of the club pulsed around me. I felt it burrow deep into my stomach, an invitation—a dare. One that I wanted to run from just as much as I wanted to take.

"Humans." The man's dark eyes darted from me to Sora, assessing, his brows lifting slightly in curiosity, like he expected to read the word printed across our foreheads. "Head over to the front desk, they'll get your paperwork ready and explain the rules."

"Seriously?" the girl behind me whined. "We've been here for over an hour."

Her long blonde hair was curled to perfection, not a dust of her makeup out of place. It made her large blue eyes pop; the dark pink on her lips a shade that highlighted their natural color while adding a juicy sheen. Her dress was midnight blue and accentuated every curve. She looked the way women looked in movies and magazines—too perfect to be real, like she'd been photoshopped before my eyes.

The kind of girl who never had to wait to get into a club.

What kind of power did this Rex guy have?

"They're on the list," the doorman said, unbuckling the rope behind him and ushering us through to the dark hallway behind him. "You know the rules, Reza. It's not like they change."

I wondered how many nights she spent like this—devoting hours of her day primping to perfection, just to wait all night at the entrance, arguing with the bouncer.

Guilt seeped through me that something I didn't even want was handed over with such ease. If it weren't for Sora's excitement, I'd have offered to trade spots with her.

My stomach tightened with each step we took down the dark hall, the lighting dark and tinted in pinks and blues.

"Oooh, bisexual lighting." Sora wiggled her brows, her fingers lightly grazing the dark, velvet walls. "I like it already."

I snorted, unable to find words as a rush of power flared over me, like the building itself was probing beneath my skin. Assessing.

Sora let out a rushed breath. "Just wait until we get in. I've heard rumors that just standing in the main room is like a lick to the clit."

"Poetic."

Nervous laughter spilled from my lips, and I tried to relax into it.

I used to be good at this. Letting loose. If I stopped being so goddamned uptight and leaned into it, I could learn to be that girl again. At least for tonight.

I pressed my hand against the wall, my head light and airy, like I stood up too quickly. The wall vibrated at my touch, purring the way that buildings did when music pulsed through the air. But it was quiet here.

As my fingers lazily traced the velvet filigree, a wave of clarity rippled through my bones, rooting me to the floor.

Sobering.

I closed my eyes, and when I opened them again, my vision shifted—doubled. There was the hall we stood in, warm and humming with muted lights, but there was somewhere else too —a forest of trees in grayscale.

And nested between two of the trees was a door.

"Woah," I groaned, leaning against the wall, as nausea rolled through my body.

I blinked.

The world righted again. The strange, ghostly forest gone, along with my dizzy spell. An illusion of some kind, maybe? Or maybe I didn't eat enough today.

"You okay?" Sora turned around; her brows pinched. She grabbed my shoulder, steadying me when I started to sway. "Is it too much? We can leave if you want?"

The lights seemed to flicker at the suggestion, but if Sora noticed them, she didn't say.

A quiet calm trickled through the air, as if the walls themselves were asking me to stay.

As if this was where we were meant to be.

As if leaving was the most preposterous idea in the world.

Normally, that kind of thing would send me hightailing it out of here, but for some reason, I leaned into it, comforted almost.

"I'm okay," I said, my smile tight, as I walked further down the hall, the feeling of rightness increasing with each step, like my body was growing stronger, the power of the building infusing me somehow. Perhaps that was how humans were able to withstand this place—it bolstered us.

"This way," a cool, calm voice echoed from an open door just ahead, right in front of the desk we'd been directed to.

It belonged to a woman. She was tall, white, with black wavy hair and full lips. Her blue eyes were almost surreal in their pigment, her features exaggerated in such a way that made the girl outside, Reza, pale in comparison.

She wore a black dress that hugged her curves and stopped just short of revealing the flesh of her ass. Her lips were painted in a cool shade of red that suited her so well, it was as if the color had been designed with her in mind.

Power emanated from her, so strong and sultry that I could almost taste it—like chocolate and cinnamon, but with a deadly twist.

One quick glance at Sora showed that she was just as captivated with the woman. Her lips parted in a soft "O" as her gaze locked on her.

It was a rare occurrence, rendering Sora speechless.

That, alone, was a testament to this woman's effect.

As if used to this reaction, the woman only smirked. It wasn't an unkind smirk, but it also wasn't friendly. A reminder, mostly, that in the supernatural world, beauty was braided with danger—the sharpest tool of a predator, to be wielded whenever they felt like using it.

"Humans need to meet with me or one of my partners before they are permitted entry," she said, her voice a sultry lick that had my stomach tightening—whether with arousal or fear, I wasn't entirely sure. One seemed to fuel the other in this place. "I'll assess your compatibility with my establishment."

Sora took a step toward the woman, as if getting swept into her orbit was inevitable.

My jaw clenched as I stood there, rooted with my hand against the wall, silently asking it for strength.

"My name is Villette," the woman purred, her lips curving into a more playful smile this time, one laced with a sultry challenge. She stepped back into the dark room behind her. "Please follow me."

Sora took a step toward her, and I reached for her wrist, pulling her back. Her skin was warm. A soft, static shock sparked where we touched; the energy kinetic. "You're sure this is safe?"

"Yes." She turned to me, threading her fingers through mine and offering a soft squeeze, the shock shaping into a lulling buzz. "This is why I know it's safe, Mars. Rex warned me about this part. Villette owns this place. Her protocol for humans is extensive—we'll be kicked out if she's not certain we can withstand it. Trust me. I wouldn't bring you here otherwise."

I took a deep breath and nodded. If there was anyone in this universe I trusted with my life, it was Sora.

We followed the woman into what was a remarkably unremarkable office for someone so magnetic.

There was a large leather couch, a luxurious armchair, and decor that oozed money.

But for a club that built its reputation on illicit encounters and sensuality, the paperwork and clutter littering the mahogany desk didn't look much different from the desk in our apartment, where I poured over ledgers and receipts for Frank's.

The lights flickered, the blues turning into deep reds. Villette rolled her eyes.

"You'll have to excuse the dramatics of this place. We have quite a packed crowd tonight and the building is overindulging a bit."

She gestured toward the couch as she moved to the armchair next to it, somehow managing to sit elegantly, despite the short dress. That seemed like a superpower in and of itself.

"The building?" I asked, taking a seat next to Sora.

"It has a power of its own. That's how this place works the way that it does." Villette leaned against one arm of the chair, her hand resting beneath her chin as she studied us. She had just the slightest southern drawl that peeked out at the edges, like it spent most of its time hiding. "Popular theory is that it either trapped a succubus when the realm split or stripped one of her power. It's infused with a magic very similar to ours." She tilted her head, and I noticed that her eyes seemed to almost swim with a hundred shades of blue—like an entire night sky existed in their depths. "The building"—she paused, considering—"amplifies lust. That lust functions as an entry point for energy transfer. As the building absorbs it, so do those of us who thrive on it."

"We being succubi and incubi?" Sora leaned forward, her eyes wide as she held on to Villette's every word, as if her next breath required it. "Lust demons, I mean?"

The woman nodded, her expression indulgent as she studied my friend—her gaze so steady and intimate it felt as if she were undressing her. And judging by the seductive smile in her eyes, it was clear that she liked whatever it was that she saw.

Sora crossed her legs, shifting slightly. Her cheeks heated with a pink flush as she met Villette's stare and tried to hold it.

It was strange to see her rattled. Usually when Sora found someone attractive, she approached the situation with a confidence I'd never been able to master myself.

Not this time.

Honestly, I understood the attraction. Villette was hot—sultry and powerful and mysterious. I'd probably be into her too if I wasn't so acutely aware of how fucking easy it would be for her to kill us.

"So," I cleared my throat, "the building feeds from us, you mean. After making us horny?"

"Mars." Sora shot me a look, uncharacteristically shy.

"What? It's weird?" I shot back, my voice a barely contained whisper.

"Yes." Villette only grinned, her gaze dancing between us, before lingering again on Sora. "And you're right it is weird. But so are many things about this world now. The building and the lust demons connected to it will indeed feed from any energy you exert within these walls. Look," she leaned forward, her focus shifting to me now, "there aren't any secrets here. If you enter this club, you'll make that choice of your own volition, giving your full consent—and only after you've agreed to our rules. We've put them into place for your safety, not ours. If you are uncomfortable with the form of payment we take, I can assure you that there are many other places to spend an evening in this city. Especially on a night like tonight. We don't beg here—" She paused, the corner of her mouth curving into a wicked hook. "Unless that's negotiated first, of course."

"And what exactly are the permanent effects of this payment?" I asked, ignoring Sora's breathy laugh.

Villette pursed her lips, considering. "It's hard to say. We only opened the doors to humans a few weeks ago, after we felt certain we could ensure their safety. It was an offering—an attempt to merge our societies a bit more. This is a simple business—and a place where people come to unwind. The last thing we need is to get the high-and-mighty religious vigilantes on our case. No human has died from the energy pulled through these walls. In that sense, I can promise you that it's far safer than being under the thrall of a lust demon one-on-one."

I twisted my ring as I considered her. "How, exactly, do you ensure our safety?"

"The building functions as a bit of a buffer. And we'll give you a bracelet that will track your vitals throughout the night. Generally, the humans affected most by a night here, simply wake up the next day feeling a bit sluggish, their moods a bit lower than usual from the drop—nothing permanent. The rules are simple, and if you follow them, you'll be fine." She held up one finger, her nail sharp, shaped, and painted a burgundy so dark it almost looked black. "You can enjoy your time at the club, so long as you wear one of our cuffs to signal to our staff that you're human and to help us keep track of you." She held up a second finger. "You stay on the first floor of the establishment." A third. "We understand that . . . release can't always be controlled, but humans are asked to refrain from having sex in this building." A fourth. "You stay for no more than two hours." A fifth. "And you may not return for a minimum of three weeks—an extra precaution to make sure you've replenished your strength. No exceptions."

Villette let her rules sink in for a moment, and I felt some of the tension disperse from my shoulders. The structure of her demands and the clear no-nonsense, dominatrix attitude she projected erased most of my unease and fear.

"So," she arched one dark, perfectly shaped brow and stood up, "do you agree to my rules?"

"Absolutely." Sora's knee was bouncing with excitement against mine.

I nodded my agreement, surprised that I meant it.

"Then if you pass my test and sign our release forms, you'll be on your way to an evening you won't soon forget."

She reached for Sora's hand, and I watched my friend stand on shaky legs.

"Don't worry, little human, this won't hurt," Villette whispered, her voice a caress that made my breath catch.

Sora swayed toward her, her eyes glazed and awe-struck. Her free hand grazed Villette's arm, tracing lightly until it reached her neck. She pulled the woman toward her until their lips were a hair's breadth apart.

"I understand the temptation," Villette whispered against Sora's mouth. She held her gaze, her voice breathy. "But for now, try and resist to your best ability."

Sora let out a low curse, then stepped back, almost panting with exertion.

"Good." Villette's fingers trailed briefly along Sora's arms, then she dropped contact and stepped back. "Very good. You're quite strong for a human. An ideal candidate for our establishment."

Sora flushed, whether from the compliment or the forwardness of her own actions, I couldn't tell. She fell onto the couch, sinking into it as if her legs could no longer support her.

When Villette turned to me, her hand extended, I stood on my own, my pulse beating a hurried drum.

Her fingers wrapped around my wrist, and I fell into her gaze.

A pulsing need thrummed through my veins, but it was no different from what I'd felt since the moment we'd stepped past the bouncer.

"When does the test start?" I asked after a few drawn out seconds, expecting my body to react as Sora's had.

Villette blinked a few times, then dropped my wrist. "Interesting."

"What is?"

"You're just not very susceptible to my power." Her hands smoothed the front of her dress and then she took a few steps back from me, her perfect composure breaking for only a fraction of a second before her gaze met mine again. "I don't encounter that often." She narrowed her eyes, studying me as if I'd offended her. "Were you . . . affected by The Undoing?"

I ran my hand awkwardly through the tips of my hair. "Free balayage for life."

As welcoming as Villette had been, there was no way in hell I was getting into the weeds about the occasional visions I had.

She cleared her throat and nodded, her half-grin less inviting this time, more pinched. "Right."

"So . . ." Sora stood, her arm pressing against mine as she turned to Villette. "We passed?"

"You passed." After a few beats, Villette blinked, then walked over to her desk. She retrieved two bands and a clipboard. "Read and sign this contract please."

Sora and I read together. And then I read through the entire thing a second time.

There were no secret promises that we were selling our

souls to a demon or that Incendiary would own our bodies for the night. Just the same rules that Villette had already laid out and a brief paragraph at the bottom that explained that any lust we experienced was an enhanced version of what we already felt; that the building's magic acted to lower inhibitions, and we were encouraged to make choices accordingly.

Sora grabbed the pen, the scratches of her signature the only sound in the room.

She handed the clipboard to me, and I did the same.

"Great." Villette grabbed Sora's hand, any of her sudden iciness now dissolved. "The bracelet will prick you when I put it on; it's powered through your blood. It will dull your susceptibilities to our magic, and it's how we will monitor you. Do I have your consent to put it on?"

Sora's neck flushed red. "You do."

Villette turned to me once Sora's bracelet was on—black with a silver "H" embossed on it. "And you? Do I have your consent to put it on?"

"Yes," I said, wincing slightly as the bracelet drew its price.

"If you feel uncomfortable at any time, just press the small button on the back of it and hold down for three seconds. A member of staff will escort you out immediately and see to your safety." Her smile widened and she walked to the door, then opened it. With a heated wink at Sora, she ushered us out. "Enjoy your time at Incendiary."

6

———

MAREENA

PRESENT DAY

"Holy shit," I whispered.

When I glanced at Sora, I knew my expression likely mirrored hers—wide-eyed and filled with awe.

The main room opened before us, the lighting and music moving together until the room seemed to almost pulse with the beat of it. A dark, oval-shaped bar was in the back half, manned by several bartenders as they mixed a range of drinks, working effortlessly together like a perfectly arranged assembly.

Most restaurants and bars I frequented since The Undoing ran like shadows of their former selves with electricity that didn't always work, fewer customers than I'd been used to, pared down dining and drink options.

Not this one.

The place was packed, with people spread wall-to-wall across the dance floor. Many were dressed in almost nothing, their bodies languid and alive as they touched and moved together until it was just a blur of parts.

There were dancers, too—professional from the looks of

them—in cages above us and on a platform that lined the entire left wall.

The rest of the dance floor was surrounded by small, intimate clusters of velvet chairs and tables—large enough for two to share. Couples sat twined together in the chairs, their bodies moving together, skin against skin, as they whispered into each other's ears, or kissed down each other's necks.

Strangely, I wasn't uncomfortable with the intimacy, even though a few of them looked like they were all but fucking. There was an odd peace to the sensual energy of the room, like it was here for all of us and therefore belonged to us all.

Heat enveloped the air, and I felt it tingle along my spine, lingering—a silent promise to sink into my skin if I only invited it in. The energy in the room was intoxicating, and I swayed with the music, my body loose, as if I'd already had a drink or two.

"It feels like a dream," Sora said, her cheeks flushed with the same heat I felt climbing up my neck.

I nodded. Dream was a good word for it. This room was different than any I'd ever been inside before. The power of it seemed to soak into the walls, into the floors, until I felt it sink into my feet, vibrating throughout my body until I couldn't tell where the room ended, and my body began.

If the building seemed strange when we'd walked into it, then this was ten shades past that.

It made sense to me now, for the first time—why Sora was so fixated on the supernatural, so drawn to this world. She didn't see the undertones of death and loss that infiltrated everything the way that I did. She saw this place, these people —and others like them.

And it wasn't just the sex, the intoxicating heat of Incendiary—it was the promise of a heightened everything, of something new. There was a pure, unbridled magnetism here—full-blown technicolor whereas the rest of our lives was cast in shadow.

The quiet fear that trailed the streets of our everyday, the desperate attempts to hold on to the world of before—was this what awaited a world brave enough to reach out and grab it?

"Should we get a drink?" I asked, my voice huskier than usual, like even it wanted to give in to the hedonism the room promised.

Sora nodded, then grabbed my hand and pulled me across the dance floor. She dragged me through a tangle of bodies, and I felt the joy of each of them cradled in the places where our skin briefly touched.

My eyes snagged on a man whose stare sparked fire—dark and shining with a silent invitation.

His hand grazed along my arm, and I shivered at the touch, my gaze caught on the fullness of his bottom lip. A sudden urge to suck it into my mouth surged through me.

As if he could read my thoughts, his mouth twisted into a smirk, a silent promise to transform that thought into reality if I only had the courage to ask.

And tonight, maybe I would let myself find it.

Sora tugged me, and my focus shot back to her. She glanced behind me and chuckled. "One drink first, then we can work on getting you laid."

I opened my mouth as if to deny it but then closed my lips and nodded. She was right. It had been a while. And a little fun tonight was needed. Desperately. It would feel good to let loose for once.

The bar was busy, though most people seemed to only be drinking water, using the bartop as a space to cage themselves against another body, the air here slightly less heady than it had been on the floor.

We watched a man pay for two large glasses of wine and carry them back to his friend a few feet away.

The bartender turned to us and raised his brows in question.

Sora shot him a flirty grin. "We'll take two of those as well."

His eyes narrowed, then shot to our wrists. Chuckling, he shook his head. "No, I don't think you will."

Her brow furrowed, ready to argue the point, but I grabbed her hand and squeezed, clocking the bartender's amused reaction.

He'd put the bottle of red back into a small fridge. The label was white, blank, except for a sharpie-scrawled AB+.

Blood.

"Oh," she said, catching on just as I did. "What do you recommend then?"

He slid a menu across the bartop, pointing to a short list of cocktails for humans, most of which were non-alcoholic.

"We generally don't recommend that you consume alcohol on the premises," he tilted his head studying us, "especially if this is your first time here. It can take a bit to figure out just how the power of this place will affect you. And," he winced apologetically, "no offense, but we've found that most humans are pretty lousy at handling their liquor in the best of circumstances."

"Waters," I said, then held up two fingers. He was probably right. I already felt buzzed, just from being in this room for a few minutes—but not like I usually would after a shot or two of tequila. This was slow and luxurious, a heady sort of buzz that usually came after a solid fuck or a deep-tissue massage.

Sora grabbed the waters, not putting up a fight, and handed me one.

I downed nearly half of it in one gulp, savoring the cool sensation as it swept down my throat.

"Damn." Sora lifted the glass up, studying it. "This is the best glass of water I've ever had."

I took another sip, nodding. If water tasted and felt this

good, I'd have no problem hitting my daily ounce goal. But I knew it wasn't just the water. It was this place. Everything felt heightened in here—every sip like the first gulp of cool water on the hottest day of summer, every graze against a stranger the promise of something more. The music was slow and sensual, and I felt it move through my body, as if it were emanating from me and not the stereo.

And, most importantly, since we'd walked in, my thoughts had been silent.

No spiraling.

No loops.

No intrusive thoughts.

Tension eased from my body, like a pool float being deflated, and I settled against the bartop, soaking in the sensation for a few moments.

Was this what it felt like—the absence of anxiety? Of fear?

The man from the dance floor made his way over to us, and a nervous, excited energy flooded my lower belly.

He was cute—a few inches taller than me, South Asian, with thick dark hair that lined his head and jaw.

Sora nudged her hip against mine, winking when I caught her eye.

"Talk about a tall glass of water," she whispered into my ear, her voice light and airy with the lilt of barely contained laughter.

When I glanced down at her, I could tell she was just as infected with the headiness of this place as I was. She swayed gently to the music, her body loose, happier and more relaxed than I'd seen her in a while. Maybe months.

Seeing her like that eased whatever lingering tension I held on to, until it was gone altogether.

"Hi." The man glanced between us, his gaze settling on me. "I'm Ren."

His voice was smoky and smooth, like silk against skin.

I glanced down at his wrists, not seeing a band, and a spark of fear fluttered briefly in my chest. Not human.

Studying his face—sharp jaw line, flawless golden-brown skin—I tried to parse what kind of demon he might be. Unless a demon flashed fang or transformed into a werewolf, it was generally impossible to tell.

"I'm Sora, and this is my friend Mars." She elbowed me in the hip.

"Mars?" He tilted his head slightly, his gaze dipping to my mouth briefly, before trailing back to my eyes.

Blinking, I cleared my throat, extending my hand. "Mareena."

Mars was reserved only for my close circle, and hot as he may be, this man was definitely not in it.

When his hand closed over mine, I shivered, the feel of his skin against mine far more intimate than it would have been in any other setting. "Care to dance with me, Mareena?"

He said my name like a purr, and my stomach dipped at the sound.

It took a lot to tear my eyes from his, but I managed it as I turned my focus to Sora. "I'm here with my friend actually."

"Go." Sora shoved me forward, shaking her head. "Have fun. We'll check in with each other in a bit, okay? Relax and try to have some fucking fun for once." The last part was a quiet plea, to me only, her glare piercing as if to cement the demand into reality.

When I nodded, Ren settled his hand on my lower back, the weight of it doing nothing to calm the low arousal that had been coursing through me since the moment we walked in.

I let him lead me out to the floor, as the song transitioned into something slower.

"Your first time here, Mareena?" he whispered the question against the shell of my ear as our bodies moved—twining as they responded to the music and each other.

"Mhm," I hummed, relaxing a little as the beat pulsed through me. I'd never been a particularly smooth dancer—at least not in public. But something about this place tore away those inhibitions, that fear of being perceived.

"And are you enjoying yourself?"

I nodded, shifting closer to him as a group of people slithered around us.

Ren smelled like power and promise—a spicy combination of cinnamon and clove.

Breathing it in, I let him pull me closer, until my body was firmly against his, his thigh sliding between mine as he effortlessly moved us to the music.

We were below one of the caged dancers and I watched them with rapt fascination, their limbs flexible and lithe as their body married the music, so smooth and filled with so much ease that it was almost impossible to figure out which was in control—the music or the dancer.

"They're something, aren't they?" Ren's breath grazed my neck, and my body erupted with chills. His fingers trailed along my arm, my back, featherlight—the barest suggestion of more.

I looked up, my focus latching on his mouth. Pressure sparked in my body, the slow building need, now almost impossible to ignore.

Ren's lips parted and he inched his face toward mine, waiting for me to pull back.

But I didn't.

Instead, I glanced up at his eyes, nodding at the question etched in them.

He closed the distance, the warmth of his mouth merging with mine as he sealed us together.

Heat flooded me as I sank into the kiss.

Fuck, I hadn't realized how right Sora was, how badly I needed a release—to just fucking let myself go.

To forget about The Undoing.

Frank.

The diner.

My past.

Him.

For one night.

I could survive one night of pure, unadulterated hedonism —couldn't I?

More than that, I could let myself enjoy it.

I deepened the kiss, my chest tightening at his responding groan.

Ren's fingers dug into my back, holding me against his thigh as heat pooled low in my belly.

With a teasing grin, I pulled back, turned around, pressed my ass against his obviously erect dick, and danced, letting the music move my body wherever it wanted to go. I felt strangely powerful, knowing that this stranger—a demon, no less—was as affected by my touch as I was his.

A woman around my age, tall and curvy, with red hair, green eyes, and a fuck-me shade of crimson lipstick on her mouth swayed toward us, until she caged me from the other side.

A dark chuckle spilled from Ren's lips, against my ear, as his fingers dug into my hips—not letting me stray too far from him as she sandwiched me between them. "This is Lenora—a good friend of mine."

For the rest of the song, the three of us danced together, our bodies hot and twined as they both ran their hands along my sides, my arms.

I glanced down at Lenora's wrist, noting the absence of a band again. How many humans were here tonight? And how many of the people here were something . . . more?

When she pressed her mouth against my neck, I froze, half expecting her to bite me. Instead, she sucked and licked, and I eased against her, swallowing a soft moan.

Ren's hand swept up my right thigh, curling toward where it met my left.

Screw it—maybe I'd fuck them both tonight.

My vision blurred, until I saw both the club surrounding us and the faint etchings of more—the trees I'd seen in the hallway, dark and gray.

I blinked again, and they vanished, the chaotic hunger of the dance floor blurring it out.

But my focus caught on a man leaning against the bar, his eyes latched on mine, burning me. Silvery-white hair, a dark shirt that made his pale skin stand out in contrast.

It was him; I was sure of it.

His expression was unreadable, but I froze under his stare, my connection to the dancers and music snapping like a severed cord

It had been six years since I'd seen him, but now twice in one day? That couldn't be a coincidence.

"You okay?" Lenora whispered, her voice dripping with the same heat I'd been swimming in just two seconds ago.

I turned back to her, nodding.

"Yeah—" I said. I cleared my throat, straightening. "Yes. I just need to use the restroom. You guys go on without me."

She furrowed her brows, her hand still against my hip. "You sure? Want me to go with you?" She glanced at Ren, her expression teasing. "Or maybe both of us?"

I shook my head, unfolding myself from them both. "I'm good, promise."

Ren laughed, the sound dark and deep. "I think she's wondering if you wanted more than just an escort, Mareena."

Oh.

I glanced back at the bar, but the man was gone.

Dammit. What was with his constant disappearing act?

I scanned the floor, but I couldn't spot him in the sea of bodies. I did, however, spot Sora. She was seated at one of the tables, her arm around a girl, both laughing as they whispered to each other. Even from here, I could see her eyes sparkling, her entire face lit up with excitement. She was having fun. I didn't want to interrupt that. Sora needed to let loose as badly as I did.

But I also needed to find this guy.

I shot Ren and Lenora a quick smile. "No, I'm good. I'll be back in a few minutes."

I left them to each other, then made my way to the edges of the crowd. When I glanced back, they were both entwined together, dancing as if I was never there between them, their lips fused together.

Fuck, they were hot.

I momentarily resented myself for getting distracted by the stranger.

The bar had a line now, so I let myself watch them until they were swallowed up by the crowd.

When I got to the front, the bartender handed me another glass of water before I even had a chance to ask him for it. A god amongst mortals.

"Bathrooms?" I asked, guzzling it until all that was left was ice.

He nodded behind the bar.

I pressed the cool glass against my neck, savoring the sensation. The chill of it was like a balm, settling me back into myself. After the initial shock of the place, it was easier to focus —where the room had felt like being hit with a harsh wave of power at first, now it was more like a still swimming pool, one I could wade through easily.

There were two separate halls back here, but I took the first.

It was quiet and dim, lit only by the back glow of some red sconces, their flare flickering along the black walls like fire.

A familiar song started, but it was softer here, muted. No louder than I'd typically play music in my room.

Humming along to the slow, sultry lyrics, I trailed my fingers over the wall, the glass still pressed against my neck with my other hand. Though I was more used to it now, I could still feel the buzzing power ebb and flow through the building, its lure gentle but unmistakable.

The bathroom was giant. The sort that had individual floor-to-ceiling stall doors and, judging by the moans coming from a few of them, I was pretty sure they were currently occupied for more than peeing.

I splashed some water on my face, taking care not to ruin my makeup any more than my sweat already had.

With a deep breath, I leaned against the sink, steadying myself. Thank god I stuck with water tonight. This place was getting under my skin, burrowing deep.

When I caught my reflection in the mirror, I jumped.

It was my face, of course, though I looked a bit more disheveled than I had when we got here. My pupils were blown wide, the eyeliner I'd been so careful to apply now slightly smudged.

The problem though, was with the scene reflected behind me. It wasn't the ornate, gothy vibes of the luxurious bathroom. Instead, the color was flattened, like the saturation had been sucked out of the room. Dark, dead-looking trees surrounded my reflection—trees that were absolutely not in the room with the me standing in front of the mirror.

I blinked, focusing on the familiar gold ring of my septum piercing, using it as an anchor.

"It's not real. It's not real," I muttered to myself. Even after six years, I still hadn't grown accustomed to these occasional visions—their distortions bled with reality until it became nearly impossible to identify the real from the not.

It was truly such a useless side effect of The Undoing.

I would've much preferred teleportation or the ability to fly.

Instead, I got two-toned hair and double vision.

When I had the courage to look up again, the strange forest was replaced by an elaborate painting. The same painting that was attached to the wall behind me.

My shoulders sank with relief.

Get it the fuck together, Mars.

I made a goofy face at the me in the mirror, relaxing when she made the same face back. The world had righted itself in my brain again.

My focus latched briefly on the column of my neck. There was a crimson smudge where Lenora's lips had been.

My body heated when I thought about where else her lips could be right now, if she'd come with me. Where maybe two sets of lips could be—all I had to do was ask.

With a heated smirk at myself, I tossed one of the small ice cubes from the glass into my mouth, then set it down on a tray near the door.

I needed to cool down. To chill the fuck out and go have fun.

A moan echoed from the stall at the far end of the room.

"Fuck, yes, just like that." The voice cracked into another, louder groan of pleasure.

Heat shot through me. Bathroom stalls weren't really my style but, fuck, I needed a release. Less than half an hour in this place, and my body had done nothing but make me excessively aware that I needed to give it some proper attention. Or, rather, have someone else give it some proper attention.

It was officially time to forget the mysterious disappearing dude and get back to Ren and Lenora.

My vibrator was great, but tonight, I wanted . . . more.

"Right," I muttered to myself. "Fun. I can do this."

I left the bathroom, but instead of turning back to the dance floor, I stopped at a large door, the word 'basement' emblazoned on it in an elaborate gold font. A woman—bald, pale, and wearing a body-con dress that highlighted her every enviable curve—walked over. Her hand was clasped around a tie, and the tie was attached to a man who had what looked like a trail of blood dribbling down his chin.

Another glance at her, and I noticed she had blood along her neck, seeping from a very obvious, very recent bite.

I pressed my hand against the lipstick kiss on my neck, reassuring myself that it wasn't also weeping blood.

The woman gave the man a sultry tug, before shooting me a wink and slipping behind the door.

A brief flare of different music and voices filtered into the hall, silencing when the door closed behind them.

Another club?

Curiosity had me reaching for the golden handle, but when I opened it, the door snapped closed again.

"I don't think you're supposed to go down there, actually." The voice was deep, crackling with an Irish lilt. The owner's breath brushed against the shell of my ear, sending a wave of shivers down my spine.

"Says who?" When I spun around, I found myself caged against the door, a familiar pair of hazel eyes holding mine in their stare. Those eyes were somehow even more mesmerizing than I remembered them being, like my brain couldn't quite concoct their exact shade. It didn't have the artistry, the shades necessary to get them just right.

"You," I said, though the word was more a soundless breath than anything with shape.

I'd thought of this man more times than I could count, wondering what had become of him that day. The Undoing and his rescue were tied irrevocably in my brain, and he showed up in my dreams often because of it.

Still, those dreams hadn't done him justice.

He had more tattoos now than he had a few years ago—or maybe my memory could only hold so much of him. Intricate patterns of ink snaked up his neck, along the arm pressed above my head, where it held the door closed behind me.

His ears were pierced, his pale hair mussed on top but still somehow perfect in the chaos of it.

"Me." He arched one of his dark brows, the corner of his mouth twitching briefly as he studied me.

"I, um—" I swallowed, trying to find strength under the weight of his gaze, remembering earlier—Mrs. Pederson. "Were you at the medical center earlier—in Wallingford?"

His expression didn't shift, and he didn't pull away from me. With a shake of his head, he leaned a few inches closer. "Nah, you must have me confused with somebody else."

There was a teasing quality to his tone that made whatever gymnastics my stomach had been doing before go full-on Olympics level now.

"And six years ago?" I licked my lips, my chest tightening as his eyes clocked the movement. "You saved me from being roadkill. The day of The Undoing. I remember you."

"Now that," he said, his gaze lingering on my mouth. "Definitely doesn't sound like me. Not really a rescue the damsel sort."

I narrowed my eyes. "Good thing I'm no damsel, then."

There it was, that almost smirk again. Why the hell did I suddenly want to feel that smirk pressed against my skin? "No. I don't suppose that you are. This isn't really the place for damsels, is it?"

I held his stare as fire pooled low in my belly. I thought, briefly, of those bathroom stalls, of how I could maybe become a bathroom stall kind of girl, under the right conditions.

"Hey, Mareena," a voice called from my left.

He stiffened.

I turned toward the voice, though I felt his gaze still drilling into me.

Ren walked closer, Lenora leaning against his side. Her

perfectly crimson pout was now feathered and smudged around the edges, like it had been partially sucked off. I had no clue how she managed to pull it off, but somehow the disheveled look only made her prettier.

Some things just weren't fair.

"We uh . . ." Ren's focus darted to the man, then back to me, his smile uncertain. "We were just coming to find you. You coming back to the floor?"

"Sorry." When it became clear that my captor had no intention of moving, I ducked underneath his arm. "I got caught up on my way back."

"Yeah." Ren glanced behind me, where I felt the man's presence like a blazing inferno at my back. "I see that."

Lenora studied him with more interest than Ren did, her lips curving into a sultry smile. "Who's your friend? He can come, too, if he wants."

A stab of something unfamiliar, almost possessive, shot through me.

Not jealousy—but maybe jealousy's second or third cousin.

I had no intention of dissecting why her obvious appreciation of him had my chest feeling uncomfortably tight—especially when I'd been all team more-the-merrier just a few minutes ago.

"Um, this is . . ." I turned around, my breath catching when I realized that he was all but glued to my back. His face was unreadable, eyes latched on mine as if we hadn't been interrupted. It became immediately clear in the echoing silence that he had no interest in helping me with a name. I narrowed my eyes and smirked. "Sir Broods-a-Lot."

A deep, quiet sound, half growl, half chuckle reverberated in his chest, and I found myself desperate to hear it again, the urge to press my palm against his black shirt so I could feel the vibration of it so strong I had to use all of my will power to resist it.

"He's not really one for words." I took a step back, toward Ren and the girl, and it was like resisting the lure of a strong magnet—every inch away from him demanded effort on my part.

A muscle in his jaw tightened, and I had to forcibly turn away from him to keep from staring at it with a hunger I couldn't explain.

"Well, good thing it's not words that I want right now," she said, her voice soaking in lust. She watched him ravenously, and I resisted the urge to step between them. "What do you say, Sir Broods-a-Lot? You want to join in on the fun? There are private rooms we can rent if that's more to your taste—a private dance, maybe. Of course, Mareena has some restrictions." Her gaze dipped to the band at my wrist. "But that doesn't mean she can't participate or watch."

"We enjoy sharing." Ren trailed his fingers up the girl's side, and she shivered, her eyelids heavy as she leaned into him and watched us.

My heart hammered in its cage at the offer. Any attraction I'd felt toward either of them before had withered up like a grape left out in the sun. Nothing sounded less appealing than the thought of Ren's fingers on me, or Lenora's on Mr. Mysterious.

"I don't," he said. "At least not with you."

"Boo." She pouted playfully. "No fun."

"Suit yourself." Ren shrugged, his focus returning to me. "Mareena, you coming?"

I shook my head. "I should check on my friend."

I could see Sora from here, and she seemed just as cozy as she had when I'd left for the restrooms, but now a night with Ren and Lenora was the farthest thing from my mind.

An annoying mystery enshrouded the man standing at my side—one I'd been oddly fixated on solving for years. I didn't fully understand what it was about him, but now that he was in front of me, I knew my curiosity wouldn't relent tonight until I saw it quenched.

"Fair enough, another time then." Ren pressed a kiss to my cheek as he squeezed my shoulder, and I flinched at his touch. It had been one thing while dancing, but it was another now.

His grip was ripped away almost instantly though, as the man shoved him back and stepped between us. "She doesn't like being touched."

The memory of that day came flooding back more vividly than it had in years. His hand on me, pulling me back from the bus. My adrenaline-flooded attempt at gratitude coming out instead like a chastisement of his grip.

"My bad, man." Ren raised his hands up in surrender. "She didn't seem to mind earlier."

"Well, she minds now," he ground out.

"You're right." Ren studied me, his brows furrowed in concern as he nodded. "Sorry, Mareena, I didn't mean any offense."

"It's fine." I winced. The group closest to us on the dance floor had stopped moving to the music. Instead, they were watching us. We were drawing attention. I caught the bartender's eye and gave him a nod, a silent promise that I'd deescalate the situation. "I'm not offended."

It was the truth—and Ren was right. I had more than welcomed his touch earlier.

My dislike of being touched had little to do with my own comfort and everything to do with my fear that I might somehow contaminate those closest to me.

It had taken years of work, but I'd gotten a little better at identifying where my anxieties and fears diverged from the curse. I was still absolutely convinced that death was haunting me—or those closest to me—but it hardly seemed transferable through touch, like a particularly gnarly infectious disease.

And if it was, something told me that demons could withstand the curse in a way the humans in my life might not be able to.

"We'll catch you later, Mareena." Lenora glanced between us, then twined her fingers through Ren's. "Enjoy your night."

With a wink, she turned and led him down to the basement.

When they were gone, I turned back to the man, every molecule in my body aware of his presence. I wasn't sure if it was the power of this place or just him. Maybe a mix of both.

"So, you do remember," I said. "That day."

He ran a hand through his hair, not meeting my stare. For the first time, he looked uncomfortable, not entirely in control.

Maybe I wasn't the only one feeling the intoxicating effects of this place.

"You should be careful, Mareena."

I shivered at the sound and shape of my name on his lips. He pronounced it slowly and softly, almost to himself, like he was tasting it.

I forced my focus up to his eyes, though they were just as disorienting. "Of what?"

"If you don't keep your wits about you," his eyes burrowed into mine, a silent plea, "this place can cast a charm that's not exactly easy to break."

I felt the timbre of his voice reverberate in my chest, its own kind of mesmerizing music.

He stood close to me, but I wanted him closer. My interest in Ren and Lenora had dissolved entirely, but he'd somehow managed to magnify the need coursing through my body like a livewire set aflame.

"Who said I wanted to break it?" I heard the desire in my voice, didn't even bother disguising it. There was no sense trying. "Maybe that's why I'm here."

He let out a low laugh, though there was no humor to the sound—just the edge of resignation. "Is it now?"

"Is that so wrong? To want a night of fun?"

"No." He shook his head, something passing in his expression. "That's not wrong."

"And you?" I asked, my voice a husky whisper as I leaned closer to him.

He swallowed, and I couldn't tear my eyes from the movement. "Me?"

"Are you here to have. . .fun?" I wasn't usually shy about wanting sex—it was often just an exchange for me, a release. I had rules, kept emotion out of it. But I felt bolder than usual tonight, and right now, I wanted nothing more than for him to say yes. "Or just to brood on the sidelines?"

"Oh, I like fun." He took another step closer and then another, until my back was against the wall. His arms pressed on either set of my head, caging me there, but it wasn't lost on me that he made sure, even now, not to touch me. "If it's fun that you want."

This close, his body consumed my senses. He smelled like mint and morning dew mixed with something entirely mouthwatering that I couldn't find a name for in my lust-addled brain.

Heat pooled low in my belly, and I felt my nipples stiffen where his chest just barely brushed up against them—a whisper, the smallest breath of a touch.

He leaned down until his lips were at the shell of my ear. His breath against my neck tore a whimper from my throat. Whatever arousal I'd felt while dancing with Ren and Lenora was nothing more than a shadow compared to what his mere presence was doing to me right now.

What the fuck was it with this guy? And why, when he was around, did everything else just fade into the background?

"It's Kieran."

I blinked, fighting to focus. "What's Kieran?"

"My name."

"And do you like to dance, Kieran?" Because if we were

going to stand here like this for much longer, I was liable to do something ridiculous, like try to climb him like a tree.

"Not really." He shifted closer, until his mouth was just barely a breath from mine, the ghost of a smile sparking in his eyes. "But I'd like to dance with you."

I grabbed his hand, my skin humming where it met his, and then led him the few remaining feet to the dance floor.

He pulled me closer, now that I'd initiated contact, his eyes on mine the whole time, like he was waiting for the slightest signal to carve distance between us again.

Distance was the last thing I wanted right now.

There were a million questions I wanted to ask him.

Why did he disappear that day?

Where did he go?

What had the rest of that day been like for him, The Undoing?

How did he know Mrs. Pederson?

Did he live near here?

But the desire to berate him with even one of those questions quickly shaped itself into a very different, very demanding desire.

We moved together, the slow, sultry beat of the song pulsing between us.

His hand was featherlight on my waist as he pulled me in, his leg sliding between mine, like he needed as much of us twined together as I did.

Heat clung to my skin as we danced, slow and steady, until it felt like we were the only two people in Incendiary. The only two people in the world.

His right hand grazed my cheek as he threaded his fingers through my hair.

I shivered as tingles exploded down my body, then I leaned into his touch, craving so much more.

He swept his thumb across my bottom lip, tracing it with a quiet reverence that squeezed at my chest.

I gasped at the sensation, at the feel of his skin against mine.

He froze; his gaze locked on my mouth.

Not breaking eye contact, I slid my tongue forward until I tasted him. His skin was cool and salty, tinged with the lightest layer of smoke.

His lips parted as he watched me, clearly just as affected as I was by the spell weaving between us.

Emboldened by his evident desire, I pulled his thumb into my mouth, swirling my tongue over it as I sucked.

He hissed. "Bloody fecking hell."

Heat blazed in his eyes, and I gasped when he pressed me closer to him. He was hard against my pelvic bone. Very hard.

For a moment, we stood still, both holding our breath and waiting, until I couldn't wait a second longer.

Leaning up, I pressed my lips to his.

He didn't move at first, didn't react.

I pulled back, embarrassed. "Sorry, I—"

And then, like a rubber band that had been pulled too tight, he snapped.

His lips crashed against mine as he dug his fingers into my back, my hair—like he couldn't get close enough.

When his tongue parted my mouth and found mine, I groaned at the warmth and taste of him.

Fucking hell, I couldn't remember a time I'd ever felt desire this strong—this demanding.

One hand gripping my waist, he slid me up his thigh, and I nearly came from that small pressure against my clit.

A low, needy moan pulled from my throat as his lips sucked their way over my jaw, down my neck. I didn't even care who might see or hear us.

"Tell me what you want?" he whispered against my skin and

the ache between my thighs deepened at the clear heat in his tone.

"Touch me."

He froze for a moment, his lips at the hollow of my neck, his hand tangled in my hair.

The hand gripping my waist pulled back, and I instantly felt the loss of his touch. Until I felt his fingers trail down the outside of my left thigh, my entire body erupting in tingles wherever his skin met mine.

He slid his hand beneath my dress, tracing up my inner thigh until his fingers met the lace of my underwear.

I gasped as he pressed down on me, my desire liquid hot and obvious as hell.

He groaned against my neck as he slipped a finger beneath the lace, stroking me.

"You're fecking soaked." His voice was strangled as he slid his finger inside of me.

I whimpered when he pulled it out, then stepped back, putting a few inches between us.

His breathing was heavy, his eyes a violent storm.

My protest must have been clearly etched across my face.

"I can't fuck you," he said, his eyes wide and wild with need as he glanced around.

I followed his gaze and noticed the bartender watching us, body stiff, head tilted as if in warning.

"But—"

"Not in here." Kieran shook his head, his eyes darting down to the band on my wrist.

Right. Villette's rules about humans. No sex.

"Where?" Because right now, I would follow him into the depths of hell if it meant he would ease the impossibly tight pressure building in my body right now.

His mouth curved into a soft smirk as he slid his finger into his mouth and sucked, considering.

"Fuck, you taste good." He shook his head, letting out a soft chuckle. "Literally anywhere else."

"Then take me." My legs turned to Jell-O at the liquid heat in his eyes.

"I really shouldn't—" His eyes darted down, his face unreadable when they locked on mine again. "It can only be once. Only tonight. That's all I can give you, do you understand?"

"Okay." I nodded, ignoring the sudden pressure tightening my chest. That was my rule, too, there was no reason tonight should be any different. "I get it, just once. Fine by me."

His jaw muscles flexed.

"No strings, just sex," I whispered, suddenly terrified he was going to change his mind and leave me here in a puddle without him. I sounded desperate, but I didn't care—right now, I was desperate. "Kieran, please."

He made a strangled sound in the back of his throat, then grabbed my hand, pulling me through the crowd.

I bit back my victorious grin, hardly even paying attention to where he was leading me, every ounce of my focus locked on where he touched me—on how fucking good it would feel when he was touching me where I needed him to be.

Cool air licked at the sweat on my neck.

We were outside, in an alley between Incendiary and whatever building was next to it. It was dark, I couldn't see any signs.

He ran a hand roughly through his hair as he looked around, searching—probably for somewhere more private. Inside.

"Here," I said, tugging on his hand.

"People might see."

"Let them watch."

He swore, then pressed me up against the wall, his hand loose against my throat as he searched my face. "You're going to be the death of me."

His mouth twisted into a small, sad smirk, a joke that my lust-addled brain was too preoccupied to follow.

Whatever it was he was looking for—desire, consent, demand—he found, because with a single nod, he dropped to his knees in front of me, his hands disappearing beneath my dress as his gaze held mine.

My breath stuttered in my chest at the arrogant teasing in his eyes.

With agonizing slowness, he slid my underwear down my legs.

I stepped out of it, my hands clasped on his shoulders for balance since I'd clearly lost all control over my body the moment he touched me.

He slid the black lace into his pocket, a cocky smirk carving across his face. "I'll be taking these."

Before I said anything, his head disappeared underneath the tulle, and I gasped when the heat of his lips found my clit.

"Fucking kill me now," I hissed, my body sliding against the wall.

With his forearm pressed across my hips, he held me there.

And then he sucked me into his mouth, my entire body throbbing at the sensation.

We weren't even in Incendiary anymore—the power of the place no longer in play—and I'd still never been so turned on in my life.

I clung to his hair, my body lost to the oncoming orgasm.

People were laughing and walking nearby, but I didn't care.

If anything, the thought that they just had to look down the alley to see us made the whole thing hotter.

My bodyweight fell against him as I came, the orgasm rolling through me with an intensity that had my vision blurring.

He licked up every last drop of my arousal, like a man dying of thirst.

He pressed a kiss to my thigh, then my leg and stomach as he crawled back up, my body tingling under every press of his lips and tongue.

"You are magnificent," he whispered against my neck, then pulled back to look at me, his eyes drunk on desire.

"Fuck me," I begged. I pressed my hand against the thick bulge of his pants, then met his eyes. "Please."

A deep groan resounded in his chest. He pressed a kiss to my neck, his teeth grazing the sensitive flesh as I unbuckled his pants and slid my fingers over him.

He was smooth and hard, his dick pulsing in my hand when I rubbed his pre-cum over the silky tip.

"I'm on birth control," I whispered against his mouth, my teeth tugging lightly on his bottom lip.

He nodded; his eyes locked on mine. He slid his dick against my clit, through my heat, coating himself in my desire. Then, with a shiver, he sank into me.

I swallowed the groan on his lips, my body molding against his as he fucked me with a punishing pace that already had me on the edge of another earth-shattering orgasm. The rush of pleasure and urgency made me dizzy. Greedy, even. We'd agreed on the one night only thing. . .but damn if I wasn't already craving another, desperately afraid to crash down from this high.

A blur of voices grew louder, but we were both too lost to care.

Kieran picked me up as I wrapped my legs around him, his mouth carving a delicious trail of heat along the column of my neck—punctuated occasionally by a low, guttural groan and a reverantly whispered, "Fucking hell."

I dug trenches into his back as another spark of euphoria spread over me, only vaguely aware of a flash of movement from the corner of my eyes. For a moment, I thought my vision was just blurring from the intensity of my impending orgasm—

that he was making me see literal stars—until I saw the faint outline of a couple of figures.

My peripheral focus locked on—holding there. Something about the profile of one of them was familiar, but the shadows were too thick, and I couldn't make out their face.

I hardly cared. The soft scrape of Kieran's teeth at the base of my neck demanded all of my attention, and I clenched around him—savoring every inch of where his skin brushed mine.

The orgasm tore through me just as the shadowed figure inched forward—familiar gray eyes that I hadn't seen in nearly seven years met mine briefly as I buried my face into Kieran's shoulder, riding the intense waves that rippled through me.

Kieran bit down on my shoulder, muffling his moan as he followed me over.

He pulsed inside of me, and I found myself desperately thankful he was holding me up.

I'd have been a puddle at his feet if he hadn't been, my body nothing but sated putty.

As the magnitude of pleasure coursing through me faded, my brain caught up with me.

Slowly, I unwound my legs from Kieran's waist and leaned back against the wall, searching desperately through the alley as I recalibrated my balance.

Whoever had been here before, whoever I thought I'd seen, was gone.

The alley was as empty as it had been when we got here, no one else in sight.

I clutched the wall, still panting.

It couldn't have been him. I had to have been seeing things—a lingering effect from Incendiary's power.

Kieran took a few steps back and winced, his eyes narrowed as if in pain.

"Fuck." He stumbled slightly, grabbing his arm.

I took a step toward him, but he stepped back. "Are you okay?"

"I'm fine. Sorry—" His eyes met mine as he straightened up—there was regret, maybe anger etched across his face. "I have to go. You should—" He took a breath, steadying himself, the maelstrom of emotions draining into a strange, distant apathy. "This was a fun night—you should go home and get some rest."

My head swam as I fought to find words, to understand what the hell he was talking about.

By the time I opened my mouth to say something, I was alone in the dark alley.

He was gone.

7

MAREENA

APPROXIMATELY NINE YEARS AGO, THREE YEARS BEFORE THE UNDOING

A man walked into Frank's.

He was my age—maybe a year or two older—white, tall, and carved with lean muscle that caught my attention long enough that my stare was probably noticeable. Dark wavy hair curled across his forehead, landing just above his eyes. It was thick and just a bit crumpled—sticking up in odd directions, like he'd been running his hands through it in frustration. His dark gray eyes latched on to mine for a moment and my stomach tightened under their attention.

There was something unreadable—unreachable—in that look; a darkness, almost, that resonated deep inside of my chest and lingered there, a fishhook refusing to catch and release.

It felt almost like staring into a haunted mirror. One that I usually did my best to avoid.

He sat on one of the barstools at the counter, just a few feet from me, spinning around until he faced the mess of pots and pans Frank hadn't gotten around to cleaning since the lunch rush.

For a moment, my gaze lingered on his back, his shoulder blades and lines of lean muscle visible through a thin black

T-shirt that left little to the imagination—though my traitorous brain had no problem filling in the gaps. There was a menu in front of him, but he didn't bother looking. Instead, he buried his head in his hands, elbows perched on the counter.

I felt a strange urge to reach out and comfort him, something I'd usually never do for a stranger. Or even a non-stranger.

"You haven't touched your food."

I jumped, nearly upending the glass of water on the laptop in front of me—one that would have had little chance of surviving the spill.

Which would've been extra bad because the laptop wasn't mine.

"Sorry?" I blinked at the screen a few times as the lawyer-speak masquerading as a rental application came back into focus. Without thought or hunger, I shoved the wilted BLT into my mouth, before peering up at Frank with chipmunk cheeks. "I have. See."

The sandwich was dry, and I'd taken way too big of a bite. I chugged a few desperate gulps of water, in an effort not to choke, while he grunted and turned back to the man who'd come in, leaving me to my work.

With more effort than it should've taken, I dragged my attention from the man and back to the screen.

Now that I was eighteen, Sora and I could officially get out of the studio apartment we'd been living in and into a proper apartment. Maybe even one roomy enough for two beds. Dream big, right?

That was what we'd been hoping for anyway.

I glanced at the bottom of the application, where the monthly cost of the one-bedroom was listed in bold print. Maybe not.

This was the most affordable option we'd found so far, but

the obscene price tag still made me queasy. It didn't even include utilities or Wi-Fi.

I swallowed the obnoxious lump of sandwich and groaned, snapping Frank's refurbished laptop closed.

How the hell were people supposed to survive in this city, let alone furnish an entire apartment? At this rate, I'd need to work twice as many shifts to make ends meet. That, or we'd have to finally give in and move out to the suburbs . . . which would mean a two-hour bus commute each way to work. Not ideal.

But honestly, as much as I loved Seattle, moving out of it was better than spending another month in Oleg's garage. A few years in that shithole was already more than I could stomach.

When Sora and I piled off the train three years ago, bleary eyed, broke, and trying like hell to leave our pasts back in southern Oregon, we'd been desperate.

Technically, we were wards of the state, on the run, and without a responsible adult to cosign for us—let alone vouch for our existence. If we wanted to stand even the smallest chance at staying together and moving on from everything we'd been through in our own way, we had to essentially disappear—from school, from social media, from everywhere—until we were eighteen and could legally live on our own.

For a chance at starting over? We gave it all up. Happily.

That first week had been . . . bad. And our options of where to go from there had been even more bleak. But desperate times called for desperate choices, and we just had to suck it up and suffer through if we wanted to make this new life work somehow. That, or give up, go back, and face what we'd left— something neither of us was willing to do.

Instead, we scoured housing ads at the closest library, hoping for just a sliver of a fucking break. Eventually, we landed on Oleg and his call for *a symbiotic living situation in an upgraded studio—rent negotiable.*

The ad didn't include pictures—the first bad sign—but we were desperate, and we definitely couldn't afford to be picky.

And the phrase "symbiotic living situation" conjured images that only became more cringe-worthy the longer I let my brain run wild with the possibilities. The second bad sign.

There were, of course, many more.

Oleg had 'upgraded' the shed in his backyard into what can only be described as a studio apartment to someone who'd never actually *seen* a studio apartment before. The kitchen consisted of a broken microwave and a dorm-sized fridge that never got cold enough to keep perishables fresh for more than a day. Two during the winter.

The bathroom was the size of a closet. Even Sora, short as she was, had to bend and contort to fit her head beneath the shower spout. And the living-room-kitchen-bedroom space was just large enough to fit *one* full-sized bed.

There wasn't room for anything else, not even a table. We had to set our stuff on top of the mini fridge if we wanted to keep the bed free from clutter—the only stipulation Sora ever had about the housing arrangements. Clean bed, and she could make almost any living situation work.

And somehow, the smell was even worse than the space.

Oleg handled the renovations himself, which largely meant slapping a fresh coat of paint over questionable stains, and the single-paned window he installed was so thin and poorly fit that there was no escaping the mold or unrelenting *wet* during the rainy season. We were in Seattle, which meant half the year was spent sopping up water and black sludge from the windowsill, the scent of mildew and musk a constant, inescapable perfume that permeated everything.

Truthfully, we should have been grateful for the window at least. It was the only source of ventilation we had. Who knew what would eventually come of our lungs, breathing up all those mold spores?

So, yeah, the place was a shithole, but Oleg only charged us a hundred bucks total a month, let us move in without references, proof of salary, or identification, and, most importantly, he looked the other way when it became abundantly obvious that we were both truant, clueless minors attempting to live off grid until we were old enough to age out of the system.

He didn't ask questions, which made him the best landlord we could have hoped for.

Plus, he even offered up his kitchen whenever we wanted to use it. All we had to do was dress up in his mother's old nightgowns when we did and tuck him in twice a month before he went to sleep. He'd originally requested nightly lullabies, but Sora was a master negotiator and threatened to report his deeply illegal 'studio' to the city if he pushed for more.

Though shitty, the setup proved pretty smooth—it was surprising how much ick you could live with if you cast it out of your mind and pretended like it was normal.

Whenever his neighbors shot curious glances at us, he told them we were his nieces, staying with him while our parents traveled, and we finished school online. Whether or not they ever questioned this white dude's familial relation with the Lebanese and Japanese teens living in his backyard remained to be seen, but if they did, nothing ever came of it.

Oleg's wasn't ideal, but compared to the alternative, it was the best option we had.

Until now.

Maybe.

Then again, now that I saw the prices proper landlords were asking for, I was starting to think that Oleg was the less predatory option.

The door swung open, and Sora rushed into the diner, the smile on her face carved so deep it actually looked painful. She slapped a rain-soaked flier on the table in front of me, the sound reverberating through the entire restaurant.

"Found one," she barked, the soft trembling of her fingers the only sign she was actually trying quite hard to contain her excitement—she just couldn't. The golden retriever energy was strong with this one.

Frank handed a glass to the man seated at the counter, not even sparing her a glance. He'd grown very used to her theatrics over the years.

"Didn't I tell you?" She jabbed her finger against the paper, smearing the ink. "Things would start looking up for us—and they have."

I shoved another bite of the sandwich into my mouth, chewing slowly as I studied the paper. It was a flier for a punk show at a local dive, covered in Sora's chicken scratch. The ink bled together with the rainwater, making it entirely indecipherable.

"Sor, it's a shitty band. Looks like there's a steep cover too."

Well, to be fair, ten bucks wasn't necessarily steep in the grand scheme of things, but it was for us.

She scrunched her nose in disgust. "What?" She grabbed the flier from me, shook her head, flattening the paper against the table until it stuck to the surface. "Not the band." She tapped the flier. "The address. It's Penny's ex's place—Becca. I've met her a few times, she's cool. More importantly, she's got two rooms available. Well, technically I guess it's one room and a small office." She arched her brow, the edge of victory in her grin as she studied me. "*But* we can actually afford it."

"Penny. . .as in your girlfriend, Penny?" I squinted at the paper until I could just start to make sense of Sora's lines and scrawl. "And she's okay with you living with her ex?"

"Eh." Sora shrugged, leaning back against the booth. "Probably not, but I've been thinking it's time to call it anyway. She's getting too clingy. Even started suggesting I move in with her."

I froze, my body going into panic mode at the mere suggestion that Sora might move out and in with someone else. We'd waited so long for our chance at a normal life. Now that it was finally within our grasp, I hadn't even considered the possibility that she might want to do something else. That her vision of the future might have changed, expanded—without me.

When I glanced up at her, my body relaxed, the anxiety immediately shifting to guilt when her expression made it clear she hadn't given her girlfriend's offer more than a passing thought.

"And you say I have commitment issues," I said, voice deadpan as I studied her, silently scouring her face for cues that I was wrong, that maybe she actually *wanted* to move in with Penny.

The only thing worse than her moving out would be her staying with me for my sake.

"Don't worry, pookie." The corner of her lip curved into a hook. "You're the only one who doesn't send my avoidant attachment issues into a raging death spiral." She grabbed the other half of my sandwich, biting off more than she could close her lips around, as she added, "Besides, Penny eats chips in bed. Can you imagine? Permanently sharing a bed with someone and their crumbs like that? Disgusting. Whenever I stay over, I end up spending half the night debating the pros and cons of dipping out while she's asleep and coming home." She sighed. "Trust me. That relationship's been on its way to the grave for weeks now, I just haven't gotten around to putting the final nail in the coffin yet." She drummed her pointer finger against the flier again. "This'll do it."

"You're sure?" I asked, keeping my face measured, blank.

"Abso-fucking-lutely I am. Ran into Becca after class." Sora was six months older than me, which meant she'd already reclaimed her identity, got her GED and enrolled in some cosmetology classes—a maelstrom of paperwork and appointments I'd been working on since my birthday. "She's not terrible. Quiet, works first shift, and spends every weekend in Portland visiting her boyfriend. The common areas are partially furnished. It's literally the perfect setup." She finished off the sandwich half, leaving the crust and a few pieces of wilted lettuce, then shot me a big grin. "We stay there for a few months—a year tops—save up, and then we can get our own place for real—just us. This is like the perfect little lily pad to help get us across the pond, you know? Next lily pad will be even bigger and better." Her smile, if possible, widened even more. "Just you wait—it's a bright future, kid. No more hiding, the world is our oyster."

I snorted. "Are we frogs or pearls in this scenario?"

Sora had a way with mixing metaphors and turns of phrase. Usually, I just sort of had to close my eyes and go with it, gauge the general vibes and hope they didn't lead me astray.

"Exactly." She waved a cold fry in the air, pointing it at me with emphasis. "You're getting there, Kermit."

The man sitting at the counter chuckled, the sound barely a sound, more the suggestion of one.

Sora turned, studying him with interest. Her eyes narrowed as she glared at his back.

It was a damn good back, but she didn't seem quite as taken with it as I'd been.

She shifted her attention back to me, her smile more tame.

I glanced down at my phone and swore. "I'm late."

I was covering part of a shift at the pub down the street, and I was technically supposed to start in five minutes. Tonight, the manager's son, Chase, was working—and he hated me with a fiery passion.

I shoved the rest of my fries at Sora, told her to call Becca and tell her I was in, before collecting my shit and shoving the laptop across the counter toward Frank.

"Thanks—you're a lifesaver, old man."

He grunted, then grabbed the computer without lifting his head up from where I knew he kept his phone perched, watching whatever local game was playing on the cracked screen.

When I turned to leave, I noticed the amber liquid in the mystery man's glass—and the half-consumed bottle of Bulleit sitting next to it.

I froze.

"Frank, since when did you get your liquor license?" I turned to him, tapping the counter when he didn't answer.

Frank's head shot up, brows pinching as his gaze dipped from me to the bottle. "I, uh—" He pursed his lips. "I didn't."

The man next to me went still as ice, his moody eyes shifting to mine as he held the glass—the nice stuff that Frank kept in his apartment, not here in the diner—to his lips.

His upper lip was full, slightly bigger than the bottom, and my mouth went dry when his tongue peeked out against the rim as he took a sip.

I blinked, swiped the bottle, and handed it to Frank.

Frank grabbed it, his face bent in confusion as he held it, like he wasn't sure how it had gotten there in the first place.

"That's your good stuff," I said, more to the man than to Frank. The diner didn't serve alcohol, and Frank rarely drank, save for holidays and after a particularly bad shift. He went through maybe one bottle of Bulleit a year. I knew, because Sora and I saved up each fall and bribed someone to buy one for us so that we had something to wrap up and give him on Christmas that he wouldn't hate. And this guy looked like he'd already thrown back a few glasses in the few minutes he'd been here.

"It's fine," he said, his voice low, smooth, with just a bit of bite—not unlike the bourbon he'd been drinking. He turned to Frank, eyes narrowed. "Isn't it?"

Frank blinked a few times, then nodded. He set the bottle back on the counter, sliding it toward the man.

"No." I stopped him, shoving it back. "It's not."

The last thing Frank needed was a citation.

The man froze, his full attention on me now as he turned, his kneecaps lightly brushing against my hip bone.

My stomach flipped, but I shoved the sensation away.

I turned toward him, meeting his eyes as I gestured in Frank's direction. "He doesn't have his liquor license," I said, my words slow and clear so that there'd be no confusion. "If you want to drink, there are plenty of other places to do so without risking someone's job stability."

Honestly, I was mildly impressed with myself that my voice came out cool and collected, and not at all betraying the way this man's stare had completely unraveled my composure.

I wasn't even sure why I was fighting this so much. If Frank wanted to give this dude his booze, that was his business—but for some reason, I couldn't bring myself to stand down.

Frank may have been a grumpy asshole sometimes—okay, all the time—but he'd been there for Sora and me in ways no one else had. As far as we could tell, he didn't have anyone fighting in his corner—except for us.

The possibility this guy was taking advantage of him rankled my nerves.

"Everything okay?" Sora rounded the booth and stood next to me, her arms crossed, signature glare glaring overtime.

"Fine," the man said, his eyes locked on mine.

I swallowed, inching back from him, but I was caught between his legs, Sora, and the stool at my back.

His lips twitched, the shadow of a smile, there and then gone.

My fingers twisted into fists—whether to punch him or keep myself from brushing that curl of hair from his eyes, I wasn't sure.

I didn't know what the hell was wrong with me, but something about this dude had my instincts going haywire.

"Okay." Sora glanced between us, then relaxed. "Great."

I narrowed my eyes, studying her from the corner of my eyes.

She didn't usually back down so easily.

"What—"

"Do you have any suggestions?" the man asked, cutting me off. His eyes cut into me, and I found myself getting lost in the bleed of grays that washed against the black of his irises. They reminded me of a thunderstorm on a warm summer night—both chaotic and oddly calming.

"What?" I blinked a few times and took a step back. There was more room this time because I'd been unconsciously moving toward him, until I was standing with his knees bent on either side of my thighs.

"Of places to drink." He arched a brow, the hair dark and thick—a perfect frame for those haunted eyes of his. "Legally, I mean. I didn't mean to cause trouble for your friend."

"Yes. She works at one. In fact," Sora said, her gaze dipping between me and the stranger, a devious grin on her face, "she's going there now. So she can take you."

My breath caught at the thought of spending more time in the man's proximity—as if a walk down the street was as intimate and vulnerable as showing him to my bedroom.

I swallowed, trying to find a way to politely decline.

"Great," he said before I could, his lips twisting into a soft, teasing smile. He stood. My eyes were level with his chest and shoulders—both lined with the same smooth muscle as his back. "Lead the way."

When I didn't respond, Sora shoved my arm. "You're running late, remember? Get going."

"Right." I cleared my throat, my stomach dropping when I realized that I'd wasted the few precious minutes I had before my shift picking a fight with a stranger. I glanced up at him, not quite meeting his eyes. "Let's go then. Like she said, I'm late."

The walk to Mac's Tavern was a quiet one.

But the quiet did nothing to ease my discomfort.

If anything, it just made me hyper aware of the few times the man's arm brushed against mine as he matched my stride, step for step.

I felt his gaze on me, like lasers burning holes, even though I refused to look at him. My brain went all loopy every time I did.

Was I breathing too loud? I counted the seconds between each breath that I took, trying to even it out, though I suddenly wasn't sure how to judge a normal break between inhales. Could he hear the absurdly loud beat of my heart as it drummed against my ribs?

I pressed each of my nails, one by one, into the tip of my thumb, counting to four over and over again, relying on the brief flares of pain to center me.

When I swung open the heavy, wooden door, Chase's hawkish gaze tracked me instantly—a predator homing in on his favorite prey. There was a grin hidden in the creases of his eyes, not because he was happy to see me, but because he was pleased he'd have a chance to scold me for being two minutes late.

He tossed the bar rag on the table he'd been pretending to clean, then closed the distance between us in three wide steps. "You're—"

"Late." I swallowed back my annoyance, offering a sheepish grin instead. "I know. I'm sorry."

"Sorry doesn't get your prep work done, does it?" he grunted, his nose curling. It was a more malicious version of one of his father's tics. "My father might bend over backwards for your excuses, or whenever you bat your eyelashes, but I won't."

Never mind that I was doing Chase a favor today. I wasn't even supposed to work this shift. I got called in because Rick was sick, though judging by the loud music on the other end of the line, he was actually just at a party he didn't feel like bailing from.

"He took a chance on you," Chase continued, hitting a stride in his righteous fury. "Always had a soft spot for charity cases. And you—what do you do? You continuously take advantage of his kindness." That cut like a blade through my gut, and try as I did to hide the sting, the gleam in Chase's eyes confirmed he was more than aware that his blow had landed. But he wasn't done. "He might pity you, but I won't have someone fuck up this business—my grandfather built it ground up, you know? You're not worth the trouble, not if this insubordination keeps up. Your lateness affects us all, Mareena—"

"I'm two minutes late," I snapped, then took a deep breath, fighting back the urge to lash him right back. It would be so easy to point out how everyone who worked here hated him, how the back of house always used shifts with Chase as punishment for whoever lost the biggest bet that week, or how in the quiet of closing, after a particularly busy rush, his own father would often confide in me about how frustrated he was with his son—about how entitled he was, how he wasn't ready to take over the business. Instead, I dug my pointer fingernail into the flesh of my thumb and swallowed the words back like bile. "I'm sorry, Chase. It won't happen again. You have my word."

Five hours. Not even a full shift. I just needed to get through five hours without killing him, and then I could go home.

"Your word is only worth as much as you live up to it, Mareena." Something about the way he said my name—stretching it out on his tongue—always made me want to snarl. He arched a brow, eyes pinning me like I was a frog he was eager to dissect. "Two minutes or not, I'll be noting this on the record, and I'll be sure to have a word with my father about it next time I see him."

I had no doubt that he would.

I bit my tongue, nodding as I pulled my apron belt from my bag. The dining room was empty. We still had an hour before the dinner rush even started—and it was Monday, our slowest night. Most bars in the area took the day off.

Someone cleared their throat behind me, and I jumped.

One anxiety bled into another until I'd momentarily forgotten about the icy stranger at my back.

Heat crawled up my neck as I realized he'd witnessed all of that.

Well, this guy had been a bit of a dick as well. He and Chase would have a lot to bond over.

I shot him a tight grin, though I couldn't muster any true kindness behind it.

"Well, welcome to Mac's," I said, gesturing absently at the empty room as I tied the apron around my waist, tugging the strings a little too tight. "You can grab whichever seat you want at the bar and Chase will fix you a drink. Legally."

Though truth be told, I wouldn't complain if he got Chase in trouble with the city. Of course, then, that would fuck with his dad—who I actually really liked—and my job—which I very much needed. Especially now that a pricier apartment was on the horizon.

"Not in your section?" the stranger asked.

"I'm eighteen. I don't work the bar."

Until I was twenty-one, I was technically not allowed to serve drinks. I just ferried them to my tables whenever my customers ordered. And since Chase was on tonight, that meant I'd get most of my drinks about ten minutes slower than if anyone else was working behind the bar. Half because he was a shitty bartender, and half because he was a smarmy dickhole who took advantage of the fact that my tips were negatively affected by his slow and mediocre service.

I fished absently in the wide apron pockets, searching for a pen.

Empty.

Of-fucking-course. Why were my pens always disappearing? I swore it was magic. Didn't matter if I had five in my pocket or fifty—one way or another, I always ended up with exactly none by the end of a shift. I'd forgotten to check before leaving Frank's.

Chase glared at me, nodding his head toward the man, like I was the rude one in this situation.

I sighed, flattening out the wrinkles in my apron. I wasn't even clocked in yet but leave it to Chase to refuse doing even the bare minimum of his job.

With a deep, grounding breath, I forced my temper down.

While I'd love nothing more than to break Chase's nose one of these days, I reminded myself *again*, as I did every shift I shared with him, why I couldn't. One, I needed this job. Two, as much as I hated Chase, I deeply appreciated his dad. And his dad probably wouldn't like it if I broke his son's nose. Three, without his dad, I wouldn't have a job.

Chase wasn't entirely wrong—his dad had broken a lot of the usual rules for me. Frank introduced me to him awhile back, and he took a chance on me when no one else would. He was also willing to pay me under the table. Illegal, sure, but it was the sort of law skirting I was desperately thankful for.

"Right, um, follow me, I guess." I grabbed a menu and walked him over to the bar, grimacing slightly when I realized it was still sticky.

Chase never cleaned when he knew I was coming in.

I felt both of their stares on me as I wiped the faux wood surface down, then left them to it. Chances were Chase hadn't done any of his own prep work necessary for the dinner service either, which meant that I had more than usual to get through.

As expected, it was a slower night, and I caught myself staring at the stranger more than once in the long stretches between seating my next table. He hadn't moved from his stool once during my shift, but it looked like he'd transitioned away from booze and on to water and food instead. Probably smart and would also explain how he was still relatively clear-eyed.

More than once, I noticed him whispering to Chase, the ever-present frown lines etched along Chase's forehead mysteriously absent. That almost never happened when I worked with him. He looked oddly . . . kind when his face wasn't contorted in constant, righteous anger.

Curiosity piqued, I found myself making excuses to pass by the bar, hoping to pick up on a sliver of their conversation—but whenever I got within hearing distance, they stopped talking.

Generally, I had to run my drinks from the bar to my tables, but Chase handled the drop-offs on his own—a bizarre occurrence in and of itself. He'd even bussed half of my tables, something he literally never did, even when his station was slow and mine was bustling.

In fact, I was usually the one taking *his* customer's empty dishes to the guys in the back.

I did my best to ignore the man for most of the night, but something about him kept drawing my focus. I caught myself staring at the back of his head while wrapping silverware or peeking out at him behind the kitchen doors while prepping side dishes for my tables.

When I ushered my final table out the door, I expected Chase to kick the guy out or cut him off. He didn't.

We closed early on Mondays, but Chase switched the sign to 'closed' a full hour before usual.

He nodded to me. "You can take off when you're closed out."

My head shot up. "Really?"

There was a flash of annoyance in his expression, but it dissolved with one glance at the stranger. "Really. I appreciate you coming in and covering tonight. You didn't need to. I'll handle the leftover closing work—you go enjoy the rest of your evening."

I froze, lost for words—my mouth gaping open like a fish.

The stranger glanced at me out of the side of his eyes, the corner of his mouth curving up as he took a long sip of water, draining the glass down to ice.

Chase started shutting down the bar, and I watched him for a full minute, half-expecting him to vomit up whatever alien had possessed him.

But no alien emerged, and when he stopped working to glare at me, I decided to just go with it.

First time for everything, apparently.

I shot Sora a text, letting her know about the extraterrestrial event and that I'd be done in ten minutes.

When I closed out my final tabs and pulled out some cash to tip Chase out, she walked in, ignoring the red "closed" sign at eye-level.

Her eyes were dry, but I could tell from her expression that the breakup had gone poorly. Sora was never the sort to wear her pain where it could be easily dissected by outsiders.

She clutched a bottle in a large paper bag at her side, shooting a wary look at me when she noticed Chase.

"Sorry," she mouthed, "forgot he was here."

Typically, Chase kicked her out whenever she came in after closing, but today he just smiled at her and waved her in before getting back to the dishes. As in . . . he was actually washing the barware . . . on his own.

Her brows shot up, shocked, and she waved back, the movement stilted and awkward. Spotting the stranger, her face lit up and she slid onto the stool next to him. She shifted slowly, keeping her attention on Chase, as if afraid that she might jostle the *real* Chase back into his body with any sudden movements.

"Almost done, just need to grab my bag from the back." I slid the envelope of tips toward Chase, but with a quick glance at the stranger, he slid it back to me, an odd, forced grin on his face. Odd because I'd never seen him smile without a tone of maliciousness behind it. This smile was almost . . . earnest.

"Keep it all, you earned it tonight." His brows bent in confusion, as if his words were as much of a shock to him as they were to me, his tongue unfamiliar with shaping them.

My fingers froze around the edges of the envelope, but I muttered a quiet thanks and shoved it into my apron before either of us had a chance to second guess the gesture. With the move-out drawing close, I wasn't going to question Chase's sudden conscience. Who knew how long it would last, and I needed all the cash I could get my hands on.

Sora's stare drilled into the side of the stranger's face until, no longer able to ignore it, he turned toward her.

"You're still here," she said, a teasing lilt to her voice.

He glanced down at himself, then shrugged. "Apparently."

Their eyes locked, the two of them caught in a silent battle of wills that I was way too exhausted to intervene in.

I left them to their riveting conversation while I said my goodbyes to the guys in the back, warned them about Chase's uncharacteristically good mood—if they wanted to ask for vacation time, tonight was the night to do it—and then grabbed my stuff.

When I made my way back to the dining room, the stranger was standing next to Sora, Chase nowhere in sight.

"Levi's going to join us," she said, mischief sparkling in her eyes.

I swallowed a groan. I knew that look.

It was her matchmaking look.

My least favorite of all.

When I shot her a glare—a clear, silent, knock-it-off—she just shrugged, an exaggerated, oblivious expression on her face.

Great. It was going to be one of those nights, and I couldn't even fight her on it because I knew the breakup was weighing on her. If this dude hanging around would help ease even an ounce of her grief, I'd suck it up and deal.

"Levi?" I studied him, rolling the sound of the name over the strange man I'd been weirdly fixated on for hours. Figures, I'd barely heard the guy say two words all night, but Sora already had his name and likely his whole life story. She was good at peopling. I, obviously, was not. I turned back to her. "Join us for what?"

"Celebrating." She took a big swig of whatever was in the bottle, before passing it to him. "We got the apartment, I'm newly single, and you got off early. Plus, neither of us has to work tomorrow. No excuses."

Levi glanced down at the bottle before handing it to me. "If it's cool with you that I join, that is?"

I considered him for a moment, then brought the bottle to my lips for a sip, hissing at the sharp burn that clawed over my tongue and down my throat.

Tequila. The cheap stuff. Sora's go-to for a messy night.

I took another swig, then nodded. Fuck it.

Sora's smile brightened, any of the lingering sadness about her breakup boxed up and compartmentalized, at least for now. She never lingered on disappointment for long. "Canal? It stopped raining and the sun will be setting soon."

"Works for me." Summers in Seattle were my favorite thing in the world. The sun stayed high in the sky until well after nine, making the day feel like it stretched on forever.

"Chase said he'd lock up and you're free to leave whenever," Levi said, shifting awkwardly from foot to foot, like he was unsure what to do with his body.

I nodded. Whatever had come over Chase, I hoped it would

last through the next shift we had together. Other than the fit he threw when I showed up two minutes late, this had been the most pleasant few hours I'd ever had with him in the vicinity. He'd been downright amiable.

"What did you two talk about?" I asked, then handed Sora back the bottle. If we were going to the canal with a dude neither of us knew, at least one of us needed to stay reasonably sober.

He shrugged, his expression unreadable. "Just small talk— nothing notable."

I narrowed my eyes. Something about his general standoff- ishness told me that Levi hadn't entertained small talk with a stranger a day in his life.

"So..." Sora turned her devilish grin on me. "Shall we?"

8

KIERAN

PRESENT DAY

I pressed the cigarette to my lips, wincing at the taste.

Mostly because it didn't taste like much. A shitty facsimile of the real thing.

Everything here was a shitty facsimile.

That was the fecking point.

A shadow of the real thing kept us craving the things we couldn't have.

It'd been a week since my little vacation in the mortal realm and I was still somehow hungover, still chasing that high.

At least today the headache had died down a bit and I was more or less able to string a thought together.

This was a dangerous world to spend so long lingering in that liminal space, recalibrating to the stench of death.

Odds were higher that one of the young, eager-fecking-beavers would see the moment of weakness as an opportunity. One wrong move and I'd be dead.

Again. But permanently this time.

Leaning back against the wall, I took a drag, relishing the memory of that night.

Fuck, I wanted to go back.

Of course, I also hadn't wanted to leave in the first place. That was sort of the point of these little vacations, wasn't it?

Gave us something to look forward to when everything around us was otherwise so fecking bleak?

I still wasn't sure if it was because I cashed out all my vacation on the anniversary of The Undoing, when the barrier between our worlds was thinnest and our power the strongest, or something else about that night that made it feel so different. So real.

Maybe it was just her. There was something different about her.

It felt like I'd flown too close to the sun at the end, like I'd tapped into something I wasn't supposed to. For a moment, I almost felt like me—the me that existed before the me in the Between anyway.

So, yeah, the hangover was shite. But it was also fecking worth it.

I pulled the crumpled lace from my pocket and pressed it to my nose—a sweet little souvenir I'd swiped at the last second.

The material didn't still hold the vibrancy of her scent, not like it did in her world. But like with the smoke, the shadow of it was there, and that shadow would be enough to sustain me for a little while at least.

Hell, it'd been a week, and I'd wanked every day since with her panties in my mouth. Even with the hangover, they'd been the best wanks of my death.

Bit of a genius move on my part, pocketing these.

Anything we brought with us during our brief trips into the mortal world usually made its way over to this one. There were exceptions, of course, but that was part of the lure of the job. We could bring things back with us. Little reminders of what we couldn't *actually* have.

Fecking masochists, the lot of us.

Groaning, I pressed my forehead against the stone wall,

letting the chill soak in through my skin. In all my years, I'd never had a humanity hangover quite like this, had never been so drained from a fuck.

I hadn't even lasted that long. Not quite a two-pump chump, but I'd been pretty damn close to earning the title.

Two hours. That was all I'd been granted in her world.

And like the dickhead that I was, I'd wasted the first one sucking down a pack of proper smokes and enough booze to burn the memory of the taste into my tongue for a few days—to sustain me until the next vacation.

Though if I'd had any fucking clue what lay in front of me for the second hour, I'd have started there. The taste of her tongue still lingered on mine—far sweeter than any booze had ever been.

I adjusted my pants, my dick hardening at the memory of it.

She'd remembered me, too, which I still didn't get. We'd always been told that was impossible. On the rare occasions that mortals engaged with us, they weren't supposed to remember. We were kind of like the faces people conjured in dreams —snapshots of NPC's, filler faces that weren't grounded in the real. In the living.

Then again, I rarely spent my vacation time chasing after people I'd encountered before.

I always wanted something fresh, something new. I didn't like lingering in the past.

Of course, when I saw her that night, tangled up between those two lusty twats, I couldn't keep away. Couldn't let them have her.

"Mareena." I whispered her name, just so that I could taste its shape on my tongue again. She was just a girl, but something about her lured me in, turned me stupid. I made bad choices around her. Dangerous choices.

I still had no idea why I'd saved her the day of The Undoing. But I was damn glad I had. Maybe, on some level, I'd sensed what was coming, the strangeness in the world. The fabric of the shadow realm coming apart at the seams.

Whatever it was, it happened. Maybe some spark of the shadow magic had lodged itself inside of her that day, gave her a bit of a safeguard against the memory tug. Weirder iterations of the power had grabbed hold of the mortal world.

It hardly mattered. I'd never see her again.

The stranger, more annoying part of it all was that I wanted to. Desperately.

Futile as it was, I'd already done the math, thought about how long it might be before I'd earn another traipse in her world. It'd probably be at least a year, maybe two. Still, the brief moments of reprieve between the hangover and wanking at the memory of her were spent plotting and daydreaming about my next vacation. That, and trying to contrive opportunities to steal some extra power—rush the process along faster.

Of course, with the trials coming up, I wouldn't have quite so many opportunities.

Maybe I could convince Rafi to get me out of it. He'd be glad for an excuse to get me out of his hair anyway.

"You look like shit." Thorne stood at the opening of my little alley, his face etched with its customary look of disdain.

"Morning to you too, sunshine," I said, forming the words around the cigarette still hanging between my lips.

"Rafi says you have two days to pull your shit together." Thorne's lip curled as he studied me. "We've been summoned for the new recruits, but if anyone sees you this weak"—he nudged his chin up—"looking like this, you're fucked."

So was he, which was what he was really getting at. Thorne hated everything about everyone, but he hated me especially. His fate was tied to mine—a cage. And under his absurd doctrine, he owed me a debt.

Something that only made that hatred flare.

And something I enjoyed lording over him whenever I got bored. Which, in this place, was pretty often.

"New class of the dead." I inhaled another drag. "How exciting."

It wasn't and we both knew it.

Time spent with the Order was dangerous.

Especially now.

If we survived the next month, it'd be a miracle.

Normally, I wouldn't be fussed—the call of the void wasn't usually something I feared. But if I was stripped of my power now, then I wouldn't get another vacation. There'd be no coming back. Which meant no more real cigarettes. No more real booze. No more her.

"Stop fucking around," he said. "I mean it. What the hell did you do last week? Spend every last ounce?"

Yep. Literally.

I'd never been pulled so violently from a stint before. Suppose I should have been grateful I at least got to finish.

But fuck, what I wouldn't give for another thirty minutes, or a round two.

The memory of the desire in her dark eyes, hot and hungry, resurfaced.

I exhaled, grinning when the cloud of smoke made him snarl. "Worth it."

"What happened to showing the kid around, imbibing in something briefer for the holiday, like the rest of us. Exercising fucking restraint."

"You," I chuckled, "imbibing?" We both knew that he hoarded his power like a dragon hoarded gold. "And I did—hung with the kid for a few minutes, brought him to the club." The mortal spot—Incendiary—tapped into the same power we fed on, which meant that it gave us a bit of an extra boost. Useful, for a night like that one, especially with the veil between this world and theirs thinner than usual. "Then I went on my own way. Said I'd take him there; didn't say I was signing up for babysitting duty."

"Just"—Thorne's nostrils flared as he glared at me, about as close as he got to keeping that rage of his in check—"get your shit together. And do it quickly."

"Yeah, y—" I hissed as a shot of pain sliced through my arm, coalescing in my veins, the sensation sharp and burning. One of the few things we could fully feel in our world—pain. Fucking figured.

Like I said, this place made masochists of us all.

I dropped the remaining inch of the cigarette to the ground, then stubbed it out with my boot.

The tattoos along my arm flared, cutting down my hand to the rings.

"A charge?" Thorne asked. "Figures the fates would take pity on you."

Pity? Perhaps. Right now, my throbbing head was an afterthought, overshadowed entirely by the pain of the call. That was one form of pity, I suppose.

I shot him a sarcastic salute and then left him to his general dickishness, chasing the twisting pull toward wherever I was being called.

The Between was a strange land—everywhere and nowhere at once—and, generally, when our power was drained, we could only make our way back to the realm of the living when we were tethered to a life there.

In the state I was in, I didn't anticipate getting another charge any time soon—and, without one, it might have otherwise been months before I could find my way back there, even in my transient form. Right now, the only way for me to leave was through a door located in the middle of a lake on the outskirts of the Order's grounds. It was a dangerous path to carve, with so many of the dead around, but I was generally pretty decent at staying under the radar when I wanted to.

When you were around for as long as I'd been, you got used to finding the small pockets of protection.

Besides, the danger was always worse upon return—when the job was done—than it was when leaving.

Tethers were controlled by the fates. They weren't transferable by theft. Not until you were paid out could the power be taken.

Still, I put my hood on—better if I wasn't recognized by anyone while in this state.

I waded through the water, until I was waist deep, the door's entryway in front of me. My arm throbbed as I stared at the familiar, unremarkable wood. It sensed where we were going, brought us to our charge.

My veins pulsed with the need to unite with whichever sorry shite I'd have to guide.

The door was a strange bit of magic, one very few of us understood. Then again, the Order never saw fit to allow us to understand. We were only given the barest scraps of information to survive on.

Without any pomp or preamble, I opened it, stepping into the technicolor vibrancy on the other side.

The transition was disorienting, but I gathered my whereabouts more quickly than I usually would.

Mostly because I recognized this place. A small, familiar building stood down the block, my fingers tingling with awareness that the other end of the tether was near.

It was unusual, getting sent to the same area in such quick succession—but who was I to question the fates or their games?

Maybe Thorne was right. Maybe I had earned their pity. Maybe I'd even get a glimpse of the girl again while seeking out my charge.

I moved through the world with ease, passing unnoticed by the handful of people walking about.

The world was so different like this than it had been when

I'd actually been a part of it, gotten to interact with it—to pretend, for a moment, that it still belonged to me.

Now, I was nothing but a trespasser here, one that existed on the margins, invisible to them all.

I stopped outside the door, looking in through the window.

The place was busier than it had been last week—the small, dilapidated building that passed for a hospital in these times was overrun and deeply understocked.

I scanned the faces, waiting for the sense of rightness I would get once I spotted my charge.

And when it happened, when I locked in, I nearly choked on the shock of it.

There, amidst the chaos, was a woman.

Luxurious waves of hair that bled from black to silver. Dark, unreadable eyes. And lips that—well, they were fucking perfect. And I knew for a fact that they tasted perfect too.

Mareena.

My new charge.

Which made her officially off-limits. . .and me officially screwed.

This was going to be fecking agony.

9

————

MAREENA

APPROXIMATELY NINE YEARS AGO, THREE
YEARS BEFORE THE UNDOING

Our short bus to Fremont and the following ten-minute walk to the canal was stilted and awkward on my part, though Sora worked her magic and ate through most of the silence.

She detailed her short, dramatic breakup—unsurprisingly, Penny didn't take the news about us moving in with her ex well —and then spent most of the time running through color palettes and decor options for the new apartment.

Levi, though quiet, didn't seem disinterested, and he did a decent job of offering opinions whenever Sora shoved pictures of various rugs and art prints under his nose. None of them, of course, were items we could actually afford, but Sora loved digital window shopping.

By the time we reached our favorite spot on the canal— between two thick trees that were perfect for setting up a hammock, my earlier tension about Sora trying to force something romantic between me and Levi had eased. She was good at making friends, and maybe that was all she was hoping for from this evening—a distraction from Penny. By her estimates, one person out of our life probably just made room for another to enter.

There was a cool breeze coming off the water, and we stood there for a moment, watching as a family of ducks and a kayaker drifted past us.

"It's beautiful here," Levi said.

"It is." I sat down on a smooth, dry patch of dirt, and let my legs dangle over the side of the ledge, feet hovering above the soft current.

The canal was a long, narrow stretch that connected the lake downtown with Puget Sound.

My favorite part of Seattle—and one of the reasons Sora and I chose it in the first place—was that it was nearly impossible to find a neighborhood that wasn't a short trip from the water. When I closed my eyes and focused on the smell of salt in the air, I could almost feel myself back with my aunt, the memory of her salt-and-pepper hair in the wind as we collected rocks along the shore suddenly vivid and clear.

"Best city in the world, didn't I tell you?" Sora plopped down on my left and took another long pull from the bottle before shoving it into my hands. "You lucked out finding us when you did you know—we can show you around. We've gotten pretty good at scavenging up cheap and free stuff to do in the city. At the very least, we can save you time going through the trial-and-error period."

Sora had a habit of spotting and befriending strays. We had a difficult first few months when we moved here, and she seemed convinced to make sure others had it easier.

"So," I took a small sip as Levi sat down on my other side, trying to ignore the gentle pressure of his arm against mine and the way it shot warmth through my body like a lightning bolt, "I take it you're not from around here then?"

He shook his head. "Just passing through."

"Where's home?" I passed him the bottle, glancing out of

the corner of my eyes as he pressed his mouth to the glass and took a swig.

"I don't know." He shrugged, something unreadable in his expression. "Is that weird? I've kind of lived all over the place."

"No, not weird." I'd moved a lot over the years, and each time, it felt like that feeling of home had to be rebuilt. It was often very grueling work. "Sometimes home isn't a place."

Mine had always been people. First, home was with my aunt in her cottage by the water. And then, eventually, it just became Sora. Still was, regardless of where we ended up crashing.

"Damn right," she said, her shoulder bumping playfully against mine. "How long are you planning to stay?"

He considered for a moment as he watched a duck dip its head beneath the water for some food. "Not sure yet. I'm in the area for a work thing."

"Well then, you'll absolutely have to come to our house-warming party if you're still in town," she said.

"I think we should sign a lease and move in before you send out invitations," I said, though I couldn't help but grin. Her excitement was contagious. We were this close to getting out of Oleg's shed and building the life we'd been dreaming about for years.

"Yeah, yeah." She scrunched her nose, glancing at me from the corner of her eyes. "You think I should invite Penny?"

Levi made a sound that was stuck somewhere between a laugh and a cough.

"Are you guys going to try being friends?" I asked. It wasn't unusual, not for Sora. I didn't know a single person who'd managed to stay mad at her for long, even when she broke their heart. She was just one of those people you did everything you could to keep in your life for as long as you could, even if that meant swallowing your pride.

"Maybe." She shrugged. "She makes a mean spinach dip

and she's great at party games, so friendship isn't off the table as far as I'm concerned."

I snorted. "Give her some time to fall out of love with you and to make sure Becca's cool with her stopping by the apartment. They're exes, too, you know? We can't all be as"—I thought for a moment—"evolved, as you."

Levi took another sip of tequila, his expression somehow smooth, as if he was drinking water and not liquid fire.

"Maybe I can set her up with one of my friends. Fastest way to fall out of love with someone is to fall in love with somebody else."

Levi chuckled again, the sound low and oddly melodious.

Sora studied him for a moment. "What about you? You ever been in love, Levi?"

He coughed, choking more at the question than he had at the booze, and handed the bottle back to her.

"Jesus, Sor." I massaged my temples, feeling almost bad for the guy. Sora didn't do subtlety; she saw no point in it. I turned toward him. "Feel free to ignore her. She does well with boundaries. Sometimes."

He was quiet for a moment, then said, "No, I haven't."

"You should try it some time." Sora sighed, leaning back. "I love being in love."

I felt his stare on me. "And you?"

"Me what?" I asked, tossing a twig into the water and watching the impact ripple.

The sky, a stretch of deep pinks and oranges, so vibrant it hardly looked real, was starting to darken.

"No," Sora snorted, "Mars doesn't even do romance, let alone love."

I shot her a glare.

"What?" She shrugged. "It's true. You're all dark and moody and anti-love."

"Not true." I flicked some dirt at her. "I love you."

She rolled her eyes. "Yeah, and do you know how much work that took—worming my way into your life? Good god, I can't imagine even rocket science being more difficult than that." She leaned forward, turning toward Levi. "But fair point, I stand corrected. Mars loves me, but only because I forced her to. She otherwise acts like it's an affliction and refuses connection on any and all levels." When I started to protest, she pressed her hand over my mouth. "She won't even adopt a dog despite being obsessed with them."

I licked her hand, and she tugged it back toward her chest with a half-disgusted, half-amused squeal.

"Well, we also couldn't afford one. And it's not like there's room in Oleg's studio for a single other thing. *We* can barely even fit in there." I straightened my posture and shot her a look. "Some people might call the no pet rule a responsible choice."

"Shut up." She snorted. "You know that's not why you have a no pet rule."

Levi's lips twitched, and I saw the light outline of a dimple from the corner of my eye. "Why would someone refuse love . . . or dogs?"

"Because"—Sora wiggled her brows, eyes dancing with mirth—"she's cursed."

"Sora." I shot her a warning look.

"Well?" she pressed. "Do you deny it? Because if I'm wrong, tell me I'm wrong."

Heat crept up my neck. Hopefully the shadows cast from the trees surrounding us were dark enough that my blush wasn't obvious.

Other than Amto Amani, who'd vehemently opposed my developing theories about the death curse, Sora was the only one I'd ever voiced the fear to out loud. Partially because she'd been around for its resurgence in my adolescence and had witnessed the heavy weight of that guilt firsthand. How else could I explain the fact that my first girlfriend, at age thirteen—

a sweet, brief romance in the way romance often was at that age —died from a heart issue, or that my first boyfriend, at age fourteen, died in a hiking accident less than three weeks after we started 'dating.' Safe to say that after that, I gained quite the reputation at our school.

And then of course, there was Rina—the death that struck deeper than all, save for my aunt's. It burrowed into my chest, setting up a permanent residence there. Any lingering doubts I had about my curse disappeared entirely that night, even with Sora's insistence that if I ever were *actually* cursed, that was the night it was broken. Since that night, she'd made it one of her lifelong missions to prove it to me.

Rina was my best friend, but she was Sora's sister. Still, even with the evidence stacked up against me, Sora refused to blame me for her death. She also adamantly resisted every single one of my attempts to refuse her friendship, to push her away. Eventually, I grew exhausted trying, and allowed myself the hope that the universe saw fit to let me keep her.

I hadn't let myself add any other close relationships since— platonic or romantic—nor did I have any plans to. Sora was alive and here—a reality I still couldn't quite let myself feel safe in—and that would be enough. I didn't need anyone else. I wouldn't risk anyone else.

"What kind of curse?" Levi asked, the stretch of silence oddly heavy now, where it had been light and playful just a moment ago.

"She's convinced that everyone she loves is doomed to die an early death." Sora dropped her head on my shoulder. "I've never really believed in curses myself, but I can't imagine a more tragic one than that."

"Well," he shifted next to me, and I felt his stare like a flame against my cheek, "you clearly managed to get past her defenses, didn't you? And from what I can tell, you're still very much alive. So, if there was a curse, surely, it's broken, no?"

"You'd think." She tried skipping a stone, but it landed with a heavy plop, just two feet in front of us. "At least that's what I've been trying to tell her. For years. But apparently not. And she refuses to let anyone else in to test my theory that if she was cursed, she's not anymore. Frank's the closest thing she has to a friend outside of me, which is just absurdly depressing."

"How'd you manage it?" he asked, the two of them carrying on with the conversation as if I wasn't here, even though I was quite literally lodged between them. "Get her to be your friend, I mean."

"Sheer stubbornness," I muttered, "and a relentless lack of self-preservation."

"Pure persistence, an iron will, and an absolute rejection of every attempt she made to push me away." Her voice was full of pride, but I could read the layer of sadness in her expression when her eyes briefly met and held mine.

For the most part, Sora was an open book, at least when it came to the joyful and adventurous parts of herself she wanted to share with people. Her response to everything we'd been through was to love with abandon and wear her heart on her sleeve—the exact opposite of mine. It was like the moment she lost Rina, she became determined to live her life to the fullest for the both of them.

Still, open as she was, it was rare for her to be quite this forthcoming, least of all with someone we'd been on a first name basis with for all of an hour. Usually, her lack of filter was one of my favorite things about her. Right now, I'd give my left kidney for her to stop talking.

When she opened her mouth to say something else, I pressed my hand across her lips—the vibration of her groan tickling my fingers.

"I think you've hit your tequila limit tonight." I grabbed the bottle from her, taking a long pull from it myself—a failed attempt to dispel how uncomfortable this conversation was starting to make me—and then set it down next to Levi, where she couldn't reach it.

She pulled my hand away, her nose scrunched in a pout. "No, I didn't. That bottle is still practically full."

"If it helps," Levi said, his voice almost a whisper as he picked up the bottle and started to pick at the label, "sometimes it feels like I'm cursed too."

When I turned toward him, I expected to find a teasing grin on his face. But when I studied him, the final rays of the tired sun delicately framing the shadows in his expression, I swallowed back my retort. He wasn't mocking me or poking fun.

All I saw stretched across the sharp contours of his face was a familiar, suffocating grief. He wore it the way that I did—a well-loved uniform that he could disguise or temporarily transform, but at the end of the day, when you took off the mask, the base of him was this.

"What kind of curse?" Sora asked.

"I don't know." He considered for a moment, likely trying to temper how much he should share in a way that Sora had failed to do. "The kind where my entire life leads in exactly one direction—no matter how hard I try to veer it in a different one." His eyes held mine with a determined focus. Something about the way he looked at me felt like he could see through me, like he could shuffle through the pages, reading every thought—even the ones that I fought to keep hidden from myself. "And that particular path is, unfortunately, a lonely one. Not one that I can drag anyone along for anyway." He let out a humorless chuckle and shook his head, an attempt to brush the thought away, or maybe just frustration with himself for revealing a wound he wasn't ready for strangers to see. "I guess that's not really a curse. Maybe more so fate."

Fate.

The word brushed against my brain like a caress. I'd never really believed in fate or destiny. My life has been a series of simply trying to survive one moment long enough to reach the next. But now that he mentioned it, the lines between fate and a curse appeared rather fragile.

If anything, fate seemed worse—inevitable and inescapable—more suffocating even than a curse.

A curse, at least, could be broken.

Shrugging, he peeled away a thin layer of the label, his focus locked on the nearly translucent strip of paper like it held the answers to the universe's most confounding questions. "Sometimes fate can have a way of feeling as hopeless as a curse, I guess. Unavoidable, like I'm a pawn in my own life."

I felt a strange urge to reach out for his hand, to ease the heaviness that seemed to suddenly shroud him, to pull him back from wherever his thoughts had carried him away to.

"Who says that you don't have agency in constructing your own fate?" Sora sat up, her eyes clear and firm—any sign of the tequila's effects dissipating instantly. Her jaw clenched as she studied him, like she was angry on his behalf. "Your life belongs to you, Levi, and you alone—don't let anyone box you in somewhere you don't want to be. If there's something you want, go after it—fuck anyone who gets in your way. Even fate."

She delivered the speech with the focus and determination of a general leading a crew into battle. I felt the familiar flare of her protectiveness. Her iron will and stubbornness extended far beyond her own benefit.

A heavy silence fell over us all for a moment.

"Maybe fate is real," she said, her voice quieter now. "I don't know, and I suppose I never will. But if I do have a fate and it leads me somewhere I don't want to go, at least I know I won't go down without a fight. Sometimes just the illusion of free will can be enough."

For most of her life, Sora had been dragged through the mud, held there by rules and people who fought to keep her down. In some ways she had it far worse than I did.

I was lucky enough to have Amto Amani for the first decade of my life, to feel the power of that kind of love and protection —but Sora had been shuffled through the system longer than her memory could place. Still, she always had such a clear vision of what she wanted, and, even more impressive, the belief that she'd achieve it. For as long as I'd known her, she'd devoted every ounce of her being to chasing after the life that she wanted, the life that she deserved. It was a devotion she extended to those less fearless in cultivating the same kind dreams.

"Is it possible," Levi said, his words slow and tentative, as his stare found mine, "that maybe you aren't cursed? That maybe these people you've known were always destined to die when they did? That they were lucky to have you in their lives at the end—a final nod of gratitude from the world they were leaving?"

Sora gasped, her eyes wide. "Now *that* is a reading of the situation I can actually get behind."

Breath lodged in my chest as his words rolled over and then through me. It wasn't a frame I'd ever considered before.

But at the end of the day, did it even matter?

Curse or not, I still always ended up in the same position every time—alone, with the people I cared about gone.

The three of us sat in silence for a few minutes, until Levi stood up and brushed the dirt off his pants. "I should get going."

"You sure?" I asked, feeling partially responsible for the turn in conversation. "We didn't mean to scare you off with Sora's Ted Talk. If you want, we can officially veto any more fate or curse conversation." I grimaced. "That would be my preference generally, if I'm being honest."

"No, you didn't scare me off. This was—nice, actually. I should get back though. I've been out for a while and people will be looking for me. Thank you for inviting me to join you both. I had fun and this was certainly a better turn from where my day started." He smiled down at us, though there was something almost sad in the downward dip of his eyes as they locked on Sora, and then on me. There was an intensity in his stare that seemed to crawl over my skin. "You won't remember me or this night, but I hope you both get everything you want out of life. And good luck with your move."

There was a strange finality in his words, but he was hiking back up toward the trail before either of us had a chance to respond.

10

MAREENA
PRESENT DAY

"Hear me out," Aidan said, blocking my path. I didn't usually stop by the med center this early, but since I stayed up most of last night experimenting with some baked goods, I figured it was best to clear out some room in the diner. "You and I—dinner and one drink tomorrow. I could use a night out, and I think you could use a meal that you don't have to cook as well."

My stomach dropped at the earnest plea on his face. Something about saying no to Aidan felt like finding a dog and dropping it off at the shelter. There was no feeling good about it, no matter what the circumstances were. Even if, odd as it may seem, the shelter was the safest place for the dog, its best chance of reuniting with its family.

"I told you before," I said, shifting around him to start organizing some of the supplies a few people brought in this morning. I didn't work here anymore in any sort of official capacity, but old habits were hard to kill, and if I was going to be here, might as well make myself useful. "I don't think it's a good idea. We're better off as friends and," I turned around to face him, hoping he could read the sincerity in my face as clearly as I tried to infuse it in my words, "I really don't want to complicate things. You're a good guy, a great one, even, but I'm not in the space for dating or anything serious right now."

It was the truth, for all the reasons I'd originally turned him down the first time he asked, but also because, for the last week, my thoughts had been incessantly circling around Kieran and that whirlwind of an evening at Incendiary.

In fact, memories of that night had been occupying my thoughts so thoroughly that I'd half-convinced myself that I saw him creeping at the window a few minutes ago. It was just a brief flash, there and then not, but enough to prove that Kieran had gone from plaguing my dreams with spicy flashbacks of that night, to haunting my waking reality as well.

Fucking figured.

Best sex of my life, and the guy immediately bailed.

Like, what the hell was that? Feeding me some line about getting home and then just dipping before I even got the feeling back in my legs? Who did that?

More than anything, I was annoyed with myself for being so annoyed with him.

Hadn't he told me that it was a one-time thing?

Hadn't those always been my rule anyway?

Hell, wasn't that the exact thing I was trying to outline for Aidan now?

No attachments, casual.

But to go from intense, life-changing sex in one minute, to leaving me alone in a dark alley the next had been more than a little jarring, and I'd be lying if I didn't admit that my ego was a little bruised.

Maybe that was just how demons fucked. The whole point of a club like Incendiary.

Not that I knew what kind of demon he even was. The possibilities had been plaguing my thoughts though. There'd been no wristband on his arm signaling he was human.

"I never said I was looking to walk you down the aisle, Mareena," Aidan said, his entire face lighting up with the kindness baked inside of his smile. "Casual works for me, but so does friendship. I like talking to you. Do you like talking to me?"

"I do, but—"

"And I would like the chance to maybe talk outside of a building filled with my patients. That's all. I don't have a ton of friends or free time, and I just think it might be a nice change of pace for us both. To get away from here, away from Frank's for a night." He shrugged. "I'm not asking or expecting anything more than that. A change of scenery."

"That's all?" I asked.

"Look." He sniffed, his smile turning coy. "I'm not *not* hoping you might change your mind on the dating front at some point. But I'm also good with just friendship." He grabbed the pile of bandages I'd sorted through and started placing them in the different bins he liked to keep stocked in the various rooms. "And to be clear, I don't mean to suggest that friendship is a consolation prize. I like talking to you. I think we are good at talking to each other. I would just like to be good at talking to each other somewhere that isn't here."

I laughed, considering him for a moment. This broke my rules, but would chatting with him over a meal really be all that different, more dangerous, than what we did every day in the med center? "Okay, Aidan."

"Okay?" He straightened; face drawn in shock. He hadn't really expected this approach to work, had he? "As in you'll go?"

"Tomorrow." Truthfully, a little company wouldn't be the worst thing in the world.

Sora had been so busy in the last week that I'd hardly spoken more than a few words to her outside of the dinner shifts.

Between the diner, her salon, and a new mystery person

she'd been seeing, but refusing to talk about, we'd been like two ships passing in the night.

Some ships sink, not all ships sink, I reminded myself.

Aidan was right, barring the slight awkwardness between us since the first time he'd asked me out, our conversation had always been easy. Enjoyable. There was no reason we couldn't go back to that. Maybe a different setting would even help—shed some of the heaviness that came with working at the med center, surrounded by pain and death all day long.

My walk back to Frank's had been an odd one.

You know that very strange prickling sensation, the one you only got when someone was watching you or following you? Well, I had it the entire time. A sixth sense tingling at the back of my neck.

Twice, when I looked back, I noticed a strange man.

Both times, he kept a few blocks behind me, like he was trying to keep some distance, and I couldn't see his face. He wore a hood—an odd choice for June in Seattle, but whatever—and between that and the early morning rays of the sun, it was difficult to get a proper look at him.

When I got to Frank's, he'd disappeared, but I locked the front door, just to be safe.

I doubted we'd have any customers for a few hours, other than maybe Claudine in a bit, so I ran upstairs to see if I could spot the hooded figure from the windows and the safety of our apartment.

Sora left after the early breakfast shift and wouldn't be done with her clients until late tonight, which meant I had the place to myself.

Again.

I used to enjoy the solitude, but lately it was starting to feel almost like a prison. There were no distractions when I was alone with my thoughts.

And it wasn't like the old days. We now had generally reliable electricity, but the internet hadn't reached the capacity that it had in the past. I couldn't doom scroll or watch videos from my favorite creators, people I'd never met but somehow convinced myself I cared about—the things I used to do create the illusion of connection. In some ways, it was better this way, but in a lot of ways, it was worse. Especially since I did my best to keep my in-real-life relationships surface level.

I opened the window in the kitchen, letting in some fresh air, and stepped out onto the balcony to survey the street below.

No mysterious, ominous stalker.

I relaxed against the railing, feeling a little ridiculous for being so paranoid in the first place.

The whole being-alone-so-much thing was clearly getting to me.

Dinner with Aidan would be good. Necessary, maybe.

Oddly, despite the fact that we lived above a diner, there wasn't much food in our place, so I grabbed a glass of water and sipped it while I watched the people pass below.

Something soft brushed against my hand, and the shock of it sent the glass spiraling to the ground. The crash of it shattering against the pavement echoed through the street.

Fuck. I loved that glass. It was from the Before, and it wasn't like I could just order another one online and have it delivered to my doorstep in a day or two.

Black feathers eclipsed my field of vision, and I took a few steps back to let the little hellion in through the sliding door.

"You scared the shit out of me, Menace," I announced, as if my overreaction wasn't abundantly obvious to the both of us. "A little warning next time, yeah?"

But the crow didn't go for his usual welcoming nuzzle, nor did he attack the small cup of peanuts Sora had left out on the small balcony table.

Instead, he went soaring into the kitchen, the crack of his caw amplified by the silence of the apartment.

If I'd still been holding the cup, I would certainly have dropped it now.

The hooded figure from the street stood in the kitchen, cursing and trying to dodge Menace as he flew toward him.

Fingers trembling, I stepped inside, reaching aimlessly for the closest thing that might be used as a weapon. Realistically, in a kitchen, that should have been a knife, but we kept those downstairs where they got the most use. We almost never cooked up here. No need when we had access to a much more efficient kitchen in the diner.

That left Sora's metal water bottle as the best option, so I grabbed it and thrust it in front of me, wielding it like a sword. "What the hell are you doing in here? Get out. Now."

The man had regained his composure, though he turned toward Menace as if it was him I was interrogating.

"Not the bird," I snapped. "You." And, because for some reason my brain decided it needed to be clarified, I added, "The crow lives here."

Slowly, as if he still wasn't sure, the hooded man turned back to me, his face still hidden from sight. "Me?"

"You see any other creepy cloaked men in here?"

He slid the hood off, and I found myself looking at familiar hazel eyes.

My bottle-wielding arm relaxed. "Kieran?"

"Uh"—his gaze darted about the room like he was just as confused as I was—"yeah. So you—uh..." He wet his lips and my focus stalled on them briefly. "You remember me then?"

"Do people usually forget you after you fuck them against a wall?" I studied him, not entirely sure whether I was terrified or angry or confused by his intrusion. Probably all three, if I was being honest. And a tiny, traitorous part of my brain was maybe even a little excited. I didn't think I'd ever see him again. "What's with the cloak? It's summer."

"Bad hangover. Sun and,"—he gestured vaguely around the

room, not pointing to anything specific—"this can all be a bit abrasive until my eyes have had a bit to adjust." He blinked. "And I don't feel warm."

"I—" I didn't know what to say in response to that, so it was probably better to move to the more pressing issues. "How did you get inside? I locked the door behind me."

He shrugged. "Locks aren't a problem for me."

"And you think what"—I narrowed my eyes—"that makes it okay to break into people's places, just because you can?"

"I didn't break anything." He arched his brow, the earlier surprise evaporating from his expression to make room for something more . . . smug.

"Not the point," I shot back. My pulse was fluttering like a hummingbird, and I couldn't be entirely sure how much of it was from fear or how much was from the way his eyes roved over me, the echo of hunger from last week still preening at the surface. "Why are you stalking me? When I was walking home" —and then, recalling even earlier than that, I lifted the water bottle higher—"and at the med center. You were there— looking in through the window, right?"

"Hm, so it's not just this building that breaks through then." He tapped the wall, as if inspecting for a hollow spot. "Thought it might be infused, similar to the club but"—he shook his head, gaze landing on me—"it must just be you."

What the fuck was he on about?

"I don't remember you talking in half answers and riddles last week."

There was a wicked glint in his eyes as they narrowed on me. "As I recall, we didn't do much talking last week."

I swallowed, lost for words at the taunting smirk on his face.

He tilted his head, studying me like I was a puzzle he couldn't quite parse, and I felt suddenly like a mouse cornered by a cat. "You're an unusual girl, Mareena."

"You followed me home and then broke into my apartment." I jostled the bottle in his direction, the water sloshing in a way that was not at all threatening. "All while dressed in sorcerer cosplay—and you think I'm the unusual one?"

"A fair point." The side of his mouth twitched, briefly, into a sharp hook that had my stomach tightening. That particular smirk, and the memory of how it felt pressed against my skin, had had a recurring role in my dreams this last week. "If it makes you feel any better, I didn't think you would remember, let alone see me."

"In what world would that make me feel any better?"

"Perhaps only in mine," he said, though it was spoken in the gentle rumble of a whisper.

"Get out of my apartment," I snapped, "and leave me alone."

Great sex or not, there was no way my libido was going to win the war with my brain on this one.

"I'll give you some space for a bit, sure,'" he said, as if it was his idea, and a magnanimous one at that. Without another word, he turned and left.

I waited to hear the door in the living room open and close, but after a long stretch of nothing, I charged in, water bottle lifted and at the ready. "I mean it, Kiera—"

The living room was empty, the door closed, no intruder in sight.

I took a few steadying breaths, then opened Sora's water bottle, draining it in one gulp, half convinced the last few minutes were nothing more than the combination of a bad night's sleep and a figment of my imagination.

And if not, he was gone, so maybe it was best not to linger on the intrusion.

After greeting Menace, properly this time, and refilling his water bowl, I made my way downstairs, ready to start prepping for the next rush.

The door was locked, just as it had been when I'd run inside.

Did he go through a window when he left?

Or was this just more proof that I'd imagined the entire thing?

It wouldn't be the first time my brain conjured up a hallucination—though this had certainly been more involved than I was used to. My visions didn't usually speak to me or interact with my environment.

I unlocked the door and shifted the sign to open, forcing my thoughts away from all things Kieran.

Normalcy. Routine. That was what I needed.

"You look bothered, dear."

"Oh." My head shot up and I found Claudine and Greta sitting in their booth. I was so lost in the cadence of my thoughts, the gentle rhythm of my knife cuts, that I didn't even hear them come in. "Sorry, I'm fine. Weird morning. How are you both? Do you want your usual?"

"Please," Claudine said, shimmying her shoulders in excitement when I started the kettle.

Greta glanced at her friend, amusement etched into the lines of her face, before turning to me. "Nothing for me, thank you."

"So, tell me dear," Claudine said as I set the tea in front of her, "what've you been up to this week? How's the journal work coming? Any new gossip in the pipeline?"

"It's coming." I walked behind the counter and then leaned on it, watching them as my own cup of tea steeped. It was a slow day, as Tuesdays always were, and I was clearly desperate for conversation, so the rest of the prep could wait a few minutes. "Most of my week has been uneventful, but I have a not-date set up for tomorrow night."

"Ooh." Claudine hunched closer, while her stoic friend sniffed hesitantly at the steam coming off the tea. "Tell me, tell me." She clapped her hands together. "Is it that nice boy you mentioned before? The one at the med center?"

I bit back my smile, nodding. "We're getting dinner."

She wiggled her brows suggestively.

"As friends," I clarified.

"Youth is truly wasted on the young." Claudine took a deep breath. "If I was you, and had those legs of yours, I'd spend every night with them wrapped around a different man."

I choked on my own tea.

Greta barked out a laugh. "Don't scandalize the poor girl, Claudine."

"I did meet someone last week though," I added, suddenly feeling the need to defend myself and my well-used youth, though I wasn't sure why. "One-time fling."

Claudine's eyes widened, a large smile cracking her face in two. "I knew there was something different about you today. You've got that glow about you. The kind only a good naked tango can unleash." She leaned forward; the steam of her tea abandoned to the periphery of her attention. "Well, go on, give us the details, dearie."

I took a sip of my tea, letting the water scald my tongue rather than loosen it. "There's nothing to tell. Like I said, one-time thing. What's new in your lives?"

Claudine batted her hand, as if it was of little consequence. "You need to work on your storytelling skills. How are we supposed to live vicariously through you when that's all you give us to work with?"

"Perhaps she wants to discuss something other than her sex life, Deenie," Greta said, and I found myself wanting to hug her with relief at the suggestion.

I nodded. "Literally anything else."

The woman pouted; the expression so childish that I laughed at the odd contrast with the wisdom in her eyes. "At least tell us what he looked like?"

"Like an adonis, I'm sure," a deep voice said.

My blood froze at the familiar Irish lilt.

Kieran stood at the door. A door I hadn't even heard open.

He'd ditched the cloak in our brief time apart and was now dressed in a much more sensible black T-shirt and jeans.

The inviting gleam on Claudine's face had dried up, replaced by a scowl. "Get out of here, boy. Leave her be. I mean it. She's ours."

Greta's gaze darted between the intruder and me; her expression unreadable. She patted her friend's hand. "This isn't our business, Deenie."

"Sure, it is," Claudine said. I was pretty sure the woman thought everything was her business. "I mean it, Kieran. You leave her alone. This is my one afternoon of enjoyment."

"You know I can't do that," he said, though there was a softness to his tone.

"You all know each other?" I asked, though judging by the alarm his presence had inspired in the women, I wasn't sure that they were exactly on friendly terms if they did.

"Something like that," he said, his focus locked on them. "You certainly attract an odd sort, don't you, Mareena." Then, back to them, he added, "I'm not even sure how you two found her—or got here altogether. There'll be hell to pay if anyone finds out."

"Don't threaten them," I snapped, my brain catching up to the chaos from earlier. "And stop stalking me. I mean it. Get out of here, Kieran or I'll—" Well, I wasn't sure what I would do. It wasn't like I could call the cops or anything. Even in the Before, they usually caused more harm than good.

Luckily, I was spared the necessity of landing on a solution.

"Oh my god, I'm so late." Sora burst through the front door, her face coated in a sheen of sweat, like she'd run here. And Sora didn't run. "Please tell me my client hasn't shown up yet?"

"Not that I've noticed," I said, "but I haven't been downstairs."

"Good, that means one thing is going my way today at least." She walked past Kieran, not sparing him so much as a glance, and pointed at the cup of tea in the booth. "Cool if I grab this? I haven't had any caffeine yet and I don't have time to deal with a headache or start a pot of fresh coffee."

Without waiting for a response, she swiped the cup and took a sip, her nose scrunching in distaste. "Mint. Not my favorite. And no caffeine." Her eyes lit up. "Does that mean your therapist already came by today? Damn, was hoping to finally catch a glimpse of her and introduce myself. Let her know I'm a big fan of her work. Next week, maybe. Anyway, catch you later, okay? Feel like we haven't properly spoken in ages. So, tonight? After the dinner rush. We can open a bottle of wine or something, hang out with Menace. I even miss that old rascal, which is really saying something." Then, without waiting for a response, she disappeared into the back hall, where there was a staircase into the basement and her little studio.

"I—" I opened and closed my mouth several times, trying to put words to the confusion. It wasn't like Sora to completely ignore customers, even if she was rushed—let alone steal their drink.

She hadn't so much as spared a glance at any of them.

"Ladies," Kieran sighed, "are you telling me she doesn't know?"

And Claudine had been sitting right in front of her. Was she so out of it that she'd missed the woman entirely?

"Know what?" I asked, half locked in a daze.

"Sorry, dearie," Claudine winced, "it was just so nice to pretend like it was the good old times again."

"Good old times?" My brain was molasses as I tried to make sense of the different threads.

"She means when we were alive," Greta added, patting her friend's hand again.

My chest tightened, and I stared at them, really looking at them this time.

They were both seated at the table, and while Claudine's position was mostly normal, practiced, Greta's leg had sunken into the booth, like there was a hole it'd passed through.

Catching my stare, she shifted, her leg reappearing as it hovered above the floor.

Then, my focus latched onto the now-empty table, where the tea had been.

She'd never taken a sip. In all her visits, never once had I seen her touch something. Now that I thought about it, I'd never actually even seen her come through the door.

She was always just seated in the booth.

I'd assumed it was because she had a knack for arriving when I was busy or distracted, only half paying attention to the dining room, but maybe it was something else.

Sora hadn't noticed her and, looking back now, whenever Claudine prattled on about the few customers who'd come in during her visits, they'd always ignored her. I'd assumed it was because she was being nosy, poking into their lives, making observations and offering unsolicited advice.

But maybe they hadn't seen her.

"You're ghosts?" The word felt strange on my tongue. "Dead?"

Claudine shrank into the booth, her face contorted into an exaggerated guilt, the way a child's might be when their parents caught them lying. "Sorry, dearie." The guilt morphed into a wince. "But oh, I do hate that word."

"Technically"—Kieran crossed his arms over his chest and leaned against the wall—"they're phantoms. Ghosts aren't real. At least not as far as I'm aware."

"Phantoms?"

"Kind of like shadows of their former selves, captured and stuck in the Between. Most will slip away slowly, disappearing altogether within a few years," he said, his tone nonchalant as if he was simply explaining how two plus two equals four and not cracking my entire ontology at the seams. "Almost like a polaroid image in reverse. Happens most commonly with demons who've met a particularly violent death. Though, in very rare circumstances, I've encountered humans who've experienced it, too. The Undoing changed the game a bit, with humans absorbing the shadow magic. The specifics of it are a bit blurry now." He shrugged. "Those of stronger resolve occasionally stick around a bit longer. It's rare for them to make it to this realm, to interact with the living." He shrugged. "Like I said, you're an unusual girl, Mareena."

Claudine stood and walked over to me.

Well, *walked* might be a poor way to describe it. It was more like she floated, shifting through air, her feet hovering above the ground.

Eyes soft with concern, she pressed her hand to my cheek—only I didn't feel it, I didn't feel anything except a soft, breathy chill.

"You're dead," I said, the words stiff. My brain felt numb.

Claudine nodded. "I'm dead."

Figured, finally had free access to a therapist and she was dead. Sora would at least get a kick out of that. "And ghosts are real?"

"Phantoms," Kieran clarified.

I shifted my focus to him, stepping away from Claudine's chilly not-touch. "But you can see them, too?"

I wasn't sure whether this made me feel better or worse.

"Yes," he said, his expression unreadable, "I can."

"And you?" I let the question drift off for a moment.

His stare snagged on mine, holding me in those eyes until time seemed to stop. "I'm dead, too, yes."

My breath caught as the different pieces of a puzzle I couldn't yet identify started to shift into place.

The fact that, like Claudine and Greta, he didn't seem bothered by doors or locks.

Did that mean he could shift through walls too?

I don't feel warm.

Wasn't that what he'd said earlier? I'd been struck by the odd phrasing at the time, but there'd been more pressing issues.

Like the fact that he was standing in the middle of my kitchen, uninvited.

He wasn't *exactly* like Claudine and Greta though.

Now that I knew what they were, now that I let myself really see them, the differences started to emerge. The women weren't quite as vibrant and *here* as he was—their skin papery and grayer, their movements more fluid than any human's would be. They weren't transparent or anything, but there was something strangely . . . airy about their appearance. Ephemeral, almost.

And the longer I stared, the more the image of them collapsed into the visions I occasionally had—another world, transposed on top of this one.

Did that mean it was real? This world I'd been conjuring for years, trying like hell to ignore.

Was it this Between place he mentioned?

And what about Kieran?

People could see him. Lenora and Ren at Incendiary— they'd even spoken to him.

But then just now, Sora had walked by without giving him so much as a glance.

And well, while Sora was only rarely interested in men, Kieran was the sort of guy who kind of demanded a second look.

His touch had also felt nothing like Claudine's had—like a

shadow against my skin, a distinctive lack. His had been solid, heated.

"Give her some space, ladies." Kieran gestured to the women, and they faded away. Gone entirely.

His stare rested on me, not without compassion, but also devoid the heat I remember from last week.

"You're different than they are." I swallowed the waver in my voice. "I touched you."

"I am," he said, a brief, self-satisfied smirk cracking through his otherwise unreadable expression, "and you did."

"What are you?" Though I wasn't sure I really wanted the answer to that question. "And why are you here? Why are you following me?"

He sat down in the booth, occupying Claudine's usual spot, his arms spread wide over the back ledge as he studied me.

"Think of me like a guardian angel of sorts," he said, the corner of his mouth flickering into a soft frown, there and then gone, just as quickly, "and you, thanks to a cruel twist of the fates, are apparently my new charge."

11

MAREENA

APPROXIMATELY NINE YEARS AGO, THREE
YEARS BEFORE THE UNDOING

The music was loud, the kind of loud that drilled into the soles of my feet and vibrated all the way up, until it settled somewhere inside of my ribs. The kind of loud that made you feel like you were a part of it, participating in the sound.

I loved it.

My date? Not so much.

"I'll grab us a drink, sound good?" he asked, his breath warm against my ear as he leaned down. It took everything I had to not flinch at the sensation.

"Great, thanks." I offered up a grin, though it stretched uncomfortably across my face, and I hoped he didn't sense the force behind it.

According to his profile on the app, his name was Joseph, though when we met up, he insisted that I call him Ace. At first glance, the date should have been okay. He was cute—athletic, dark hair, tall, good smile—but the conversation had been stilted and awkward and he just kind of gave off one of those vibes. The sort that I wouldn't have said yes to if he'd asked me out in real life, without the veneer of a screen.

We grabbed a quick dinner before the show, and he'd spent nearly the entire time talking about the frat he was pledging, the coolest parties he'd gotten into, and complaining about a never-ending list of bad dates he'd been on thanks to the apps.

In the entire forty minutes I'd spent with him so far, he'd asked me exactly one question about myself. That question was about my major, even though my profile very clearly stated that I didn't go to college, though I hoped to start taking classes at one of the local community colleges next semester.

Disappointing didn't cover it. I'd only agreed to go out with him in the first place because he'd messaged me about the books I had listed in my bio.

Of course, it became clear once meeting in person that he'd never actually *read* them—he'd clearly used the internet or his more bookish friends to initiate a conversation that he had no interest in continuing once we were on the actual date.

Was there such a thing as emotional or intellectual catfishing?

Because I was pretty sure that was what this was.

And somehow it was so much worse than if he showed up looking entirely different from his pictures.

As it was, I was trying to salvage the night anyway. It was Friday, I'd suffered through the intricate negotiation between eyeliner and makeup remover that led to a killer cat eye, and I'd already gone through the tedious effort of actually leaving the apartment.

The bar was cool at least. And since I never went out with anyone more than a couple of times, it hardly mattered if his company was less than desirable. In some ways, it was almost preferable this way.

Ace was a student at the local university, and I loved any excuse to come to this part of town. There was something appealing about sinking into the college crowds, walking through campus, eating at the restaurants the students frequented, combing through the bookstore's lists of textbooks —though damn those prices were ridiculous. Thank god I preferred fiction.

Would I ever have the money and freedom to go to a school like this? Absolutely not. But it sure was nice to dream occasionally—to imagine what my life might have looked like if things had been different. If I had a family, stability, and the comforts that went with those things growing up.

So, in different circumstances, I would have absolutely bailed on the date after scarfing down our mediocre burgers. But Ace pulled through in one way at least. He had tickets for a small show on the outskirts of campus and I knew the music would at least drown out his mindless chatter. His roommate apparently knew the band, and he'd used that hookup to sneak us in without IDs—something I was grateful for and couldn't do so easily without him.

While I wasn't vibing with him, I was absolutely vibing with this venue. It was dark and grungy—the floor the sort of sticky that no mop could strip, the wooden booths lining the perimeter carved up with initials and plastered with stickers from the bands that had played here in years past, the bar lined with gray-haired dudes, who all gave me the sense that they'd been regulars since their college days.

It was the sort of place I would have hated working at—the stick alone, built up from years of beer spills, would have been a pain in the ass to deal with—but I loved getting to exist inside of it for one night.

According to my quick research on the place, it had been around for nearly seventy years and was a frequent haunt for Seattle's literary and music scene. It was grimy and dark and something about being here made me feel settled in the city, just knowing that I was existing in the same place where so many artists had their start.

In short, I could happily suffer a less-than-perfect date for the chance to linger in here for a little while longer, listening to a newly formed band as they fought to find their sound amongst a cluster of college kids who were searching for their own sense of self with a similar sort of rigor. Fake it 'til you make it, babes.

The band started a new song, this one slower than the last, and the lead-singer-slash-bassist crooned a soulful tune that drew in the crowd's attention more than the previous songs had. She was talented, radiant, and it was clear that the band had a promising future—she just had to wait until the rest of them caught up to her.

My body moved to the beat, as if of its own accord, and I let myself sink into the sound, to connect to the chaotic atmosphere and the captive audience.

Until I felt my skin prickle with the sort of awareness that came with being watched. When my eyes snapped open, I expected to find Ace watching me from the bar—a thought that sent a shiver of discomfort down my spine.

But, instead, my eyes locked on Levi.

I froze when I saw him. It had been a month since that day on the canal, and we hadn't heard from or seen him since.

He stood with his back propped up against the wall, half-hidden in shadows. Like before, he was dressed in black pants and a black T-shirt, his hand dangling a beer bottle next to his leg.

Eyes on me, he pressed the bottle to his lips and took a drink.

My stomach dipped under his attention, but I brushed the feeling away.

I offered a small wave, giving him the opportunity to pretend he didn't see me if that's what he wanted. Part of me hoped he ignored me, though I wasn't sure why.

Instead, his brows lifted, and he spun around, as if expecting someone else to be standing next to him.

I smiled, my body still buzzing with adrenaline as the crowd around me swayed to the music. Who the hell else would I be waving to?

He nodded once, his lips twitching into a barely-there grin, but stayed where he was, as if giving me the same opportunity to bail. Usually, I would have.

Whenever I ran into a random acquaintance in the wild, I almost always did the normal thing of pretending I didn't see them and continuing on my way. Seattle was a town of introverts, so that was usually the expected and preferred practice anyway

But the ambiance of the place put a spring in my step, and I found myself suddenly desperate for company more riveting than my date's.

A quick glance over at Ace showed that he was still in line at the bar, so I maneuvered my way to Levi.

"Good to see you again," I yelled, my voice getting swallowed up by the gravelly sound system.

His brows furrowed as he watched me.

He took another sip of his beer, and I couldn't stop my eyes from tracing the liquid down the smooth column of his throat.

"You remember me?" He bent toward my ear, his words somehow undercutting the music where mine had failed.

"Yeah, of course," I yelled back, my voice way less smooth than his as it tried to compete with the noise. "I wasn't quite as drunk as Sora that night."

Truthfully, Sora had been *way* more intoxicated than I'd initially realized, which I felt kind of bad about. Usually, I was better at gauging her pacing, but that night had been a strange one. We'd made it home without any particular issues. In fact, she hadn't stumbled once or even slurred her words. But when I mentioned Levi the next day, she had absolutely no recollection of him.

Blacking out was rare for her, and her hangover hadn't been

particularly terrible, but apparently the tequila had done its job of helping her drown out her post-breakup angst.

"Hm." The sound was like a low growl, and my stomach twisted as he studied me. It took everything in me not to squirm under his steady perusal. "Interesting."

I wasn't sure what was so interesting about that. Levi wasn't the sort of guy someone could easily forget.

"So, you're still in town then?" I hated myself as soon as the words were out of my mouth.

Obviously, he was still fucking in town, Mars.

He nodded, the expression on his face unreadable.

"Right." My smile faltered slightly.

Levi's posture stiffened, his nostrils flaring ever so slightly as he watched something behind me. He honestly seemed completely disinterested in continuing this conversation, but I had no idea how to bow out of it gracefully.

"You come here a lot?" I asked, kind of thankful when the drummer started a solo, effectively canceling out my voice.

Levi didn't seem to hear me. That, or he did and just didn't bother answering. Either way, he clearly didn't feel like talking. Not like this was exactly the right venue for a stimulating conversation.

And it wasn't like I wanted to pick up on our fate-versus-curse chat either.

"Thanks, by the way," I yelled.

"For what?"

"Whatever you said to Chase that night—at Mac's Tavern? He's been way less of an asshole since the night you came in."

It was true. Shifts with him had become downright pleasant. I wasn't sure what kind of magic Levi wielded with his conversation, but we were all incredibly grateful for it.

He shrugged, his expression flattening. "Wasn't me. I didn't say anything."

He fell back into silence, his focus lingering behind me—

not even toward the stage. Part of me regretted walking over to say hi, now that I was just adjacent to his whole dark and broody vibe. It was somehow even more uncomfortable than if he'd just ignored my wave hello altogether.

I stood there for a moment, debated finding Ace, or just calling it a night, the trance of the music now long lost on me.

"Right." I gave him a tight grin. "Well, see you around, I guess." When I turned around to leave, I nearly ran into Ace.

Surprisingly, I found myself oddly excited to see him, if only so that his presence could act as a buffer for Levi's stiffness.

"Hey man," Ace shouted, the music picking up again and swallowing his voice. He handed me a beer, then placed a hand on my lower back. He nodded at Levi with a tight smile. "I'm Ace. You a friend of Mareena's?"

I took a step to the side until his hand dropped away. I may have been glad that he saved me from rambling endlessly and embarrassing myself further, but that didn't mean I wanted the tool to touch me.

Suddenly all I really wanted was to dip out of this place and curl up in my bed with a good movie or book. Salvage whatever was left of my night off.

Levi's dark stare slid from me to my date, his eyes narrowing. "What did you put in that drink, Ace?"

Ace's grin faltered for a moment, then doubled in size until it made my fake grin earlier look downright deserving of an Academy Award in comparison. "Not sure what you're talking about, man."

Levi grabbed the beer from me, and I jumped when his fingers brushed against mine.

He lifted the rim to his nose and sniffed, not once shifting his glare from Ace. "Let me be clearer this time, *man*. I saw you drop something in this beer. And then you gave it to Mareena. What did you spike it with?"

"It was nothing," Ace said, though the color drained from

his face when Levi took a step toward him, positioning himself between us. Ace held his hands up and took a few steps back, bumping into a random girl behind him. "Look, it's no big deal, okay? Just a little something to help loosen her up, you know? We're just trying to have some fun."

My jaw clenched and a wave of fury shot through me—most of it directed at Ace, but there was a decent reserve saved for myself, too. Why the hell had I let this asshole I didn't even know get my drink? I'd seen enough movies and news headlines to know better. I should've gone with him, watched the bartender open the bottle and taken it directly from his hands.

"You tried to drug me?" I asked, my voice crackling under my anger. "Are you fucking kidding me?"

"Dude, chill out, you don't need to blow this out of proportion," he shot back.

Levi was tense, and he shifted toward Ace, positioning himself between us.

"Out of proportion?" I yelled, completely unconcerned with the looks we were drawing from the cluster of people surrounding us.

"I'm sorry, okay," Ace said, then started to move toward me. "It was a mistake. Won't happen again."

I snorted. Again? This dude actually thought I'd stick around with him long enough for there to be another opportunity?

"Stay the fuck away from her." Levi's voice was low, but the threatening growl of it somehow carried over the music.

"This isn't your business," Ace shot back, his expression twisting into something darker. "This is between me and the girl—stay out of it."

The girl. Who the fuck did this guy think he was?

Levi shifted so that one second he was standing between me and Ace, and the next he had Ace flattened against the wall, his forearm pressed against his neck.

The panicked look in Ace's eyes and his mouth's fish-like mawing made it clear he was struggling to get a gulp of air in.

I grabbed Levi's shoulder, aware that the attention we were drawing was slowly growing more interested in us than the band, but he didn't budge. "Levi, stop."

He glanced back at me, the question and surprise clear on his face.

"Let him go," I said. "I appreciate the assist, but I don't need your help. I can handle it from here."

A muscle in Levi's jaw pumped, and I could tell he wanted to argue.

"Let him go," I repeated, my voice firm now.

Ace was turning purple, his hands clawing at Levi's arm, though to little effect—Levi hardly seemed to notice, even though Ace had started to draw blood.

Slowly, not once taking his eyes off me, Levi removed his arm, letting Ace slide down the wall, gasping as he fought to suck in a breath.

"Thank you," I said, then I turned my fury on Ace. "You actually spiked my drink? And you have the audacity to act like my anger is blowing this out of proportion? What the fuck is wrong with you? How many people have you done this to?"

"That dude is fucking nuts." Ace coughed as he found his footing, his hand massaging the base of his neck. "Look, Mareena—"

Before he had a chance to fire whichever excuse he was going to pull out of his ass, I pummeled my fist into his face with every ounce of strength I could muster.

In my head, it seemed like a good idea, but several things happened at once, proving me wrong.

Ace fell to the side before landing on his ass, his nose blossoming into a fountain of blood which, to be fair, was pretty great.

But pain, hot and angry, shot through my hand, and the

momentum of the punch dipped me forward until I went spilling down on top of him—stopped only by a firm arm around my waist that held me steady.

The music faded, then stopped altogether when the drummer realized he was playing alone.

Whatever cover we had here in the shadows, on the perimeter of the dance floor, was now long gone. The bouncer at the door came barreling through a shocked crowd that was torn half between backing away to give us space and inching closer to see what might happen next.

"What the fuck?" Ace yelled, his fingers delicately tracing his face, where his nose was now bent at an angle that it hadn't been before. "My nose—you fucking bitch." He turned to the bouncer. "She fucking hit me. Don't just stand there. Do something. Get them out of here."

The bouncer was a large, bald, white man, stacked with muscle so thick it cannibalized his neck. His face was etched with a scowl so deep that I actually flinched when he turned it on me.

"He drugged her," Levi said, his voice was calm and carried smoothly now that the room was shrouded in virtual silence. His arm was still around me, keeping me in place even though I was no longer at risk of falling. He shoved the bottle in his free hand toward the bouncer. "Check the beer if you don't believe me. This wasn't her fault. The prick got what he deserved." Levi glanced down at Ace, his face carved into a dark scowl. "Far less, if I'm being honest."

There was so much loathing in that look that I wondered, briefly, if Levi would've suffocated him to death if I hadn't asked him to let up.

Whatever color was left in Ace's face immediately fled the scene as the crowd started to whisper around us, their curious expressions now shifting to disgust. His teeth were lined with red, and the front one appeared chipped from this angle. "Look man, I'll go, okay. She's an uptight bitch—and he's an asshole. Don't believe them. I didn't do anything. She didn't even drink it."

The bouncer held the bottle loosely at his side as he surveyed the scene, clearly at a loss for how to handle the situation. How often did this sort of thing happen?

Ace took his momentary pause as an opportunity. He kicked the bottle out of the bouncer's hand, shattering it at our feet. The liquid poured everywhere, dissipating and sinking into the already wet, beer-coated floor.

Ace shot me a satisfied smirk, made ridiculous by the smear of blood smeared across his mouth.

With a sinking feeling, I realized what he'd done. The dickhole destroyed the evidence. He was going to get away with it.

I lunged toward him, my vision swimming with a visceral, hot rage I was desperate to release, but Levi's grip held firm.

"Stop," he said, voice low in my ear. "You've already hurt your hand. He's not worth any more damage."

"I don't give a shit about my hand," I screamed back. Right now, I hardly even felt it. The only thing I felt was the violent bloom of anger that was making my head swim.

Levi said something else, whether to me or the bouncer I couldn't tell. I didn't care.

All I saw was red, the injustice of the situation flooding my system with such a furious wave that I could taste it on my tongue.

I wanted to dig my nails into the creep's smug face and claw at him until it was unrecognizable.

The reality of the situation settled over me, hot and searing. What would have happened if I had taken a sip of that beer? If Levi hadn't been here, hadn't said something? What if Ace got away with this and tried it again on someone else? His parents were rich, he had everything he could possibly want—why wasn't it enough? Why was it *never* enough? Why did men do this shit and why did it feel like they always got away with it? Why did men—

Nope, that was the end of my thought. Just why did men? Period, full stop.

After a moment of burning heat, the fight slowly bled out of me, leaving only an aching soul-deep exhaustion. There was no winning in this situation. Pricks like Ace always got away with this shit—if not tonight with the bouncer, then tomorrow with his parents paying off whoever they needed to in order to make the accusations disappear.

What was the point in fighting it? All I got in return was a now-throbbing hand.

When I stopped resisting him, Levi let me go.

He bent down over Ace, though I couldn't catch what he said.

Ace's expression flattened into fear, like he'd seen a ghost. His body trembled on the ground, but he only nodded, the smug look in his eyes now blank.

Levi glanced back at me, making sure I was still exercising restraint, then spoke briefly with the bouncer.

I didn't really want to stick around long enough to catch the highlights of their conversation. I had no intention of waiting for the bouncer to escort me out or call the cops. The last thing I needed was to deal with the police. Fuck that.

I'd only just gotten my life and identity back. I wasn't about to throw it all away.

When I tried to leave, my body chose that exact moment to lock.

My chest was tight, like it couldn't suck in a full breath of air. Though the music had stopped, the whispers and sounds suddenly felt too loud and chaotic to stomach for another second longer. They slurred together until it felt almost like I *had* been drugged.

The people and lights and noises surrounding me blurred at the edges until the scene came to me in stilted clusters.

I felt like I was going to scream or pass out if I didn't get a fresh breath of air in my lungs—maybe both.

When a hand grabbed my upper arm, I flinched.

Something flashed across Levi's expression when he came back into focus. He let my arm go, then took a step back. "Sorry."

I shook my head, my limbs suddenly mine again, then wound my way through the crowd, not stopping until I made it outside. I sucked in a breath, relishing the feel of the cool evening breeze on my skin.

For a minute, I simply stood there, trying like hell to regulate my breathing.

I'd had enough panic attacks in my life to know that I was on the edge of one right now. I dug my nails into my palm, fighting like hell to focus on the sensation of it.

I wanted to go home.

No, I wanted to rewind time so that tonight never even happened in the first place.

And I wanted Sora.

But she would be out late for a work thing. She'd ditch it immediately, of course, if I called her and told her what happened, but that was why I didn't want to. No sense ruining her evening. There'd been enough collateral damage already tonight.

My hand pulsed, like it had a heartbeat of its own, the pain flaring now that my body was settling back into itself.

My knuckles were already swollen, two of them cut and bloody. I must've hit Ace's teeth.

And my thumb—I hissed when I tried to bend it.

Fuck, it hurt.

Why did punching someone always seem so simple and

easy in the movies? From the look of it now, I'd probably done just as much damage to myself as I had to Ace.

"Let me see it."

I spun around, only to find my eyes level with Levi's chest. I stepped back, shaking my head. "It's fine. I'm fine."

"Mars, let me see it."

"Don't call me that," I snapped. "Only Sora calls me that."

I was being ridiculous, given the events of the evening, but I couldn't bring myself to care.

Sora gave me that nickname years ago, the night we ran. When I'd bristled, she'd insisted.

"You give someone a nickname when you're close. We're going to be close, Mars. Whether you want to be or not. You're not getting rid of me, especially not now. Not after everything. We're all we have."

When she'd said that name—Mars—my chest had cracked open. I hadn't heard it in years.

Not since Amto Amani. After losing her, and then Rina, my first real friend in a long time, I'd been desperate for connection. Sora had seen the worst of me—had seen me literally take someone's life. And still, she wanted to stay. In fact, she demanded it. Any other circumstance, and I'd have been better about pushing her away, keeping my distance. We were starting fresh, somewhere new—it should have been easy, walking away from her. But for some reason, some undeniable weakness, I didn't.

Nicknames, especially that one, were reserved for people who stuck around, or at least intended to. There was a permanence there, a familiarity. I didn't have the capacity for any more connections. Nicknames were for friends.

Whatever Levi was, he wasn't my friend.

"Sorry." He offered a careful smile and took a slow step toward me, the kind of hesitation you'd find with someone approaching a feral animal. Maybe I was. "Mareena, can I please take a look at your hand?"

I pulled it against my chest and stepped back. "I said I'm fine. My hand is fine."

He sighed, then ran his hand through his hair. "You're going to make this more difficult than it needs to be, aren't you?" His eyes locked on mine, his expression flattening into a strange stiffness. "Let me look at your hand."

"No."

Surprise flickered on his face. "How do you do that?"

"Do what?"

His eyes held mine for a beat, but then he shook his head. "Never mind."

I stared at him, my blood pumping angrily into my hand until pain was the only thing I could feel.

He smirked. "Unclench your jaw, okay? I promise I won't hurt you. Please just let me take a look, I'm used to assessing these kinds of injuries."

I exhaled, watching him, then shifted my jaw from side to side. It was tight. He was right, I had been clenching. For some reason, that only annoyed me more. Slowly, I extended my hand toward him, figuring this would be the quickest way to get him off my case. "It's just a cut. I'll be fine."

He arched his brow, then took my hand. "You're not used to people trying to help you, are you?"

I hissed, pulling my hand back when his thumb brushed over my knuckles.

"Sorry," he whispered, almost absurdly gentle now as he examined my bones, the pads of his fingers pressing down with a light pressure, his eyes shifting between my hands and my face as if trying to gauge how much each movement hurt. "You know, you have almost comically bad punching form. First time, I take it?"

I pulled my hand back with a snarl.

It wasn't, but the last time hadn't gone so well either. Not that I was going to tell him that. "Haven't had a ton of practice.

I'm not usually a violent person." I bit my lip, before adding a grumbled, "But the asshole deserved it."

"Yeah, he did," he said, his jaw tight. "He deserved worse than that, actually, but he'll get what's coming to him."

"Unclench your jaw," I said with a smirk, then narrowed my eyes. "What did you say to him anyway? He looked more afraid of what you said than he'd been of my fist."

"Doesn't matter."

I studied him for a moment, not entirely sure why I was being so stubborn. It wasn't Levi's fault that Ace tried to drug me. It also wasn't Levi's fault that I hurt my hand. If anything, I owed him.

But something about him just made me want to wear an extra shield, a coat of armor.

"Thank you," I snapped.

"You know"—his face broke into a grin that had the outline of his left dimple making a guest appearance—"I can really feel your gratitude." He rubbed his chest, his eyes brimming with constrained mirth. "Truly, like the rays of the sun. Maybe even warmer."

Instinct had me ready to lash out again, but I swallowed the urge back and winced. Might as well have swallowed razor blades.

I took a deep breath, ready to try again. "Sorry. I didn't mean to take tonight's events out on you. None of this was your fault." My gaze dipped down, unable to hold his stare. Once my body and brain were in defensive mode, it was nearly impossible to pull them quickly out. "Thank you for calling him out. I don't know what would have happened if—if—"

The thought died on my lips, and when I was brave enough to look back up at him, his expression was grim.

"Thank you as well."

"For what?"

"For stopping me," he said. "I'm supposed to be keeping a

low profile, and I don't know what I would have done if you didn't tell me to let him go."

I nodded, remembering the look on his face when he held Ace against the wall.

How far would he have gone?

After a long, tense moment, he cleared his throat, his gaze dropping down to my hand. "Well, I don't think you broke anything, but it's not a bad idea to swing by the ER just to make sure. I can take you—"

"No."

While I was truly grateful for my job at Mac's, it didn't exactly come with winning benefits. And any free insurance I had through the state was basically trash. The only thing that would make the rest of my night worse than it already was would involve sinking into debt because some prick tried to take advantage of my momentary lapse in judgement.

Levi shoved his hands in his pockets and studied me. I could tell he wanted to press the issue, but whatever he saw in my eyes must've convinced him not to. He glanced down the street, then back at me. "Alright. No hospital. But there's a convenience store down the street. Let me get your hand cleaned up at least, put some ice on it."

Though my knee-jerk reaction was to fight him on that, too, I relented. I needed to take the wins when and where I could. "Fine."

We were silent as we made our way down the block, and I followed him awkwardly while he grabbed a bag of frozen peas, some bottled water, alcohol, and bandages, mentally calculating how much this concession was going to run me.

But when we got to the counter, he refused to let me pay.

After two minutes of arguing the point and a glare from the overworked cashier, I bit my tongue and let him fork over the cash.

He pulled me under a lamppost, the yellow glow illuminating a swarm of insects flying above our heads.

With gentle hands, he got to work cleaning the wound.

I only flinched once, which I was proud of.

He placed the bag of peas over my hand and my body relaxed with relief. "Keep this on."

"Thanks," I mumbled, glancing up at him.

He grinned. "No problem. Can I walk you home?"

I shook my head. "No, I'll be okay."

"For my peace, not yours." He shrugged, sending that teasing smirk into his eyes again. "I get very few opportunities to be chivalrous. Please don't take this from me." His lip twitched as he watched me. "It's the least you can do, to repay me for saving your life and all."

"Oh please." It took everything I had not to roll my eyes, so there was no restraint left to bite back my grin. "Fine. But then we're even."

"Deal."

It wasn't a ridiculously long walk by most standards—just twenty or thirty minutes—and I'd make sure to ditch him a block or two before I got to the apartment. There was no reason he needed to know my exact address.

If anything, after tonight, I was doubling down on my trust no one rule.

"I can teach you how to fight," he said, a few minutes into our walk. We'd both been silent, lost in our thoughts. "If you want, I mean."

I arched my brow. "Yeah? And what exactly would you get out of that?"

Levi was nice and had so far proven not to be an axe murderer, but there was an edge to him that made it clear that nice didn't mean he wasn't dangerous. And he definitely didn't seem like the sort of person who went about his day with altruism as his north star.

"Does it have to be transactional?" he asked.

"Everything is transactional."

"Then"—the corner of his lips curved before flattening again—"I guess I just want more exposure to that prickly personality of yours."

"I'm not prickly," I snapped back.

He let out a bark of a laugh.

"I'm . . . guarded." My cheeks flamed. "And for good reason. In fact, if I'd been more guarded tonight"—I held up my hand and the pitifully wet bag of peas attached to it—"maybe this would have never happened."

A fresh wave of shame, coated in a healthy helping of anger, surged through me. Why was it always like that? The one night I actually tried to just go with the flow for once, to have fun, this shit happened. I was actually enjoying myself, too. Not Ace specifically of course, but the bar, the music, the students. I'd even been almost happy to see Levi standing there, all broody and mysterious on the perimeter.

It was like the universe was scolding me for letting loose, letting my armor down.

"Fair enough." He shrugged, the shadow of a smirk flattening into something sadder. "It can be a trade then."

I glanced at him from the corner of my eye. "I'm not sleeping with you."

"That's not—I'm not—" He made a weird sound in the back of his throat. "That's not what I'm suggesting. I don't really know anyone around here. And it looks like I'll be stuck working near town for a bit. It would be nice to see a—" He paused, searching for a word, then smiled when he found it. "Friendly face."

I grunted at his choice.

"And," he continued, "I meant what I said that day. I enjoyed hanging out with you and Sora, getting to see a small sliver into your world. It's rare, you know—having someone like that who looks out for you, who you look out for?"

"I'm not in the market for more friends."

"Clearly." He smirked. "Not friends then. Colleagues. I'll give you a lesson on how to punch assholes without hurting yourself. You give me a tour around the area. Win, win."

"They have tour guides for that."

Levi didn't wear designer labels or anything that screamed money, but I could tell from the look of his clothes that they were made of good, probably expensive material. And he was here for work, which probably meant tech, and he carried himself with the sort of confidence that comfort conveyed. Something told me he wasn't hurting for money—paying for a guide was probably in his budget.

"Tour guides are too"—he slid his hands in his pockets, considering—"perky."

Fair enough, I couldn't argue with him there. "And you'd prefer prickly?"

"Every day of the week."

"Fine." I sighed, almost regretting the decision already. "But if you want to see anything that requires admission, that's on your dime, not mine." I held out my good hand. "Give me your phone."

He didn't bother reigning in his victorious grin as he did.

I plugged my number in, setting my name as Prickly Rick Steves.

It took me longer than usual to punch in, my right hand was now both sore and numb.

"Thanks"—he glanced down before pocketing it—"Rick."

"No problem." We came to an intersection, and I turned to him. "This is where we part."

He glanced at the gas station on one side of us, and the fast-food restaurant on the other. "I don't see an apartment building."

I shot him a look. "After the night I had, you didn't really expect me to show a stranger where I live, did you?"

He bit back a grin. "Reasonable point."

I lifted the now-soggy bag. "Thanks for the peas."

"Any time."

When I got home, I had a new text:

Levi: "Home safe?"

Me: "Yes."

Levi: "Good. See you soon, Rick."

Levi: "P.S. Feel free to save this number under "Hot, Mysterious Savior."

I smiled to myself, then logged his number under Discount Rocky Balboa instead.

12

MAREENA

PRESENT DAY

For a full minute, my only reaction was to laugh. "You honestly expect me to believe that you're my guardian angel?"

Kieran continued to watch me, a bemused look on his face. "Yeah, actually, I do."

I waited, expecting him to break into a raucous laugh, too, and then, hopefully, to offer a real explanation as to why he was stalking me.

But he didn't.

"Wait"—I held the warm cup of tea between my hands, focusing on the heat of it to help ground me—"seriously?"

He arched one of his dark brows, the color in such contrast with the silvery-white hair on the top of his head. He nodded. "Seriously."

I took a long pull of the tea, savoring the burn as it coated my throat and chest on the way down.

When I thought of angels, chubby babies and blond-haired harp players came to mind.

I studied Kieran, my eyes locking on his piercings, his tattoos, that fuck-me-smirk he often wore like a dare. He looked like a drummer in a punk band more than some winged protector.

Not to mention he didn't exactly fuck like an angel either.

"You don't look like the type," I said.

"Yeah?" He shot me a devilish grin. "Type, eh. How many angels have you known exactly?"

Okay, fine. We could play this game if he wanted to.

It wasn't like I was busy—he'd quite literally gotten rid of my only two customers. And they didn't even want anything other than steam. Now, I understood why.

"And do you regularly fuck your charges?"

The curve of his lips flattened.

"No, that's not exactly allowed." He considered for a moment. "Or at the very least, if it's not directly punishable, it's incredibly taboo."

"But you fucked me," I said, as if he needed reminding.

"I did."

"So ..."

"You weren't my charge then," he said with a sigh, as if this whole conversation was growing very tiresome. He spread his arms out. "Now, you are. Meeting me before was just an ... unfortunate coincidence."

Ouch. Way to knock a girl when she's down.

"But the day of The Undoing—" I frowned. "You saved me from becoming a human pancake. That's a very guardian angel thing to do, assuming I believed in such a thing."

He tilted his head and, just like that, guardian angel or not, I felt like his prey again. "So it would seem."

"What were you doing there that day then? And why did you save me if I wasn't even your ... charge?"

"I was seeing to a different charge." He sniffed, then drummed his fingers soundlessly on the booth. "And then you were there, and I just ... stopped you."

"How many charges do you have?"

"One at a time."

"Say I believe you; how long will you be my guardian angel?"

He shrugged. "Until my job is finished."

"What exactly is your job? Have I always had a guardian angel?" I asked, slowly starting to come around to the fact that maybe he wasn't fucking with me. "And also, angels are actually real? Does that mean that there's a heaven and hell? Is hell different from the world that opened up in The Undoing?" I leaned over the bar, considering. "Is *this* hell?"

"You're a lot chattier than you were earlier. I think I preferred you then."

"That's not an answer."

He exhaled, closed his eyes, then leaned his head back against the booth, exposing the dark tattoos that lined the column of his neck. "No, not as you know them but, yes, there are dead people who take on . . . jobs of sorts. I don't know, I don't know, definitely not."

It took me a moment to track which answer went with which question, especially because he conveniently ignored the first two. "How can you not know if hell is real but also be sure this isn't it."

He swallowed, and I hated how intently my eyes tracked the movement. "I've been to realms far worse than this one. So either this isn't hell, or the definition of hell as you know it is an inaccurate one."

I walked to the door, turned the sign back to closed, locked it, and then sat at the booth opposite of him. "Why didn't Sora see you? And why can I?"

"I don't know." He opened his eyes, tilting his head until his stare latched onto mine. "*You're* not even supposed to be able to see me. You shouldn't be able to see Claudine or Greta either. And I sure as hell don't know why you're able to. You shouldn't have even remembered our . . . encounter last week, or at least not that I was the one you had it with anyway. Like I said, you're an unusual girl, Mareena. It's a bit agonizing, but I imagine it has something to do with The Undoing. You must have absorbed some shadow magic that day, and it's given you this unfortunate sixth sense into the world of the dead."

"Ren and Lenora saw you."

His brows furrowed.

"The couple from the other night. They"—I felt the blush creeping up my neck—"the ones that invited us to the private room." My stomach sank. "Oh god. Are they dead too?"

"Oh," he said, "them. That night was different. I was on"—his nose scrunched up—"vacation of sorts."

"Vacation? Guardian angels get vacations?"

"Why? Shouldn't we? Or do you expect us to be worked to the bone?" He grunted. "Fecking capitalism. Doesn't even stop when you're dead, eh?"

"I don't know, do you even have bones?" I took a sip of tea, less because I was thirsty and more for something to do. "So you can turn it on and off then? The seeing and not seeing you thing?"

He shook his head, then held up one finger. "The boundary between our worlds is thinnest on the anniversary of The Undoing." He added a second. "Incendiary functions as a bit of a catalyst for shadow magic, which is what my power pulls from, making it an ideal space to be corporeal." A third. "And I used up all of my strength to sustain my body in the human realm that night. I won't be strong enough for another proper foray into the world for a very long time."

"But you look more—" I studied him, searching for a word. "I don't know, more solid than Claudine? Once I knew to look for it, I mean—she seemed more ephemeral than you do." I kicked my foot out beneath the table, testing a theory, and winced when it crashed into his shin with a little more enthusiasm than I'd been intending. "Sorry. I can still touch you, I mean. Claudine couldn't touch me."

"You're my charge," he shrugged. "You're the only one I can touch without using up power I don't have. And like I said, you're unusual, Agony."

"Okay, Casper," I shot back, "say I believe you," I fidgeted with my ring, focusing on the familiarity of it. "Why do I have a guardian angel? Why now?"

Why not when I'd needed one most. Why not when I lost my aunt? Or Rina? Or when Sora and I were barely scraping by those first few years on our own?

Relative to the rest of my life, I was actually doing okay right now. I was stable—more or less anyway. There were so many people in need of protection and guidance more than me.

He was silent for what felt like a much longer time than it probably was. "I'm here to help you lead a better life. A happier one."

"I . . ." Whatever I was expecting, it wasn't that. "Um, what?"

"You don't have enough fun, I'm here to help you live a better version of the life you're currently living. To push you to do things."

"I like my life."

"Do you?" He didn't ask the question like it was an accusation or a challenge, but for some reason I couldn't shake the feeling that was what it was anyway. Then he reached forward, pointing to the space between my eyebrows. "Because you've also had that particular frown on your face all day. You seemed much more relaxed, some might even say happy, last week."

"Last week was a kind of vacation for me, too," I said. "And you're starting to sound suspiciously like one of those guys who goes around telling women that they look prettier when they smile."

"Your frown is just as pretty as your smile, Agony."

"Stop calling me that." I stood, glaring down at him, as frustration flared from my chest to my feet.

"There she is," he said, his mouth curving into a vicious grin. "I don't think I will, actually. Now that I know it brings that out of you."

"We can't all just go fucking strangers outside of demon clubs every day of the week you know," I said, ignoring his comment. "I have responsibilities. Not every single day has to be filled with euphoria."

"Euphoria?" he asked. "Was last week euphoric for you then?"

"Oh, shut up." I grabbed my empty teacup and took to tidying up the place. "My point is, I don't want a . . ." I gestured at him. "One of you. A guardian angel. I'm good. Go fix someone else's life. Someone who needs your . . . services."

"That's not quite how it works. I'm tethered to you until my job is done."

"You're what?"

"Tethered to you." He shrugged. "Like it or not, I'm here until I'm called away. Can't leave your side for extended periods of time. Consider this the official notice of your life audit. See" —he smirked—"even in my world it holds true—the only things you can count on are death and taxes. I just happen to have one foot in each field at the moment."

"I'm happy," I shot back as I made my way behind the corner. With a huff, I started washing the dishes that were already clean, just for want of something to do other than look at him. "Overjoyed, some might say."

"Clearly," he said with a sardonic look. Then, after a moment, he crossed his arms over his chest and leaned back against the booth. "Okay then, prove it."

"I—what?"

"Show me what a day in your life looks like. What's that

phrase humans started using a while back?" He narrowed his eyes. "What sparks joy for you, Agony?"

"Definitely not that nickname."

He let out a low chuckle. "Joy—perhaps not. But it definitely sparks something, and for now, I'll take what I can get."

I scrubbed the mug, taking my frustration out on the poor ceramic.

"Claudine and Greta weren't wrong," he said, his face two inches from mine as he leaned over the counter, studying me.

I jumped at his sudden proximity and soap suds went flying like splattered paint, all over my shirt.

"Life is wasted on the living." His shoulders sank slightly, not in a release of tension, but like something was weighing them down. "You don't even understand what a gift it is. To be alive."

"What do you want me to do, go back to Incendiary and spend my days getting high on pheromones and mood lighting?"

"No, not that place. Like I said"—he gestured to himself—"I'm off-limits to you now that we have a . . . working relationship. You can't fuck your auditor, and I'm not entirely convinced you'll have the restraint to resist me once your inhibitions are lowered."

I bit the inside of my cheeks, a half-assed attempt to hold in my retort.

Truth was, it was possible he was right.

As annoying as I currently found him, he was also just as delectable looking as he'd been last week. And once Incendiary worked its magic, who knew whether I could keep my desire from leaking out all over him.

"Life isn't supposed to be sunshine and rainbows every day, you know?" I said instead. "And this whole guardian angel scheme sounds a lot like that toxic positivity bullshit plaguing the world before The Undoing. Who gets to decide how I'm supposed to live my life? Who told you to come to fix something that isn't broken?"

He pressed his hands to his chest in mock surprise. "Did you just ask to speak to my manager, Agony?"

I considered him for a moment. "Do you have a manager? Is there, like, a head guardian angel or something? Do you have colleagues? Could I get a different one? Someone less . . . insufferable."

Read: someone who hasn't already been inside me or featured heavily in my fantasies this past week.

"Unfortunately, we're stuck with each other for the foreseeable future." He shot me a wicked smile that did unfortunate things to the knots in my lower belly. "Like I said, we're tethered." He took a deep, dramatic breath, as if he found me just as tiresome as I found him—except for the fact that while I was radiating anger, he appeared deeply amused. "Look, do I seriously look like a harbinger of toxic positivity to you?"

No.

But, as I'd already noted, he didn't exactly look like an angel either. He was walking sex on a stick, and I'd have way sooner believed him to be the devil.

Then again, according to most lore, Lucifer was an angel too.

"I'm not asking you to smile until your depression disappears. I've been dead a long time but, believe it or not, I do remember that life wasn't all, what did you call it—sunshine and rainbows? I'm simply asking you to show me around a day in your life. It's so rare that I get to converse with someone on the job. This could be fun, if you let it. At least for me anyway. What makes you tick? What makes you happy? Like I said, consider today an audit. The faster you appease me, the faster I'm out of your hair." He leaned in closer. "Assuming that's what you really want, of course. Not that you'll get much of a choice either way."

"Very much," I said, my tone clipped, though I couldn't bring myself to meet his stare. Those eyes had an unpredictable effect on my brain.

"Great." With a clap of his hands, he ushered me from behind the counter. "Let's take the day off work then, go do something more enjoyable than . . . this."

"I can't just leave."

"Got to say, Agony. . ." He surveyed the empty restaurant. "Don't think anyone will miss you anytime soon."

I couldn't exactly argue with that, and maybe the sooner I did as he asked, the sooner I'd be rid of him. I *had* just been complaining about wanting more company, hadn't I? "Fine. How does this work then? What do you want to do?"

"Good question," he considered. "My top choices for fun have always been vices, and," he scanned me head to foot, "like I said, we're keeping things professional. So why don't you show me what an ideal afternoon looks like for you. Seems like as good a place as any to start, doesn't it?"

"Vices? You don't really fit the angel mold. Not exactly what I would expect from an angel anyway."

That wicked smirk again. "Maybe you need to adjust your expectations."

"So, what? I'm just supposed to wander around town with some dude that only other random ghosts and I can see?"

"Phantoms. And yes, that's exactly what you're supposed to do."

I stalled, not because I was against the plan, but because now that I was thinking about the things I liked to do best, I realized how long it had been since I'd done them.

We were well into paddleboarding season, and I hadn't been out once yet this year. In fact, I hadn't been out last summer either.

And I hadn't gone swimming in the lake or gotten exuberantly drunk with Sora while we watched seals and sea lions chase salmon down at the Ballard Locks in ages.

Hell, even my biggest me-time hobby, reading, had been conspicuously absent from my life recently.

All my time went to managing Frank's, lingering at the med center, and volunteering with whatever else was needed at any given time in the community. Trying to keep people alive and staying as busy as possible so that the chaos of this new world didn't force me into an isolated, spiraling cave of doom.

"Tell you what," Kieran said, probably sensing that I was starting to spiral into a zone very far from joy, "why don't we start out simple?"

I glanced at him. "Simple is good."

"Close your eyes."

"What?"

"Close your eyes, Agony."

I exhaled sharply at the ridiculous nickname but did as he asked. "Now what?"

"Ah, ah, ah," he tsked, "patience is a virtue."

"Thought you said vices were more your speed." My eyes sprang open. "What's the afterlife like?"

He shook his head like I was a child who'd stepped out of line. "Let's get this out of the way now—we're not doing the 'twenty questions about what happens when you die' thing. Anything you ask me about death or my job will just be met with silence." He sighed. "Besides being forbidden, that's not why I'm here—and there's no use lingering on death and what comes next when my whole purpose right now is to get you to live in the moment. To enjoy your life while you have it—the good and the bad." When I opened my mouth to argue, he added, "Close your eyes, no talking."

Jaw clenched, I did as he asked, though I didn't see the point in hanging out with my guardian angel if I couldn't even probe him about his death and what came after . . . this.

"Now," he said, tone playful, "try to picture yourself the last time you were doing something just for you. Not for your restaurant, not for that shabby little center you pretend is a hospital, not because someone asked or forced you to do it. Something you did for yourself, nobody else. Picture it. Your body feels light, the tension in your shoulders is drained away, that perpetual scowl nowhere in sight."

I popped open one eye. "Don't push it."

"Eyes closed, Agony. You want me gone, then you need to do things my way."

I groaned but did as he asked. Demanded.

"Where are you?"

Heat exploded in my belly when the image of Kieran outside Incendiary, bent on his knees as he ducked under my dress shot into my brain like a bullet.

He cursed. "Whatever has that blush on your cheeks, clamp it down. We are keeping this PG, Agony."

The fact that he could see my blush just made my cheeks heat more. Could angels sense arousal? "In the water," I shot out, pulling the first non-sex-related activity from my arsenal.

"Like a bathtub?" he asked, his pitch rising in surprise.

I snorted. "No, the lake. On my paddleboard."

"Right. And that's . . . different than a surfboard, I take it?"

"Yes, different than a surfboard. You stand on it and . . . paddle." I opened my eyes, studying him. "How long exactly have you been dead?"

"Too long," he said, brushing the question to the side, just as he had the others. "Sitting on a plank in the water seems an odd choice for what's supposed to be an exciting bunk off work." He mussed my hair in that way adults often did when they were trying to appease a child. "But okay, Agony. Let's go take a drift on your board thing." Then, he added, "And maybe after we can have a discussion about what, exactly, constitutes a craic."

I fixed my hair. "Are the dead always this judgy?"

"No." He smirked. "Consider yourself lucky. You could've gotten stuck with one of the old boring guardians."

"Maybe boring suits me." I shot him a smirk. "Feel free to swap charges with another guardian at any time, Casper."

"No." His eyes dropped to my mouth, where they lingered for a beat. "I most definitely won't be doing that."

13

MAREENA

APPROXIMATELY NINE YEARS AGO, THREE
YEARS BEFORE THE UNDOING

With a heavy tug, I managed to pull the paddleboard down the dock, plopping it less gracefully than I normally did in the water.

It was more difficult than usual since, though mostly healed, my hand still wasn't back to tip-top shape. Pumping the board up had been a test in patience that I almost didn't pass.

At least it was healing. My knuckles were pretty much back to their normal size and, based on the improvements these last few weeks, I was confident my hand would be fully functional in another week or two. Seemed Levi was right, thankfully—nothing was broken, and the cuts had already scabbed over.

The sun beat down on my back as I velcroed the strap around my ankle and then wiggled onto the board.

It was my prized possession and the single most expensive thing I'd ever purchased for myself. Even though I got it second-hand, I still cringed whenever I thought about how much I forked over.

Worth every penny though, if I was honest.

Plus, it was on its third summer—patch tape worked wonders on all the inevitable holes.

It was one of those absurdly perfect Seattle days. Not a cloud in the sky. Hot, but tolerable near the water. And since it was a Wednesday afternoon, the small, secret cove I flocked to wasn't too busy. Two guys scarfed down their lunches near the ramp, trying to soak in a few minutes of sun before they got back to work. At the end of the dock, there was a couple, both laying out in highlighter-bright bikinis while they played fetch with their golden retriever. Peels of their laughter and cheers ricocheted around the little bay, each time the dog bravely dove into the water and eagerly swam after his orange ball.

With a giant smile on my face, I leaned back on the paddleboard and floated near the dock, soaking in the feel of the sun on my skin.

This was one of my favorite places in the entire city. It was physically impossible not to feel a shooting wave of happiness here, on a day like this.

"Tell me, Rick," a deep voice sounded above me. Startled, I wobbled on the board, nearly tipping into the water, then steadied myself at the last second, wincing when I used my bad hand to stabilize. "How exactly is this touring?"

I sat up and found Levi staring down at me—dressed in black, as usual, a hesitant scowl on his face as he glanced from the dock to me.

We were doing my portion of the deal first, since he didn't want to start Punching Asshats 101, as I'd dubbed it, until my hand looked less like a blob with five sausages attached.

"You're like," I shuffled through my dry bag and pulled out my phone, "half an hour early."

I'd deliberately come down here before we were set to meet so that I could get some solid introvert peace and quiet beforehand.

He shrugged, a soft smirk teasing his lips. "Didn't want to be late. And I needed to make sure I could find this spot based on your . . . colorful directions."

I swallowed my grin. Instead of giving him an address, I'd sent him on a bit of scavenger hunt that forced him to explore a park and small shopping district on his way to me. Figured it was a good way to smash two tours into one, plus see if he would actually follow through.

"Well, you made it." I scanned his clothes. Black pants, black T-shirt—surely, this was a uniform at this point—and a backpack dangling at his side. "Thought I said bring a swimsuit and prepare for a day out on the water?"

Maybe he wasn't so great at following instructions after all.

"Trying to get my clothes off already, are we?" He winked, kicked off his shoes, then peeled off his socks. "Have to admit, I honestly thought you were fucking with me. But I came prepared in case you weren't."

When he started to unbutton his jeans, I shifted my focus to the other side of the dock, suddenly deeply interested in the colorful, sun-bleached houseboats lining the water.

"So why the water?" Levi asked. "Thought today was supposed to be a tour day?"

"Best place to see the city, in my opinion." I glanced back at him, finding myself very thankful that my sunglasses were oversized. Hopefully that meant they hid some of the blush on my cheeks, or the fact that I couldn't tear my stare from him.

Not only did Levi have a pair of swim shorts under his pants —black, his signature color, of course—but he was also now shirtless.

And, unfortunately, it was as perfect a sight as I'd imagined it would be the day I first saw him at Frank's. Smooth, lean muscle, every inch carved to perfection. It was honestly ridiculous.

He smirked, no doubt fully aware of how hot he was, and lifted his bag. "Er, what am I supposed to do with this?"

Right. I could do this. It took me a moment to unfluster myself and lift my dry bag up to him. "Put anything essential in here, and then just hide your bag behind that bush over there." I nodded toward the main ramp, which had a bush and small cove underneath, a few feet above the waterline. "Should be safe until we get back. Probably."

"You really know how to set a guy at ease, don't you?" Still, he did as I suggested and hid his bag under the bush. It, like everything else he owned, was black, so it would blend in well enough. When he made his way back to me, I had one leg dangling over one side of the board and used the paddle to anchor me to the dock.

I'd gone with a one-piece and pair of shorts, so that I wouldn't feel too exposed. Still, when his gaze dipped over me, it felt like I might as well have been wearing nothing.

Some of his cocky expression waned when he stared at the paddleboard. I wouldn't call it outright fear, but he was eyeing it with the sort of suspicion I'd be eyeing every beer that dudes tried offering me in the future.

Should I have warned him?

While I often felt more in control on the water than I did on land, that didn't necessarily translate for others.

"Sorry, I should have checked with you first. If you're not comfortable, you don't have to get on. Do you know how to swim?"

"I'll manage." He grinned. "Hopefully. I mean, how hard could it be?"

Then without warning, he took a running jump and leaped over me and into the water, clearly unconcerned about the wave he sent splashing up in his wake.

He stayed under longer than I anticipated, and when I glanced around, expecting rippling rings to signal his emergence, I saw only still water.

"Levi?" Leaning over, I tried to see through the murky depths of the water, but all I saw was my own reflection staring back at me. "Levi!"

Before panic had the chance to fully settle over me, my board tipped, sending me plunging into the water.

Ice surged through my veins. While the water was safe to swim in, it was still cold. The Pacific Ocean was always frigid, no matter how hot the temperature on land was—and even though this lake was freshwater, not salt, the two still connected. Now that fall was ushering in, it wouldn't be until next summer that a swim in this lake didn't send a bolt of cold through my bones.

When my face broke the surface, I found Levi, his head resting on his arms, which were folded over the board to keep him effortlessly afloat. "Whoops."

I brushed my hair back and grabbed my sunglasses before they disappeared into the lake, never to be seen again. I'd lost three pairs, two shirts, and a book to these depths over the years. "Dick."

He shrugged, a wicked grin on his face. The sun made the water droplets on his face sparkle, like they were laughing too. "Sorry, couldn't resist."

As much as I fought to keep it there, my scowl twisted into a laugh. "Whatever, you're paddling. Get on."

He slid himself over the board with more grace than I'd anticipated and leveraged his weight while I climbed up myself.

Once I steadied us both, I handed him the second ankle leash. "Put this on."

"Yes, mam."

When I glanced at him, my breath caught in my lungs. If he was hot dry and on land, then wet Levi was two stages past scorching.

Water glistened over his skin. The dark curls that were always half in his eyes were pushed back now—the gray pools clear and filled with a mirth that the sun gravitated toward and only seemed to accentuate more, like it was his own personal ring light.

I cleared my throat, and glanced down at the board, realizing how very little room there was between us. "Right. Safety first. Let's teach you how to stand."

Pushing off from the ramp, I positioned us a few feet away, ensuring that if and when we fell again, neither of us would end up getting a dock lobotomy.

Like most people, Levi fell the first time he tried standing.

And since we were both on the paddleboard, that meant I fell, too.

I talked him through it, giving him the spiel I wished someone had given me: don't lock your knees, stand on either side of the line to center your weight, and when it's time to stand up, don't look down, look out on the horizon instead.

He was wobbly at first, but he had a good awareness of his body and center of gravity, and, once he had a feel for the board, a solid balance followed soon after that. It was always more difficult with two people on here, so I was impressed with how quickly he picked it up.

The water rippled around us, and when I glanced to the right, I noticed a furry, golden head making its way toward the board.

The golden retriever swam up to me, no doubt excited to have playmates in the water. He held the orange ball in his mouth like a prize as he collected a few well-deserved scratches behind his ear. He plopped the soaking-wet ball between us, and Levi tossed it out into the water, for the little land-seal to go fetch.

We watched him collect it, then head back to his moms on the dock, pride brimming when he climbed up and shook off all over them.

Feeling lighter than I had in a while, I handed Levi the paddle and gestured for him to kneel. It would be easier to move us both that way than if we were both standing. Then, I waved my hand out toward the expanse of water. "Alright, let's go see the city."

Paddling two people wasn't exactly the easiest thing in the world, but Levi made it look like it was. He moved us through the water evenly, with an impressive speed that didn't seem to cost him any effort.

"You're different out here, you know." He averted his gaze when I looked at him, almost shy. "Happier. Freer."

"Less prickly, you mean?" I arched my brow.

He laughed. "Yeah, less prickly. Though don't get me wrong, I like the prickly you, too."

My chest tightened at that admission and, clearing my throat, I gestured absently around us—the blue sky, the warm sun, the picturesque water and houseboats lining the coast. "Kind of hard not to be happy out here."

"You come here a lot then?"

I nodded. "As often as I can. I've always loved being on the water."

Sometimes, after a particularly bad day, I'd find my way to the dock we'd left from and just go for a swim, alone, letting myself become one with the water and night sky. Not exactly the safest safety blanket in the world, sure, but my little cove never failed to make me feel better—less alone, even when I was. Out here, the weight of the world just felt lighter—no matter how heavy it was on land.

The water was also where I felt closest to Amto Amani. When I closed my eyes, I could almost imagine that I was back on our little shoreline, just out of reach of where her voice would carry. That if I opened my eyes, I might see her standing there on the dock.

Though, of course, I never could.

I studied him as he maneuvered us away from the small bay and out into the canal. We weren't too far from where Sora and

I had taken him before. "You sure you've never been on a paddleboard, or were you just fucking with me?"

His lips tipped into a small grin, that dimple of his making an appearance again. "I pick things up pretty quickly."

It took a non-small amount of effort not to stare at his chest and abs as he moved us effortlessly through the water. The constant shifting from one side of the board to the other did major things for the expanse of muscle on display.

"This canal splits the northern half of the city from the southern, which makes it a unique way to understand and calibrate where a lot of the neighborhoods are. So," I said, jutting my chin to the west, "if we went that way, we'd eventually hit the Locks in Ballard and, from there, the Sound." I pointed to the buildings on the opposite side of the water. "Over there, you have Magnolia and Queen Anne." I pointed east. "We're going this way. We'll hit Wallingford and Lake Union, and if we keep going beyond that, the lake will eventually spill into U District and Lake Washington."

He nodded, maneuvering us in the direction I suggested.

After a few minutes of silence, he glanced down at me. "Your hand looks better. How's it feeling?"

I opened it, flexing. "Better. Figure I should be in perfect punching form in a week or so."

He grinned. "I'll keep that in mind."

Surprisingly, he hadn't texted much in the weeks since getting my number. Just enough to confirm a time and place— and for me to send my directions. And he usually took hours, sometimes days, to respond to the few back and forths we had managed.

It made sense. Levi wasn't the sort of person who was stuck to their phone—a trait I admired. In fact, the only time I recalled it making an appearance was when he shoved it under my nose to punch my number in.

"So," I said, feeling slightly bad that I wasn't contributing much to the actual labor of the paddle. Least I could do was come up with some conversation. "What part of town are you staying in while you're here."

His grip tightened on the paddle, the smooth cadence of his stroke breaking just a touch. "Um, I'm outside the city, mostly."

I studied him. "How far outside of the city?"

He shrugged. "It changes. Sometimes I'm close, but otherwise, I'm a few hours out."

My jaw dropped. "Hours?"

His eyes shifted to mine, then back to the water, like he was embarrassed. "There's not much to do where I'm working. I don't even have cell service." That explained the infrequency of his texts. "So I drive into the city for a night or two when I'm off. Clear my head away from—everything."

I thought back to that day at Frank's. He'd been drowning his sorrows in liquor. He was also stiff and moodier than now. "What kind of work do you do, exactly?"

He was silent for a long stretch, like he was searching for the right words—something that instantly had my hackles up, because why did he make it seem like it was such a difficult question? "My family works in protective detail. And right now, my mom is spending a lot of time with a small town in the mountains. I can kind of come and go when I want, but sometimes she sends me out of the state, too—for other clients and stuff."

"Protective detail," I repeated, rolling the words over my tongue. Like a bodyguard? What the hell did that mean? And who needed security in the mountains? "How long have you been doing that?"

He shrugged. "As long as I can remember."

I narrowed my eyes. "You can't have been working that long. You don't look all that older than me, and I doubt your family let you go all secret service mode as a minor."

His lips twitched, but he didn't say anything.

"And you don't know how long you'll be around the area?"

He shook his head. "Not forever, just until my skills are needed elsewhere."

"And those skills are?"

A smile stretched across his face, that dimple making an appearance again. "Teaching girls how to punch asshats."

I chuckled, though I recognized the clear attempt to change the topic for what it was. "You won't tell me what you do, where you're from, how long you're here. What will you tell me?" When the silence stretched between us again, heavier now, I became abundantly aware of the fact that I was in the middle of the water with a virtual stranger. I was a strong swimmer, and was pretty confident that I could get away from him if I needed to—that was one of the reasons I'd suggested we do the tour here instead of in a car—but he wasn't exactly offering trustworthy vibes. "You've got to give me something, Levi, otherwise I'm just going to think that I've embarked on a transactional venture with a serial killer."

He stopped paddling for a moment, and we watched a crew team pass us, their soft chants fading with each pull. "I can't tell you a lot about what I do or why I'm here, Mareena. I could lie, make shit up"—his eyes snagged on mine, an emotion I couldn't parse flitting across his features—"but I really don't want to do that."

That night at the canal, he'd been oddly easy to talk to. At least Sora seemed to think so. And he didn't seem to have trouble chatting with Chase or the bouncer at the party. Just me.

He was an indecipherable puzzle—one that occasionally made it seem like it was solvable, only for you to step back and realize that there were twice as many pieces than when you first opened the box.

I dipped my feet in the water. "Okay, then tell me something about you. Or about your family. Just—" I watched a seagull dive into the water, fishing out its lunch. "Tell me something true." I flicked at the water. "It's only fair. Sora spilled one of my darkest secrets within, like, twenty minutes of talking to you."

"To be fair"—he sat down on his calves, giving up on paddling altogether now—"you're more a closed book than you think you are. Maybe the most locked down person I've ever met, and I've met a lot of locked down people." He shifted, letting out a breathy laugh. "Besides, Sora hardly revealed anything. She just told me that you thought you were cursed. That you believe, on some level, that those you're close to die. I wouldn't really call that a particularly soul-baring secret. If anything, that tells me more about the people around you than it does you. Plus, for all you know, I brushed it off as a joke."

"You didn't." I was suddenly incredibly aware of the fact that his knee was only an inch or two away from mine.

He shook his head. "No but, in the interest of fairness and keeping things transactional, I also gave you one of my own fears in return."

The way he lingered on the word 'gave' made me realize that that moment had been more soul-baring for him than I'd realized.

"You really believe that you have no say in your destiny?" I asked.

He arched his brow. "You really believe you kill people by association?"

"Touché."

"What will convince you that I'm not a serial killer?" He shot me a coy grin. "Since apparently saving you from a drugged beer isn't cutting it."

"Oh please." I grunted. "Everyone knows that serial killers enjoy doing the killing part themselves." I flicked some water on the board at him. "If anything, you were just saving me from Ace so that you could get me off yourself." Heat crawled up my neck as I instantly realized my mistake. "I mean off me," I corrected, flustered. "*Off me* yourself."

"Off you," he said, then he let out a deep and husky chuckle that did strange things to my stomach.

I couldn't bring myself to look at him, choosing instead to focus on the yacht coming toward us, and the obnoxious yuppies dancing to shitty music on the deck.

"Tell me about your mom," I said, shifting the conversation in a direction that most definitely would not send my mind in dangerous directions.

"I don't really know what to say about her. No one's really asked me about her before," he said, almost surprised by the revelation. "She's a . . . mom, I guess." He shrugged. "Tough, kind of standoffish around other people, but warm around me. Funny when she lets her guard down—which is pretty rare when it's not just me and her. She's also extremely protective." He paused for a moment. "I owe her a lot. She gave up a big part of her life when she found out she was pregnant with me. I've always kind of felt shitty for that."

"What do you mean?"

"She had an affair," he winced, then dropped his leg in the water, letting it dangle over the side. "And the guy who impregnated her was not the guy she was married to."

"Ah," I said, "and judging by the fact that you called him 'the guy who impregnated her,' I'm guessing you and he aren't exactly close."

He ran his hand through his hair, which was now almost dry again from the sun's heat. "Nope. It was just a fling—with my mom. He wasn't around."

"I'm sorry." And I was. I knew what it was like not to know the people you came from. It wasn't a loss in the traditional sense—it was hard to miss someone you never had—more like an emptiness, a piece of yourself that was forever cut off from you. "I never met my dad either."

He glanced up at me, a softness in his eyes that wasn't there before. "And what about your mom?"

"She uh—she died giving birth to me." I swirled my leg through the water, needing the distraction. I never let myself linger on my parents for too long. There was too much guilt, too much shame—both because giving birth to me killed my mother, and because when it came down to it, I missed my aunt far more than I'd ever missed the parents I never even met. Sometimes, even though it didn't make any sense, that felt like a bit of a betrayal. "What about your mom's husband, from before? Is he still in the picture? Are you two close?"

Levi shook his head. "No, they had another son." He looked shy suddenly, the callous, cocky mask he usually wore slipping away. "Before me, I mean. So, I guess I have a half-brother technically. I've met him, but we aren't really close. I tried, when I was younger, to reach out"—he exhaled sharply—"but he made it very clear that he had no interest. He hates me, but I can't say that I entirely blame him."

"Why would he hate you?"

"Isn't it obvious?" His leg brushed against mine under the water, but he pulled it back just as quickly, as if the touch had stung. "I broke up his perfect family. If I hadn't been in the picture, I'm sure my mom and her ex would have worked things out—whatever their problems were. She's never really discussed it with me. I think thinking about that part of her life hurts too much."

"Hey." I nudged him, waiting to continue until he looked up at me again. "That wasn't your fault. I'm sure what happened was shitty. But if he blames you, then fuck him. He doesn't deserve to have you in his life."

"What about you?" he asked, watching me now with a focus that made me squirm. Maybe drawing his attention back to me had been a mistake. "Who raised you, I mean, if not your birth parents?"

"My aunt," I answered. "Well, technically my father's aunt and my great aunt, I guess. After my mom—" I shrugged. "Well, you know—after what happened—I moved in with my mom's sister, but I wasn't there for very long."

She was my mother's only family, an older sister she was never close with, but she took me in anyway. I didn't have any memory of her. Or any memory I did have, I suppose, was cobbled together through a handful of photos I found online years later—memories that were half shadow and false memory, a record more than anything I felt particularly connected to. It seemed silly, holding on to a memory of what I couldn't keep.

"It didn't work out?" he asked.

"She died, too. Overdosed a few days before my first birthday. And her own daughter, just two years older than me, fell ill not long after she passed. Her husband—my uncle—sent me away after that. Thought I was cursed." I gave him a wry grin. "My cousin got better after I left—or at least I assume she did, since she's still alive anyway. According to the internet." And a drunken night of social media sleuthing with Sora.

I never tried getting in touch with her though. Protective services reached out to them after Amto Amani died, hoping they could place me with them. But my uncle made it clear that I wasn't welcome.

I was dead to them, no matter how alive I was.

It stung, maybe, but I understood. Bad omen, curse, or just plain bad luck—it hardly mattered at the end of the day. My presence had done very little to protect the people closest to me.

"But yeah, I guess that's where the whole curse thing started, now that I think about it," I said.

"That's ridiculous, you know that, right? A string of rotten luck, sure, but what happened to them wasn't your fault." His brows were furrowed, like he was angry on my behalf. "You have to see that."

I shrugged. "Yeah, maybe. I mean, I don't know, I know the curse theory is all woo-woo and out there, and maybe it's not real. I hope it's not. Trust me, no one hopes that more than I do. But there's enough evidence that it is—or at least that it could be."

I dipped my hand into the water, letting the cool, gentle waves pull it under. Oddly, I wasn't panicking. Maybe it was because I was in my element out here, or maybe it was just something about Levi—he'd certainly had a way of getting Sora to open up, I supposed I shouldn't be surprised he'd been just as successful with me. Or maybe it was easier to be open with him because I knew what this was—a transaction. Two days, and we were well on our way through the first.

There was no danger of things going any deeper than surface level, not really.

In some ways, that made him the easiest person to talk to. Things I spoke into existence out here would be swallowed up again by the sea and a stranger.

"It just seems easier to assume it's true," I said. "Safer. For other people, you know? I don't blame my uncle for sending me away."

He didn't know me. He wasn't even my blood. And he certainly didn't owe me anything. He did, however, owe his daughter protection and, rational or not, it was entirely possible that shipping me off was what saved her in the end. Almost like he had been holding onto her at the edge of death's cliff with nothing more than fatherly desperation and a white-knuckled grip—and the only way to pull her up was to let me go.

In her story, he was a hero. In mine, he wasn't even a villain. Just a fleeting footnote.

Levi didn't look convinced, but he decided to be merciful and drop it. "And after that—you lived with your father's aunt?"

I nodded, the tension easing from my body. "Amto Amani. She's the reason I'm on the West Coast. I was born in Ohio, but I moved to a small isolated town on the Oregon coast when she took me in."

"What was she like?"

"Warm. She had a really great but kind of dark sense of humor. And she didn't give a single fuck what anyone thought about her." I smiled, remembering her fierceness, the confidence she radiated in every room she walked in. Now that I was older, I wondered how much of that was innate, and how much was a shield or weapon she could wield when she needed it most. "Which was really impressive, considering she was a bit of an outsider, and we lived in a super small community. The sort filled with judgmental assholes just looking for someone to cast out. People thought she was a witch." I laughed, my chest feeling light and free with the memory. "They hated her for it, but that didn't stop them banging on her door in the middle of the night, begging for spells and talismans for whatever misfortune had fallen on them. We had a lot of fun over the years, collecting random things and pretending to enchant them."

During my time with her, I never once felt like I was cursed, though I'd asked her about it when I was older—like as I grew, the more aware I became that death was close. She often brushed it off, called my fears unwarranted, but sometimes I'd catch her watching me when she didn't think I noticed, her features carved into a frown, lost in thought.

Of course, after I arrived, and throughout the nine or so years I lived there, people in our small town grew mysteriously ill. Several even died, but no one cast the blame on me.

Who would blame a child? Especially one orphaned so tragically?

No, it was far easier to blame my aunt, a woman who'd always lived on the outskirts of their community, as mysterious as a stranger.

My memories of the town, even now, were laced with the sharp sound of their whispering behind our backs—an occurrence that took place nearly every time we walked down the main street of shops. They swore that she was a witch, cursed; threatened time and time again to have me taken from her and sent away to a more suitable guardian. Someone who could give me a family, a future, a more palatable life.

Or at least one that better suited their idea of a palatable life.

I loved living with my aunt, and never once felt like my life was lacking in any way.

She'd always pull me tight against her side, gluing us together when those threats would resurface—her warmth sinking into me, a calming promise, the vicious hiss and nonsensical chanting she shot back at the pearl-clutching townspeople a dark dare.

It was enough to keep their threats just that. And their fear never stopped any of them from haunting our driveway in the early hours of the morning, begging for a love spell to draw back a cheating spouse, or a protective talisman to keep their investments from slipping through their fingers.

She would always acquiesce, whispering gibberish over her table of found objects and rocks—most discarded trinkets I'd collected from oblivious tourists during the summer months. Worthless.

Then, when the townspeople threw her a few wrinkled bills, noses crumpled in disgust—disgust that seemed directed half at her and half at themselves—they'd stow away their useless talismans and the cloudy vials of water they'd assumed she'd 'blessed' and brought back from the Mediterranean Sea. They had no idea that I'd collected the liquid from the shoreline just a few steps from their very backyards.

Of course, those moments of desperation also never stopped them from whispering behind our backs the next day when we'd go in for the week's groceries or keep them from hugging their children close to their bosoms whenever we passed by.

I'd asked her once, why she did it, why she fed into their fears and carved space for the lies they harbored to root and grow, but she only laughed, her answer so clear and so her, that I remembered every word to this day.

"Fear is a powerful tool, habibti," she'd said, her words filtered through the soft curves of the accent that only occasionally made itself known. *"Don't underestimate it. Their money spends the same, no matter what names they might call me. And it's far better for their ignorance and hatred to land on me than on you. I can make better use of it."*

Her fearlessness wrapped around me like a cloak, and I grew to revel in her cleverness, amplifying her fake chanting with my own whenever I was feeling particularly brave.

"She sounds kind of like you," Levi said, drawing me back from the recesses of my thoughts.

With slow, steady strokes, he started pushing us down our path again.

He had no idea how very wrong he was—or how much I wished that he wasn't.

"I can tell you really loved her." He smiled, and this time it stretched all the way to his eyes. "You light up when you talk about her."

My cheeks warmed under the weight of his gaze. "She was just that kind of person, you know? The start of my life was chaotic, but when I was with her, it never really felt like I'd suffered some great loss."

Even with the solitude of our town, made more obvious by the disdain of the people who lived there, I loved my childhood with her. Possibly, in part, because I didn't know anything different, but mostly because she had a way of infusing warmth into every room of our small cottage—her every exhale breathing comfort and light into each crack and cob-webbed corner.

As long as I had her, I hardly noticed the things I lacked—friends my own age, my parents. She was all I needed. And she put my needs before anything else, even when they created more work for her.

"During my first week of school," I said, recalling the memory with a sudden urgency, "I'd been picked on so badly for living with a witch that I begged to be homeschooled. It was a request she'd refused, at first, until the afternoon I came home with a black eye and a gash a few millimeters short of my eyeball where the sharp edge of a rock had hit. She gave in instantly after that, securing a stack of textbooks and various homeschool curriculums. Just like that, she sacrificed so much of her time and so many resources to keep me safe, to keep me happy."

Our life went back to being cozy and quiet after that day. Just us. She never let me go a single day without knowing that I was loved, without making sure I understood that my life was a gift, not a curse. That I was not defined by what I'd lost but forged stronger because of it.

"How long did you live with her?"

"About nine years, give or take," I said. "She died on my tenth birthday. And then I ended up in a group home and foster care. That's where Sora and I eventually met a few years later."

If I believed in such things, I'd think Amto Amani had sent her to me—like she knew I'd need someone to hold onto when she was gone, someone too stubborn to let me isolate myself entirely.

"I'm glad you had her," he said, his expression soft, the hard edges from earlier erased entirely. "And I'm sorry that you lost her so young."

"Thank you." I swallowed; my throat tight with the loss of her. "I don't talk about her much."

"Why not?"

"I don't know." I shrugged. "Sometimes it's hard."

"I get that." He nodded, his lips lifting into a small smirk. "Sometimes it's easier to talk to a stranger you've only agreed to hang out with twice."

I snorted. "Precisely."

But it was also more than that.

After my aunt died, I didn't speak about her very much. Partially because, at first, I didn't know what wearing the grief of her loss would feel like. The more I grew into it, the less I felt equipped to unpack it, to put it on display for people—even Sora, which was absurd, because she would have understood better than most. But she held her own pain just as closely, like a second skin.

In some ways, it was easier to dance around the other's pain, a silent promise that we knew that it was there, that it festered—neither of us able to look the other's loss in the eye, because if we did, we might have to let it go.

And we both understood the truth—that letting go of that pain was the only thing more heartbreaking than feeling it. That pain was the final tether we had to the people we'd loved the most. It had to be guarded, protected, at all costs.

The days after my aunt died had been easier in some ways. People treated me with understanding, their eyes soft, their voices quiet as they ripped me from the only home I knew, placing me in a different, colder one, where I was untethered from any connection to my life before then. Still, while their words were filled with false sincerity and wishes for my wellbeing, they didn't fight back against my tears, didn't tell me to toughen up or get over it.

In those days, my grief was a deep wound, an incision I could point to, that they could all see and understand, on some level. But as the days turned to months, and then years, that wound closed, becoming nothing more than fading scar tissue to those viewing it from the outside.

What they didn't see or understand was that, though invisible to them, the ache left by my aunt's death festered beneath my skin, growing and rooting into my veins and bones, cocooning me completely. Where grief had been acute and sharp before, it had morphed into a gentle—though no less painful—throb. One I couldn't escape. One that became like a second heartbeat, as necessary to me as my own breath.

The loss engraved in me by her death was so much more than just the loss of her person. She'd been the only anchor I had to myself. With her, I lost my community, my culture—the frail connections to family and blood were completely eviscerated. With her gone, I didn't know where boundaries of myself started and ended. I didn't know who I was without her. Without the one person in the world who understood me, who'd seen me—through me, down to the core of who I was.

I knew it was the same for Sora, after Rina died. Perhaps that was why we never spoke about it. Both of us recognized the echo of a pain we tried desperately to cover in the other. It was the sort of agony that only multiplied when you looked at it, like speaking it into the world would only infect the other's wounds, make them worse—impossible to feign recovery from. If we tried to wrap up each other's grief, we'd be left sitting on the discarded paper, drowning in it.

"Well," I said, clearing my throat and shoving the weight of loss back into the recesses of my mind where I usually kept it covered, "this is Seattle."

The already-wide canal opened up into Lake Union, the large lake that traced the skyline.

Something about the immensity of it here, existing in the middle of it, made me feel so small. But not in a bad way, just one thing that reminded me how very full and exciting the city really was outside of my small world.

Behind us stood Gas Works, an old industrial plant that had been repurposed into a public park in the sixties. It was such a strange mix of nature and industry, the large metal structures were still on display, though they were ruins now, as grass and plants reclaimed the area surrounding them. There was a giant hill that tourists and children climbed, their kites soaring like birds through the sky.

As cool as the park was on its own terms, it was generally visited because it looked out on one of the best views in the city.

In front of us, tall and looming, as sea planes took off and landed around us stood the Seattle skyline—the famous Space Needle on the right, closest to where we were floating.

"Beautiful, isn't it?" I asked.

"Breathtaking," he said, his voice almost reverent as his eyes held mine.

14

MAREENA
PRESENT DAY

Instinct had me resisting everything about Kieran and this little midday field trip, but I pushed all of my energy into ignoring it. If this was the only way to stop being haunted by his presence, it was best to just get on with it.

And, honestly, a nice cool dip might be just the thing to keep my slutty little thoughts about our hookup last week from overheating.

After letting Sora know that I was heading out and that we'd catch up after dinner, Kieran and I found ourselves at one of the many boat launch points in Wallingford.

It wasn't my favorite part of the lake, but I did my best these days to avoid the dock I always used to frequent. Sometimes it was impossible to divorce a memory from a place.

I set my paddleboard in the water and climbed on, watching Kieran expectantly. "You okay?"

He squinted up at the sun. "Yeah, it's just so . . . bright. I'm not usually out in the sun this long."

"Still hungover then?" I asked.

He nodded.

"Weird to think that angels get hangovers."

With a grunt masking as a response, he climbed onto the board.

It hardly even responded to his weight. I pretended to accidentally brush my knee against him, just to convince myself that he was, in fact, corporeal. At least sometimes. Sort of.

My brain latched on to the impossibility of it all, but I reined it back in. "So, you can sit on solid objects, but you can also go through them?"

He nodded, then swiped his hand through the board and into the water to illustrate the point. "I can interact with the world, in a limited way, but I can't touch any living thing except for my charge. Unless I want to waste whatever meager energy stores I've saved up trying to shove some random guy down the street or something."

"Why?"

A couple with two kids passed by us in their kayak, all four of their faces bright with the exertion and excitement that came with the activity. It was a beautiful day, and the lake was more crowded than I'd anticipated.

For some reason, I'd unconsciously assumed the rest of the world would have abandoned their old hobbies after The Undoing. Like I had for the most part. That the world would be irrevocably split between Before and After, like it had been for me.

But that wasn't the case. People were more resilient than I gave them credit for.

Maybe they were better for it. There was a strange kind of peace in existing as I did before. Out here, it was almost easy to pretend the chaos of the last six years had never happened. The world changed, sure, but it didn't feel like it here. Everything was just the way that it was in the Before.

Then again, that could have been a family of vampires for

all I knew, so maybe not. From what I'd gathered, they weren't affected by sunlight like Hollywood had led me to believe. Didn't sparkle either.

"Giving us limited range in this world gives us something to work toward," he said, his hand lingering in the water. "Right now, I can't really feel this. Not in the way that you can, that is. The sun, the water, the board, they all feel like the same thing. They're just . . . there."

"The sun is annoying you though."

"In my world, the bad things come more easily than the good."

"But when you get your vacations"—I stood up, adjusted the paddle, and started guiding us out along our path—"you can feel things more intensely then?"

It'd certainly seemed so anyway, unless he'd been faking his desire last week.

He nodded, studying me while he leaned back on the board, settling in.

It took a few minutes to get my stroke into the cadence, but once I found that groove, it was like no time had passed at all since the last time I'd been out here. Of course, I'd certainly be feeling it tomorrow, discovering aches and pains in muscles I'd long neglected.

We didn't speak for a few minutes, and I slowly let the familiar ease that always settled over me out here seep into my bones. The world was quieter, made more sense than it did on land, during all the daily turmoil of survival.

And while I didn't exactly enjoy the forceful delivery of the message, Kieran was right—it had been too long since I'd let myself indulge in the things I loved.

After a while, when we were away from some of the roots and debris closer to the shoreline, I set my paddle down and jumped into the water, letting the icy chill lick and bite along my skin.

Since The Undoing, there were hardly any commercial ships to worry about. None of the boats that came through this way these days had a motor, which meant there was more space to spread out and enjoy the water. No constant worry that some rich tool's yacht was going to come speeding through, cut too close, upend the board, and chop me up into ceviche with its propeller.

When I broke the surface, my focus was drawn immediately to Kieran.

Even with his demanding personality, and the whole dead guy thing, I couldn't deny that he was still just as stunning as he'd been at Incendiary. Hell, I'd been fixated on the memory of his features for years. In that sense only, did the whole angelic thing seem plausible. Why else would he be so fucking beautiful? Or feature so frequently in my thoughts?

The sun highlighted all the angular perfection of his face, the strange, almost iridescent ink of his tattoos, the mesmerizing flecks of gold, amber, and green in his eyes.

He watched me with such yearning, but it was different from the yearning at Incendiary. This wasn't motivated by sex or lust. This was different.

He looked almost sad.

I found myself wondering what his life was like, about the plane or realm or world that he spent most of his time in. But not for the same reasons as before—not to satisfy my own curiosity.

I was curious about his life for his sake.

"What does it . . . feel like?" he asked, his voice so low and quiet that I almost didn't catch his question. "What do you like about it out here?"

"It's cold." I closed my eyes, focusing on the specific sensations. It had been so long since I'd taken the time to really notice them. "But not in a bad way, not freezing or anything. It's the kind of cold that shocks you, wakes you up, like a livewire running through your body." I pulled my arms through the water, focusing on the feel of it. "Like even though I know this lake is probably filled with hundreds of dead fish and other gross things, there's something remarkably refreshing about it, something that feels rejuvenating—pure."

"And," I continued, "I can feel the temperature shift and change as I move through it. The water on the surface is a few degrees warmer because of the sun. But I almost can't feel the bottom half of my legs from the cold. And I think I'm more aware of my senses and my body in the water than I am on land. Not sure why. There's something really cool about going below the surface, and even with my eyes closed, I can sense my way back up. And it's quiet, isolated. Even when people swim or pass by, most of them tend to preserve the peace of it out here. Sometimes it feels like I'm watching the city from the outside, part of it but also not, between two worlds, almost, or in another one entirely."

Which was maybe how I felt most of the time—caught between two worlds—but out here that didn't scare me in the same way it did when I was surrounded by people.

I shifted onto my back, floating as I used my arms to move me parallel to the board, Kieran just above me. I closed my eyes again, letting the sun kiss my skin.

"But more than the way the water feels, I think I just really love how *I* feel when I'm in it. The way it makes me feel weightless. It's freeing, how little effort it takes to move through it, to float. How it squeezes and forms to me, like that feeling of pressure from a really good hug. And I guess it's a little terrifying, too, how vast and powerful it is; how small or irrelevant it can make you feel to be a person floating in this giant, connected ecosystem. But those are the same things that make it exciting." I opened one eye, squinting against the sun. "I don't know, does that make sense?"

He leaned over, studying me, until his face was hovering

just above mine, blocking the worst of the sun from my eyes. "Yes, Agony, that makes sense."

"Good." I started to smile, but it wavered. My stomach tightened as our eyes locked, his unreadable as always, but also unexplainably tender, and I found myself strangely wishing that I could reach up and kiss him.

But then I remembered that this was not last week, and the circumstances of our nearness now were entirely different. So, instead of leaning into the impulse, I took a deep breath and went back under water, not surfacing again until the tightness in my stomach loosened.

I swam for a while, never going more than twenty feet away from Kieran and the paddleboard. Each time I let myself glance back, I found him watching me, the lines of his body oddly tense, and when I swam a bit further out, he called me back, his voice strained with traces of concern.

It reminded me a bit of when my aunt used to do the same.

If you're not careful, habibti, that current will steal you away from me far sooner than you're meant to go.

Which was maybe the biggest reason I liked it out here. I felt closer to her, closer to who I was before I lost her.

Only when I pulled myself back onto the board, soaking it in icy dregs, did Kieran finally relax.

He worked a muscle in his jaw, his focus suddenly on everything but me.

"You okay?" I asked.

He nodded, the dark expression slipping back into his more familiar mask. He'd been guarded last week, but he was so much more so now. He was stiff. Unreachable. "Great."

I paddled us back to the launch site in silence, my body looser and lighter than it had been before making this trip.

"Thank you," I said, finally breaking the quiet.

"For what?"

"I think I needed this." I shot him a look. "I mean, don't get all cocky or anything, but maybe you're not the worst guardian angel in the world."

Something shifted in his eyes, until the gentle teasing that had been slowly making its way back to the surface, slipped back under, like it had been taken down by an invisible anchor.

He watched like a silent sentinel, while I deflated and packed up my board, and exchanged pleasantries with some other people heading out into the water.

For a moment, I'd almost forgotten that Kieran was invisible to them and there'd been several times where I had to swallow my use of "we" back at the last second.

It was only just before we made it back to Frank's that we spoke again.

"Thank you," he said.

I glanced up at him from the corner of my eyes. "For what?"

"For letting me hang out with you today. It's not often that I get to really interact with my charges or their world. It was. . ." He paused, as if surprised by the word when he found it. "Nice."

"Yeah." I smirked. "You're not terrible company for a dead guy."

"This is so weird." Sora cupped her face in her hands, her elbows leaning against the kitchen table while she stared at where she imagined Kieran to be. She was about a foot off. "What does he look like?"

I'd explained the situation to her—leaving out the part about him being the guy I hooked up with last week—when we got back, just before the dinner rush. Which meant that I'd had to field her questions for a few hours, while we served our guests and Kieran looked on with amusement.

At first, he didn't understand why I chose to return to work.

Didn't see how it could be, in a lot of ways, just as fulfilling as the afternoon off had been. But as I moved through my shift, greeting our usuals and feeding them the recipes I'd spent months perfecting, I realized that working here was more thrilling than I'd noticed before. Fulfilling in a way that was different from my time spent on the water. As burned out as I sometimes got, I genuinely liked helping the people in this community. Liked making their day better, giving them a safe space to relax for an hour or so.

In some ways, it helped ease some of the guilt I carried about the curse—and let me interact with people without getting too close, without risking their lives.

After a few minutes of watching Sora and I juggle the dinner rush, Kieran's confusion started to fade, until he seemed genuinely interested in everything—asking me questions about the food, the people, the taste of things.

It had been difficult, not cracking a smile when he started making observations about our customers, trying to guess their illicit pasts or construct entire stories of their lives from one cursory glance.

I turned back to Sora and shrugged. "He looks . . . I don't know, like a regular guy."

Kieran grunted. "Liar. Tell her I'm a smoke show."

"Ask him what it's like to die," she demanded, her eyes wide with excitement.

"He won't answer. Very illusive and uptight about the whole thing."

He shot me a glare, but I just grinned.

"Do all people become guardian angels? Or ghosts?" Sora fiddled with the pendant around her neck. Since Menace had stolen it, she'd taken to wearing it daily to ward off his thievery. I was pretty sure she even slept and showered with it on now. "Is there, like, a network of dead people that he can reach?"

My stomach dipped. Why hadn't I thought of that? Could we reach Rina or my aunt through Kieran?

When I turned to him, he shook his head. "Ghosts as you probably conceive of them don't really exist. Only phantoms or echoes, like you saw with Claudine and Greta. But humans can't become one of the dead or phantoms. Occasionally those who absorbed a lot of power during The Undoing can, but that's very rare. And as for my kind—only those with supernatural blood can be reborn in the Between."

The shot of adrenaline ebbed from my system as I translated for Sora.

She narrowed her eyes, considering. "What about bringing someone back though? I've heard rumors that the Sect of Azrael has found a way to commune with or even bring back the dead."

I sat up in surprise. Sora had never mentioned this to me. We always did everything in our power to stay away from the compounds. They were all infiltrated with greed and manipulation.

After The Undoing, people went feral trying to find meaning and explanation amongst the chaos. Most of the old human governing bodies and religions fractured into cults. Only six of them seemed to survive beyond the initial surge of splits.

There were five main arms named for the followers of Azrael, Gabriel, Michael, Raphael, and Lucifer.

Each of them crafted their own ethos around what was known about their archangels through the various Abrahamic religions, all of them determined to find a way to either manipulate, eradicate, or obtain the power pouring into our world. I couldn't keep up with their belief systems or rules, or who hated who this month. It all seemed so . . . arbitrary.

But in the last few years, Lucifer's followers split into The Seven Sons—each sect radicalized and named for one of the seven deadly sins, all in competition with each other for their prophet's blessing and power.

The sixth arm was founded around a supposed new prophet: Rob. He was just some random guy before The Undoing—a college student studying philosophy or sociology or something. But his following had grown surprisingly large in the last few years.

All of them were bullshit, as far as I could tell. Which was why I was so thrown that Sora mentioned them with legitimate interest. We'd always done our best to steer clear of the religious zealots. They were just as dangerous as the local militia groups and the worst parts of the old governments.

Whatever expression was on my face softened her own. "My friend from the market, Rex? He mentioned it to me recently. He spent quite a bit of time with Azrael's followers a while back, but I didn't want to get your hopes up if it was just bullshit."

I offered her a smile that felt too stiff as I waited for Kieran's answer.

"Those ridiculous little cults?" He snorted. "Total Bullshit. I mean"—he ran his hand through his hair, considering—"like, Azrael was a real person—so I'm told anyway. Probably the others, too, though I've never met them or known anyone who has. I can promise you that if they're alive, they're not wasting their time around power-hungry humans. And they aren't all powerful. They live and die just as every demon does."

"So they might be alive? They aren't angels in the way you are?" I asked.

Kieran stiffened. "No, they're not like me."

"What do you mean Azrael *was* a real person? Did he die?" I asked, after conveying his words to Sora.

"No one knows. We were told that he used to be the primary conduit between my world and yours. Heard he was a total dick—most with that kind of power are. But he disappeared decades ago. Even still," he added, "the mythologies that humans hold are so deeply fractured and contorted, they're all but meaningless. It would be like"—he narrowed his eyes—"like trying to understand Ireland's entire history, everything the country embodies and has ever embodied, through nothing more than taking a bite of cereal, the kind inside the leprechaun box, the one with those wee marshmallows. It's completely fanciful. Reductive to the point of absurdity."

Sora's shoulders sank when I finished translating. "So there's no reaching the dead then?"

"I didn't say that," he said. "I'm here, aren't I? I know Azrael used to commune with the departed, even those who weren't awakened into a death of service like me. My kind are very rare." He shot me a smug grin. "Most of the dead immediately move on to whatever comes next. I haven't any idea what that is though. I'm in the dark like the lot of you, I suppose. Though I have my theories." His expression grew more serious. "I've heard of human witches fiddling around with spells—parlor tricks more like—but some might be able to speak to the dead. It would be rare, of course. Better chance with a phantom or an echo; by their nature they hold onto a small flash of themselves. Otherwise, the dead don't tend to hold their living memories."

"You don't remember your life before you died?" I asked, surprised by how much he was willing to share now, after an afternoon of refusing me any of the answers I wanted.

"No, not really." The corners of his eyes pinched. "When I woke up, I was me. I had my personality, general likes and dislikes—but the people in my life, the specific experiences I had when I lived in this realm? All gone. It's better that way though."

"How so?" I couldn't imagine all of that being erased, everything that made me . . . me.

"Better if we aren't tethered to this world, to the connections we used to have. It would make everything harder. Some things come back over time. But I've never chased after my memories. I prefer to exist in the now—not want anything I can't have. Makes my job easier; makes the occasional vacation less devastating when it's over." His expression shut down, like he'd said too much. "Anyway, that's as far as I'll go with your answers. Tell your friend that those cults want what cults and religions have always wanted—power and control. They won't help her, not without a price she won't be willing to pay. Her time is better spent on the living; the dead have moved on. For their sake and for hers."

Sora's expression was uncharacteristically closed off to me as I relayed Kieran's thoughts.

She sat, silent, drumming her fingers noiselessly on the table as she processed.

But then, just as I stood to get ready for bed, she said, "Wait." Her eyes darted to mine; her brows lifted in excitement. "The curse!"

"What?"

"Ask him about your curse. If there's such a thing as a death curse. Or omen or whatever." My breath hitched, but she went on, turning toward where she imagined Kieran to be sitting—though he was now across the room, studying Menace's picked-over dinner with curiosity, as if it were a museum exhibit and not some abandoned nut shells and homemade kibble. "Ask if he's ever heard about someone who's been cursed to lose everyone they love to some tragic, early death."

Again, I was shocked by her question. Partially because I hadn't thought to ask it first myself, and partially because I was terrified to hear the answer.

There were two options, as far as I could see.

Either way, I'd lose.

I'd find out that everyone I lost was, indeed, dead because

of me, or that I'd spent a lifetime pushing people away for no legitimate reason.

Neither option filled me with anything less harrowing than dread or regret.

Kieran's brows furrowed as he considered her demand, his gaze darting between the two of us as he stitched together an answer. Then, as if realizing something, he shook his head. When his eyes locked on mine, I saw something flit behind them, pity maybe, or something close to it that I couldn't quite parse. "I've never heard of a curse or omen like that, no."

After saying goodnight to Sora, I got ready for bed, surprised when I found Kieran lurking in my bedroom, an ever-present shadow that not even Peter Pan could shake.

My neck heated when his eyes fell on my vibrator.

"Well—" I cleared my throat. "Good night, I guess. Will you —er—be back tomorrow? I'm not really sure how long this whole guardian-angel-life-audit thing is supposed to last."

"Back?" His brow arched in question. "Oh, I'm not leaving tonight."

"Don't you have more important"—I waved my arms like wings—"angel-y things to do than watch me sleep?"

His eyes glittered with amusement. "Not in the least."

"How long will you be stalking me then?"

"Until my job is done."

"And you're not going to give me any more hints as to what that job is or requires from me to speed along?" I asked. His face remained as impassive as always. "Right. Of course not. Why be helpful when obstinance is an option."

He smirked, his eyes snagging on the vibrator again.

I shoved it into a drawer.

"Well, you're not sleeping in here," I said, my words rushed and flustered as I tried to shove away the very small part of me that almost wanted him to stay. "Do the dead even sleep?"

"Not well." He tilted his head, studying my pile of books

now, as if he were trying to commit the titles to memory. "But yes, we sleep."

"Well, where do you usually sleep when you're on assignment?"

He froze, then straightened his posture. "Like I said, this is an unusual case."

I wasn't sure what he meant by that, but I could tell from the narrowed line of his mouth that he wouldn't offer any more details than he already had tonight. "We have a couch. You're welcome to it, I guess."

"If that's what you'd prefer," he said, the corner of his mouth curving into a small, soft hook again that had my stomach tightening. "Do try to exert some self-control though, yes? No crawling out in the middle of the night wearing nothing but bedroom eyes and lace, begging to cuddle. I won't be tempted." His stare dipped, lingering on my mouth for a beat, before scanning the rest of me as if envisioning the sight. He clicked his tongue and shrugged. "Like I said, I'm off limits. So you'll have to make-do with your fantasies."

I shot him a glare.

He chuckled, the sound raspy and deep. "Good night, Agony. Sleep well."

I did not, in fact, sleep well.

At least not at first.

I spent a solid hour replaying the absolute chaos of the day.

Then another hyper-fixating on the fact that the guy I slept with was not only dead, but sleeping on the other side of the wall. And that awareness, unfortunately, led to a never-ending loop of the night we'd spent together at Incendiary on repeat in my mind.

After doing everything I could to push the memory from my thoughts, my body refused to unclench the desire that had been slowly building all day—with every touch, every teasing smirk.

With a frustrated sigh, I opened my drawer and grabbed my vibrator.

I let that night replay in my mind, properly this time—uninterrupted and without shame.

And when I finally approached the release I'd been chasing all week, I pressed my face into my pillow and bit down, silencing his name on my lips.

15

MAREENA

APPROXIMATELY NINE YEARS AGO, THREE YEARS BEFORE THE UNDOING

"Thumb goes on top, like this." Levi tightened my fist, shifting my fingers until they were properly positioned. Given the violence of the activity, he was surprisingly gentle. The heat of his hand sank into my skin. "Whatever you do, make sure you don't strike with it at the side. You risk breaking it like that."

"Or just turning my fingers into giant sausages for a few weeks," I said, fighting a grin. My fingers were back to their normal size now, all signs of damage erased entirely, save for a small white scar on one of my knuckles.

"Or that." With a featherlight touch, his thumb traced the small mark. His eyes darted up to mine, the hues of gray darker than I remembered them, or maybe they were just more striking today against the vibrant oranges and reds of the changing leaves sprinkled over the ground.

The sun was still out, though it was setting earlier and earlier each day, and the parks weren't as busy now that the temperature was dropping. Still, there was a crispness to fall in Seattle that I loved almost as much as the summer. Everything looked sharper, more vibrant, the air less hazy now that the final intense weeks of the wildfire season were ebbing.

It'd been nearly a month since we'd last seen each other, his mystery work keeping him away longer than he thought it would. Part of me was convinced the long stretch of his silence was his way of backing out of his side of the deal, that I'd never see him again.

When my phone vibrated with a text yesterday, I found myself unexpectedly happy to find that he hadn't.

"Is it . . ." He cleared his throat, his usual snarky confidence absent, as his hands hovered over me. "Is it okay if I position you?"

I nodded.

He brought my arm level with my shoulder, bending my elbow as he stood behind me.

"When you start—" His voice was soft against my ear, and I fought to focus on the words, rather than the soft tickle of his breath against my skin. "Your pinky should be closest to the ground, index up." He brushed my first two knuckles, lingering again on the small scar. "This is where the point of impact will be, not your entire hand."

I nodded, my mouth too dry to find words.

"You want to stay grounded, keep your wrist straight," he continued. "You'll do more harm to yourself than to your opponent if you're too loose or wild with it."

I swallowed, then nodded. Though I hadn't run into Ace since the day the asshole tried to drug me, I sure hoped he'd walked away that night the worse of the two of us.

Levi nudged his foot against mine, widening my stance a bit, until my feet were lined up against each of his insteps. With my back pressed against his chest, his arms brushing alongside both of mine, this demonstration was suddenly far more intimate than I'd imagined it being in my head. "Feet should be under your shoulders, pointing toward your target."

Currently, my target was a small red balloon floating a few feet in front of me. Too soft for me to injure myself again, but visible and solid enough to give me a small target to aim for.

"You're right-handed?" he asked.

I licked my lips, the cool autumn breeze chilling where my tongue just touched. "Yes."

"Dominant foot is back, and you'll swing forward, like this." He took a few steps back to demonstrate the motion, his perfect form so casual and effortless, I wondered how often, exactly, he found himself needing to use it. "Your power stays in your lower body and travels up, through your arm."

I watched him move through the motions a few more times, then emulated them myself. With a soft pop, the balloon sprang away, only to immediately boomerang back, popping me in the nose.

Swallowing my pride, I flicked it away. Suppose it was only fair the balloon got a shot in too.

"Good," he said, his lips twisting into a small grin, "that's a good start. Don't be afraid of your opponent, and don't pull back before your fist reaches them. Instead of imagining hitting them, try and picture yourself hitting through them."

It was strange, trying to muster power against a small piece of air-filled rubber, but I tried to focus on something I wanted to hurt. Though it had been nearly two months since that night, my brain had very little difficulty conjuring Ace's smarmy face. Complete with that arrogant-as-fuck grin of his.

I struck again, the balloon jutting harder and farther this time, as the string fought against the small sandbag keeping it from flying away.

"Great." Levi smiled, nodding his approval. He came closer, lifting my elbow slightly. "Bend your knees a little, it will help stabilize you when you jab. Give you more power." He gripped my hips, the pressure so light I almost didn't feel it—like he was trying hard not to invade my personal space or box me in. Still, my body seemed to come alive at his closeness, my skin tingling at the points of contact. "Move your hips and chest as one, twist them toward your target. Your fist will follow the path, but make sure you don't lean forward too far in the follow through. Otherwise, you'll go sailing over your opponent and lose any of the headway you had."

Something else I'd done incorrectly that night. The memory of Levi's grip, ironclad and strong around my waist, as he pulled me back from falling on top of that asshat came rushing back to me.

Following his instructions, I hit the balloon again. This time, I felt more stable, more connected.

Over the next hour, he ran me through various positions, teaching me to jab, uppercut, and defend myself from someone throwing fists at me.

Even with the chill in the air, my skin was laced with a layer of sweat. My hair had also largely fallen from the tight ponytail I wore it in, and I could feel my baby hairs curling around my face in a halo.

Even though Levi ran through every exercise with me, he still looked pristine—not even the suggestion of sweat, or like this required any more effort than a casual stroll through the park.

It was infuriating, but I also caught myself stealing glimpses of him whenever he wasn't looking.

As usual, he was dressed head-to-toe in black. Though today, instead of jeans, he had on a pair of joggers that showed off the hard curves of his ass to such a degree that I had to actively force myself to keep my gaze up.

Then again, maybe not.

Our deal would be up after today, after all, meaning that for all intents and purposes, Levi and I would never see each other again. That made him an ideal candidate for a casual, fun hookup. No strings, just two bodies seeking a bit of comfort and release.

I'd spent an embarrassing amount of time during his demonstrations silently debating the merits of asking if that might be something he'd be into. After a shower, of course. I was downright disgusting right now.

"Now let's work on getting out of a hold," he said, the only warning before his strong arms came around my body, tightening in a vise until I was sealed against him, his body locked around mine. "If someone grabs you, it's important to know how to get free. Proper form with hitting is important, but this kind of maneuver can be the difference between life and death."

My heart raced at his closeness, but for an entirely different reason now. I blinked a few times, my vision blurring slightly in my peripherals, as dots of light slowly eclipsed the quiet park around us.

I squirmed against him, but his hold only tightened with each movement I made until, eventually, I could hardly move at all. His chest was like a rock against my back, his arms, though lean, were stacked with corded muscle I couldn't budge.

Panic clutched at my chest, my lungs were tight as I tried to find my breath, to inhale. When I couldn't, my heartbeat raced even faster in response.

The vibrant scenery around us disappeared, until all I could see were dark, vibrant flashes of the past.

Eyes squeezed tight, I fought for control; to keep the memories of the last time I'd been held like this at bay for as long as possible.

A soft buzzing noise reverberated through my ears, drowning out any other sound—a soft buzz that I couldn't shake. I tried desperately to swallow, to get my throat working if I couldn't force my lungs into action, but my mouth was impossibly dry, my tongue coated with a metallic taste that made me want to gag.

My legs shook, my knees ready to give up altogether and abandon their post. Levi's grip was the only thing keeping me up.

"No." I swallowed, the sound deep and haunting as I tried to make my mouth work. "Let me go."

"Mareena?" The brace of Levi's arms loosened instantly at the command.

I fell to my knees, dug my fingers into the soft green grass I'd been standing on all afternoon.

Fucking get it together, Mars. You're not there. You're not there anymore. You will never be there again, not another day in your life. You made sure of it.

Finally, I managed to suck in a full breath of air, my body almost sore from clenching so hard.

I was at Greenlake.

It was just Levi, it wasn't him.

"Mareena, please—look at me." Gentle hands brushed my cheeks, then tilted my chin up until the sun's fading rays beat against my eyelids. "Are you okay? I'm sorry, did I—did I hurt you?"

I shook my head, then slowly opened my eyes, blinking back the film of tears until Levi's steady gaze was all that I could see—swirling shades of gray that were darker around the center and lightened the further out from his irises.

His thumb brushed my cheekbone, and I felt the smallest trail of liquid there.

Fuck.

Tears.

I was fucking crying.

One of my biggest rules was to never let anyone see me cry. Except for Sora.

Tears meant pain, and witnessing that kind of pain gave people too much power.

Vulnerability meant closeness, and I did not do closeness. I did not *want* closeness.

I fell back on my ass and propped my elbows on my knees as I glanced up at him.

The look of concern was so sharply drawn over his features that I actually winced at the sight of it. There went any chance of me getting Levi into my pants later tonight.

"I'm okay," I said, my voice tight as I offered him an unconvincing smile. "Sorry. Really, I'm fine."

"Don't apologize. Please, just tell me what's wrong. Did I hurt you?" His eyes darted over every inch of my skin, assessing for injuries, for some kind of physical marker that *something* had happened to cause that kind of reaction.

Sorry, bud, just my brain.

Shaking my head, I wiped my cheeks, and stood up—legs still shaky, but strong enough to keep me up.

He reached forward to stabilize me, but I stepped back.

"I said I'm fine," I snapped, unable to keep the irritation from my voice.

"Right," he said, eyes soft, hands raised palms up between us. "I'm sorry."

"Not your fault." The words were cracked, stiff, and I could hear the anger buried inside of them.

Anger that, judging by the crease between his eyebrows, Levi assumed was directed at him.

As if he'd been anything other than perfect in this situation.

That just rattled me further, adding a hefty dosage of guilt to the embarrassment already sinking like an anchor into the pit of my stomach.

"Sometimes—I just don't like being held like that is all," I said, my voice hollow and strange as I fought off the final vestiges of the panic attack. "I don't like being constrained. I should have said something earlier. I'm sorry. It's hard to know when my body will react like . . . that."

"Don't apologize." He studied me with a still kind of focus that made my skin prickle. "I should have checked in before grabbing you like that. I'm sorry. I wasn't thinking."

An awkward, heavy silence fell over us, and I couldn't bring myself to shake it, to meet his stare and brush this off, to get back to his demonstration.

Sometimes this was my least favorite part of the panic attacks. The aftermath. The actual wave itself had been brief, relatively speaking, but now I felt like an intruder on the scene, all traces of the ease between us before now long gone.

My body no longer felt like mine, like I'd stretched someone else's skin over my bones and tried to pass it off.

I felt the familiar numbness settle over me, until the unease and embarrassment faded into a cool nothing. This was a regular part of the programming—like my body could tell when my emotions were bouncing around like a ping pong ball, impossible to control or predict. Instead, they would just sort of shut off altogether, the plug pooled from the wall until the fancy lights and loud sounds bled into a quiet, merciful nothing.

As if sensing my absolute stuckness, Levi walked over to the base of a large tree, where we'd parked our stuff earlier.

He shuffled through his bag and presented me with a water bottle.

I took a deep breath, closed the distance between us, and grabbed the bottle, draining half of it in one gulp. The water was still cold, and I focused on the startling sensation as it carved an icy path through my body, my brain still hyper alert and working in overdrive. "Thanks."

"No problem." He offered a small smile, then shuffled through his bag again. "I made us some sandwiches too. Probably as good a time as any for a break. Didn't realize how long we'd been at it. I tend to get a bit distracted when I'm training—I shouldn't have pushed you so hard."

I shook my head, brushing off his apology.

He pulled a thin, checkered, black and white blanket out and, with a flourish, spread it evenly at our feet.

I stood there, unmoving, as he produced a pair of sandwiches wrapped in cling wrap, a container of grapes, and a bar of chocolate.

"Did you bring a picnic?" I asked, stunned momentarily out of my daze at the sight.

His shoulder blades shifted as he crawled over the blanket, smoothing the corners down. He froze, turning back to me. "I uh—hope that's okay? You don't have to eat any of it," he added, as if I might be concerned he was like Ace and attempting to drug me. "I'm just always starving after a workout and if I don't eat, I turn into an asshole."

My mouth opened as I tried to find words. No one had ever made me picnic before. It was an oddly thoughtful gesture, and absolutely *not* part of our deal.

Still, while I wasn't exactly hungry, I knew that food usually helped me settle back into my body when I got like this. Closing my mouth, I nodded, then took a seat next to him, far enough away that we weren't touching, so that my ass ended up half on the blanket and half on the prickly grass.

He handed me a sandwich before quickly unwrapping his, looking uncharacteristically shy and uncomfortable as he took the first bite and chewed.

I watched him swallow, staring at the smooth column of his neck.

Catching my stare, he shrugged, misinterpreting my hawkishness. "It's nothing fancy. I'm not really a cook. You can stick to the grapes and chocolate if it's not good. Promise—" He made an X over his chest. "No hurt feelings."

"No, this is good. Thank you." My fingers, still a little stiff and trembling, fumbled their way through unwrapping the sandwich.

Relaxing a little, he popped the lid off the grapes and nudged a second bottle of water toward me, as if he could sense how parched I was.

My mouth always got excessively dry whenever my anxiety spiked like that.

We ate in silence for a few minutes, neither of us sure what to say.

I made my way through half of the sandwich, not even tasting it, lost in my thoughts. The grapes went down a little easier—the cool, crisp juice of each bite was harder not to notice.

When he was done with his sandwich, Levi leaned back against the trunk of the tree, eyes closed.

The park was particularly peaceful right now. The lake sparkled a few feet to the north of us, and except for the occasional runner or dog-walker on the trail that circled it, we were mostly alone.

I was oddly annoyed with my body and brain for throwing a wrench into such a beautiful day. There wouldn't be many more before Seattle's winter season left the days dark and gray, the promise of rain on every forecast.

"Do you get them a lot?" Levi opened one eye, glancing at me briefly.

"Get what a lot?" My voice was cracked and flat to my ears.

"Panic attacks?"

I clenched my jaw, then nodded. "Sometimes, yeah. They used to be worse though. This is the first I've had in a while."

He nodded, then, as if just remembering, shoved his hand back in the mystery tote bag and pulled out a box of mints. He gave them a shake, the sound of candy against tin ringing through the park, then tossed them into my lap. "Should have thought of it earlier. Mints—or, really, anything with a strong taste always help me when I get them."

I popped the top off and shook one into my palm. "You get panic attacks?"

"They're rare now, but I used to get them pretty regularly a few years ago." His lips twitched. "Not fun."

"Not fun," I agreed, rolling the mint over my tongue. He was right, the intensity of the flavor—cold and spicy—helped ground me. "I usually try to do the whole 'five things' thing— you've probably heard of it. The one that's like, think of five things you can see, four you can touch, etcetera, etcetera. But sometimes in the thick of it, it's hard to remember. Doesn't always work either, you know?" I clicked the mint against my teeth, focusing on the feel of it. "Thanks though, this helps."

"Any time," he said, and when I tried to hand the box back to him, he shook his head. "Keep it. I have more."

Instinct had me ready to refuse, to press the issue, but I fought it down. Sometimes when a person was trying to do something nice, the kinder thing was to let them, even if it went against your nature. I pocketed the box. "Thanks."

"Do you—" He ran his hand through his hair, like he was fishing for something to do with it. "Do you want to talk about it? What triggered it, I mean?"

I grunted; half laugh, half absolutely fuck no.

His mouth hooked into a grin. "Yeah, I figured."

"Anyway," I stretched the word out, as if it might help me land on a good change of topic, but my brain was spent. I glanced down at my phone. Fifteen minutes until my next bus, but I didn't see the point in extending this further. I held out my hand, awkward and unsure how best to end this. "I feel like I can fully break a guy's nose without fucking up my hand now. So, thank you. It was—uh"—I shoved my arm closer to him for a handshake—"good doing business with you. I hope you—"

How was that supposed to end?

I hope you have a good life? I hope you enjoy your time in Seattle? I hope that your fate is more open to free will than you think it is?

They all seemed like such ridiculous, strange things to say to someone who now felt far less like a stranger than I'd intended him to be.

He stared at my hand for a long moment as if stunned, then closed his around mine. His skin was warm and calloused, and he didn't let go right away. "So that's it, then? You're just going to leave? Dine and dash?"

I stared at him. "Well, yeah. That was our deal, wasn't it? One tour of the city, one training session? Mission accomplished, we did it."

"Wow." A rakish grin stretched across his lips, his eyes widening in shock. "I have to tell you, Mareena, I've been dropped by a lot of people in my life, but no one has ever been quite so business-like about it."

He still had my hand in his, his grip gentle, very easy for me to pull back from if I wanted to.

"I mean, did you want another tour?" I supposed I hadn't really shown him much, when it came down to it. Seattle was composed of different micro neighborhoods that stretched well beyond the few we'd seen. "Different part of the city, maybe?" Every time we met, we'd mostly stuck north of the cut out of convenience. There was still a ton to see south of downtown. "A museum or something?"

He shook his head, and I hated myself for feeling just slightly disappointed. "No, I don't want another tour."

I pulled my hand back, smoothing my features into a blank mask.

Right, that was for the best.

"Okay then." I attempted a soft smile, but I felt it bristle and knew it probably came off stiff, maybe even slightly annoyed.

What was the point of him pressing me then? "Have a good life, I guess."

"This might come as a shock to you," he said, "given my devilish good looks and winning personality, but I don't really have many friends."

I shrugged. "You're new in town, I'm sure you'll make some. Just maybe try to be a bit more humble when you go about it."

"I don't just mean in Seattle. I mean that I generally don't have many friends, period. Not really any, except for my mother, now that I think about it." He shivered, before adding in a softer voice, as if more to himself than to me, "Which is just about the most depressing thing I think I've ever said out loud."

My chest tightened at that revelation, at the clear loneliness suddenly so achingly obvious behind the teasing mask he often wore. "You're a likeable enough guy, I'm sure you'll have no problem making friends."

"You flatter me." He smirked, leaning back against the tree with a dramatic sigh. "But you're also, unfortunately, incredibly wrong. You see, I've been trying to befriend this girl. She's making it very difficult though."

I arched my brow. "Maybe she's just smart."

"Maybe she is." Some of the playfulness in his eyes evaporated.

"Friends are overrated," I said.

They weren't. Without Sora, there was no telling where I would be in this life, but I was acutely certain that it wouldn't be anywhere good.

"I agree, probably," he said, considering. "But don't you think I should get the chance to see for myself if that's true?" He shot me a smirk. "Look, all I'm saying is that you don't have a monopoly on surly and standoffish approaches to relation-ships. And maybe we can be surly and standoffish in the same vicinity as each other again."

"Surely there are better options for you out there."

"No," he said, "I don't think that there are."

I opened my mouth to say something, then closed it again.

"Do you want to see me again?" He asked the question as if it was the most logical thing someone could possibly ask. "It's really very simple, if the answer is yes."

"I, uh." I glanced down at my phone, ten minutes until that bus, then back at him. "I thought you understood after that first night. I'm not really in the market for a new friendship."

"Right," he said, brows furrowing with faux concern, "the infamous curse."

My lips tightened into a stiff line.

"What about Frank?" he asked. "You consider him a friend, too, don't you? And he's not Sora. And he's still alive."

No, Frank was nothing like Sora. But he also was nothing like Levi.

My relationship with Frank was a standoffish sort. We saw each other every day because we were in the same neighborhood, and while I enjoyed his general existence, it wasn't like we were *close*, close. He was Frank, I was Mareena, and that was that. We existed in each other's orbits, but it wasn't like we talked about life's enduring trials or gave each other dating advice.

Although Frank had tried the latter exactly one time, and we were both so deeply uncomfortable with his attempt that neither of us could even look the other in the eye for a week.

"That's different," I said. "Frank's just—Frank. We aren't really friends, per se."

"And I'm just Levi."

"Fair point. In that case, I fully endorse you becoming friends with Frank. I'll even put in a good word."

Levi smirked. "I had a—pricklier contender in mind. Don't want an old softy like Frank getting all attached and needy."

"Frank is plenty prickly."

"Do you always make everything so difficult?" He let out an exasperated groan.

"Everything."

"Fine, not friendship. What would I do with a friend anyway?" He narrowed his eyes, the weight of his gaze unrelenting. "But what if you and I tried something else?"

"Like?"

"Like—" his mouth curved into that grin again. "Like diet friendship."

"Diet friendship?"

"Yeah, you know, like diet soda." He shrugged, searching for the words. "It's the shadow of the real thing, or the suggestion of it more than the thing itself—derivative. No one loves it, it's no one's first choice, but they tolerate it. Or at least they pretend to."

"Speak for yourself. Regular soda's too syrupy-sweet for my taste."

"That," he said, "doesn't surprise me at all."

"Well," I started, not entirely sure why I was even entertaining this ludicrous tangent right now, "what makes a friendship . . . diet?"

"I don't know. I've just invented it. I guess it's just whatever version of friendship you find tolerable enough to convince you to admit that you actually *want* to hang out with me again."

I stared at him, stunned and speechless, trying to materialize some sort of response—but I had nothing.

His eyes were teasing as they met mine in the silence. "Gods, Sora really wasn't kidding, was she? You really do need an iron will to get you to relent even the slightest bit." He let out a ragged chuckle, but when I stood up and grabbed my things, he stood, too, hands up in surrender. "Okay, okay. Hang on, just don't go. Not yet. What if we make some ground rules? As many as you'd like. I mean it—the sky's the limit. Just consider the

possibility that on the scale of Frank to Sora, there is somewhere I might possibly fit."

"Ground rules?"

"Yeah, like," he paused, searching, "like okay, how about this
—I promise not to call you Mars until you ask me to. And . . ."
He held up a finger when I started to protest. "And, we will
never hang out more than once every few months or so. Surely
everyone who's been taken out by your curse has been around
more frequently than that, right? Risk averted."

He wasn't wrong.

"And," he continued, sensing that I was wavering, "just to be
sure that we don't divert into something less—diet—you
should make a vow that you won't fall in love with me."

I snorted. "No problem there at least."

"That's what you think." He smirked. "I can be pretty damn
irresistible when I want to be."

"You clearly don't want to be very often," I muttered.

"See," he said, "this is what I need in my life. You keep me
humble."

"Why do you want to be my friend so badly? I'm sure you
could very easily find someone else, someone you don't need to
negotiate with—someone normal, someone way less, I don't
know"—I searched for the word, landing on it with an icy smirk
—"prickly."

"I happen to like prickly. In fact," he shot a far friendlier
smirk back, "prickly is my favorite flavor of diet friendship."

I fought against the genuine grin threatening to take over
my mouth. When I finally won that surprisingly difficult battle,
I shook my head and sighed. "Look, I'm not being an asshole on
purpose, okay? Trust me, the whole no friendship thing is for
your own good—"

"Diet friendship."

"Whatever." I groaned and glanced down at my phone
again. I had three minutes to get to my bus.

If I wanted to make it, I needed to leave now.

Why was I even entertaining this? All I had to do was gently turn him down, turn around, and go home. It was such a simple, easy thing to do.

And yet, here I was. Actually toying with the idea of breaking my well-defined rules.

For him.

Why?

"It might seem like a joke to you, this whole"—I waved my hand awkwardly between us—"curse thing. I get that. It probably sounds fucking absurd. But I swear that it's not. And I can't have another person's death on my shoulders. It's too hard, okay?"

Hard didn't even begin to cover it. I honestly didn't think I would survive that kind of pain or guilt again.

"I don't think it's ridiculous," he said, his face more sober now. "I just think that you're the type of person who's maybe, I don't know. . . " His eyes slid to mine, lingering there for a beat past comfortable. "Worth the risk."

"Levi—"

"And," he said, cutting me off, "this isn't like the other situations. I, for one, am profoundly aware of the risk, probably even more than you are, if I'm being honest. But I'm interested in testing the boundaries of this supposed curse—and I'm doing so of my own volition. If I end up kicking the bucket early, I promise not to blame you."

"You'll be dead, I won't really be concerned about your blame at that point."

"Yeah, but you get what I mean." He shrugged. "In my . . . field," he paused, as if tasting the word on his tongue, "people die all the time. It's a dangerous job."

"Then why do you do it? Why not do something safer?"

"I'm not afraid of death, Mareena." His shoulders fell, like there was some invisible weight there that he'd suddenly been asked to carry. "There are things far more terrifying than that."

There were.

Like being the one death left behind.

The words were on the tip of my tongue, but I pulled them back, swallowing them down as I always did when they got too close to the surface.

That was the worst part about this curse—it made me self-ish. It wasn't just that the people I loved always died. It was that they died and left me here—alone and missing them so much that I sometimes couldn't so much as breathe under the weight of it.

They died, and I had to go on living.

There was something so profoundly cruel about that.

"Please," he said, his voice soft, almost defeated. He scrubbed his hand over his forehead, then through his hair, looking like even *he* was confused by why this silly proposition mattered so much to him. "Mareena—I—" He shrugged. "I could just really use a friend."

"Diet friend," I corrected, my throat thick and tight as I tried to swallow back the grief threatening to choke me.

"Right." His lips twitched, sensing victory in his grasp. "We take it at your tempo. I'll text you next time I'm in town. We don't even have to talk in between my visits to the city. In fact, we can make that a rule, too. I'm usually out of service range anyway. And if at any point, one of us wants to cut off the diet friendship, they can just fade into silence, no questions asked. So"—he sniffed, eyes hopeful—"we have a deal? Are these terms agreeable?"

He extended his hand toward me with the same rigid awkwardness that I'd employed just a few minutes ago.

"Our first deal went pretty swimmingly, didn't it?" he added when I hesitated. "Who knows, maybe this one will be even better."

For a moment that seemed to stretch into infinity, I stared at his hand, considering the offer. A voice inside my head screamed at me to just turn around and leave while I had the chance, while his absence didn't sting. To pretend I'd never met him. To lock our few hours spent together in a box in the back of my mind where I stored all my fleeting acquaintances. Future me would be better off for it.

A softer, smaller voice, one that hadn't quite gotten its legs yet, whispered a gentle suggestion that maybe instead, I extend my hand just a few inches forward and take his—a quiet, hopeful 'what if.'

What if Sora was right?

What if the curse had broken that night a few years ago?

What if I could negotiate with death—could find a way to keep people at arm's length, but allow them to exist in my life? On the peripheries, yes, but closer than I'd let them get before in some sort of liminal way.

Before I could question it a second longer, I wrapped my fingers around his hand, ignoring the warmth of his skin and how my own responded greedily to the sensation. "Deal."

16

MAREENA
PRESENT DAY

I choked on the smoke, the back of my throat raw and burning as I tried to suck in a proper breath of air.

"I can't believe you like this stuff." My voice cracked on another cough. "This is seriously the thing you miss most about being alive?"

"One of them." Kieran shrugged, his eyes alight with amusement. "You don't exactly make it look as desirable as I recall it being. They should really consider trotting you around as a walking advertisement for kids."

"Too bad there isn't any after school programming in the After. Sounds like I'd have the potential for stardom." I took another puff, wondering if maybe it got better the more you partook, but it only heightened the burn.

He watched the tip flare, a small smile tugging at his lips as the smoke curled in front of his face.

It reminded me of Claudine and her mint tea—the way she would sit for half an hour, sniffing at the steam, like that was how she consumed it.

Honestly, it was a bit ridiculous that I hadn't immediately realized she was dead.

Was I really that oblivious? That caught up in my own bullshit that I completely missed the fact that one of my customers wasn't even amongst the living?

"What's it like?" I asked, flicking the ashes over the side of the hammock. We were lying out by the canal, wedged between two trees that provided some protection against the scorching rays of the sun. "For you now, I mean. Can you smell it?" I reached over so that he could take the cigarette if he wanted. "Could you smoke it? In your current state?"

"My current state being dead, you mean?" he asked. For a moment, it looked like he might grab it, like he might try, but then his hands stiffened at his side, one resting against my calf. He was sitting in the hammock with me, both of us facing each other. There wasn't a lot of room to move, and it was impossible not to touch. Still, it was strange, the unexpected chill of his body against mine, so different from how he'd felt against me last week. "I could smoke it, but it's not the same in this world as it was when I was among the living."

"How so?"

"Unless I'm on one of my rare, embodied vacations, everything in this world is watered down to the point of being almost worse than not having it at all." His nose curled in disgust. "Sort of like if you were to take whiskey and then mix it with so much water that all of the effects you might like from the alcohol— the buzz, the burn, the taste—were gone, and you were just left with a glass of water that tasted a bit rank. At that point, I'd rather just have a glass of water, you know? The drop of whiskey only serves to make it fouler."

I put the cigarette out against the tree.

Well, one more thing to cross off the bucket list anyway. I tried it, hated it, and wouldn't be forcing the rest of it on my lungs.

My tongue slid over my teeth as I tried to swallow away the

taste. I had a feeling it wouldn't be going anywhere until I got hold of my toothbrush later.

I set the dead butt on the ground, next to our things, and sent myself a mental reminder to take it with us when we left and dispose of it properly. "Can't believe smoking is one of the things you miss most. I can't imagine even tolerating it, let alone loving it. Not that I enjoy whiskey either. So maybe the analogy was always going to be lost on me."

He shrugged. "It's an acquired taste."

My nose wrinkled at the scent that still lingered in the air. I should've tried this while we were on the trail, now we'd be stuck with this stale, almost rotten smell, until the wind chose to disperse it.

"Is this how you died? From lung cancer?" I immediately regretted the question as soon as it left my mouth. "Sorry, that was probably a deeply rude question, feel free to ignore it."

"No." He flexed his hand, the one that was dressed in a set of silver rings, as if he had a cramp. "That's not what killed me."

There was an air of finality to the sentence, and I knew he wouldn't be providing more information. "What did you like about it?"

"I don't really know." He closed his eyes, considering. "That's one of the cruelties of my kind's condition. We wake up as ourselves, but also not. My likes and dislikes are divorced from the contexts that created them. The specific memories they're tied to are gone."

"I don't know that I fully understand—how could you still like the thing, but not know why?"

"Yesterday," he said, "when you were swimming in the lake. You got this kind of far off look at one point, and I could tell you were thinking about something. Something that made you happy—you were smiling."

Was I? I thought back to yesterday afternoon, trying to

remember all of the things we spoke about, but also what I hadn't said aloud.

"Probably Amto Amani," I said. "She's one of the reasons I love to be near the water. So much of my childhood was spent on the shoreline near our house."

"Good," he said, nodding, "so it would be like that. Imagine that you know you love being near the water, that it's an essential part of you, but you wouldn't fully understand why. You'd have no recollection of your . . ." he paused, as if trying to remember the name, "Amto Amani?"

I nodded. "My aunt." I had a habit of always referring to her by name, letting the alliteration of it roll over my tongue and through my thoughts—like that kept her closer, somehow.

"You'd have no memory of her, of the time you spent together near the water, you'd just know that every time you saw the shoreline, that it was important to you in some fundamental way. And there'd be this ever-present ache, drawing you to it, but you'd never truly discover why. You'd get close, every now and then, but it would slip away, the core of it forever elusive. All that's left is the yearning."

"That sounds fucking awful."

He shrugged again, but I got the sense that he was more bothered than he let on. "That's just the way of my kind."

"But those memories can come back? Eventually?"

Something shut off in his expression, the breeziness of the afternoon eclipsing for a moment. "In part. They can come back—slowly, and over many years—but only if you want them to. You have to work for it, chase them. And that kind of relentless pursuit brings its own kind of danger. I've seen it spell doom for many."

"Do you? Let them come back, I mean?" Going years without understanding yourself sounded miserable. "How long have you been in your line of work, anyway?"

His mouth tightened into a stiff smile, and he tapped the

book resting on my stomach. "No more questions about me. Like I said before, we're not really supposed to interact. We're here to do one of the things you enjoy." He leaned back again, his eyes closed. "Read your book now, Agony."

I studied him for a moment, trying to parse the blank expression on his face, the half-answers he'd given me. Then I sighed, knowing that I wouldn't get anywhere by pressing for more information. Kieran seemed in a constant battle—desperate for companionship, but cagey about engaging in it all the same.

AFTER THE BREAKFAST rush and lunch prep earlier, Sora kicked us out, told me to take the rest of the day off—tomorrow, too.

"It's not every day you get a hot guardian angel," she'd said.

"How do you know he's hot?" I'd asked, thankful at the time, that Kieran hadn't been within earshot. He'd been sitting next to a pair of our regulars, unbeknownst to them of course, watching with a bored sort of enthusiasm as they argued about whether vampires could turn humans if they chose.

A devilish smirk had crossed her features, and she poked between my eyes. "Because you get this look on your face whenever you stare at him."

"How do you know when I'm staring at him," I'd shot back, swallowing my embarrassment and hoping like hell Kieran couldn't decipher my expressions as well as Sora could. "You can't even tell where he is."

"Well," she'd said, a wicked gleam in her eyes as she followed my gaze, "he's either over near the Fitzes, or you're suddenly very attracted to our eighty-year-old regulars."

"I—" I swallowed. "You're sure that you're good for the shift tonight? And breakfast tomorrow?"

"Yep," she said with a knowing look, "no more clients today

and I can call in backup if need be." We often hired some of the teens in the area to pick up extra shifts when we were slammed and could afford it. They were always glad for the work, but mostly I think they just liked to feel like they were part of something. The ritual of doing something so mundane was comforting in a world split with chaos. "Did he say how long he'll be around?"

I shook my head. "He's not exactly forthcoming with how this whole guardian angel thing works."

"Mysterious." She winked. "Exactly your type."

AND THAT WAS how Kieran and I had come to be here, along the canal, listening to the slow rush of water as I thumbed through my book—because it was the only thing that came to mind when he'd asked how I liked to spend my time when Sora wasn't around.

It took me a few minutes—to ignore his proximity and the strangeness of the whole scenario—but, eventually, I fell into the steady lull of the story, getting swooped up in the whirlwind romance and heart-pumping mystery of the book.

"I never understood the appeal of reading books," Kieran said, after an hour or so of silence.

I set the book down, which required serious restraint. I'd just gotten to a particularly unexpected twist. "You don't read?"

He shook his head. "Don't think I liked it much when I was alive either. Think I preferred real-life experiences, not the kind that exist in books."

Several of my favorite dark romances and horror novels came to mind, and I bit down on my smile. While I loved to read about certain . . . adventures, I was more than happy that they stayed between the pages of a book—a contract between me and the characters in which I got to experience the highlights of their lives without accumulating the wagon of trauma that came with all the rest.

"It's the same as watching a film," I said. "You wouldn't want to live in a slasher movie, would you? But the adrenaline you get from watching the events transpire is exciting. Especially since you know that you're experiencing it from the safety of your couch."

"I suppose."

"And with books, I feel closer to the characters. Like I'm reading about the adventures and experiences of a friend. I just feel like I'm a part of their lives, I guess?"

"Wouldn't you rather just talk to your friends?"

"I—" I closed my lips, not entirely sure how to structure my response to the directness of that question.

This was something I hadn't unpacked before, that books had sort of been my stand-ins for connections when I kept myself from having them. With books, the dangers of getting close to someone were blissfully absent.

"I don't have many friends," I said, after a few seconds of silence, "other than Sora, I mean."

"Seems to me you have an entire restaurant of them," he said. "Your customers all seem to know and adore you."

"Know me, yes," I said, "but it's a different kind of knowing. They're acquaintances. Some are closer than others, and we help each other out when we can. Especially since The Undoing. But Sora's the only person I've really let in."

"Why?" He shifted slightly as he studied me, until my leg lay over his. When I started to move away, to give him more room, he set his arm down on top of my calf, preventing me. "Friends and family—that's what people love most about being alive, isn't it? The comfort of connection? Isn't that what people spend most of their lives chasing?" A look of amusement passed over his expression. "Suppose, even in death, many chase after it still."

Perhaps this was ultimately why he was here, why I'd been handed a guardian angel in the guise of a broody stalker. Perhaps this was the path he'd been sent to guide me on, to show me the ways that I'd been wasting my life, living it incorrectly, guided by fear.

How very Dickensian.

"When you get close to people," I said, searching for the right way to put it, "it makes losing them more difficult." I shrugged, hoping I pulled off my feigned nonchalance better than he did. "And I have a habit of losing the people I get close to."

He considered me for a moment. "The curse that your friend brought up last night—you really believe it, don't you? That getting close to someone will edge them closer to death?"

"Well—" I took a deep breath. "It's been true, historically." After reciting the list of people I'd lost over the years, the number only increasing in the years since The Undoing—though the more recent losses had been mostly surface-level acquaintances—I closed my book, no longer in the mood to continue with my vicarious adventure. "Aside from Sora, Frank is the person I'm closest with."

"And where is this Frank?"

"In the medical center. Very sick," I said, as if that alone proved my point, "though we don't know what's wrong with him."

"I don't know, Agony"—Kieran ran his thumb over my calf, though I wasn't sure he was doing it consciously—"sounds like bad luck and coincidence to me. Nothing more than that."

"Yes, I've heard that a lot. Sora's been trying to convince me of as much since I confessed the fear to her." I shrugged. "But whether it's bad luck or something else, I'd rather not risk it."

"If it helps," he said, his eyes narrowed as they focused on mine, "I was honest last night. I've never heard of someone having a death curse. And death is sort of my industry." He winked. "Some might even call me an expert, in fact."

"You've said yourself that after The Undoing, you've hardly kept up with how much the world has been changed by magic," I said. "So how could you know? Maybe curses and omens appeared in the epilogue of your life, not the meat of it."

"But this supposed curse has chased you long before The Undoing, hasn't it?"

True. There was something about having undeniable evidence though—magic was real—that just solidified the thereness of the curse. "Yes, but magic existed before The Undoing. The Undoing simply revealed what was always there. Made it incontrovertible."

"Sure." He dropped his hand over the rim of the hammock, letting his fingers trail over—and through—the blades of grass. "Sounds a bit like you want to believe in the curse though. That you want it to be true."

I sat up straighter. "Why would I ever want that?"

"Gives you an excuse to keep people at arm's length, doesn't it?"

I blinked, breaking the hold of his stare.

"It's strange though," he continued. "You speak of death as if it's a person. As if it's alive."

I narrowed my eyes and nodded, though I couldn't bring myself to expand on that. To put into words that I knew I was right. That I'd met Death, seen him with my own eyes—caught between a dream and reality, in the cracks and crevices where a memory started to blur. That I knew him to have dark hair and amber eyes, and a crooked mouth built for taunting.

I'd just never been able to say the words out loud, as if giving them voice would make them irrefutable.

Until then, Death could exist in some liminal space, where he was perhaps less powerful.

"So," Kieran continued, his eyes sparkling with so much life that it was hard to remember that he was dead, "if we assume Death is a person—and, you know, also real"—he tipped his chin down playfully—"don't you think it would be a bit below their pay grade to spend their time haunting some girl, cutting off her connections, one by one, until she's left all alone? For the sake of what—cruelty? Boredom? It's just—and don't take this the wrong way, Agony"—he squeezed my calf—"but this theory of yours seems a bit self-involved, don't you think? To assume someone with that kind of power over the world would use it to torment a young girl before she's even born."

He was teasing me, that much was clear. But there was also something in the way he spoke so plainly about the absurdity of the curse that eased something inside of me I'd never been able to ease on my own.

Not since the days when my aunt would hush my fears and couch them in what she always assumed them to be—manifestations of grief, a pain so amorphous that I couldn't contain it. And so, I let it bloom and blossom—into a being so unwieldy I could never shake myself loose of it.

Maybe it was because Kieran was dead. If anyone could speak of death, could slash through the truth of it all, it would be him.

Whatever the case, I leaned back in the hammock, watching the web of leaves high above us, as a small sliver of a life-long tension started to unknot and unfurl itself, before it slowly seeped from my body.

17

MAREENA
PRESENT DAY

"You're not seriously going to follow me tonight, are you?" I whisper-yelled from the corner of my mouth, trying not to attract too much attention to the fact that I was talking to myself. Luckily, the street was mostly empty.

"Like I said—" Kieran's lips twisted into a dark grin. "You're my charge. I'm tethered to you until my work is done. Even if you're on a date."

"It's not a date," I said, patting the invisible wrinkles from my skirt as a couple across the street shot me an odd look. "It's dinner with a friend." After another quick look at the couple, I relented, no longer caring if strangers thought I was talking to myself. Odder things had happened in the last few years, and I didn't know them. "I thought after our conversation earlier that this might be a good idea—that maybe this would fix the"—I gestured abstractly in his direction—"you know, situation."

"Situation being. . ." He arched his brow. "That you're being tailed by a devastatingly good-looking guardian, you mean?"

"I didn't say that."

He smirked. "Didn't have to."

"You're insufferable." I shook my head. "Maybe I should cancel. Reschedule for another time." Sora hadn't been at the apartment when we'd returned. Other than a hastily scrawled note taped to the front door of Frank's alerting our customers that we'd be closed for the evening, but that breakfast service would start as usual, she hadn't left word of where she was. "It's not too late to get something together for the dinner service."

"Not a chance," Kieran said. "Don't get me wrong, I enjoyed people-watching at your restaurant last night, but I can't handle another evening cooped up with everyone ignoring me."

"They couldn't see you. And it wasn't like I could talk to you in front of them."

He shrugged. "Well, still, I want to see this Aidan guy you're so fond of. See what kind of a night out you can get up to when amongst the living."

My neck heated at the memory of the kind of night I'd gotten up to amongst the dead just last week. "You do realize that I'll still have to ignore you? I'll just be ignoring you in a different restaurant than my own."

He shot me a rakish grin. "We'll see how long you can resist my conversation."

I exhaled, ignoring the teasing look in his eyes—and the way that look made my stomach tighten into knots. "So you think this will work? Going through with tonight, I mean?"

He furrowed his brows. "Work?"

"If I go tonight, if I put myself out there, chase after connections like we talked about—do you think that'll fix the whole. . ." I sniffed. "You know, life-audit-dead-stalker thing."

"Do I think fucking someone is going to spark joy? Only one way to find out, Agony." He rolled his teeth over his bottom lip and winked. "Though if memory serves, it definitely seemed to spark *something* last week."

"Yeah," I deadpanned, "regret."

"That would wound me"—he pressed his hands to his chest

in mock pain—"truly, if I wasn't so very confident in the fact that you've been pleasuring yourself to that memory all week." His face split into a devious grin. No doubt because my exaggerated expression of revulsion was fooling no one. "Pretty sure I heard the familiar rumble of a Bob last night."

"Bob?"

"Battery operated boyfriend."

I glared at him, though it probably had no heat compared to the blush spreading across my cheeks. "You know, you're a bit insufferable."

"So I've been told." He smirked. "Twice by you, in fact, just this afternoon."

I sped up, getting a start on the evening's most tiresome task —ignoring him.

"What are you doing?"

"Practicing for tonight," I sniffed. "Pretending you don't exist."

"Oh fun." He glanced at me from the corner of his eye. "Let's bet on how long it'll be until you break." He pressed his hand to his chest. "Personally, I give it thirty seconds into your date. His company will be so"—he closed the gap between his thumb and his pointer finger until they were less than an inch apart—"bland in comparison to mine that you won't be able to stand it." He clicked his tongue. "Bet you'll be glad I came along then, eh, Agony?"

I took a deep breath and did my best to pretend that a tall, tattooed, thoroughly infuriating angel wasn't glued to my side.

But my thoughts immediately went to the lingering anxiety that had been rolling through me since we left Frank's.

Ditching the diner was uncharacteristic for Sora. In the months since we'd been manning Frank's, we hadn't closed for a dinner service once.

Even more uncharacteristic was leaving without telling me where she was headed.

Phones didn't really work as effectively as they used to, sure, but we'd made a habit of jotting our whereabouts down on paper, sticking them to the bathroom mirror, whenever plans came up. We kept each other in the loop. That was how we kept each other safe.

What if something was wrong? What if something happened to her?

Was this just me doing it again?

I fidgeted with my ring as I tried to confront the discomfort.

Was this just me making mountains out of mole hills as usual?

Being unduly anxious out of fear?

Imagining hypothetical what-ifs until I couldn't think straight?

Why did I always imagine the worst possible options, never the good ones?

Maybe Sora had left a note, and I just missed it.

Maybe Menace had stolen it. He had been in the habit of moving things around the house lately.

"Relax, Agony." Kieran's thumb pressed down gently on my lip, releasing it from where my teeth had been holding it prisoner. "I shouldn't have teased you about your not-date or your battery-boyfriend." He arched his brow, as if surprised by the revelation. "And I don't think I *like* it when you ignore me."

Then, as if shocked, he dropped his hand, flexing his fingers again like he was in pain.

Did angels even feel physical pain?

"What do your rings mean?" I asked, my fingers reaching out of their own accord to touch them. They were dark silver, but in certain lights there was this strange iridescence to the metal—black and blue and green, all woven together. Fluid, like an oil slick.

"No." Kieran pulled his hand back, shoving his hand

behind his back, all remnants of his earlier teasing instantly sapped. "Nothing. They're nothing."

"Right, sorry." It felt as if I'd overstepped, though I wasn't entirely sure why. He'd been overstepping all day. "I didn't mean to offend you."

He shook his head. "You didn't." He glanced at his hand, his expression heavy as he flexed his fingers, then the muscles in his wrist and forearm, as if they were all stiff. "It's just—the material is dangerous to human touch. My kind awakens with these bands. They are the catalyst for much of our power." With a deep breath, the sudden tension in his body sank away, replaced by a shadow of the ease from before. "Suppose you could think of them like my wings."

I nodded, struggling to tear my stare away from the strange metal, now that I let myself fully look.

As if thinking of wings drew them to us, Kieran ducked and swore.

Menace landed softly on my shoulder, his head turning slightly so that he could get a better look at the angel.

He dropped a small stone in my palm—it was swirled with blue and gray, almost like a marble with sharp edges. Pretty.

I dropped it into my pocket and fished out one of the pieces of kibble I carried around, offering it to him as a thank you. I'd be sure to add it to his collection when I got home tonight.

"What's with the crow?" Kieran eyed him with a strained curiosity. "Is it the same bird from before? The one that tried to lob my head off in your kitchen—and last week, at that medical center of yours?"

Menace let out a deep, startling caw.

"Yeah." I scratched the back of his neck, trying to calm him. "He's usually pretty chill. Maybe he senses you?"

"He can more than sense me." Kieran narrowed his eyes, studying the bird. "He can see me. And touch me." He tilted his head, revealing a series of shallow scrapes. "Maimed me, actually. Possibly even tried to take my life before your eyes. Yet you're just . . . petting him as if he were nothing more than a harmless house pet."

I snorted. "He barely touched you."

"Little does he know," Kieren smirked, "that I don't have a life to take."

"Can animals normally see and touch you?" I asked.

"The occasional critter will sense that something's near when I'm around. Animals are often more in tune with the dead than humans." He shook his head. He studied the crow with renewed focus. "But they can certainly never touch me."

"Oh, um—" I held my hand up, waiting for the soft pinch of his talons to grip my fingers as I maneuvered him between us. "Menace is kind of . . . dead, too. Or at least he died and then came back to life. Sora sometimes calls him Frankenstein, but that never fits right because she really means Frankenstein's *monster*. Victor Frankenstein himself never came back from the dead—plus, he was an asshole." I ran my fingers over the side of his neck. "I prefer to think of Menace more as a crombie."

"Crombie," Kieran deadpanned. "Am I supposed to know what that is?"

"A crow zombie," I said, before adding a quieter, "Seems obvious enough to me."

He ignored the barb. "And this crow of yours came back from the dead?"

"The Undoing." I shrugged. "He was dead, and then. . ." I mimed an explosion with my free hand. "After everything settled, he was . . . not dead."

"Must have one foot in both worlds then." Kieran pursed his lips, his chin resting on his fist as his stare shifted between us. Then he reached forward and ran his fingers over a patch of my hair, where the black bled to gray. "Perhaps you both do. Curious. The Undoing has certainly made for a more interesting mortal world."

"No more curious than talking to a dead guy in the middle of the street," I said, lifting my hand in the air as Menace took flight.

"You grow more intriguing by the hour, Agony."

Menace landed on a nearby tree, close enough to watch us from safety. It usually took him a while to warm up to new people. Though something told me he was just as intrigued by Kieran as Kieran was of him.

Maybe Menace was the reason I was . . . the way that I was. Why the world sometimes blurred into two; why I could see Kieran and Claudine. I'd been touching him when magic poured into this world. Maybe his crombie-ness infected me, too?

I studied him for a moment, considering the possibility. If he could see Kieran, did that mean that he'd be able to see and interact with Claudine or Greta?

Then again, they might not come back after Kieran shooed them away.

As we approached the medical center, my thoughts clouded with another memory. "Mrs. Pederson." I turned toward Kieran. "You were here. The day that she died."

Something flickered in his expression, but it was gone before I could decipher the reaction. "I was."

"Why? Do you know what happened to her?"

His lips flattened into a tight grin. "Just paying respects to a former charge was all. I was in the area."

When I tried to ask the series of questions tangled on my tongue—why then, when was she his charge, why hadn't he been there in the weeks she'd been catatonic—Kieran shook his head, stopping me before I could voice a single one.

"We won't discuss my other charges. I'm a gentleman. And everyone deserves their privacy, Agony."

Before I could push back, the door to the center swung open.

"Mareena." Aidan's expression softened into a smile. "Good, you're here. I was afraid you might have changed your mind."

"*This* is your date?" Kieran eyed him head-to-toe, nose curled. "First impression?" No one had asked, but that clearly wasn't stopping him. "You can do better. You *have* done better. Quite recently, too."

This was not a date.

This was two friends grabbing dinner and a few drinks.

And it was looking more and more like a ridiculous idea by the moment.

I shot a discreet, warning look at him—apparently not *everyone* deserved their privacy—then returned Aidan's smile. "Nope, I'm here."

Aidan had chosen a small restaurant, just a twenty-minute walk from the med center, and I'd spent nearly the entire time with my attention divided between making conversation with him, while trying to ignore the guardian angel stalking us.

Kieran refused to give us more than twenty feet of space, and I could practically hear his running commentary about Aidan, even though every time I glanced back his lips were sealed—nothing but the dregs of mirth in his eyes.

Menace seemed to be tailing Kieran just as discreetly as Kieran was tailing us.

Every few minutes his loud caw would ricochet through the mostly-empty street, and he'd occasionally hover just above the angel's head, as if he wasn't entirely sure whether or not he was real.

"The crows in this city grow bolder every day it seems." Aidan ducked as Menace flew between us. He landed on a crooked post above the restaurant, the chains holding the sign attached fluttering under his weight. He let out another loud caw that cracked in the wind. "Pretty soon they'll be running it."

I offered him a small smile, widening my eyes at the crow in question, silently demanding that he behave himself. "Better them than the compounds, I suppose."

Aidan opened the door for me, ushering us both across the threshold, and when it slammed closed behind him, I took that as a hopeful sign that Kieran might back off for an hour or two and go do . . . whatever it was that dead guys did when they weren't haunting someone.

But of course, not to be deterred by such an obvious signal that his presence wasn't wanted, he simply walked through the door, a cocky smirk plastered on his face.

Ten minutes into the meal, Kieran seemed to understand that I wouldn't respond to his running commentary; and only after draining my second glass of wine was I able to semi-ignore his presence long enough to properly engage in conversation with Aidan.

Kieran sat at the empty table beside us, his head propped up by his hand, as he watched us the way that people passively watch a dull play.

Aidan pressed his napkin to the corner of his mouth. "Jo tells me Frank was awake for a bit this afternoon."

My fork, which was halfway to my mouth with a scoop of rice and curry, fell back to my plate. I winced at the soft, metallic clang of the metal. "When? What happened?" I stood up, ready to go see him, but then the past tense of his words sank into me like lead, so I sat back down. The one day I wasn't around would of course be the day that Frank was awake. I'd missed him. "Did Sora get to speak to him?"

The corners of Aidan's eyes pinched. "No. Jo ran by the diner, hoping to catch one of you, but it was closed." He must've seen the guilt etched across my expression because he added, "He was only awake for a few minutes from what I understand, so even if Jo was able to reach you guys, I think you still would have missed him. By the time I went to check on him, he was asleep. Vitals were good though, and Jo told me he was in good spirits."

A wave of guilt rolled over me. "Still no idea what's wrong? How The Undoing transformed his illness?"

Aidan shook his head. "I'm sorry. I did hear word from a small clinic across town that they've heard of a couple of similar cases. They've promised to reach out if they have any more information." He reached across the table and placed his hand over mine, squeezing gently. "We'll get to the bottom of it, Mareena. I'm sure of it. Jo's got an in with the compounds— they might have something for us soon. We're not giving up hope. Until then, he doesn't seem to be in pain and his numbers are stable, which are good signs."

My eyes glazed over with the threat of tears. Blinking them back, I nodded.

"Thank you," I said, offering his hand a soft squeeze in return. "I can't even begin to tell you how much Sora and I appreciate everything you've done for him. For all of us."

He threaded his fingers through mine and smiled. "Least I can do. You two help us keep the place running. You know—" He grunted, then shook his head. "Before everything happened, I considered dropping out of med school. Going a new path altogether."

"Really?" He was so good with the patients, with everyone, I couldn't imagine him doing anything else. Aidan was one of those people who seemed to thrive in this new world. Every day that I saw him, he was alive with purpose, like it flooded him.

"Yeah, I thought about going into tech or accounting or something else. I don't know, there was just so much more bureaucracy in the medical field than I imagined there being when I was younger, you know? Took away some of the magic of the whole idea. It was only a passing thought at the time." He grinned, his eyes darting to mine, almost shy. "Obviously now, I love what I do, and the people I get to work with, so I'm very happy I stuck it out."

"So am I," I said. I caught sight of Kieran from the corner of my eyes and jumped.

He'd been so uncharacteristically silent that I'd almost forgotten he was here.

"You okay?" Aidan asked, his thumb gently stroking the back of my hand.

"Like I said before, Dr. Mediocre wants to fuck you," Kieran said, his tone laced half with teasing, half with a dark edge. "Surely, you can see that now, Agony? But I can't fathom why you'd let him."

I choked out a cough and tried to cover my shock with another large gulp of wine.

"I mean, it's not that I care or anything," Kieran went on. "It's not my job to pass judgment on the lives of the living. You're free to fuck who you want, I suppose." He paused for a moment, clearly fighting the silence I wanted so desperately for him to succumb to right now. "But it's just. . .this guy? Really? You can do so much better."

That sounded like the definition of passing judgment to me.

When I turned to shoot him another warning glare, I found his face only a few inches from mine.

At some point during his one-sided conversation, Kieran had abandoned his passive spot in the audience entirely—and was sitting instead in the chair to my left.

At our table.

With his arm wrapped around the back of my chair.

He was also clearly no longer bored, though his expression was otherwise unreadable.

A muscle ticked in his jaw as his stare snagged on the spot where Aidan's hand touched mine.

"Yeah." I pulled my hand back, though I wasn't entirely sure why. Aidan and I hadn't done anything wrong. We were two friends offering each other comfort. And if it became more than that, was that so bad? "Sorry, I'm fine. Spaced out for a second there. It's been a. . .weird day."

Aidan was a good guy. Kind. Thoughtful. Smart.

Alive.

His soft smile dipped for a fraction of a second, and I grabbed my fork, as if I'd only meant to scarf down another bite of my dinner and not recoil from his touch.

Wasn't this what Kieran had been on about earlier? That I needed to make connections, stop shielding myself? Wasn't that exactly what I was doing? But then why did I suddenly feel flushed and guilty, like I'd just been busted for something unseemly. And why did Kieran now look even less like a guardian angel than usual, and more like someone who very much wanted to remove Aidan's head from his spine?

More importantly, why the fuck did one look at Kieran tie my stomach into more knots than Aidan's lingering touch had?

Kieran's sudden nearness alone had my heart rate speeding up and my stomach fluttering with. . .something.

Fucking traitorous brain. The bitch was never on my side.

There was a perfectly nice guy sitting right in front of me, but all I could seem to focus on was my obnoxious, dead, stalker.

"Mareena?" Aidan's brows pinched with concern.

"Yeah?" I cleared my throat and noticed that my forkful of food was chilling somewhere between the plate and my mouth, as if my brain had forgotten the performance midway through the task. Setting it back down, I tore my focus away from my stalker and back to my date. No. Not date. My friend. But maybe it should be a date? Maybe this was how I could prove that my life was on track, how I could get rid of my stalker for good? But did I really want to get rid of him? I shoved the thought away before I had the chance to dissect it any further and offered Aidan a tight smile. "Sorry. I'm fine.

It's just been a bit of an off week. Must be catching up with me."

The rest of the meal went as smoothly as the first half of the evening.

Kieran went back to his sullen silence, only occasionally grunting like a moody teenager when he found Aidan's conversation boring or when he choked back his snarky commentary.

Though when Aidan insisted on walking me back to the apartment, Kieran couldn't resist responding with, "The woman's only got her own *literal* guardian here, but yeah, sure—walk her home. I'm sure *you'll* ensure her safety."

"Well, this is me," I said, when we reached the diner, wincing at the cheesiness of the line, as if Aiden didn't walk by the place almost every day. When did I get so fucking awful at this?

"So it is," he said, his eyes roving over the diner and then up to the apartment windows. When his gaze fell back to meet mine, there was a wistful smile on his face. "This was fun. I really needed a night out. Away from—" He made a vague gesture. "You know . . ."

"Everything?" I finished.

Nodding, he let out a soft laugh. "Exactly."

"Me, too."

"So," he said, face scrunching in question, "does that mean you'll consider having dinner with me again? Sometime soon?"

Kieran sighed, then kicked a rock into the street.

Aidan turned around, searching for the culprit of the soft echo.

"Yeah, that'd be good," I rushed out, an attempt to distract him. "Maybe next week?"

And maybe next week, we wouldn't have a third wheel and I could give him the full attention that he deserved.

Though the thought of that sent a sharp pang through my chest.

Apparently, I'd grown reluctantly accustomed to the grumpy guardian.

Bad habits were so much easier to pick up than good ones, it seemed.

"Yeah? Next week is great. Have a good night, Mareena." Aidan smiled and pressed a soft kiss to my cheek.

I held my breath, hoping like hell that I might feel some kind of flutter or desire at his nearness, but all that I felt was his warmth, and the gentle scratch of his five-o-clock shadow.

And then, when he walked away, all that I saw was Kieran.

His forehead was pressed against the wall of the diner, and he rolled it over the surface, like he was trying to scrub the tedium of the night from his memory.

Uncharacteristically quiet, he followed me up to the apartment, a silent shadow as I locked the place up and replaced Menace's water dish.

Sora still wasn't back. Another anxious search of the place turned up no note, but I choked back my anxiety and fiddled with my ring while I got ready for bed.

My brain was swimming with a million 'what-ifs' and possibilities of where she could be or of what could have happened to her, when I found Kieran lying on my bed, the book I'd been reading earlier opened on his chest.

"What are you doing?" I asked. I pulled back the covers to nudge him off, but he didn't budge. After two more tugs, I gave up with a huff and slid myself beneath them. "You're not sleeping in here."

"Your friend is okay, Agony." He put one arm behind his head and stared at the ceiling with so much focused attention, it was like he was trying to memorize every imperfection in the plaster.

"What?" I turned on my side and studied him. "Is that your angel Spidey-sense tingling or something? Do you actually know where she is?"

He shook his head, and a small crease formed between his brows. "No, I don't know for sure. And she's not my charge, so I don't have a read on where she is."

"Then why would you say that?"

"I don't—" The muscle in his jaw ticked as he searched for the words. "I don't think that I like it when you feel worried." His lips pursed, as if he was surprised by the admission. "And I thought it might help to have another voice weigh in on the matter—one to combat the voice catastrophizing in there." He pressed his thumb between my brows, and I felt his touch sink into my bones and carve a crater inside of my chest. When his eyes met mine, there was nothing of the teasing or snark from earlier in the night. Only a soft, steady clarity. "So no, I don't know for sure that your friend is okay, but it seems far more likely that she is than she isn't." He smoothed the worry lines with his thumb, and though it shouldn't have worked, it did. "Perhaps you inspired her to take the day off—to find her own joy. Perhaps she's out chasing it."

Nodding, I swallowed back the sudden tightness in my throat. "Okay."

"And if, in the morning, you're still concerned, we can look into it."

"Okay." I hated how small and broken my voice sounded in the space between us.

"Okay," he said. He opened the book back up and pointed. "I think you were here?"

When I nodded, he started to read.

And though I fought the tug of sleep for as long as I could, and though my mind occasionally drifted away from the story and started to spiral, the lull of his voice always brought me back—until his smooth lilt finally pulled me under into one of the deepest sleeps I'd had in years.

18

—

MAREENA

APPROXIMATELY NINE YEARS AGO, THREE
YEARS BEFORE THE UNDOING

"So . . ." Sora bumped her hip against mine before dropping a five-pound bag of ice into the sink, "party started an hour ago. When is he coming?"

"Who?" I asked, playing dumb as I took a sip of her latest party drink. It tasted like lemonade mixed with rubbing alcohol and something distinctly herbal, and it was a true mark of our friendship that I managed to mask how bad the concoction was.

She scrunched up her nose. "That bad?"

"Um," I said, searching for a description. Apparently, my masking wasn't so great. "Strong."

"Good." She grinned, then slammed the bag down, breaking the ice up into smaller chips for her next batch. I'd be sticking with my classic vodka and soda for the rest of the night. "And what do you mean 'who'? You know who. Your friend." I shot her a glare, but she shrugged it off. "What? It's not every day that you bring home a friend unprovoked. Usually, I have to beg you to help me fill out these nights."

"I don't know what you're talking about." I glanced down at my phone, like I was checking the time, though I knew damn well what time it was, and that Levi said he'd be here around now. "I bring people over all the time."

We both knew that was a bald-faced lie, but it was the sort of thing you were supposed to say to an accusation like that.

She pinched my cheek with her freshly painted manicure. "Of course you do, pookie."

A knock sounded at the door, and her mocking smile turned into a legitimate one. "Never mind, I'll bet that's him." She wiggled her eyebrows at me. "So, he *is* real then."

The urge to roll my eyes was powerful, but I held strong. "Dick."

She winked, then took to stirring her mixture in a bowl that was half the size that she was.

Jen, one of Sora's friends from cosmetology school, opened the door. I could tell from Levi's smug expression, that she was giving him one of those appreciative, head-to-toe appraising sorts of looks.

Honestly, I didn't blame her. Levi was the kind of hot you had to actively try not to notice. Part of me deeply wished he wasn't.

"Hi, uh—" He held up a bottle of something. "Is Mareena here?"

"Go save that poor boy," Sora whisper-shouted, "before Jen runs him off."

Propelling myself with a deep chug of Sora's glorified jungle juice, I made my way back into the crowded living room. It wasn't crowded in the traditional sense one might think a party could get. There were only ten or so people here, mostly Sora's friends, though, at her insistence, I'd also invited two people from Mac's Tavern.

When Levi's gaze landed on me, his face stretched into a grin—one wide enough to showcase that damn dimple of his. I practically saw Jen swoon when it made its appearance. Again, a very understandable response. "Hey."

"Hey," I said back, ushering him in and away from Jen's hungry stare that was not-so-discreetly lasered in on his ass, as he made his way into the cramped living room.

He glanced around, nodding at everyone as they ran through their names in the way people always did in these situations—as if Levi, or anyone really, could be expected to remember a dozen new names, let alone correctly attribute them to the right faces.

"I can take your coat," I said, holding my hand out as he tugged it from his long frame. "There's not much room, but we're keeping people's stuff in Sora's bedroom for now."

We'd been living with Becca for more than six months, but it still felt so strange to think that Sora had her own room. That *I* had my own room. I'd taken ownership of the small office space. There was enough room for a full-sized bed and desk, and even a small bookshelf. No closet, but I made do with the one in the hallway just fine. My favorite part was the large sliding door that led to the small balcony and let in a gentle swath of the sunlight that was so rare this time of year.

As far as bedrooms went, they were pretty tight quarters, but compared to what we dealt with in Oleg's studio, it felt like a damn penthouse suite in comparison.

"Can't believe I've actually been invited into the famous new apartment," Levi said, his voice low against my ear, so that only I could hear. "Honestly, I half expected you to text me the address of some nearby intersection before blindfolding me and walking here."

"Kinky," I teased. "To be fair, I did consider going that route, but when I suggested it to Sora, she made the very good point that if we really wanted to keep the location a secret, we would need to murder you and then dispose of your body, which would make the entire tedious process far more work than it was worth."

Levi grunted and when I spun around to face him, the reason for it was immediately clear.

Sora had attached herself to him, her arms stretched around his waist in one of her signature hugs. The kind that made breathing a thing of the past.

For being so tiny, she had one hell of a grip.

"You came," she squealed. "I'm Sora, though apparently we already met and spent half the night together a while back." She glanced up at him with a devilish smirk. "Tequila really must have worked her magic that night—you don't even look vaguely familiar."

"What now?" Rose, one of Sora's cosmetology friends, asked from the living room, her voice filled with indignation.

Levi's eyes bulged wide as they met mine, his discomfort palpable.

"Nothing nefarious," I shouted back. "We hung out, Sora blacked out on tequila, we parted ways."

"Thank you," Levi mouthed, awkwardly patting Sora on the top of her head like he wasn't quite sure what to make of her—almost like she was a feral animal that terrified him. It was, perhaps, the most normal reaction to someone like Sora I'd ever seen.

True to his word, Levi and I hadn't really spoken in months. Last time he was in town, I had a shift at Mac's, and while he stopped by for dinner and to check in, it had been a particularly busy night, so we weren't able to catch up much. This afternoon had been the first I'd heard from him since then, and I'd already committed to making an appearance at Sora's get together.

Surprisingly, he wanted to come. Said he'd never been to a proper house party before, though I wasn't sure what exactly made a house party a proper one.

At the time, I thought he was kidding, but judging by the clear discomfort etched into every line of his body, his expression devoid of its usual snark, I was inclined to believe he'd been telling the truth.

Where he'd appeared so smooth and composed while teaching me how to throw a punch, he seemed way less at ease around larger groups.

Made total sense now why I'd spotted him lurking alone at the bar both times I'd seen him in the wild. Maybe he hadn't been kidding before—maybe he really was as much of a loner as I was.

Which meant that he was probably even less used to friends than I was—something I would have never guessed possible.

"Let's get you a drink, shall we?" I asked, making my way over to Sora's puke-green mixture.

"Yes, please."

I scooped him out a ladle's worth, then doubled it. He'd need some liquid courage to survive the mental stamina of this group.

Sora had these party nights once a month, and I usually made excuses to avoid them at all costs, sometimes even begging Chase to schedule me on those nights so I'd have an easy out. When that didn't work, I usually dipped out of the center of things after an obligatory hour or two and holed up in my room with a book until everyone took off.

Her friends were nice, but they were almost all extroverts, which meant that I was generally exhausted for days after they left.

Sora peeled herself from Levi's side and made her way back to the party where people were arguing rather animatedly about which game they should play next.

"Thanks." Levi held the questionable liquid to eye level, like he was trying to manufacture the courage to take a sip.

"It's best if you don't overthink it and just drink," I said, taking a giant gulp of mine and wincing openly now that Sora wasn't here to see. "She takes great pride in her concoctions, but they are—"

"Not good," he hissed, smacking his lips. "I didn't even know you could make alcohol taste like that."

"We all have our gifts. Be careful though—a few glasses of that will hit you out of nowhere. So. . ." I studied him, my own growing buzz making it difficult to suppress the smile stretched across my face, or my general excitement that he was here. "How've you been?"

"Still alive." He took another sip and shot me a smug look over the rim of his glass. "I guess that means your friendship hasn't killed me yet."

"Well—" I smirked. "The night is still young."

"Guess you and Sora will have to figure out how to dispose of my body anyway then."

"Hey, Mars." James, a guy who worked in the back at Mac's, walked into the kitchen. He had on a mustard-colored beanie that made his light brown hair curl around the brim. "Never Have I Ever or King's Cup? We can't decide."

Levi stiffened slightly at the nickname, his brows pinched in question as he shot me a teasing look and mouthed "Mars?" silently when James wasn't looking.

James wasn't a friend, but he'd adopted Sora's nickname for me almost instantly, much to my chagrin. But we also connected so superficially, that I almost didn't care. He started working at Mac's a month ago, and we hooked up exactly once.

It was a decision I'd almost instantly come to regret, since judging by the appraising look he shot at Levi, the whole 'casual, one time, no strings attached' stipulations I'd laid out beforehand obviously hadn't been as clear as I'd thought they were at the time.

Men seemed to take offense at my disinterest in second helpings—that, or they saw it as a challenge; like in setting my boundaries, I was inviting them to play some game I had no interest in watching, let alone participating in. Or like in saying 'yes' once, I owed them every subsequent time after.

Women, however, usually took me at my word. For example, I'd also hooked up with Sora's friend Rose once, a very long time ago, but unlike James, she hadn't tried changing my mind after. Nor had she made shit weird between us when we shared space at parties like this one.

"Neither," I said. "I have a study group in the morning before my shift, so I'm not trying to get entirely shit faced tonight."

"Don't be so responsible. Come on." James shifted closer to me—oblivious to Levi's stare which had swiftly turned from teasing to a full-on deadly—his hand brushing up against my arm, as if he meant to grab it. The gesture was probably intended to come off as flirty, but it just made my skin crawl. "It'll be fun."

When he curled his hand around mine, I flinched, putting some much needed distance between us again.

"I said I'm good," I snapped, then instantly tried to ease the annoyance out of my tone with a half-smile. James was clingy, but I also had to see him semi-frequently at work, so I didn't want to make things more uncomfortable than they had to be. That said, I mentally pushed casual hookups with colleagues under the bad lessons learned list that I kept an unofficial tally for in my head. "You guys go ahead without me; I need a breather from all the socializing."

"Right." James's eyes slid to Levi then back to me, his jaw tight, but he thankfully bit back the retort very obviously brewing on his tongue. "Suit yourself."

He grabbed another drink and nodded at us once before rejoining the party.

I needed to let Sora know in the morning that he was officially on the not-invited-back list. I didn't need that kind of energy in our space.

As soon as James disappeared, Levi leaned forward, ready to comment.

"Don't," I said, though there was no edge to my voice.

Levi gasped in faux shock. "I didn't say anything."

"Mhm." I grinned into my cup. "Let's keep it that way."

He studied me for a second, the tension in his body slipping away like sand through fingers. "So, house parties, huh?"

I winced, realizing I'd effectively bulldozed Levi from playing whatever game the group landed on. "Shit, I didn't mean to shut that down. We can go join in on their game if you want. Generally, they can be pretty fun if you're in the right headspace for them."

"Nah," he said. "I'll hang back with you, if that's okay. I don't think big crowds are really my thing."

His gaze traveled over the kitchen, mentally clocking every design choice with a soft nod.

Sora would be pleased. She'd put a lot of work into making this apartment feel like a home. Becca, our roommate, was hardly around, and had pretty much used the place as a landing pad to crash in when she wasn't at work or with her boyfriend.

"Mine either. Sora mostly hosts these as a stand-in for how she imagines college parties would be if we lived on campus somewhere." I shrugged. "She doesn't want us to miss out on any quintessential age-appropriate experiences." I glanced up at him. "Her words, not mine."

It was something she took very seriously. There was a four-page list in one of her old journals that tracked different experiences and events that Rina had either made passing mention of when they were younger, or else random things Sora imagined her sister would have loved if she was still here with us.

Rina had always been the most adventurous and outgoing of the three of us. Back then, Sora was quieter, kept mostly to herself. Sometimes that meant she got swallowed up by her sister's shadow. But after Rina's death, it was like she'd taken on some of her traits and transformed them into something that made more sense for her—a way to honor her memory, like she was still with us.

We tried to tackle at least one thing on her list a month. The frat-house style game night sort of stuck though, and while it wasn't my favorite way to kill an evening, I liked doing what I could to help Sora feel closer to Rina.

I nodded at the bottle hanging at Levi's side. "What'd you bring?"

"Wine."

I let out a low whistle. "Fancy."

Not exactly the illegal beverage that came to mind for a party hosted by eighteen-year-olds, anyway.

"Not really." He held it up, studying it. The bottle was dark, the label an almost comically loud range of colorful cartoon dog faces. "I know nothing about wine. I always just go with the coolest label. And this one had dogs."

"I like dogs," I said.

"I know."

"Well, we can either go join the party and share your dog wine," I shot him a look, "or we can ditch them entirely and hoard the whole thing for ourselves while we sit on the balcony and people watch like a pair of curmudgeonly gargoyles."

"The latter sounds like my ideal house party, actually."

"Mine, too."

I glanced at the bottle. Twist off. Perfect.

I didn't think we actually owned a bottle opener, now that I thought about it.

I grabbed a few blankets from the hallway closet and nodded for him to follow me through my room to the balcony —and then instantly regretted that I hadn't bothered cleaning in here. My room was usually off-limits at these things—Sora always made sure I had a place to escape to in case I needed one—so it hadn't even registered.

He took in the room, his eyes tracing every inch of it, as if he was trying to catalogue everything, filing away each tiny detail.

My cheeks heated under his appraisal, and I fought the urge to justify my haphazardly selected posters and precariously arranged stacks of books. There was a particularly spicy novel opened on my nightstand and I desperately hoped that he didn't catch the title.

I slid the balcony door open and waited for him to pass through, the frigid air like a balm to any lingering vestiges of embarrassment.

The chill went from welcome to downright wintery in a matter of seconds though, and I curled myself up in one of the blankets before handing the second to Levi and claiming one corner of the wicker couch.

We'd gotten the couch used for our favorite price—free—in some neighborhood group, but it had definitely seen better days.

I held my breath when Levi sat down, hoping like hell it didn't collapse under our collective weight. The wicker creaked and groaned, but after a few seconds, it silenced its protest beneath us.

"I like your place." Levi twisted the cap off the colorful dog wine and offered the first sip to me, while he settled his blanket over his legs.

Shit. I'd forgotten to grab glasses.

When I glanced at him, I expected to see the lie in his eyes, but all I saw was earnest approval. He hadn't directly mentioned it, but sometimes you could just look at someone and know that they were used to wealth. Or at least moderate comfort. Levi had that vibe.

And while I adored the home that Sora and I created here —it truly was shaping up to be everything we'd dreamt of—it was far from glamorous. Most of our things were mismatched, used to the point that they were on their last legs—well-loved as Sora liked to frame it. Neither of us came with much, so the place was also pretty barren. Becca's previous roommates had taken their things, and they'd clearly been the ones in charge of most of the shared furnishings. But every week, it seemed like Sora would find something special to add—like she was collecting little puzzle pieces throughout the city in a scavenger hunt only she could complete.

"It feels like a good home," he added, threading his fingers through the small holes in the crocheted blanket. Sora picked it up for three bucks at a thrift store last week. She couldn't bear the thought of some, likely dead, old woman's hard work sitting on a shelf and collecting dust, not getting the love it deserved. And neither of us would ever be getting hand-made items from a doting grandmother, so by her logic, we were the perfect adopters.

"Yeah, I guess it is." It was definitely on its way to becoming one, anyway. I felt more at ease here, more stable than I had in as long as I could remember. Like for once, I could come up for air and let my lungs take their fill of it.

For the first time in a long time, Sora and I could exist as loudly as we wanted. No one was going to find us and toss us back into a system that had already failed us too many times. We had jobs, we were figuring out what we wanted out of life, and we were no longer dressing up as Oleg's dead mother while he lived out his quirky fantasies.

Still, as good as things were, I couldn't ever quite shake the hollow ache in my chest. Sometimes I felt it so sharply, it was like it existed entirely separate from me, the way it clawed and screamed at night, and I had no way to ease its pain.

"What's your home like?" I asked, pushing the fleeting thought down.

Levi took a long sip of the wine, his stare locked on the

small dish Sora set out on our balcony. It was for the crows. She was determined to befriend one of the city's many murders—so far to no success.

"Honestly, I don't know that I really have one anymore," he said, whispering the words into the night, as if speaking them out loud manifested them into truth. "Or if I ever really did."

There was such a quiet sadness in his tone that it was almost hard to look at him—like if I did, I might find it etched into his skin, a bleeding, festering wound.

"Home doesn't have to be a place," I said, echoing a conversation that came back to me as if in a dream, one we'd had many months ago, sitting along the canal.

"No." He glanced down at his lap, his mouth hooking into a soft grin. "It doesn't."

"What have you been up to?" I asked, suddenly impossibly curious about what his life looked like when he wasn't here, in these strange, isolated moments with me.

"A lot." He shrugged. "Work has been—I don't know—just a lot, honestly. I feel like we've been trying to build a dam with nothing but a few twigs—less, even. With nothing but some strands of hair."

I couldn't imagine private security fitting into the metaphor, but I supposed it could be a life-or-death kind of field in some situations.

"I'm sorry," I said, knowing that he wouldn't or couldn't say much more about work. "That sounds miserable."

He nodded, then turned to me. "What about you? Did I hear you mention a study group or something?"

"Yep." I took a deep breath, trying to quell the strange mixture of anxiety and excitement the prospect conjured in my gut. "I'm going back to school. Enrolled in a class at the community college up north last month."

"That's amazing. Are you liking it?"

"It's nice, yeah." It had been years since I'd been in a classroom, so I was still getting used to the feel of it again. "I can only afford to take one class a quarter—between tuition prices and making sure I still keep all my shifts at Mac's, you know? So it'll be years before I can get a degree or anything particularly useful, but yeah, I'm excited about it."

Loud shouts echoed inside, and I had a feeling the group had moved on to a more animated game.

Levi chuckled, then shook his head. "So, what kind of party games do you usually play at these things anyway? That guy mentioned a few."

"Never Have I Ever?" I asked, surprised, but then I realized that if he didn't really go to any parties, most social games were probably also equally unfamiliar. "It's usually a game people play to get to know each other better, but when there's drinking involved it tends to warp into a game designed to get people to reveal more intimate histories. Usually about their sex lives and stuff. Sort of like the dark and twisted cousin of two truths and a lie." When he furrowed his brows, I continued, "Someone says two true things about themself, and one lie, and the other people have to try and guess what the lie is. It's a common ice breaker, I think, in classes and stuff? People act like it's fun, but it's always seemed like an unnecessarily anxiety-inducing way to get to know people better."

"I see," he said, a devious glint in his eyes, "though I can't say it's entirely shocking that a game intended to draw connections between strangers would be uncomfortable for you."

"What?" I scrunched my face in exaggerated hurt. "I can be fun. Not to mention that alerting the room that the people closest to you have a tendency of dropping dead can be a super effective way at severing connections too, not just forging them."

"Touché." He grinned. "Let's play one."

"You want to go back in?" Though the thought of returning

to the chaos emanating from our living room was about as desirable right now as going to the dentist.

"No, here. Just us."

Something about the way he said 'just us', or maybe the way his eyes snagged on mine, had my stomach tightening—whether because of the wine or something else, I couldn't be sure. "Okay. Which game?"

He slid his teeth over his bottom lip, considering. "I don't really have any interest in lies, or causing you unnecessary anxiety in trying to suss them out, but we could do two truths?"

I took another sip of the wine, the bitter notes getting stuck on the back of my tongue. "How about one?"

"Negotiations." He smirked. "You've a bit of a need to maintain control over every situation, don't you?" He exhaled, dramatically. "But I suppose that's a suitable amendment for a diet friendship. Two truths each might be extending beyond our limits. So our game can be one each—a truth for a truth." He narrowed his eyes, studying me. "But I want a good one, not something anybody else knows."

"Sora knows pretty much everything about me," I said.

"Sora doesn't count. I want something only Sora knows about you. Not something you tell just anybody."

"Deal." I burrowed into my blanket, watching the soft trickle of rain wash over the street. "But you're going first."

"How generous." He grabbed the bottle from me and took a drink, my focus suddenly latched onto the press of his lips to the rim where mine had been just moments ago.

I blinked, shoving the thought away. "Make it good."

He looked out over the balcony, watching as an elderly couple crossed the street below us, collecting his thoughts for a moment. "I brushed it off before, a few months ago when it came up—but sometimes"—he took a deep breath, an uncharacteristic vulnerability lining his expression—"sometimes I think that I'm deeply jealous of my brother. Of the life he gets to lead. He doesn't even appreciate it. But then also"—his voice softened, until it was just a whisper competing with the rain—"sometimes I wish that I grew up with him, that things were different. That we were close, like brothers are supposed to be. That there was some way to erase all the anger between us and start over. I think"—he shrugged, then took another sip—"I think I might have liked being a brother, maybe even been good at it—in different circumstances."

The deep sense of loneliness that always seemed to shroud Levi like a heavy cloak was almost suffocating to witness now. I felt it like an ache inside of my own chest.

I slid my legs closer to him, a fair compromise to the strange, suddenly intense desire I had to pull him to me in a bone-crushing hug. "What's his name?"

"Eli." He shot me a look from the corner of his eye. "Don't get me wrong, he's not perfect. Sometimes I don't even understand why I want any sort of relationship with him at all. He's arrogant as hell and can honestly be a bit of a dick. Completely full of himself. And he spends all his time constantly surrounded by his friends—all of them just as entitled and stubborn as he is. A bit obnoxious, really. But they're all so incredibly close with each other. I just . . ." He shrugged. "The few times I've seen them or Eli, my knee-jerk reaction has always put me on the defensive. That, or I just turn into a complete asshole whenever I open my mouth. He wants to hate me, and I make it extremely easy for him to continue doing so. I've never really had something like what they have. I think, on some level, I'm just jealous—of Eli, and of them. They're more his family than I will ever be."

"Does he live close by?" I asked. "It's not too late to try forging some kind of a relationship with him, if that's what you really want. Maybe now that you're both adults it will be easier?"

"Reasonably close, yeah." He passed me the bottle. "There's

a lot of baggage there though." When he shot me a flirty wink, I knew that the vulnerability of his confession was coming to an end. "For now, I think it's best that I devote my efforts on one attempted friendship at a time. Which I guess makes you my test case." He nudged his knee against mine. "Your turn, Mareena. Hit me with your soul-revealing truth."

"Soul-revealing, eh? Way to make the game sound fun and inviting."

I thought for a moment, but for some unidentifiable reason, my brain lasered in on the night that Rina died, the rest of my life blanking out of my memory as if it had never existed—my entire being suddenly condensed into that one night.

The one night I spent so much energy trying desperately to forget.

Some truths were better kept secrets. Not just for my sake, but for Levi's, too.

Plus, Sora and I had sworn to never speak of the details of that night again. Doing so now felt like a betrayal. There was also the fact that I'd killed someone that night and, if I was being honest with myself, I didn't want Levi to see me as a murderer. As resistant as I was to let him close, I also didn't want him to disappear on me altogether either.

"That one." He pressed his thumb between my brows, smoothing out the line there, his touch surprisingly warm and gentle. "That's the one I want. The one that's making you make that face."

"I can't tell you that one," I said, the words automatic. "Some secrets are good—necessary, even."

"Yeah, I get that." His lips turned down slightly. "How about you tell me the parts of it that you can? The parts that you want to tell me?"

Muscle memory had me wanting to immediately resist, to pluck something else, something trivial, from my experiences. But there was also a part of me that wanted to tell him something deep below the surface, something coveted like this particular truth. To actually give the diet friendship a chance—to test the limits of my curse and dare to imagine a future where it was, indeed, broken. Where I could build connections beyond just myself and Sora.

So, instead of fully unpacking the events of that night, something I rarely allowed myself to do even alone, I streamlined and tucked them into something that could be shared—but still something no one but Sora and I knew.

"Um—" I started, not entirely sure where to go from there. It was kind of an odd feeling. I'd pushed that night down so far, and for so long, that I didn't really know how to pull it back up to the surface, how to craft it into something I could give words to. "Sora and I were in the same foster home for a few months," I said, finding my in. "Usually, when you hear the awful stories about foster care, it's the parents you hear about." I shook my head. "But Cheryl and Joe were pretty decent for the most part. They fed us, housed us, made sure we went to school and did our homework. I'd definitely been in less comfortable set ups over the years—as had Sora. Their son, however, was the problem—there was something sadistic about him, something not quite . . . right."

A muscle in Levi's jaw pulsed and his expression grew hard, but he didn't say anything, his eyes silently urging me to continue at my own pace.

I ran through the details of the night in my mind, mining for what I could share.

Rina lived in that house with us too, and at first, she'd been fascinated by their son, Blake. She may have even had a bit of a crush for a little while.

Blake loved the attention even though he was a few years older, just shy of eighteen at the time, and shouldn't have been thinking about her in that way. But he did, and where her interest had been brief and fleeting, nothing more than a school-girl crush, he'd quickly grown obsessed with her.

When she rejected him, that—well, that was when everything started to change.

And it changed quickly.

Blake was used to getting whatever he wanted. He didn't know how to process the word 'no.'

He took the rejection out on Rina the best way he knew how, by fucking with the people she loved most—me and Sora.

His cruelty manifested in small ways at first. He'd lock one of us in the closet, or we'd wake up to find ourselves hand-cuffed to our beds, where he'd leave us for hours until his parents got home from work.

But after a month or two, his pranks got darker, more twisted.

"Things got bad," I continued, glossing over the details. "At first his parents tried to ignore it. Whether they truly didn't believe that he was capable of violence, or they just tried to convince themselves otherwise, I'm still not sure." Parents always want to believe the best about their children—Cheryl and Joe were no different. But we were the ones who had to pay that price. "Eventually, though, things got bad enough that even they couldn't pretend what was happening was okay. They sent him away for a while to stay with some extended family—hoping distance would make things better, that his obsession was just a temporary fixation that could be corrected through some distance and time. And in the meantime, they started looking into getting us set up with a different home."

They obviously hadn't explained that their son was the main reason for this sudden relocation, or they would have moved things along more quickly. Joe was running for a local office, and he blamed the intensity of his campaign on the need for a change—told them he and Cheryl could no longer provide the attention we needed. It was an unusually slow process because there wasn't any urgency.

But he clearly underestimated the depths of Blake's obsession with Rina. He must have casually mentioned that we were leaving to his son, because when Blake showed up that night, he was angrier than I'd ever seen him. Years later, and I could still remember with iron clarity, the bolt of fear that shot through me when I saw the look in his eyes. It was a darkness I'd never seen in another human before, a desire to inflict as much pain as possible.

Levi shifted slightly, until his leg was lined up against mine, the gentle warmth and pressure of him sinking into me.

I fidgeted with my nails and pressed them into the soft flesh of my palm, stopping when Levi clocked the movement, brows tipped in concern.

"Anxious habit," I said. "Don't even usually realize I'm doing it."

He handed me the label he'd already peeled from the wine bottle. "I have those, too."

I took the label and started peeling it into thin strips, as I let myself think about that night for the first time in a long time.

The first thing I remembered was waking to Sora's screams. Joe was out, and Cheryl was an absurdly deep sleeper—aided, most nights, by a few pills.

When Rina and I tore from our rooms, we found Blake hovering over Sora in the hallway, a knife pressed against her abdomen, his eyes wild with rage. I could smell the alcohol on his breath, like it had perfumed the entire hall.

Rina screamed and ran toward him, using all her weight to pull his arm away from her sister, but he lashed out. He threw her into the corner of the wall, where it lined up with the banister, his knife lodging inside of her abdomen.

There was a soft cry to my right, and I found Cheryl there,

standing in her bedroom doorway, her eyes wide with horror, frozen like her brain refused to process the scene in real time.

Blake yanked the blade from Rina's stomach, and I ran over to her, blinking back tears as I held my hands against the wound. I tried to stem the bleeding like I always saw them do on TV, but there was so much blood. More than I'd ever seen. Her shirt and the floor beneath were coated in it, and when I looked down, I found that my arms and knees were too.

Panicked, Blake pressed his ear to her chest, then started yelling over and over to his mother that she was dead.

"Gone," he'd yelled, "gone, gone, gone." Like he was a petulant child who'd lost his favorite toy.

My ears rang, and I remembered feeling like I was there, but also not. Like I was watching the scene from outside of my body. I couldn't feel anything, couldn't make myself believe what had happened.

Sora crawled over to us, her scream reverberating through the hall, but it seemed so far away, like it was outside somehow.

I remembered thinking at the time that that was good, that maybe the neighbors would hear her and come, that maybe they'd help Rina—since Cheryl was absolutely useless. But Blake's words kept circling my thoughts on repeat—she was gone, she was gone, she was gone.

Panicking, Blake grabbed Sora by the hair and tugged, his eyes wide with fear. He started mumbling about how he had to kill us all too, because we saw what he'd done.

Cheryl had tears running down her cheeks, her eyes locked on her son—but she didn't move.

She was just going to stand there and let him do it again.

Anger, deep and relentless and unlike anything I'd ever felt before seared through me, iron hot. I ran over to him, punching and clawing at his face, fighting desperately to get Sora out of his grip, to turn his vengeance away from her.

He tried to fight me off with his free hand, the one still

clutching his knife. The blade sliced along my arm, but it didn't hurt. I couldn't feel anything in that moment, only all-consuming fury. I didn't think, I just acted. In one fluid movement I placed my hand over his, wrestling for control until I twisted the blade in the direction I wanted it to be planted.

Shocked, his grip freed Sora. His eyes locked on mine as he screamed, his rancid breath hot on my face. He wrapped his now-empty hand around my throat, his fingers tight and unrelenting while I fought to peel them away. As my vision clouded, I abandoned the attempt, instead driving the knife deeper into his stomach, until he finally let go.

From his mother's perspective, my back to hers, we probably looked like we'd frozen—locked in an embrace, a temporary truce. Like he'd just lost his footing and stumbled down the stairs, the knife sinking into his stomach in the process, a twisted mirror to Rina's wound.

I fell to my knees, my fingers tracing the remnants of his grip, my throat sore and scratchy as I sucked down air.

When I turned back to Cheryl, her mouth was gaping open, like she wanted to scream but no sound would come out.

To this day, I still wasn't completely sure whether she'd seen everything, whether she knew the truth—that I was the one who'd slid that knife through his skin as if it was nothing more than butter. That I'd do it again and again without another thought.

Most likely not. Something told me that if she knew what I'd done, she wouldn't have let us leave as easily as she had.

After a long, panicked moment she fumbled her way over to her son, shaking and silent as she checked for a pulse. Only when she heard a car turning up the driveway did she stir back to life. Face pale, eyes bloodshot, she turned back to us looking more haunted and broken than anything I'd ever seen.

She mouthed the word, "Run," and Sora and I only hesitated long enough to glance at Rina's lifeless body, still and bloody on the floor, an image to gut us in our nightmares for years to come. But then we never looked back.

"One night, he attacked us," I said, editing the night down, skipping over the parts I could never put words to.

That he'd attacked us far more than once.

That I'd fought back that night.

That Blake's death was ultimately ruled a tragic accident— nothing more than an after-school special about the dangers of underaged drinking and drugs.

That there was never any mention of Rina's death at all—a final attempt on Cheryl and Joe's part to cover up for their son one last time. Why tarnish his name with murder, too, right?

That no one came looking for us. Either because no one noticed that we were missing in the chaos, or maybe they did but they didn't want to use expensive resources trying to hunt us down, or because Cheryl and Joe hid our tracks for us. It was the only shard of protection they had left to offer after failing so miserably all those times we'd begged them to listen—after pretending for months not to see the bruises or cuts, the lost looks in our eyes.

That before that night, I'd spent weeks lying awake in their home, wishing for Blake's death, for the death curse to be real, just this once—only for it to be granted two minutes too late.

That powerful people could get away with anything, could warp the world to fit whatever reality benefited them most. While the rest of us paid the price.

That Rina paid a price steeper than any of us.

Joe had even won his election, the town's pity from his son's death no doubt lifting him up in the polls. Last I'd read, he and Cheryl had started a church—no doubt to cleanse their hands of guilt. Rina would still be alive if they'd taken their son's actions more seriously.

I stopped looking them up years ago, desperate to leave that entire life behind.

"We fought back," I said, my mouth dry. I took another sip of the wine. "We made it out of the situation alive. But after that night, after that place, we didn't want to get stuck in another shitty situation and we didn't want to be split up. So, Sora and I ran." It took everything to keep my voice even—the tendrils of barely-constrained anger tugging at the seams I'd sewn so tightly over the years. "We ended up in Seattle and we laid low until we aged out of the system and could take our lives back into our own hands. The night we met you, we were looking for our first real apartment. Starting fresh, finally."

"What happened to the son?" Levi asked, his voice thick and stiffer than usual.

I gave him a small, sad smile, took another long swig of the wine, and then gave him the only truth that I would ever be able to offer where Blake was concerned. "He never hurt us again."

19

MAREENA
PRESENT DAY

The air was dry, laced with the tangy scent of driftwood and brine. And there, just on the edges, I could make out the soothing smell of musky attar and just a hint of mint. I took a deep breath, savoring the taste across my tongue, the way it filled me up, the way it made me whole.

Hazy shards of sunlight pierced through the window, framing the room in a kaleidoscope of colors.

I knew this room. And I knew it deeply. Knew the pale blue stripes of the comforter that had faded from years of washing, the poorly traced cedar trees painted along the far wall. Knew not to step on the plank of wood just before the doorway if I didn't want to announce my presence; that if I looked under the bed, I'd find a stash of books I kept hidden but still in reach, so that I could read late into the night when I was supposed to be asleep. Knew that if I opened the window, I'd hear the familiar song of the waves down the road as they crashed their greeting into the shoreline.

And in my palm, I knew that the tarnished loop of metal that rested there, tied me to this place, to this life, to this time—even though I couldn't understand why or how.

Pocketing the ring, I leaped over the door frame and out into the hall, my heart racing at the possibility that I was back, that she was here.

"Amto," I yelled, and my voice echoed out higher and more youthful than I was used to—and the laughter that spilled out at the shock of it only sharpened the strangeness. "Amto Am—"

Her name died on my tongue when she came into view.

Just as I remembered, but somehow still different.

Her gray hair, wiry yet soft, was pulled back against her neck, a few stray curls loose around her face. She had her linen sleeves bunched up to her elbows, the tawny-brown shade of her skin luminous against the sharp white fabric.

There was a large mat on the counter in front of her, where she was busy separating, stuffing, and rolling the grape leaves, her fingers moving seamlessly through the process, like she'd spent a lifetime perfecting it.

The faintest hum of a long-forgotten song trailed through the room, cutting off only when she looked up and spotted me watching her.

Her crooked smile made my breath catch.

"There you are, habibti, I thought you might sleep the entire day away." Her voice still had the soft, melodic cadence it always did, with the unexpected sharp edge that caught strangers by surprise and added a layer of depth to it.

"I'm awake," was all that I managed. I couldn't pull my eyes from hers. They were large and brown, and just as warm as I remembered them being. Just as welcoming. Just as wise. "I'm here now."

"Good," she nodded, "that's good. We'll take a walk in a few minutes. It's a beautiful day." She pointed her finger at me. It was smudged with tomato paste. A knowing smile carved across her lips, revealing the small chip in the corner of her front tooth. "Lucky girl —a beautiful day to celebrate a birthday."

And just like that, my stomach sank, though I couldn't fully understand why.

I thumbed the ring out of my pocket, my gaze caught between trying to soak up as much of my aunt as I could and staring at this ring, trying to remember why it was important. Why it kept stealing my focus.

When I looked back up at her, she wasn't alone.

"You." My voice came out a deep bellow, filled with all the threat and dread I could muster at ten years old. "Leave this place."

A man, with hair as black as the abyss and eyes the shade of crystallized amber stood behind her, his head hovering over hers as his unnatural stare met mine. There was no emotion on his face, no regret and no sorrow.

Something about him was so familiar, the recognition like a bolt through my chest, though I couldn't remember where I'd seen him before.

He slid his hand through her chest as if she was made of nothing more solid than air, and then she crumbled at his feet, the tray of grape leaves tumbling to the floor and scattering all around her.

"No," I screamed and fought to run to her, but my feet refused to carry me. Instead, they stood there, useless blocks of cement, leaving me with no other option but to scream and cry from afar.

"It's not your time," the man said, his emotionless eyes locked on mine as he drained her of her life, "but it will be one day."

This. This moment was where I recognized him from. Those eyes haunted this day with the persistence of a predator.

"Amto," I screamed, her name on my lips more the screech and metallic wail of a feral thing, than the cries of a young girl. I bent over, tried my best at clawing myself forward, hopeful that if my feet wouldn't obey me, my talons might. "Don't touch her."

But the man paid me no more heed, his focus now funneled to the task at hand. And when he was done, he left without a passing glance, leaving me alone and fumbling over a broken corpse.

Death was only good for one thing—an empty, relentless hunger —and when he demanded a meal, it was best served in cold blood.

"It's okay, you're okay," a deep, rumbling voice vibrated into my back, jangling against my ribs. "Breathe, Agony. Breathe. It was just a dream."

I choked on the whiplash of being pulled from that scene to this one. My bedding had tumbled to the floor, and my skin was caked in sticky sweat.

My arms flailed in front of me, searching for Amto Amani, but I couldn't move.

"Breathe," the voice said again, its whisper a soft caress at the shell of my ear.

Light poured through the window, and when I glanced up, I noticed Menace standing on my dresser, watching me, unsure whether to approach.

My body was caged between two strong, tattooed arms, and my heart beat a heavy protest against their firm grip.

Slowly, they relented, and I took advantage of the sudden freedom, scooting to the edge of my bed.

I brushed my hair from my eyes, wincing at how slick my skin was, and then froze when I saw him. "Kieran?"

His eyes were hard as they darted between mine, his face edged with concern. He lifted his hands between us, as if approaching a timid animal, and sat up. "You were having a nightmare."

I nodded.

It was a frequent nightmare—one with a thousand variations and shifts, though the ending was always the same.

Always that man. Always those eyes. And always Amto Amani's empty shell.

"Did you stay here all night?" I asked, not bothering to keep the accusation from my voice.

He winced. "When you fell asleep, you shifted onto my chest, and I didn't want to wake you." He ran his hand through his rumpled hair, looking suddenly shy. "I waited for a while, but then I guess I . . . dozed off, too." The corner of his lips dipped as he stared at my pillow. "It wasn't planned. I don't usually sleep much in this realm. Or much at all, really."

I stood, feeling self-conscious of the silk shorts and baggy T-shirt, and the chaotic bird's nest that was my hair.

Without glancing back at him, I walked over to Menace and stroked the back of his head. "Morning."

He nipped affectionately at my finger and followed me to my door, flying through it the moment I opened it and straight toward his bowl of treats.

Honestly, I was surprised to find him in my bedroom. Menace was usually skittish around strangers, but he seemed to be warming up quickly to Keiran.

The apartment was quiet, unusually so.

Judging by the fact that I hadn't been awoken by an alarm, and the digital clock on the stove was out, there had been another power surge.

It was rare for me to sleep this late.

I ran to Sora's room, to see if she'd overslept, too, but it was empty.

Taking the stairs two at a time, I charged into the restaurant, expecting to find her behind the counter, the chaos of the breakfast rush slowly dissipating. Without electricity, it would have been an unexciting meal, but we kept provisions on hand to keep the people fed when our cooking resources were limited.

But the restaurant was empty, shaded by the blinds still pulled over the window, the entire room looking just as it had when I'd closed everything down last night.

She hadn't opened it this morning.

My racing pulse leftover from the dream now had a new source of fear to fuel it.

When I turned around, ready to call up to him, I collided with his chest instead.

"She didn't come home last night," I said, fighting back the waver in my voice.

Kieran eyed me for a moment, his stare roving over the diner as if I just hadn't looked hard enough. Something hardened in his features, and he nodded, his gaze returning to me. "Go get ready, we'll look for her."

Half an hour later, we stood outside the entrance to the market. The single optimistic bone that I had in my body suggested that maybe she was here. I usually opened the diner on Thursdays, and Sora usually spent the morning wading through the market stalls, finding new ingredients we could work into the weekend's menu.

Maybe she was here. Maybe she decided it was best to close until the electricity was back up and take care of this in the meantime.

Generally, I avoided coming down here. The place was always packed and full of people, demon and human—all of them bartering for resources in a more tension-filled echo of what Seattle's market culture used to look like.

When phones and the internet became unreliable and unreasonably expensive, I found myself almost glad to be rid of the distraction—the permission to unplug and engage more on a local level had been unexpectedly welcome. Right now, I would give anything for my old phone, and the option to reach Sora in two seconds flat.

"Well," Kieran said, surveying the bustling crowd, "at least she has blue hair. That'll make her easier to pick out."

"Why didn't I bring a fucking picture of her?" I sighed. "Could've shown people, asked if they'd seen her recently."

For fifteen minutes, I went stall-to-stall, asking the artisans and customers if they'd seen Sora—if they knew who she was —while Kieran acted as an invisible sentinel, his eyes hunting for that recognizable ball of blue hair and energy. But the people here didn't know me, didn't trust me, and if they had seen Sora, they weren't interested in telling me as much.

My chest was tight, my fists clenched, as I fought back the impending wave of panic that I'd been trying to suffocate all morning. This was useless.

Where else could she be? Where would she have gone?

Did she go see the new girl she'd been dating, the one she met at the club? But I didn't even know her name, or where she lived. I didn't know where to even start.

"You owe me four weeks' worth," a tall, muscular man barked at a stall next to us. "I've been unreasonably patient."

A much smaller man, with deep red hair and emerald green eyes winced, nodding so intensely that he looked like one of those old bobblehead dolls. "I know, I know, I'm sorry."

The angry man grabbed the bobblehead by the front of his shirt, tugging him forward until they were nose-to-nose. "Patience isn't one of my virtues, Rex. Where's the pendant? I'll take that as payment."

"Rex," I whispered, the name sparking some faded memory.

Wasn't that Sora's new market friend?

The one who'd gotten us on the list for Incendiary?

"Hey," I said, louder this time.

"What the hell are you doing?" Kieran asked, his eyes wide with shock.

"What?" The burly guy turned toward me, dragging Rex along by his neck.

"Let him go," I said.

Kieran sighed, his mouth tight. "Never mind. Why did I ask? Of course you're picking a fight with the biggest, scariest looking guy in a two-mile radius. Why would you be doing anything else?"

"Be quiet." I glared at him.

The bully wrinkled his nose in confusion. "Didn't say anything."

"Not you," I shot back, quickly losing my temper.

"Not even a single ounce of self-preservation does she have." Kieran sighed. "Of course, this is the girl I'd get saddled with looking out for."

"No one asked you to follow me," I said, then turning to Rex and ignoring the bully altogether, I asked, "Have you seen my roommate, Sora?"

"No one asked me, actually. I don't have much of a choice in the matter." Kieran's jaw was tight as he studied the two men in front of me. "And in case you forgot, I can't touch them. Which means that I can't protect you." He shook his head. "I don't get it. Are you *trying* to get yourself killed? Because there are less messy ways."

"Don't know her," Rex said, his voice a wheeze.

I narrowed my eyes on him. "I don't believe you."

"You shouldn't," the bully said, his face smug. "He's a liar and thief. Now if you'll excuse us—"

"Was she here today?" I balled my fingers into a fist. "Did you see her last night? She didn't come home, and I'm worried about her." Maybe appealing to his own fear would help my case. Sora had called this man a friend, hadn't she?

He shook his head, though the movement was stilted by the man's grip on him. "Like I said, don't know your friend. Now get out of here."

I took a deep breath. "One more chance, Rex. Do you know where she might be? I'm not messing around."

"I said beat it," he snapped, his eyes dark and filled with malice when they landed on mine.

"Fine." I pulled back my arm and surged my fist forward, focusing on the follow-through when it met with his freckled nose. It already had a bump, like it had been broken once or twice before, so hopefully I didn't do any added permanent damage.

The crack echoed around us, and the bully dropped his hold on Rex as blood splattered across his face.

Wincing, I flexed my hand. Sore, but there wouldn't be lasting injuries.

"What the fuck, Agony?" Kieran pressed close against my back. "We need to get out of here. Immediately."

"You said find my joy, right?" I ground out, shooting a look back at him. "This is me doing that. No joy until I know that my best friend is okay."

The bully glanced from me to Rex, then swiped away a smear of blood on his pale skin. His face twitched into a vaguely impressed expression. "Not bad. Decent form."

"Thanks."

He sniffed once then shrugged. "Fine, you can deal with him for now. I'll come collect later, Rex." He started to walk away, then turned back to him, his finger extended in warning. "And don't forget, stop by the house later. Maryanne's making your favorite stew, she'll be hurt if you miss it. But clean yourself up first."

"Yeah, yeah," Rex muttered, spitting out a spray of red. He ran his hands down his pants, straightening them out, as if that was the part of his outfit that needed the tidying. Then he shot me a glare, swiped the blood from his face on the sleeve of his shirt, and with a wince and quick crack, snapped his nose back into place. "I assume you're Mars, then?"

"Mareena," I corrected, my fingers jittery now that the moment was settling. "Sorry," I added, gesturing to his face. "I think the tension of the moment got to me and I went a little overboard."

Why had I punched him? Kieran was right. What the fuck was I thinking?

The market goers walked around us, occasionally with a

lingering stare at Rex, but otherwise seemed generally unconcerned about the sudden bloodshed.

"Don't worry about it." He sighed, running his fingers gently over the bridge of his nose as if testing to see if it was, indeed, properly realigned. "I tend to bring out the violence in people." He ripped the pendant dangling from his neck off and set it down on the counter of his booth. "This fuckin' thing's more trouble than it's worth."

Some talisman of some sort. Witchcraft, maybe? Did he practice?

At this point, I wasn't sure I wanted to know.

"Here." I offered him a tight smile, then grabbed the bandana tied around my bag and handed it to him. "For the, uh —" I rubbed my nose to illustrate where blood was still pouring from his. "You know."

"Thanks," he said, blowing his nose into the cloth. I definitely would not be asking for that back. "And I was telling the truth—mostly. I haven't seen Sora today."

"But you do know her." I narrowed my eyes. "Well enough to know who I am."

He nodded, shoving the bandana in his pocket. "Yeah, she's a nice girl. One of the few regulars who's still kind to me around here."

I winced, feeling worse for the whole punch thing. "Sounds like Sora. Not a mean bone in her body—unless you crossed her."

He shook his head, then his eyes darted to mine briefly before scanning the people lurking around. "She's really missing?"

"Yes," I said.

"And you're actually concerned? You're sure she didn't just take an impromptu holiday or sexcation?"

"Sexcation?" Kieran wrinkled his nose in confusion. "The fuck is that?"

"Look, I'm certain. This isn't like her. We always check in. Do you have any idea where she could be?" My eyes started to well with tears and I choked on a sob. "Please."

"Emotions are often heightened around me." He glanced at my eyes and started to hand my bandana back to me until I vigorously shook my head. "Been that way since The Undoing. It's why I like Sora so much. Usually run into her when she's already in a good mood." He sighed, then ran his hand through his red waves. "Okay, I don't know where she is, but I do know what she might be after."

I took a step toward him. "After? What do you mean?"

He bit his lip, considering for a second. "Alright. Look, are you familiar with the Sect of Azrael?"

I nodded and my chest was so tight it felt like it was on fire.

"She came to me a couple of weeks ago. She was real down. Unusual for her, you know?" He glanced at me and shrugged. "Hated seeing her like that. She's one of my few sparks of joy around here. But when I started talking to her, she mentioned her sister—mentioned that the anniversary of her death was coming up." He winced at whatever emotion he saw reflected on my face—anger, fear, grief, maybe all three. "I might have talked to her about a ritual I'd heard of."

"Ritual," I repeated, my voice hollow.

Kieran was glued to my side, the back of his hand brushing against mine. "Easy, Agony. Breathe. Try to rein it in until you get the information you need."

"You know—" Rex shrugged and started to fiddle with the rocks and random beads on his cart. "Not a guarantee or nothing, but a possibility. There've been rumors."

"What did you tell her?" I asked. My finger pressed into my ring so hard, I was at risk of breaking it. "What did this ritual"—I spat the word—"of yours require?"

"Woah, woah." He put his hands up. "Let's be real clear. Not my ritual. I'm just the conveyor of information. Don't get mad at the messenger."

"Tell me."

He sighed, glanced around to make sure no one was eavesdropping, then gestured for me to get closer. "It requires three things. First, a shard of Michael. Second, the human completing the ritual needs to exchange blood with a vampire." He held up three fingers, the creases of his knuckles still lined with his blood. "Third, she needs to complete the ritual at a place touched by magic."

I clenched my jaw. "And this ritual—what does it do?"

"Like I said"—Rex spread his hands out—"no guarantees, but when I was with the Sect, they were certain this could help the living commune with the dead."

There was a loud caw, and shiny black wings swept over the table. Menace swiped whatever pendant Rex had just yanked off his neck, then flew to an awning across the street.

Rex tossed a rock in his direction but missed by several feet. "That fucking crow keeps jacking my goods."

"I'll get it back for you, but finish telling me what you know," I said, my focus darting from Menace back to the table of random rocks and gadgets. It mostly looked like junk. "You peddle these fake charms and talismans to people. Did you do the same to Sora?"

He clicked his teeth. "Fake? No. Who says it's fake?" He shook his head. "And I told her several times that the ritual was a long shot. I'd never seen it done, didn't know anyone with firsthand experience. Could be total crap, for all I know. But I thought I was helping—offering her some hope about some possible option in the future, when it might be feasible, you know?"

"You were helping yourself." My hands were clamped in two fists again as I took another step toward him. "Trying to manipulate her back into her cheery, hopeful self. For your benefit. Not hers."

Sora didn't trust people easily. She wouldn't charge into a dangerous situation without thinking it through, talking it out.

But she might skip some corners if it meant seeing Rina again.

I cursed, my hand curling into a fist again.

"Okay, okay." He stepped back, bumping into his table and knocking his wares to the ground. "Look, I sold her a necklace. Blue—very nice, very rare. Matched her hair and everything. Was just trying to give her some hope. Make her smile. Didn't think anything more would come of it."

Shit. The pendant Menace had swiped and stocked away in his treasure box last week.

I took a slow, steady breath, trying to calm the rage bubbling inside of me. "And Incendiary; you got us into the club last week. Why?"

"She came back a few days later, a lot brighter, a lot happier —her usual self. She mentioned the club, wanting to go. I didn't think anything of it at the time. Everyone wants to get a ticket into that place. How was I supposed to assume she wanted more than a nice night out with her roommate?" He tilted his head from side to side. "Couple people owed me favors. I called them in." He shrugged. "Like I said, I felt bad. I was trying to make her happy. I was doing something nice."

Nice. I grunted.

Incendiary was a place for a nice night out. It was also a place where someone could casually introduce themself to a vampire.

I turned to Kieran. "Let's go."

"Hey," Rex called out when we started to leave. "I really do hope she's okay. And I don't know—maybe it will be worth it. Maybe the ritual will work. She just wants to see her sister again."

I froze, my body vibrating with barely constrained anger. As if I didn't understand my best friend's motivations. As if I didn't know that she wanted to see her fucking sister again. Of course she fucking did.

But that's not what he cared about.

"I'm supposed to be finding my joy," I mumbled. "Instead, I'm only finding my rage."

Kieran glanced down at me, his mouth pressed into that smirk of his. "I don't know, Agony. Gotta say, rage looks pretty good on you, too."

"Hey, wait!" When I didn't turn or respond, Rex's voice only grew louder. "What about my pendant? You said you'd get it back for me."

I closed my eyes and sighed. Then I turned toward Menace and called him over.

When he latched onto my shoulder and dropped the warped leather and stone onto my palm, I thanked him, offering a piece of kibble that I kept in my bag in exchange.

Then I threw the necklace onto the ground.

The three of us left without looking back to watch him scramble for it.

"What now?" Kieran asked, his expression unreadable.

"We visit Incendiary again," I said. "Tonight."

20

MAREENA
PRESENT DAY

"You're not on the list." The bouncer didn't even spare me a second glance. It was the same guy who was here last week.

"I know I'm not on the list," I said. "I'm not here to party. I just need to see if my friend is here."

"What's her name?" he asked, his voice a bored drawl. When I told him, he just shook his head. "She's not on the list either."

"I know that she's not on the list. Please just let me check to see if she's here?"

"No name, no entry. It's a simple rule, girl." He nodded toward the line of people huddling behind me. "You see them? They understand that rule. Feel free to join that line, and maybe you'll be one of the lucky ones granted entry."

I pinched the bridge of my nose, begging whatever gods existed for a shred of patience. "My friend met a woman inside, when we were here last week. I don't know her name. But now my friend is missing, and that woman might know where I can find her. Please, I just need to take a quick look."

"No name, no entry," he said again, then looked me over, a

flash of recognition passing over his features. It should. I was wearing the exact same thing I'd worn last week. I had no patience to put together another outfit the club might deem worthy of granting me entrance for. "Human, right?"

I nodded.

"Humans are required to wait the required three weeks before being granted entry again. You're not above the rules."

Kieran snorted. "How many humans do you know that can talk to dead people and share apartments with crombies? This girl doesn't follow any rules."

I bit the inside of my cheeks.

Kieran sighed. "This is getting us nowhere."

"Clearly," I muttered.

The bouncer shot me a suspicious look. "Leave now, before I make you."

"Come on, Agony," Kieran said, nodding toward the street we'd arrived from. When I resisted, he added, "Just trust me. I have an idea."

"Fine," I grumbled, then turned my back on the unhelpful bouncer and followed my stalker into a dark alley.

We were silent as we passed the line of eager people, all just as desperate as I was to get into the club.

When we reached the dumpsters, Kieran shot me a smirk, then turned into a narrow alley.

The same one he'd fucked me in last week.

The flare of recognition sent a brief wave of heat through my body, but it was quickly dampened by the anger and stress of our significantly different circumstances tonight.

Kieran's triumphant expression dissolved into frustration when we found the door. "Fuck." He turned back to me. "Do you remember this door not opening from the outside?"

I shook my head as I ran my fingers over the seams of the all but invisible doorway, hoping for a secret latch or something.

"Suppose we were a bit distracted," he muttered.

"You can get through though, can't you?" I made an exploding gesture with my hands. "Just do your ghostie transparency trick and walk through the wall."

"I don't blow up." He shot me a disgruntled look as if I'd insulted him. "And like I said, I may be dead, but I'm not a ghost. Ghosts aren't real. Phantoms are as close as it gets."

"At this point, it really seems more like semantics than any—" I pinched the bridge of my nose. "Whatever, that's not the point. Can't you just . . . slip inside and see if you find her?"

"Probably." He flexed his hand again, and I noticed that the veins in his arms looked darker than usual—almost strained. "I won't be able to go very far from you, but it's worth a try at least."

"Great," I said, shoving away my questions about his arm. I rifled through my bag and handed him the picture of Sora I remembered to bring this time. It was several years old, and folded down the middle, but it would serve our purpose tonight. "Ask people if they've seen her."

Kieran studied me for a moment. "How exactly am I supposed to do that? You are the only person who can see or hear me."

Right. Fuck.

"What did the girl look like? The one you saw her with last week? Maybe I can see if I can spot her? Or I suppose we could wait at the entrance to see if she leaves? Though people often don't leave this place until well into the morning, so no guarantee that will work."

"We're not waiting until morning." I leaned back on the trick door and groaned, trying to picture the woman from that night, but I'd only gotten a brief glimpse of her. I'd been focusing more on the excitement lighting Sora's face and then, later, on Kieran.

Closing my eyes, I tried to recall the details of that night, to think of another option that might help us get into the club.

And then, as if answering my silent plea, the trick door shifted and opened—just a crack, but enough for me to slip inside.

Well, fell inside was maybe the better descriptor.

When I caught myself against the wall, the same gentle hum I'd experienced last week bolted through my body. It felt like the building was pleased that I was back, like I wouldn't have made it to this side of the wall unless it wanted me here.

The door was closed again, but there was no handle on this side either. Had it let us out last week as well?

"Curious," Kieran said, his chest glued to my back as he reached to touch the wall, "this building granted you entry. I wonder why."

I leaned into Kieran, and my entire body came alive at his nearness.

Fuck.

When we'd been planning for tonight, I hadn't even considered this part. How difficult it would be to hide my attraction to him in this place. Not that it had been particularly easy the past couple of days either, but something about this place made it impossible to deny.

"You're warmer in here," I said, turning around to look at him. Of course, that only left us chest to chest, his mouth suspiciously close to mine, as if he'd been bending his face to my hair. I cleared my throat and backed up against the wall. "More like you were last week, I mean."

His stare leveled at me, then lingered on my mouth. "Told you this place was like a power boost. The shadow magic that fuels it is the same that fuels me."

"Right." Tearing my gaze from him, I scanned the place, not entirely sure where to start, but deeply certain that I needed to not be standing in a secluded hallway pressed up against my very off-limits guardian angel. "I suppose we should start looking."

"Lead the way," he said.

After the first fifteen people glanced at the wrinkled photo without a flicker of recognition, I started to get frustrated; after the next twenty did the exact same, this entire venture seemed suddenly futile.

I scanned every face that I saw, but no flare of recognition hit me either.

That meant that the chances of me recalling the woman Sora had met last week were dwindling quickly—or that she wasn't here tonight, which seemed far more likely.

I did my best to steer through the crowd in a way that kept me out of the bartenders' view line. While I didn't think they would remember me from last night, I didn't want to risk getting tossed out of here. Something told me that they wouldn't be gentle about it.

The dance floor was just as packed, just as lust filled as it had been last week, and I had to actively fight my body's impulse to join into the lull of it.

Just when I was starting to think this was perhaps the most useless idea I'd ever had, a man next to me squinted at the photo I'd just shoved under his face.

"Do you know her?" I asked my chest aching with hope at the hesitant recognition in his eyes.

He was a lean, tall, Black man with a kind face and warm eyes, dressed in a vibrant-green pantsuit that matched his eyeliner and lashes. "Know her? No." His voice was deep and velvety, and he carefully grabbed the photo from me. The lights reflected against his sharp cheekbones as he studied it. They were highlighted in an iridescent glitter that was entrancing under the mood lighting. Something about the gentle energy he exuded soothed the anxious frustration that had been building in me. "But she does look familiar."

"She's my roommate," I yelled, leaning closer to him in a desperate attempt to compete with the heavy base. "Please, she's missing. Can you recall if you've seen her recently? Or at all?"

His focus shifted from the photo to me, his lips dipping into a small frown as he studied me. Concern or pity, I wasn't entirely sure which. With a single nod, he tapped the shoulder of the woman next to him. She was dancing with a group of three people, her deep brown eyes glazed with the energy of the crowd, and maybe something even stronger. None of them wore a band that marked the humans from the demons. "Is this the girl that your friend Lav was with last week?"

It took a moment for the girl's focus to shift, but when it did, I saw the same flash of recognition on her face as I'd found on her friend's.

She nodded. When the man bent down to whisper into her ear, her eyes darted to mine.

I held my breath, and only when I felt his fingers fold over mine did I realize that I'd unconsciously reached for Kieran's hand.

The girl leaned forward. She was white, and just as stunning as her friend, though dressed in a more muted color palette. Her breath was warm as she grabbed my shoulder with gentle fingers before pressing her mouth against my ear. "She was here last week, with a vampire named Lav." Her voice was unexpectedly high, even as a whisper, almost girlish. "I don't know if Lav is here tonight, but if she is, you're more likely to find her in the basement. That's where she spends most of her time."

"Thank you," I said, then turned to her friend, hoping my expression conveyed the depth of my gratitude, on the likelihood the music muted it, "both of you."

"Good luck," the girl said. "I hope you find her."

Kieran and I wound our way toward the back, though I noticed that he kept his hand pressed close to his chest and avoided bumping into anyone, even though he could simply pass through them if he wanted.

When we reached the door that he'd stopped me from going through last week, the one that Lenora and Ren had disappeared through, my heartbeat skipped.

"You sure this is a good idea?" he asked, and his breath against my neck sent chills down my spine. "We don't know how these rooms will affect you."

"Right now it's the only idea." I opened the door. "Let's go."

As we descended, the energy of the club changed—the power amplified so intensely that I was practically panting from it by the time we reached the bottom.

"Fuck." Kieran hissed behind me, and I felt the featherlight pressure of his fingers against the bare flesh of my arm.

I gasped at the sensation, and it took every ounce of my willpower not to lean into him.

The room was segmented with dozens of closed doors and private areas scattered around the outskirts. Soft red light glowed throughout the otherwise dark room, and the center of it was framed by tables and chairs. There were . . . performances of a sort unfolding on the stage in the middle.

A woman naked and in the feral throes of unashamed passion, was straddled over two men—both of whom seemed to be impaling her. The three of them were tangled together, a mess of sweaty limbs and moans.

I stood there, stunned as the woman sank her teeth into one of the men's shoulders, drawing blood. She drank her fill, then let the remnants of his blood slide down her chin, her neck, her chest. Her blue eyes were alive with lust, and when the orgasm rippled through her, I clenched my thighs as if it were mine.

"Just going to stand there all on your own, sweetheart?" A man approached; his dark eyes shot through with flares of yellow gold. "Or would you prefer some company? There are very few fantasies that go unrealized down here. You only have to say the words."

When he took a step closer, I felt a deep rumble vibrate against my back.

Kieran's chest was pressed up against me, and when he wrapped his arm around my waist, tugging me to him, my stomach tightened.

The man couldn't see or hear him, of course, but I leaned into his hold, liking the feel of it way more than I should.

"I'm—no thank you," I said, my voice lower and hoarser than I was used to. With trembling fingers, I held the picture of Sora with him. "Have you seen this girl?"

The man's eyebrows raised in surprise as he studied the image. "So, she's your type then?"

"I—what?" Shaking my head, I hastily added, "I'm looking for her. Or a woman named Lav, I think. Is she here?"

"I haven't seen the girl in your picture but—" His lips curved into a salacious grin as his stare dipped back to my face. "I did see Lav go into that room." He pointed to the third door on the left. "Perhaps an hour or two ago. It's hard to say. I have a habit of losing time down here. Premium membership will do that to you."

"Thank you," I said, grabbing the picture back from his reluctant grip. "Have a good night."

When I started to move toward the room he'd indicated, my legs shaking with fear or need or some combination of both, he grabbed my wrist.

Kieran tried to rip the man away from me, but his fingers simply slipped straight through him unnoticed by the demon entirely.

"You can't go in there," the man said. "Not without being invited by all consenting guests inside." He nodded toward an empty table. "You will need to wait until they are done."

Wait? For how long?

He'd said Lav had gone in an hour or two ago, hadn't he? How much longer could she take? And what . . . what exactly was she doing in there?

"Grab a drink," the man said, setting his eyes on another man across the room who was unabashedly checking him out. "Try to enjoy yourself in the meantime."

Kieran's dark glare didn't budge from the demon until he was well across the room. Only when the two men embraced, their hands greedily roving over each other, did the tension ease from his body—and even then, only slightly.

"Well," I said, my voice as shaky as my legs, "I guess we wait."

"You shouldn't stay here," he said, the lines of his jaw stiff enough to cut ice. His eyes darted from person to person, studying each one as if he anticipated an attack. "It's not safe."

"I'm not leaving until I have a lead on Sora." I made my way toward the bar, done with the debate, and ordered a water with as much confidence as I could muster. Could the demons down here smell the human on me? I wasn't entirely sure how that worked. And I didn't want to get thrown out of here before speaking to this Lav lady.

Devoting most of my focus to keeping my hands still enough to keep the water in my glass, I walked toward a small table in a dark corner, one with a good view of the door the vampire was apparently on the other side of.

"I just need to try and blend in," I said, scooting gracelessly into the deep booth, "go unnoticed."

Kieran's stare speared through me. "That's not possible."

But he sat down next to me anyway, his posture rigid and the usual indifference he wore like a mask abandoned for something stuck somewhere between fear and something else I couldn't quite parse.

What did he have to fear? He was already dead.

I took a sip of the water and groaned at the electric chill of it. I'd forgotten how amazing water tasted here, how intoxicating it felt to drink. To be alive. And down here, where the power of the place seemed to practically pulse with abandon, the whole room breathing with it, the sensations were only amplified.

Kieran stiffened next to me, his eyes locked on my lips.

I wiped them over with the back of my hand, checking to see if I'd missed my mouth.

He dropped his gaze, but his expression only looked more strained. After a long, stretched moment of silence, he hissed. "You had to wear that fecking dress, didn't you?"

I looked down at myself. "What's the matter with my dress?"

"Nothing," he grunted. "That's the problem."

A loud moan echoed through the room, and my focus latched onto the small stage, and the threesome I'd somehow forgotten about. The woman's head was bent back in ecstasy as she rode one of the men. The other stood above them, gripping himself as he watched.

"Oh," I said, my mouth suddenly dry. "Right."

The back of Kieran's hand brushed against mine and I gasped at the sensation, my chest heaving like I couldn't suck down a proper breath.

I glanced at him from the corner of my eye to find him staring at where our skin touched. It was slight enough to have been accidental, but neither of us pulled away. Instead, he shifted, as if getting comfortable; but when he finally stilled, we were even closer—his thigh kissing mine.

Jaw rigid, he swallowed. Then, slowly, as if slightly hesitant, he traced the edge of my finger with the tip of his.

My mouth went dry as the featherlight touch spread a ticklish heat throughout my body, igniting into something surprisingly fierce. When I closed my eyes—whether to block out the sensations or linger in them, I wasn't entirely certain—he started to trace along my palm. He drew long, luxurious lines that had to be pure wizardry, the way they had my body responding to him. My brain began conjuring a million different scenarios of his hands all over me—not one of them sparing a single thought to all of the reasons it couldn't happen.

Right now, in this room, it felt like anything could happen. The rest of the world simply fell away.

When I opened my eyes again, his were glued to my face. The depth of his stare was impossible to read, though I thought I recognized at least a flicker of the heat raging inside of me reflected there.

I couldn't breathe as my focus dipped from his eyes to his lips, and the memory of their taste had me desperate for another.

His jaw tightened, a small muscle clenching along the edge as he watched me.

For a moment, I thought he might lean forward—close the distance and do something about the impossible ache he'd built up inside of me—but a loud, guttural moan, followed by another, broke his trance, and he pulled back.

I swallowed, turning back to see the two men on the small stage—who I'd forgotten about entirely again—spill their cum on and inside the woman, their chests moving in ragged, sated breaths.

My heart raced a raging jealousy at their unabashed plea-sure, the ease and freedom with which they chased it.

When I turned back to Kieran, my vision blurring with desire, he stilled.

His body coiled with restraint, the kind so tight it was on the edge of snapping. After a drawn moment of silence, he bent his head down to my ear. "Tell me, Agony." I swore his whisper might as well have brushed directly against my clit for all the liquid it had coating my thighs right now. "Did Dr. Mediocre's touch make your heart race like mine seems to?"

He traced my palm again, then brushed his thumb over my wrist.

"I—" I blinked. "Who?"

His mouth tipped into a wicked smirk. "We do have some time to kill, don't we?" With an uneven breath, he trailed his finger slowly over my hand, then skirted against the outer edge of my thigh. "How do you suppose we should spend it?"

My own breath came out strangled, and my knees, working without permission from my brain apparently, dipped apart, the invitation clear.

A couple sat a few feet away from us, their lids hooded but smiles warm as they whispered to each other.

"Eyes on me, Agony," Keiran said, and the command pulled my focus back to him, like a leash only he controlled. My heart drummed with an anticipation so demanding, that I felt it pulse through every vein. With agonizing slowness, he trailed his fingers beneath my dress, and my body lit on fire when they brushed against the lace edges of my underwear. "Fuck," he hissed, "you're soaked." One half of his mouth tilted up in a smirk. "You'd be the death of me if I wasn't already dead."

"We agreed, one time," I said, my voice little more than a whimper, a plea for him to disregard it. "You were pretty adamant about that before. And I—I don't mess around with anyone twice."

No one I actually liked being around anyway. And as annoying as Kieran was, I'd be lying if I said I didn't enjoy his company for the most part.

"Fuck what I said before." He studied me for a moment. "Right." His eyes filled with daring. "The curse. Everyone you let too close to you dies." He leaned into me until his lips brushed the shell of my ear. I shivered. "Like I said, good thing I'm already dead then, isn't it?"

"I—" Whatever argument I'd been about to forge died on

my lips when his finger slid over me again. A soft, needy moan tore from my throat. I was already so fucking close to the edge.

One touch, and this man had me almost undone—in a room full of people.

"You shouldn't feel this good." His voice was hoarse, deep with restraint. Too soon, he pulled his hand back and stared at his glistening fingers. His eyes were wild and dark with desire as he stared at them, hesitating only a moment before bringing them to his lips for a taste. "Shouldn't taste this good. Shouldn't make me"—he shook his head—"feel like this. I'm not supposed to feel anything. I don't get it." When he looked at me, there was genuine curiosity in his stare, bleeding through the heat. "How do you do it?"

"It's—" I whispered before fumbling for the rest of the sentence, my entire body pulsing with need, desperate for his touch, for him to fuck me like he had last week, before everything got so . . . complicated. "It's not me that's doing this to you, it's this place."

"Trust me when I say this, Agony—" He shook his head, his expression strained, almost sad. "It's you." He blinked slowly, a strangled breath releasing from his lips. "I *can't* want you." His jaw tightened. "I can't *have* you."

"Even here?" The tightly wound control I'd been keeping over my libido since he'd bowled back into my life unwound completely. I understood the reality of our situation. I was alive, he wasn't. He was my guardian, I was his charge. This couldn't go anywhere beyond this. But. . . "Just tonight?" I licked my lips. "Who would know?"

His eyes, dark and wild, latched on to mine, searching.

"Kieran." My lungs were frozen, my gaze dipping to his mouth, then the straining bulge in his pants, my mouth ravenous to taste him, too.

As if the plea was written in script across my face, he shook his head, then rubbed his hand over his forehead, looking pained. "Fecking hell."

"Are you oka—"

He groaned, eyes meeting mine again. "Fuck it."

Without another word, he slid off the booth and onto his knees, until he was kneeling in front of me. The table hovering above my thighs moved through his chest, as if it was the immaterial thing not of this world, not him. Then, careful not to lift my dress up entirely, he slid his hands up either side of my thighs and pulled me closer to the edge, until my legs were on either side of him, then he tugged my underwear down.

"I want to taste you properly." With a wicked grin that had me clenching, his eyes met mine, waiting.

It should have been a ridiculous suggestion, an absurd scene—this dead man between my knees, with a table lodged through his body like he was made of nothing but air. A room full of people surrounding us. But he felt solid and warm and so fucking good to me. More real than anyone here.

And no one could see him. So, as long as I kept my shit together, we'd be fine.

I gave him the world's subtlest nod, half my brain aware that people could see me, the other half not giving a fuck if they did —both halves fully in agreement that they would deflate and die if he didn't fulfill whatever dark promise was hidden in that look.

He dipped his head down, and I watched in amazement as it sank through my dress, his tongue solid and confident when it met my skin.

I swallowed back a moan and fought the urge to start riding his face in the middle of this club.

My fists dug into the edge of the booth as I tried to keep my body still, my expression flat, but when he slid two fingers inside of me and brushed them against my wall in a come-hither motion, like he'd been given a 3-D map to every nerve-ending in my body, all pretenses of composure went out the window.

There was a new set of performers on the stage now, and they held most of the room's attention, their moans and screams a suitable enough soundtrack to layer over my own desperate whimpers.

When he sucked on my clit, applying just enough pressure to make my vision blur, I gripped his shoulders, digging my nails into his back.

He groaned against me, as if my taste, alone, had him on the edge.

And the heat of his breath and the feral need in that sound was all that it took to pull me undone entirely.

My body clenched around his fingers as I clung to him, as he lapped me up through the waves of my release.

We stayed like that for a long moment that stretched into two, until he slid my underwear back on, somehow making it look and feel even hotter than when he'd tugged them off in the first place.

Then he dragged himself back into the seat next to me, his expression drunk and smug as he reached into his pocket, and pulled out a black ball of familiar lace. "Suppose I can't keep every pair, can I?"

"Are those—" I let the question die on my tongue when I realized that they were, in fact, the pair of underwear he'd nicked from me last week. But then the desire squeezing my chest reshaped itself when I got a better look at the hand holding them. His veins were dark as ink, the black lines bleeding from those odd rings of his, all the way up to his elbow. "Kieran, your arm. What's—"

"It's nothing," he snapped. He slid the fabric back into his pocket, then pulled his sleeves back down, concealing his hand from my sight. "Don't worry about it."

"You look like you're in pain." I reached for his arm, all

subtlety gone as the couple next to me shot me confused stares. "Something's wrong, you're getting worse."

"I'm dead, Agony," he said. The corner of his mouth twitched into a sad smile. "There is no worse."

I heard the lie cutting through his voice. "Kieran—"

My protest was stopped by the sound of someone clearing their throat above me.

When I turned around and glanced up, I found myself staring at a very stunning, very familiar, very angry woman.

"Villette," I said, offering her a weak smile. "Um, good to see you again."

If looks could kill, I would've been dead twenty-times over with just one second under her stare. Livid didn't even begin to cover it.

"You are—one"—she held up a single finger, with a pristinely shaped, very sharp nail—"not supposed to return for another two weeks. At least. Two"—another nail met the first—"required to be on a list to gain entry. Three, you're required to meet with me for pre-approval, a wellness check, and band. And finally—" Her nostrils flared slightly, like she was losing control of the very fragile threads of her rage. "I'm absolutely positive that I made it abundantly clear that you were never allowed beyond the main floor."

"I know, but—"

"You've not only risked my business and the wellbeing and credibility of this entire establishment," she snapped, "but your own life. Do you know how lucky you are to be alive right now, human? What the hell were you thinking? Your lust is like a neon sign right now. Were you—"

"My friend is in trouble." I bottled the shame and fear vying for center stage in my stomach and met her stare. "I was told that she met with a vampire named Lav last week. That she is here tonight. And I need to speak with her. I'm—"

"Careful, Mareena," Kieran said, his body stiff as his eyes darted between me and the terrifying woman in front of us.

I took a deep breath. "I'm desperate. I need to find her. And right now, this girl Lav is my only lead."

Villette studied me for what felt like an eternity, her face icy and sharp while her eyes burned with a terrifying fire. Just when I'd thought she was going to rip my throat out for compromising her club, she asked, "Your friend—the girl you came with last week, you mean?"

"I . . ." I nodded, my throat dry. "Yes. Have you seen her here?"

She shook her head and narrowed her eyes. "Your information was wrong. The woman—Lav—she wasn't even here tonight."

"But that guy—" I searched the room for the man from earlier, but he was nowhere in sight—no doubt locked in a room with someone by now. I pointed to the door I'd been watching. "Someone told me she was in that room."

"She was." Villette nodded. "Two days ago."

"She—what?" I deflated into the booth, trying to figure out what the fuck I was supposed to do now. My eyes glazed with the threat of tears, but I pressed my fingers against my eyelids, trying to keep them back. Then I glanced back up at Villette. "Do you know where I might find her? Please—" My voice cracked, and there was no hiding the desperation or fear choking me anymore. "I can't lose her. Sora is all I have."

Villette sighed, then turned on her heels and walked over to the bar. She returned with a business card and a pen. Leaning over the table, she scratched an address on the back in blood-red ink, her handwriting as sharp and dangerous as I might've imagined it. Then she slid it across the dark glass toward me. "I don't know where Lav lives, but I think she frequents this bar. If she's not there, the regulars might be able to help you."

When I reached for the card, she pressed her finger into the center of it, stopping me.

"Listen to me very carefully," she said. "You need to understand that, where this address leads, you are not promised safety. Very dangerous people spend their time in and around this bar. It is not a place where you belong, and you should consider every other option before you enter it." Her lips pressed into a flat line. "Perhaps your friend is fine. She seemed very capable, from what I remember of her."

"She is very capable," I said, pulling the card from her grip when she finally relented, "but that doesn't mean she isn't also in trouble." I met her eyes. "There's nothing for me to consider. She's my best friend. My family."

Villette arched her brow, studying me, then, satisfied with whatever she found in my eyes, she nodded. "Very well, do as you wish. But please leave my club immediately and do not return."

As if I was a child being escorted to detention, she followed me up and to the entrance, not letting me out of her sight for a second. When we reached the door to her office, she gestured to the stairs leading out of the club. "How, by the way, did you get past my security?"

"Honestly?" I shrugged. "No idea. The door in the back alley sort of just slipped open."

She narrowed her eyes. "There is no door in the back alley." Her lips pursed, then she nodded up the stairs. "Very well, take your leave."

"Thank you." I held up the business card. "For this and for not killing me."

The barest flash of amusement flitted across her expression, before it returned to its otherwise stern mask.

When I took a few steps up, Kieran at my side, she called up to me, her voice soft but steady. "Good luck, Mareena. I don't want to see you again, but I do hope you find your friend."

The bouncer, when we emerged from the other side of his door, looked like he'd seen a ghost. Little did he know, he was staring through one.

"How the hell did you—" He shook his head, exasperated.

As we rounded the corner, I exhaled—the knots in my stomach slowly loosening enough for me to breathe properly.

"Holy shit," I said, "that was intense."

But when I turned to him, Kieran's face looked decidedly less triumphant. If anything, he seemed even more tense than he had at any point in the night.

"Hey, you okay?" I asked. I glanced down at where the dark veins slid beneath his sleeve. "Is it your arm?"

Only he wasn't looking at his hand or at me.

Instead, I followed his gaze across the street, where a man stood looking just as intense and angry as Villette had when she caught me.

He was pale, with dark shoulder-length hair and dressed head-to-toe in black.

With a sudden lurch, I realized that I'd seen him before.

Six years ago—when Sora and I stumbled upon the vampire and werewolf. He was the third man, the one Sora couldn't see.

Kieran stepped in front of me, like he was trying to block me from sight—and that was when I noticed that the man was staring daggers at Kieran, his jaw clenched.

"Can he . . . can he *see* you?" I asked.

"Of course I can," the man said, his eyes narrowing as they shifted to me. "The better question is, why the hell can you?"

21

MAREENA

APPROXIMATELY EIGHT YEARS AGO, TWO
YEARS BEFORE THE UNDOING

"Hey!" A white woman with long, red hair and impeccably applied eyeliner reached out for Sora as we made our way toward the back door of the bus. "It's you!"

She had a gentle twang to her voice that was rare to hear this far north.

"Oh hey—" Sora paused, pursing her lips, her eyes narrowed as she tried to place the girl, "You." I bit back my grin. Sora was many things, but a good liar was not one of them. She clearly had no fucking clue who this woman was. After a long moment, she gave up. "Sorry, my memory is shit. Do we know each other?"

"I thought so, maybe," the woman said, her face twisted in confusion. "You look so familiar. I just can't quite place your face."

"It is the kind of face you remember," Sora responded with a teasing smirk. "You live in the area? Maybe we've run into each other somewhere in the neighborhood."

"No." The woman's face fell. "I don't. Visiting family." She studied her, thinking for a second, then shook her head.

"Weird, I could have sworn we've met before. Church, maybe?" she snapped her fingers, realization softening her expression. "That big, culty one just outside of Portland, right? My family was sucked into it for a few months a while back."

I snorted. Sora hadn't been to church a day in her life. This was either the most awkward pick-up attempt I'd ever seen, or she had the wrong woman.

"Sorry, that definitely doesn't sound like me," Sora said, waving a quick apology to the bus driver who was sending us a death glare through the mirror above him. We were the ones who'd requested this stop and now we were holding up the route. "Must be somebody else. Sorry, this is my stop but enjoy the rest of your visit!"

He started to close the doors, so I grabbed her arm and tugged her between them before the bus took off with us still on it.

"Rude," she said, her eyes dancing with amusement as she straightened her dress and got her bearings. "I don't see your boyfriend."

"He's not my boyfriend," I said, a little too defensively.

She shot me a snarky look and shrugged. "Whatever you say. Wouldn't be the worst thing in the world, would it?"

"I don't do—"

"Relationships." She sighed. "Yes, Mars, I know. I'm just saying, maybe this time you should reconsider. What are you going to do, be alone forever?"

"Course not." I bumped my shoulder into her. "I have you."

"Obviously. Till death do us part, but you know what I mean." She narrowed her eyes, studying me. "Unless you're not attracted to him, of course?"

"I'm not." Though I knew we both heard the lie in my voice.

"Well—" She scuffed her sneaker against a gap in the sidewalk. "I'm just saying, it would be okay if you were. I just want you to be happy."

"I am happy. I don't need anyone to be happy."

"Clearly." Deciding to be magnanimous for once, Sora let it slide, then looked down the street. "Where is he anyway?"

"Right here," a deep, gravelly voice echoed behind me.

I flinched, then spun around to find Levi a few feet away from us.

How long had he been there? And was it long enough that he'd caught the last few seconds of our conversation?

Fuck. Heat crawled up my neck.

"Assuming it was me you were looking for." He glanced at me for a moment, concern on his face. "Everything okay? You seem tense."

"Yeah," I said, relaxing a little. If he'd heard us, he was doing a damn good job of pretending otherwise. "You should know better than to sneak up on someone like that though. I know how to throw a mean right hook now. If I had"—I pinched my pointer finger and thumb together—"even slightly slower reflexes, you'd be knocked out on the sidewalk right now."

"Hello to you, too," he said, his face splitting into a bemused, crooked grin that made my stomach dip.

Sora wrapped her arms around him in one of her vise-like hugs. "Good to see you again, Levi. You ready to go to the best place in all of Seattle?"

When she disentangled herself from him, he shifted toward me, arms open like he expected me to step into them.

"She doesn't do hugs," Sora said, swatting his arms down.

"I don't do hugs," I confirmed.

"Noted." He nodded, his mouth dipping down at the corners briefly, before he studied the intersection. "So. . ." He scratched his head. "This is the most magical place in Seattle?"

"Don't be ridiculous." Sora beamed up at him. "This is just near where we catch our next bus. I had a class in Columbia City earlier." Sora ran her fingers through my dark waves, a devious expression on her face. "Mars was my model today. Doesn't her hair look great?"

My cheeks warmed under his appraisal, and I found myself trying to look anywhere but at the clear approval on his face.

I shoved Sora's hands away from my head.

"It does," he said.

"Not that she let me do anything particularly fun." She sniffed. "Only cut a few inches."

"I let you near my head with scissors." I narrowed my eyes at her. "That's all the fun you get for now. We can talk again when you graduate."

She'd spent half of our trip to her studio today trying to convince me to let her dye my hair ten different shades of pink or try out the rainbow stripes a friend of hers recently got done at a local salon. And it took the second half of the trip to settle on a compromise—only a trim, but if she stopped arguing with me about it, then she could come hang out with me and Levi afterward, since he'd be in town for a few hours this afternoon.

Never mind that Levi had already asked me to invite her.

Since we'd spent most of her house party a few months ago avoiding the actual party, she'd been endlessly begging me for a chance to get to know him better.

"You know," she said, steering us in the direction of our connecting stop, her eyes sliding deviously over Levi, "I could give you a quick trim later, too, if you'd like." She clicked her fingers together like scissors. "I need to bring in more practice models. But I promise that I'm actually pretty decent."

"I can see that," he said, slowing his pace to match mine. "I'll mull it over next time I'm in need of a haircut."

"Just be—" I stopped, forgetting whatever it was I was about to say, my focus locked on a small bar. There was something strange about it, something I couldn't quite place. I had the oddest urge to walk in, even though I had no desire for a drink and knew they couldn't serve me one even if I did.

"Mars?" Sora waved her hand in front of my face when I didn't respond. "Hey, what's up?"

"You okay?" Levi asked, his brows furrowed.

"Yeah." I nodded. "Yeah I'm fine." I glanced over at Sora, though tugging my eyes away from the bar required an unusual amount of effort. "Sor, you know this place?"

"Uh—" She arched her brow, studying me. "What place?"

"This bar?" I asked, gesturing at the very large, very obvious building in front of me. "I don't think I've noticed it before."

"You mean the janky looking abandoned building with boards over the windows?" She squinted, then shrugged. "No."

I processed Sora's words, then did a double take. What was she talking about?

The building was maybe a *little* divey, but it looked clean. Far better off than Mac's or Frank's or any of the other local holes-in-the-wall where we spent our time.

A man with dark red hair walked out, lit a cigarette, and then leaned against the wall, studying us with mild interest.

"We should go." Levi cracked each of the knuckles in his left hand, his shoulders tense. "Don't want to miss the bus."

"Huh." Sora blinked a few times, frowning. "I guess it is a bar. Weird. Never noticed it."

"You coming in or what?" the man asked, his eyes scraping over me in a way that made me suddenly feel naked.

"No," Levi said, his tone clipped. "She's not."

"Suit yourselves." The man shrugged, snuffed the cigarette he'd taken maybe two puffs of out on the bottom of his heel, and went back inside.

"Let's go, Mareena," Levi said, his voice low and urgent, as he pressed his palm to the small of my back.

Normally, I would bristle at the contact, but I found that I strangely needed it. I couldn't quite pull myself away.

With quick steps, Levi ushered me toward Sora, who'd

already resumed her walk as if we were never interrupted, completely oblivious of the creepy dude.

We reached the stop in relative silence.

Levi was oddly tense, and uncharacteristically focused on his phone, while Sora checked her app for the next arrival.

The bus pulled up after a few minutes, and once we were seated, Levi relaxed a bit, though he kept darting glances out the window.

"So," he said after a few more minutes of silence, "where is it we're going again?"

"It's a surprise." Sora was in the row of seats in front of us, but she'd twisted around so that she was facing us, her chin resting between two headrests. "You're not afraid of dogs, are you?"

Levi shook his head, an amused look on his face.

"Good. Then it won't be a bad surprise."

I snorted, then leaned back, feeling suddenly exhausted and deeply grateful to get a chance to sit for the next twenty or so minutes.

I closed my eyes, listening with amusement as Sora drilled Levi with questions. He was a good sport about it and surprisingly answered most of them, only occasionally steering her gently away from whichever topics he wasn't comfortable discussing. Which, for Levi, was anything that got too personal.

More surprising, though, was the fact that Sora didn't fight him on his caginess or push for more information.

She liked him—I knew the dips in her tone well enough to tell—and something in me eased at that realization. I found that I wanted them to get along—a realization that then fucking terrified me.

Because that meant that I was getting used to Levi's presence. Growing fond of it, even.

After a few minutes of silence, I felt him leaning closer to me, his breath warm against my cheek.

"Truth for truth?" he asked, his voice quiet.

I opened my eyes and noticed Sora's head pressed against the glass.

I chuckled. She was asleep. This wasn't an entirely surprising feat for her—she had a habit of burning hot and bright with excitement one second, and then crashing the next. Kind of like a toddler. Or a golden retriever.

"Okay." I turned toward Levi, suddenly very much aware of how close he was. His shoulder brushed against mine every time the bus driver took a turn, and my stomach made an annoying lurch each time that it happened. "But I need to think of one."

"You don't like hugs," he said, the sentence on the tip of his tongue, like he'd been doing his best to hold it in all this time. "Can you tell me why?"

I shrugged, dropping my eyes. It was too hard to focus when he was looking at me like that, all wide-eyed and curious, close enough that I could see the different shades of gray bleeding into each other.

"You don't know, or you don't want to talk about it?" he asked. "I can come up with a different question, if you'd rather something else."

"No." I shook my head. "It's not that. I'm just trying to nail down the reason." Truthfully, I couldn't quite identify the boundaries of the preference. It had changed over the years, becoming an uninterrogated fact about me. My memory bubbled with a vision of Blake, the way he'd often hold me down or lock me in somewhere, just to press Rina's buttons— the acerbic terror that would crash through me like an unrelenting tide when he'd do more than simply hold me there. "In part, I think I don't really like feeling restrained or being touched when I'm not expecting it."

His expression shifted, eyes widening with concern. "That day, when I taught you how to fight . . . when I grabbed you?"

I nodded.

"I'm sorry." He hissed. "I shouldn't have done that."

Many people said the words 'I'm sorry' like an afterthought, an impulsive phrase used to brush their own discomfort away. Levi said the words like he meant them, down to the marrow of his bones.

"That wasn't your fault," I said, blinking away the closeness of him and shifting my focus to the worn plastic on the seat in front of me. "You were teaching me to defend myself. It was a very expected next step, I'm just not . . . normal about that sort of thing, I guess."

"Normal is relative," he said, then added after a beat, "But you said in part. Is there another reason? Other than feeling restrained, I mean?"

A moment that felt impossibly long stretched between us like taffy.

My chest tightened as the edges of something much sharper than Blake's cruelty curled into me—a truth I hadn't whispered into life maybe ever. One I'd hardly even acknowledged to myself before now. "Yes, but you can't laugh."

"I wouldn't," he said, his voice dripping with earnestness.

"I didn't used to hate hugs." I kept my voice even, clinical—as if I was dissecting someone else's memory. "I think I started associating bad things with hugs the day my aunt died. It was my birthday," I added, as if the specificity of the date added distance to the pain. But then I remembered the smell of her, the waft of rosewater and mint that clouded her embrace, and clinical distance suddenly became more difficult to perform.

Levi's fingers brushed against mine, the touch so featherlight and soft, there and then gone, that it could have been nothing more than an accidental brush, the natural result of the bus's winding path along the bend in the road.

"She'd just given me my present, a family ring," I continued, fiddling with the skin around my nail beds as if they held the key to compressing the imperceptible waver in my voice locked down. "The last thing I did was give her a giant hug. I ran to put the ring away, too afraid to wear it right then, like I might lose or damage it somehow, and when I came back into the kitchen, she collapsed. That's . . . when she died." I took a deep breath, dispelling the tightness in my chest and let out a forced laugh. "In the chaos of the aftermath, I didn't even grab it—the ring I mean."

Truthfully, other than the clothes that fit in one suitcase, I hadn't brought anything when I was taken from her house. It was like, on some level, I knew that anything I held onto would carry the weight of those memories—the reminder of everything I'd lost.

"Anyway—" I exhaled, sinking deep against the stiff bus seat. "I know it seems ridiculous, and I know that my hug didn't literally kill her. Of course, I understand that's impossible." I glanced up at him briefly, then turned away, trying to brush off the intensity of the moment, the way he so clearly hung on every word—as if he cared about this story as much as if it were one of his own. "But I think after that day, I just sort of internalized it on some level. That's when I started really fixating on the whole curse thing. I'd more or less ignored the whispers of it before then, not really focusing on the family members who'd discarded me or overthinking about my parents. But once I lost the one person in my life who mattered, everything just sort of . . . shifted. My aunt wasn't there to brush away the fear, to tell me I was being ridiculous. And I guess I just felt like I was, I don't know—poisonous or contagious or something. And if there was even the slightest chance that I was—"

He nodded, then finished the thought where I left it. "You'd rather not risk it."

"Exactly. And after a while, hugs just felt so . . . heavy, I guess." I glanced out the window and swore. "This is us."

The trip had flown by so much faster than it usually did.

Talking to Levi always had a way of making time feel like it was warped.

He pulled the string, requesting the stop, and I nudged Sora awake.

She jumped up, disoriented, but it took her less than a moment to realize where we were—and when she did, she grabbed mine and Levi's hands, tugging us eagerly toward the exit.

I laughed, allowing her to pull me along, her excitement contagious.

The bus let off at a seemingly unremarkable park, and Levi shot me a confused, this-is-supposed-to-be-the-most-magical-place-in-Seattle look.

"Just wait," Sora said, catching onto his doubt. "We're not there yet."

She led the way, then spun around when the trail opened up to the main event, so she could soak in his reaction.

Loud barks echoed around the parking lot, as we made our way through the gates.

Four giant dogs greeted us when we entered, a Great Dane leaving a trail of drool along Levi's thigh.

"Isn't it great?" Sora bent over to pet a pug who sounded like he was snoring, despite being wide awake.

"Your favorite place in the entire city is a dog park?" Levi tried to keep his expression flat and critical, but I could tell from the teasing tug at his lips that he was deeply amused by the turn of events.

"It gets better," Sora said, with a squeal. She waved us toward her, an assortment of dogs following along after her as if she was the leader of their pack.

I scratched behind the pug's left ear. He'd found a spot in the shade, and I had a feeling he wouldn't be joining for the next leg of our journey.

"It's kind of hard not to love this place," I said, soaking in the warmth of the sun on my face. It was the first week of May, and the weather was just starting to get good. Another month or two, and it'd hopefully be hot enough to go for a non-arctic swim in the lake.

A large gray dog slid between us, and when I reached down to pet him, I accidentally found myself running my hand over the back of Levi's.

I shifted quickly, patting the dog awkwardly on the head instead.

"Yeah." Levi cleared his throat, then smiled, his dimple out in all its glory. "Yeah, I get that."

We didn't speak for a few minutes, and I was suddenly aware of how, even here, surrounded by dozens of dogs and their literal shit, my brain still seemed to find and focus on the scent that I was beginning to think of as distinctly Levi—woodsy and spicy, with just a touch of citrus.

The dog park opened out into a long trail, and we followed it, making friends with each of the dogs along the way, their zoomies taking them in every direction imaginable—some even carving paths directly *through* their humans. At least one guy's ass was covered in dirt from a fall.

No one minded though. This place belonged to the dogs; we were just lucky enough to be a part of it for the afternoon.

Levi's excitement dipped when he checked his phone, the line of concern between his brows deepening a bit before he slid it back in his pocket. This was the most I'd ever seen him use it before.

"Um—" I glanced over at him, trying not to be nosy. "Everything okay?"

He nodded, his lips pressed in a tight line. "Yeah. Work stuff."

He seemed to carry a peculiarly heavy load of work stress for someone his age. Part of me felt like that sort of adulting wasn't supposed to come into play for another decade or so.

But I also knew that his life outside of our . . . diet friendship was kept locked down pretty tight, so I nodded and let it drop. His life was truly none of my business, and I needed to keep reminding myself that I was the one who wanted it that way.

"This is the best part," I said, not bothering to hold back my smile when we reached another set of gates.

The trail opened to a small beach, and there were at least ten dogs hopping and swimming in the lake. One had even gone so far as to greet a kayaker passing through the area.

Levi laughed, any visible tension he still carried shedding away instantly. "Dogs *and* the water?" The corner of his mouth twitched. "I can see why you love this place."

When we reached the gravelly shoreline, I kicked off my shoes, peeled off my socks, and rolled my jeans up as high as they would go. Sora tossed her shoes on mine, and we waded into the water up to our mid-calves. Neither of us minded the biting chill of the water as a black retriever of some sort dropped a ball in front of us, begging Sora to toss it farther out.

Levi joined us, and we stayed out there watching the water and dogs frolic against the mountain line in the distance, soaking in the chaos of the scene for as long as we could stand —until well after we'd lost all sensation in our feet.

The walk back to the bus was chillier than it had been on the way out, but Sora kept us laughing through most of it and we made plans to grab an early dinner nearby, before heading back to our part of town.

But when we closed the gate behind us, leaving the happy dogs to their play, and walked toward the parking lot, the laughter dried up on Levi's face, instantly, like some invisible hand had just turned off the tap, drought imminent.

His crooked grin transformed into something hard, and his posture went rigid, as a woman walked over to us, the expression on her face just as tight.

"Mom." The word came out clipped, tinny, his jaw clenched. "What are you doing here?"

Mom? She didn't look old enough to be his mother—unless she had him when she was absurdly young. Her hair was reddish brown; her skin a shade or two paler than Levi's.

She was an inch or so shorter than me, and quite slim, but there was a severity in her posture that oozed control—power. If Levi told me she was an action figure model or the newest cast member in a superhero movie, it wouldn't entirely shock me.

"You stop answering my texts and ignore my calls during a time like this, and what do you expect? Something's changed and we need to go—now. There's a chopper waiting for us."

A chopper?

Who the hell were these people?

As if just noticing us, the woman—his mother apparently—studied us, the look in her eyes flat, like she found Sora and I decidedly unimpressive. She flared her nostrils, before drilling him with that terrifying stare of hers, some silent conversation passing between them that I wasn't privy of.

"Really, Levi," she said, her sheer exasperation finally breaking it. "I don't know what's gotten into you lately."

"Mom—"

"Everything in the state that it's in—and *this* is what you're up to?" She gestured behind us. "A dog park with—" Her eyes slid to us before gripping him in her stare again. "With these girls? Stealing into the night, disappearing for days on end. You're getting sloppy—"

"How did you find me?"

"You were supposed to be prepping for a mission. You weren't. And then you stopped responding to your phone, so I tracked it."

A mission? Who the fuck did she think he was—James Bond?

"Thought something might've happened to you, or gone wrong, or—" She took a deep breath and straightened her posture, her voice quiet but firm when her eyes met his again. "We don't have time for this. Wipe them, and let's go."

Wipe them?

Sora's questioning gaze met mine and I offered a barely perceptible shrug in return.

I had no fucking clue what this was about.

"Mom," he snapped, his expression dark and so unlike anything I was used to seeing on his face.

"Now, Levi. This isn't a discussion." She shot him a look of disbelief, like whatever she was asking was the most obvious thing in the world. "I'll see you at the car. We're down the block. Two minutes. Take care of it."

Without so much as another glance in our direction, she spun on her heels and left.

He watched her silently until she disappeared around a corner, the lines of his back rigid.

"I'll uh—" Sora glanced between us. "Give you guys a minute. See you later, Levi. We'll do dinner another time I guess."

She walked back toward the fence to greet the new dogs making their way inside, until it was just me and Levi and a static silence that seemed to suck the air from around us.

"You okay?" I asked, not entirely sure where to start.

"Yeah." He scratched the back of his head, the movement stilted with frustration he was trying his best to contain. "Fine."

"Levi," I said, shifting slightly until his eyes met mine. "What was that about? Your mom—"

"Sorry about that, she can be . . . intense."

"Yeah, that's one word for it." I tried to map what he'd told me about her onto the woman I'd just met—the person he spent most of his time with. She was definitely intense, a bit terrifying if I was being honest, but she'd seemed legitimately concerned about him —worried enough to track him. Which was both peculiar and . . . intense. "What exactly does your family do, Levi? And what did she mean"—I searched for the phrase she'd used—"wipe us?"

"She didn't mean anyth—" he started to say, but then he thought better of it when he saw me readying to call bullshit. "Some secrets are good, necessary, even," he said instead, echoing my words from months ago back to me. "Can you just trust me on this, Mareena? The less you know, the better. I don't want to lie to you, but I can't tell you this truth either."

I took a deep breath, studying him, trying to decide what that meant—trusting someone who had the kinds of secrets that he and his family clearly had. At the silent plea in his eyes, any hesitation I had dissipated when I exhaled.

I'd kept impossibly big secrets—to keep myself safe, to keep Sora safe.

Maybe Levi was protecting someone he loved, too.

"Fine," I said, "but you still owe me a truth next time I see you. And you better make it a good one, or no deal."

"I can do that." His lips curved into the start of a smile, but then they dipped back down into a straight line just as quickly. "I should probably go."

I nodded, not sure what else to say into the unusually awkward void now gaping between us.

He turned to leave, took two steps, then turned back. "Can you do me one more favor?"

I arched my brow in question.

"Can you—can you not go to that weird bar we saw today? The one earlier, on the way to the bus stop?"

"I, uh—" Confusion stole any chance I had at coherence. I wasn't sure what favor I'd been expecting him to ask for, but that was as far from a possibility as it could get. "Huh?" was all I landed on.

"Promise me, Mareena." His eyes were dark and urgent, and they drilled into me with relentless desperation. "Please."

"Okay," I said, not bothering to ask, because I knew I wouldn't be getting any more information if I did. "I won't. Promise."

"Good." His shoulders relaxed slightly. "Thank you."

I held his gaze for an impossibly full moment, all of the new, unsaid strangeness churning question after question in my mind.

"I think my two minutes are up," he said, looking suddenly exhausted and so much older and more worn out than he had ten minutes ago. "I better go."

He was a few feet away before I found myself calling out his name.

When he turned back, my chest tightened at the sight of him, like something big had shifted, but I didn't understand what.

"Promise me you'll be careful," I said, hating how vulnerable my voice sounded, how vulnerable I suddenly felt.

His lips twitched. "Deal."

22

MAREENA

PRESENT DAY

"What the hell are you doing here?" Kieran asked, his voice low and laced with an edge I hadn't encountered from him before.

The man walked toward us.

Like Kieran, his arms were covered in ink, the edges of some design on his chest peeking out from beneath the collar of his shirt. His eyes were so dark that it was almost impossible to discern between iris and pupil, and there was a jagged scar etched through his right eyebrow.

He was attractive, but as he studied Kieran, his face was carved in what seemed to be a permanent scowl. He'd spared me only the briefest of glances before deciding I was apparently not worth his interest.

But it was his hands that had my blood running suddenly cold. Looped around his fingers was a set of rings. Rings that were identical to Kieran's. Was this guy another guardian angel? He looked even more dangerous and menacing than Kieran did, which meant that angels were clearly nothing like the ones in the stories we'd all been fed.

"What do you mean what am I doing here?" he snarled in a

subtle British accent. "You were supposed to report to the Order days ago. Rafi sent me to see what the holdup was." His dark gaze slanted in my direction again, before shifting back to Kieran. "And apparently, you've just been wasting our time, gallivanting with the living. Really Kieran—" He shot him a look of disgust. "Didn't have you pegged as someone who'd risk the Order's wrath for a plaything that can see the dead. Are you truly that desperate for a taste of this world?"

"Watch it, Thorne," Kieran snapped. "I mean it."

"Or what?" He smirked, which somehow only made him look more threatening. "We don't have time to pander to your every whim. You were given a job, and you haven't completed it. You don't belong here, you don't control the fates, and you should've been back two days ago."

The fates? What the fuck was he talking about?

"You've checked up on me like a good little soldier," Kieran said, inching in front of me, like he wanted to keep me out of sight. "Now go home and tell Rafi that I'll return when I'm done with my assignment."

The man, Thorne apparently, bared his teeth. "I was ordered not to return without you."

"Since when do you follow orders?"

Thorne's hands flexed into fists.

"I've seen you before," I said, stepping out from behind Kieran's shadow, attempting to dispel the visceral tension building between the two men. "A few days after The Undoing. There was a vampire and a werewolf." I took a deep breath, steeling myself under the weight of Thorne's stare now that it was burrowing into me instead of Kieran. "They couldn't see you though. Neither could my friend."

There was a woman heading in our direction, but she only shot me an alarmed look, before crossing the street to give us a wide berth.

"So," I said, glancing between the two men. "I take it that

means you're dead, too?" Which meant that, to the rest of the world, I was in the middle of a dark street, talking to myself. Great.

Well, that was one way to keep people at a distance.

Something flashed in Thorne's eyes—a watered down version of surprise, maybe. He studied me again, with slightly more attention this time. Not like I was someone worthy of his attention, but like I was gum stuck to the bottom of his shoe. A nuisance he was trying to figure out how to rid himself of as quickly and efficiently as possible.

Kieran stiffened, inching closer to me.

"I'm Mareena," I said, awkwardly extending my hand out to him.

Thorne only scowled at it.

"This is Hawthorne," Kieran said, his jaw tight. "But everyone calls him Thorne."

I gave him a tight smile, offering the vitriol he served up right back to him. "Suits you."

"Exactly." Kieran grunted, before adding a mumbled, "Been nothing but a thorn in my ass since the moment I met him."

"Are you a guardian angel, too, or another ghost-phantom-thing like Claudine?" I asked, fidgeting with my ring, as I tried to assess if this guy was a legitimate threat, or just a friend of Keiran's whose factory setting came with a stick shoved so far up his ass that it addled his brain. "Or . . . something else, maybe?"

"Fucking hell, Kieran," Thorne spat out, his eyes shining with venom as they lasered in on Kieran's hand. It was getting worse, the veins black as tar as they branched up his forearm. "You can't be serious."

"Hawthorne," Kieran said, his voice dipping into a warning growl. He adjusted his sleeve until it covered his arm.

Instead of answering me, the two of them got caught in some silent staring version of a pissing contest. That, or maybe they could communicate telepathically. Kieran hadn't exactly been expansive when describing his powers or the various forms and occupations of the dead.

"Stay here for a minute, Agony," Kieran finally said. "Thorne and I need to have a brief chat in private."

Without waiting for my response, they walked off.

So . . . apparently, they couldn't telepathically communicate then. At least that was one answer down. More than I usually got out of Kieran.

For five minutes, I watched the two of them argue down the block, just out of earshot.

They were tense, the silent threat of aggression baked into every line of their bodies.

I glanced down at the business card Villette had so reluctantly parted with, my focus split between the shady new arrival and devising the fastest route to the address. Thorne was not part of tonight's plan. We didn't have time for this.

Kieran's gaze sought me out every minute or so, almost like he didn't trust that I would listen to him, that I would wait. And honestly, maybe I shouldn't.

Judging from Kieran's absolute refusal to stop stalking me, I'd been under the impression that guardian angels were *supposed* to stick to their charges like glue. He'd said as much, hadn't he? That we were bound, and he couldn't leave until his job was finished?

Not that I knew what *finished* even looked like for a guardian angel on duty. He hadn't been particularly forthcoming about that either.

But Thorne made it sound like Kieran's constant presence wasn't actually necessary. Maybe he was just supposed to check in occasionally, see how I was doing—watch from afar. If Kieran had other things to do, he was free to leave. It wasn't like I'd asked for a perma-stalker.

I ignored the hollow dip in my stomach when I thought

about the possibility of him doing just that. I knew he wouldn't be around forever or anything, but I'd kind of grown used to his hovering, incessant presence over the last couple of days. And after what had just happened in Incendiary ...

Fuck, was I getting attached to a dead guy now?

What the hell was wrong with me?

Maybe it would be better if I just left now, while they were distracted—saved us all the trouble before things got messier.

Sora was missing; I had my own stuff to handle. I most certainly did *not* need to get caught up in the drama of the dead. And, judging by their posture and the deep snarl on Thorne's face, they weren't any closer to working out their disagreement.

Soft, laughing voices echoed down the street as a group of people, each of them dressed to the nines, made their way toward Incendiary. The night was still young, which meant that if I moved quickly, I could probably make it to the bar before last call.

Decided, I spun on my heels and started walking away, doing everything in my power to ignore the heavy pang in my chest at the thought of leaving without saying goodbye to Kieran.

I brushed the guilt away with a deep, steady breath. We were tethered. If he wanted or needed to find me whenever they were done hashing their shit out, he could. In the meantime, I had a best friend to track down.

Sora was the thing that mattered above all else. Kieran was just a temporary fixture in my life. Sora was my home.

I'd only been walking for a few minutes when I felt a presence at my back. With as much subtlety as I could muster, I slid my apartment key between my fingers and spun around, holding the makeshift claw up in front of me.

Kieran's brow arched in vacant amusement that melted into a small frown. "Thought I said don't move."

Thorne stood next to him, staring down at me like I was gum again.

"You clearly have stuff to do," I said, hating the rush of relief that flooded me at his nearness, "and I need to go find Sora. We can check in," I glanced at Thorne, "you know, later."

"No can do, Agony." Kieran shook his head, then wrapped his arm over my shoulders, turning me back in the direction I'd been walking. "I'm your shadow until my job is done."

We started walking, Thorne following behind us a few paces like a storm cloud.

"You did your job," I said. "I'm sure you've got other charges to track down and haunt. I can take things from here."

"I'll be the judge of that," he said.

"And your friend?" I glanced back at him, flinching at the dark look in his eyes.

Thorne made a deep rumbling sound. "Friend is not the word I'd use."

"He's free to do as he wishes," Kieran said. "I'm not his keeper. I'm yours."

"So," I said, after a long, drawn-out minute of silence that was starting to make me itchy from the discomfort of it, "are you a guardian angel, too, Thorne?"

Kieran started to answer, "More or le—"

"No," Thorne said, cutting him off. "I'm a reaper."

Kieran rolled his eyes, a muscle ticking in his jaw.

I stopped my stride, letting that world roll over me. "As in, like—" I tried to form the shape of a scythe with my hand, but it ended up looking more like a bad impression of Captain Hook. "Grim?"

Thorne, who'd apparently only momentarily forgotten that I wasn't worthy of his attention, went back to glaring at me in a silence that screamed rage.

"We're part of the same order," Kieran said, chewing over

his words slowly. "I protect and guide people. He devours them."

Thorne snorted.

"How—" I glanced up at the ominous figure. "Lovely."

Thorne narrowed his eyes, and I shivered under his stare. His vibes definitely suited his career path, that much was clear.

Sensing that I'd gotten all that I was going to get out of either of them, I focused on navigation, and we spent the rest of the journey in relative silence. And in that silence, I felt the heaviness of the unspoken closeness between Kieran and I fall over us both. We couldn't exactly talk about it now. Something told me that would only sour Thorne's mood more, if such a thing was possible.

Kieran made it very clear early on that any kind of relations were forbidden between a guardian and his charge, and I had a feeling that Thorne wouldn't take sex-club magic as a solid excuse for rule-bending.

Truthfully, I was almost thankful for the discomfort of the situation. It slowed my anxiety spiral that had been deepening every second since we'd left Incendiary.

Between Rex and Lav, what the hell had Sora gotten herself twisted up in? And how the fuck was I going to get her untangled from it?

Why hadn't she come to me about it?

Probably because she knew me well enough to know that I'd do everything in my power to stop her. But now look at the mess we were in. Best case, I'd show up at this bar and find her casually sipping on a beer beside Lav the vampire. Worst case . .
.

I did my best not to linger on it.

When we finally found ourselves outside of the bar, exhausted and sore from an unexpectedly long walk, I froze, the sudden flare of recognition like a knife to my chest.

Kieran glanced down at me. "Everything okay? You change

your mind?" Then, after a beat of silence, he added, "We can go home—maybe Sora came back? Or we can try again tomorrow."

"No." I swallowed, trying to bring some moisture back to my tongue. It had been years since I'd even thought of this place, but now the memory came flooding back at full force. The bar hadn't changed much, but I didn't feel that strange, intense draw to it that I remembered feeling all those years ago. "It's just . . . I've been here before. It—" I licked my lips. "Took me by surprise is all."

A burly redhead burst through the door, the loud bang of the door echoing in the otherwise empty lot. There were two men with him. He dragged them both by the collars of their shirts, as if they were a pair of unruly school boys.

"You know the rules," the redhead said with a snarl, "not in here. Lucky Claude is in yet, or he'd slap a ban on you both. That, or he'd just take your heads for pulling this shit in his bar."

He tossed them with the sort of casual force one might use to toss a bag of trash into a dumpster. A cloud of dust and gravel softened their landing. Not wasting a moment, the two men locked into a wrestling match with each other, moving with a speed and ferocity that no human could ever manage.

The redhead nodded in our direction, his eyes roving over me in a way that was very obviously assessing me beyond my threat level. "You coming in or not?"

I tugged at my dress, wishing it covered up more of my body than it did.

"This is a bad idea," Kieran said, his hands clenched into fists at his sides. "I can't protect you in there."

"We're not leaving," I whispered the words out of the corner of my mouth. The last thing I needed was the bouncer thinking I was talking to myself.

"Agony—"

"You said I needed to find my joy," I said. "There's no joy without Sora. Feel free to wait out here if you want."

I stepped around the fighting muscle tornado and smiled at the bouncer. "I am."

He gave me another weighty appraisal and opened the door.

"Well," Thorne said, breaking his silence, "at least this should move things along nicely."

A low growl vibrated in Kieran's chest as I stepped over the threshold into a bar I'd promised years ago that I would never enter.

23

MAREENA
PRESENT DAY

The inside of the bar was a lot larger than I imagined it being. The main room was filled with an inviting energy, given the aggressive welcoming party outside. Cozy wooden tables were scattered throughout the room, mostly filled with lively and laughing faces. It was hard to imagine that they were most likely all demons. They all looked so—human. I also didn't get why Villette's tone had been filled with such warning when she mentioned this place. Everything seemed so normal, so jovial.

The lights were dim, which meant the electricity was functioning, there was a group playing pool in the back, and judging by the half-full pitchers at most of the tables, there didn't seem to be any shortage of booze or beer. It reminded me so much of the time before that my stomach actually ached at the sight of it.

After all the death and chaos in the years since The Undoing, it was easy to forget that some people still lived with this level of comfort and ease. Whoever owned this place must've had some premium supplier hook ups.

Like Incendiary, this establishment didn't seem too badly affected by all the destruction. Maybe it was a demon thing.

They never relied on the same governing structures that humans did, so when those structures collapsed, their lives stayed relatively stable in comparison.

That, and probably the fact that the compounds and human cults weren't much of a match for a group of demons this large. They didn't need to worry about the raids or competition for the resources the compounds hoarded.

I scanned every face, holding my breath with the hope that Sora's would be one of them. That she was fine, that she knew Rex's ritual was bullshit. That she'd simply been so lost to the lust of a hookup with Lav that she'd forgotten to mention that she might be out for a few days, hanging with her new crush at a vamp bar. But with each face, that thin shred of hope shrank, until it became abundantly clear she wasn't here. None of the women looked even vaguely familiar, which meant that Lav probably wasn't in attendance either.

Fear, angry and sharp, speared through my chest at the possibility that I was too late. That maybe she *had* been here, searching for a cure to death, but one of the vampires, all flirtatious smiles on the outside, had slit open her vein for dinner, then left her alone and dead in an alley somewhere.

As if sensing the shift in my thoughts, the back of Kieran's hand brushed lightly against mine. The contact was brief, but for some reason, the tenderness of it only made it more difficult to hold my shit together.

"Can I get you something, dear?" a voice called over the loud hum of conversation.

Blinking away the film of tears that was threatening to break free, I turned toward it.

A white, middle-aged woman with a gentle smile stood behind the bar. Her reddish-brown hair was shoulder-length and curly, and her skin was lined with soft wrinkles that highlighted her welcoming expression, stretching it so that it was mapped across her face. When she caught sight of my barely contained tears, those wrinkles shifted just slightly, until her face shone bright with concern. "You okay, hon? Are you here on your own?"

Swallowing, I pulled out the picture of Sora and slid it across the bar, my trembling fingers betraying my attempt at collecting myself. "I'm looking for my friend, Sora. Have you seen her? Tonight, or last night, maybe?"

The woman grabbed the picture and held it in front of her face, studying it for a moment. "Not tonight, no."

My stomach sank as I sat down on one of the free stools. Where the hell was I supposed to go from here?

The woman set the photo down in front of me. "But she was here last night if memory serves."

My head shot up. "She was? You recognize her?"

The woman nodded. "Sweet girl. Was surprised to find her here." Her eyes darted to me; her face pinched with concern. "We don't get very many humans here. They're not exactly our targeted clientele, as I'm sure you're aware."

"Do you know who she was here with?" My heart thumped loud and heavy in my chest as the tenuous thread of hope appeared again. "I was told maybe some girl named Lav?"

"Yeah, she was here with Lav." She grabbed a glass, filled it with water, then set it down in front of me. "Drink this. You look like you've been through the wringer. Like you've seen a ghost or something. Let me know if you want anything stronger."

"Thank you." I ignored the offer. "Is Lav here? Do you know if she came in at all tonight?"

"Hey Marge." A tall man slapped his hand against the bar top with enough force that the glass of water trembled. "One more pitcher and a round of shots, if you will. And add them to Manny's tab."

"Quite the big spender tonight, isn't he?" Marge got to work on the order but met my eyes and then nodded toward the back of the room. "Lav hasn't been by here tonight, but that's her brother, Manny, over there in the back." She squinted, then chuckled. "The one who's about to lose another fortune at the pool table with that terrible form of his." She turned to the man who ordered the drinks. "You sure he's good for the tab tonight? Because I'll come collecting from you if not."

"I appreciate it," I said, then grabbed my picture and slid off the stool, leaving them to their discussion.

Kieran kept close to me as I wound my way through the maze of tables and bodies, ignoring all the curious stares leveled on me as I passed by.

Thorne stayed back by the bar, looking thoroughly bored.

The crowd around the pool table erupted in jeers when Manny did, indeed, miss his shot.

He handed his cue to a girl next to him, his face flushing with heat as his friends ribbed him.

"Excuse me," I said, squeezing around a seated couple who appeared to be in the awkward stages of a first date, "are you Manny?"

"Who wants to know?" There was an edge to his tone; but when he caught sight of me, his eyes dipping immediately to the deep plunge of my dress, the instinctual snark ebbed into a sleazy appreciation that made my stomach recoil. "Yeah, I'm Manny. What can I do for you?"

Ignoring the whistles and jeers from the two guys next to him, I handed him the picture. "I think my friend was here last night with your sister. Have you seen her since then? Or do you know where she might be?"

The flirtatious grin dried up immediately when he caught sight of Sora's face.

"No," he said, voice clipped, "never seen her before. Sorry."

Kieran scowled. "That smells like a lie."

"What about your sister? Lav, right?" I pressed. "Can you tell me where I might find her."

"Don't have a sister." He drained the rest of his beer. "Think you've been given some bad information."

One of the guys in the group leaned forward, until his face was just an inch away. He took a deep breath, his green eyes sparkling with teasing interest. "Human." He shot a look back at Manny. "If you don't want her, man, you cool if I have a go? Haven't had a proper warm drink in a minute."

My heartbeat drummed against my chest at the suggestion, which only seemed to amplify his interest.

"You one of those blood groupies, sweetie?" He grabbed a piece of my hair, letting it slide over his fingers. Then, when it fell back to my shoulder, he pressed his nose to the crook of my neck, his tongue lapping rough and hot against my skin. "What do you say, I promise I'll be gentle. If that's how you like it."

Kieran's arm wove around my waist, tugging me back. The vampire stumbled forward into the pool table, not expecting my sudden, jerky retreat.

"You need to get out of here, Agony." Kieran's voice was hard.

I appreciated his concern, but I wasn't leaving until this dickhole spilled what he knew about Sora.

"I'm not interested in being your blood bag." I shoved Kieran's arm away, then stepped closer to the vampire, hoping like hell my attempt at confidence didn't come off as brittle as it felt. Then, I stepped around him until I was in front of Manny. "Like I said, I'm trying to find my friend. Please just tell me what you know." I waved at the table. "Then I'll let you get back to losing your pool game."

The girl in the group barked out a harsh laugh, but Manny's expression darkened.

Kieran cursed, then stepped between me and Manny, even

though we both knew the gesture was futile. He was no more solid than air.

"She's got balls, you've got to give her that, Manny." The green-eyed vampire edged closer from behind, until I was sandwiched between him and Kieran.

"You don't belong here," Manny said, ignoring his friend. "You need to leave. And you and your kind need to stay away from my sister in the meantime." Well, he'd certainly bailed quickly on the cover story that he didn't have one. "She gets involved in shit she shouldn't. I don't want her near you, or your friend."

What the hell was he talking about?

His eyes darted to me, then to the front of the bar, like *he* was the one thinking of leaving.

If I didn't know any better, it almost looked like he was . . . afraid. But of what? Me?

"There's your answer," his green-eyed friend said, still pressed into my back. "But information doesn't come free here, Princess." His breath curled over the back of my ear. "You have a lot of nerve coming into a place like this, speaking to us with a tone like that . . . demanding something you haven't earned." He grabbed my shoulders and leaned closer, his nose trailing along the column of my neck. Then, in a dark whisper, he added, "But I do like the way bravery smells on you, so I'll give you another chance at the negotiation table if you promise to play nicely."

"Chad," a deep voice called out across the room, and the green-eyed vamp froze, then immediately put some distance between us. "Do you or do you not know the rules of my bar?"

I fought the urge to roll my eyes. Of course this asshole's name was Chad.

But when I spun around to clock the owner of the voice, I understood immediately why Chad suddenly looked like he'd swallowed a knife.

A man with swept back, white-blond hair, heterochromia, and a presence that oozed control walked toward us. He was dressed in a neatly pressed dress shirt and slacks, the sleeves rolled up to his elbows, revealing lean cords of muscle.

I found myself leaning back toward Manny and his friends, as if they offered a small veneer of protection from the ice-hot power emanating from the man.

He was like the embodiment of everything I feared most about demons. It wasn't the drunken assholes fighting outside that worried me, though I knew they could snap my neck in half a second if they really wanted to. It was someone like the man standing in front of me, who scanned over the faces in the bar as if they were nothing, mere decoration—ants beneath his magnifying glass. The kind of demon who could compel an entire room into silence with one seething look.

Chad stammered out a "Sorry, Claude," then carved a cartoonishly wide gap between us. "Would never have really taken a bite out of her in here, was just kidding. I swear." Then, at whatever look Claude leveled him with, Chad dropped his gaze to the ground. "It won't happen again; you have my word."

"Your word is only valuable to me when I believe it," the man, Claude apparently, responded, his tone clipped. His eyes —one dark brown, the other a mottled gold—snagged on me. I flinched under his appraisal. "Who are you and why are you here?"

"Agony," Kieran pleaded, "let's get out of here before this gets worse."

With a deep breath, I steeled myself, then took a step forward. "My name is Mareena." I held the image in front of him, pleased that my hand only trembled a little. "I'm looking for my friend. And I'm not leaving here until I find out where she is."

Claude arched his brow, glanced briefly at the picture of Sora, then returned his gaze to me, studying me with a focus so unrelenting that I couldn't convince my lungs to function properly. At my back, I felt Manny and the rest of his friends scatter away like frightened rats.

"You have a lot of nerve," Claude said, his voice soft and steady, but somehow more ominous because of how collected it sounded—so sure and confident, like a predator just before he launches on his prey, "talking to me like that, and in my bar no less." In a motion too quick for me to track, he plucked the picture from my fingers and flung it across the pool table. "Your friend is not here. And, assuming her puppet masters gain better control of her, she won't be back again. Her kind are not welcome here."

"Humans, you mean?" I asked, deeply confused. What the hell was he talking about? Puppet masters? Did he mean Lav?

"Humans are free to enter if they wish." His mouth curled into a snarl. "But I will not entertain a member of the Seven Sons in my establishment. They bring only trouble to our kind. I've made myself very clear in the past, but it seems they've grown more daring over time. Lav was unaware of your friend's associations when she brought her here, so I don't blame her for the poor judgment." He glanced at Manny. "It was you who escorted the girl out last night, correct?"

"Yes," Manny answered.

"There you have it," Claude said, turning back to me, his hands spread in front of him. "She's not here and she hasn't been on the premises since last night. Now please take your leave before we have another issue on our hands."

"The—" I paused, confusion cannibalizing my fear. "What are you talking about? Sora's not a member of the Seven Sons."

"The girl in that picture—" He gestured to the photo. "Is a member of the House of Wrath. And one who's made enough enemies of the other Sons that House of Lust ordered a bounty on her head just last week. From what I understand, her capture is fetching quite the reward. She's lucky no one here recognized her or turned her in before I asked Manny to remove her from the premises. I have no interest in the Sons' ridiculous spats."

"No," I said, shifting my focus back to the vampire in front of me. I assumed he was a vampire anyway. "You're mistaken."

"No." Claude's jaw was tight, every stretched line of his body so clearly screaming threat, that he might as well be wearing a sign with the word 'dangerous' plastered across it in neon lights. "I'm not. Your friend's made quite a name for herself in Wrath's fighting circuit. They've been shuffling through the city all year. She's taken a surprising number of lives, too"—his head tilted as he took a step closer—"for such a small, unassuming human, that is."

"You must be thinking of someone else." I shook my head. "My friend's not in a cult." The thought was almost ridiculous enough to make me laugh, but one look from Claude had the humor drying up instantly. "She works in a diner every night and cuts people's hair. She won't even kill those giant-ass spiders that show up every fall, for fuck's sake. Trust me," I added, "I promise you that you're wrong."

I felt the rest of the patrons' eyes on us, the room that had been bustling with good humor when we entered, was now filled with a silent, captive audience—one that watched us with bated breath. I got the feeling people didn't challenge Claude's misconceptions very often.

Even Thorne was watching us—looking, for once, almost entertained.

Dickhole probably wanted to watch this vampire drain me dry.

"I saw her there myself," Claude said, "today, in passing, when I met with one of their representatives to remind them of our agreement. That they're to stay away from my establishment if they don't want more trouble." His eyes narrowed.

"They assured me that I wouldn't find her in this part of town again."

"You saw her?" I asked, trying to imagine what the hell Sora would be doing all the way over by Wrath. It didn't make any sense. "I don't believe you."

I could understand why she might have come here last night. According to Rex's list, she needed to exchange blood with a vampire. There were plenty here if Lav wasn't up for the job.

But what did she need from House of Wrath?

"It's a dangerous game," Claude said, a muscle ticking in his jaw, "to come into a vampire's place of business and call him a liar. It appears that you're as reckless with your life as your friend is with hers."

"She's my best friend." I met his unflinching stare. "There's no risk I won't take to find her."

He was silent for a moment as he assessed me.

Kieran edged closer; his expression unreadable.

"Very well," Claude said, "it's your life to gamble with as you like. But I find that my patience with girls who dress their bad decisions in the guise of courage wears thin these days. So you'll have to lay down your life somewhere else. As I've already made clear, your friend is not here. And if she's got any sense of self preservation, she won't show her face near this place again. Now, if you please," he said, drawing the word out in a way that made it sound more like a threat than a request, "I ask that you take your leave. And don't let me catch sight of you in my bar again. There's only so much restraint I can request of my patrons, and if a human walks in, offering her life so flippantly—" He shook his head, shrugging. "I won't waste my breath protecting it again."

Jaw clenched, I reached past Claude and grabbed the photo of Sora.

"Understood." Ignoring every instinct in my body that told

me not to turn my back to a predator as deadly as Claude, I made my way to the door.

The bartender, Marge, watched on with concern as she twisted the bar rag in her hands, wringing it within an inch of its life.

There was another woman beside her now. She had long, black hair, and looked to be of East Asian descent. There was something unusual about her, almost otherworldly, and I couldn't get a read on her age for the life of me. Her dark velvet eyes were absent of the anxiety etched so clearly in Marge's.

"Don't worry," she said, her voice soft and melodic, "his bark is worse than his bite. If you do decide to return to this place in the future, you'll be under the same protection as everyone else."

Claude mumbled something incoherent, but I couldn't bring myself to turn back and look at him.

With a soft smile, she freed Marge's rag from the woman's relentless grip, then shot me a look that I couldn't begin to decipher. She watched my weird walk of shame with unblinking focus—and the way that her gaze shifted to Kieran, then Thorne, then back to me, her mouth pinched in curiosity, I was almost convinced that she could see them, too.

"Fecking hell." Kieran exhaled sharply, his hands on his knees as he bent over. He shook his head and looked up at me. "That was about two seconds away from a disaster, Agony. Can we please just go home now?"

My attention locked on a black, polished SUV—the only car in the lot. It was rare to see a car so well taken care of these days. This one looked almost new. Pristine. Not a speck of dirt on it. Something told me it belonged to Claude.

"Agony." Kieran followed my gaze, then stepped in front of me. "What, exactly, is going through that head of yours?"

"Wrath's compound is a decent trek away. And we won't make it there tonight if we go on foot."

"No." Kieran shook his head. "Absolutely not."

Sidestepping my guardian angel, I walked over to the car. One quick glance at the bar's entrance confirmed that we were alone out here. The bouncer must have gone back inside, now that the guys he'd thrown out had either killed each other or found their ways home.

When I grabbed the door handle, it opened with a soft click. Unlocked. Apparently, someone stealing from Claude was such a wild thought that he didn't even bother with the most basic precautions.

The lights came on overhead, illuminating the fancy dashboard. I took that as a promising sign. The car *wanted* me to take it.

"Do you even know how to drive one of these?" Kieran asked. He ran a hand aggressively through his hair as his gaze darted between me and the door, like he expected someone to come marching over any second now.

Cars were expensive and, since The Undoing, deeply unreliable. In the Before, Seattle's public transit system was comprehensive enough that I made do easily with buses, the light rail, and the occasional paid car service when I was particularly desperate. There'd never been an opportunity or reason to learn how to drive.

I slid onto the smooth leather driver seat. There wasn't a single speck or crumb on the inside. Smelled fairly new, too. Who the hell was this guy?

I turned to Kieran and shrugged. "How hard can it be?"

He groaned. Then his face, if possible, went a few shades even paler than it usually was.

"Seems your new toy has quite the death wish." Thorne shot Kieran a dark smirk as he stepped *through* the car door and made himself comfortable in the passenger seat. "At least I'll get to enjoy watching this disaster of your own creation blow up in your face."

24

MAREENA

APPROXIMATELY EIGHT YEARS AGO, TWO YEARS BEFORE THE UNDOING

The apartment was empty, so I decided to spend my night curled up in bed—alone, except for the company of a particularly intense horror novel that had my blood pumping overtime.

Fear was a strange phenomenon. I found that I both hated and craved it, and there was something so magical about how something as innocuous as ink on paper could strike so deeply into my bones, forcing my muscles to clench and my heart to race like a trapped bird in its cage.

Stranger still, was the fact that I actively sought this rush out. That I almost craved it.

It was late, and my room was bathed in the soft glow of my side lamp and the crackling flame of a candle.

Just as the protagonist started walking into the desolate basement—truly why did they all do this, let their attraction to danger lead them in the exact direction they shouldn't be going?—a loud knock sounded in the hall.

I jumped, tossing the book as if the monster in the story might burst from its pages.

My fingers searched for something to defend myself with,

but all that I had within reaching distance was my vibrating wand.

Defense by vibrator was better than no defense at all, so I grabbed it, hoping like hell it looked at least a little bit intimidating.

There was another resounding crash as I made my way to the front door, my eye pressed to the small peephole, lime-green wand clutched like a club.

Something slammed against the door, a hand maybe, blocking my sight. I jumped back at the ricochet of the impact, my heartbeat pounding in my ears.

My phone was in my room. Why the hell hadn't I grabbed it? Phone to call for help beat vibrator every time when it came to intruders. Every. Time.

When I turned to go rectify the situation, there was a loud groan, and then another crash.

I pressed my eye to the peephole again, finding the obstruction gone—and a dark, familiar figure leaning against the opposite wall, hair wet and curling over his eyes.

With a heavy exhale, my body relaxed.

Levi.

Grinning at my own melodrama, I slid the door chain and flipped the deadbolt. No more terrifying myself with scary stories while alone this late at night again. It was lowkey embarrassing how reactive I was tonight.

"You're breaking the rules, you know." I grinned, swinging the door open. "Pretty sure we agreed to a minimum of a month between hangouts. I just saw you a couple of we—"

The words dried up on my tongue at the state of him.

His eyes were wild and drawn, like he was in the deep stages of an alcohol bender, his skin tinged gray and clammy with sweat.

But it was his torso and arm that drew most of my attention. His usual black shirt was torn, the area around his stomach darker and wet. The smooth skin of his forearm was streaked in red.

Blood.

"Oh my god. Levi, what happened?"

His eyes shifted, unfocused until they found mine. "M-Mareena, you're here. That's good." His words were slurred as they rushed out. "Very good. Tried to call first but lost my phone." His gaze shifted down, brows furrowing. "Is that a . . . vibrator? Who answers the door with a vibrator?" A smug, teasing light flared in his eyes. "Did I . . . interrupt something?"

"I—" I glanced down at the vibrator, then back at him. "Levi, you're bleeding."

He shrugged. "A bit, yeah." Then he pressed a bottle which looked about a third full of whiskey to his lips, draining it dry in one smooth chug. There was a crumpled paper bag dangling in his other hand, the one with blood now seeping freely between his fingers. "I might need some of your help, actually. I wouldn't have come like this, but—" He took a ragged, shallow breath. "I was in the city, and then this happened, and then I didn't have anywhere else to go."

He swayed unsteadily, and the vibrator thumped on the floor, forgotten, as I rushed forward, reaching him just as his back crashed against the wall. He leaned against it, like he couldn't fully support his weight on his own.

There was a trail of dark blood through the carpeted hall.

"W-what happened?" I asked again as I pressed my hand to his cheek, unsure where to grab him without causing more pain. "Levi—we need to get you—"

He dropped the empty bottle, his large hand engulfing my cheek as he pressed his forehead against mine, the gesture so unexpected that I didn't even flinch at the intimacy of it. "Mars. Sorry, I mean—" He took a deep breath, like he was breathing me in, but then it shifted quickly to a choked gasp as if he couldn't quite fill his lungs properly. "Mareen—"

"Oh, for fuck's sake, Levi," I snapped, "just call me Mars. What the hell happened to you?"

"No more diet friendship?" His breathing shifted, becoming more shallow and uneven. Too much blood, there was no way a person should be standing and talking with this much of their blood on the outside of their body. "Regular calorie friendship?" A grin tugged at his lips as he added, in a disbelieving whisper-shout, "The good stuff?"

"Regular friendship." I nodded, my eyes blurring with a film of tears as I tried to put pressure on the gaping wound stretching across his abdomen. Though, judging by the icy fear carving a claustrophobic path through my ribs, I wasn't sure that I was willing to call anything about this moment good.

His smile swiftly turned into a groan as more of his weight fell against the wall.

"We need to get you to the emergency room. Now." My hands were shaking, my skin now soaked with blood. His blood. "My phone's in my room, I'll call an ambulance."

I hadn't seen this much blood since the night we lost Rina —and the relentless similarities between the two scenes made me dizzy as I fought to keep my focus on the present.

"No." He coughed. "No hospital."

"Yes, hospital." I shook my head, trying to understand how this was even a debate right now.

"I didn't make you go when you didn't want to," he said, with the unwavering stubbornness of a child who knew he had no argument to stand on but held to it regardless.

"I had a bruised hand."

"And?"

"My hand is practically holding together your stomach cavity right now, Levi. There's a difference."

"No," he said, sobering up. He held his hand over mine, adding more pressure to the wound, his eyes holding me with an intensity I couldn't blink away from. "Promise me. You have to listen. I can't—no doctors. It'll be all right. I'll be all right. I promise." He stood up straighter as if to prove it to me, but then just slid back down against the wall, wincing. "I heal fast. Lightning fast, in fact." He chuckled, the sound of it bizarre against the gory scene. "Trust me, you'll see."

"There's a giant fucking hole in your stomach, Levi," I said again, on the off chance my words landed this time, "you don't just heal from that. I don't understand. Were you shot?" The gash was too big for that though, not that I'd ever seen a bullet wound in person. "Please, tell me what happened?"

He grabbed my other hand, where it was braced on the wall, then twined his fingers through mine. His thumb started rubbing circles over my palm, like he was trying to comfort me, like *I* was the one he was concerned about, of the two of us. "Promise me, Mars. No hospital. No doctors. Just you."

"Levi—" A tear fell down my cheek and I pulled my hand back from him to wipe it away.

His brows furrowed as he cupped my face again.

With a gentleness so at odds with the violence of the hallway, he slid his thumb along my cheek, brushing away my tears. When he pulled it back, his thumb came away covered in blood. "No hospital. Promise."

I held his eyes, my heart racing against my rib cage.

What the hell was I supposed to do right now?

At the look of sheer desperation on his face, I nodded. "Promise."

Maybe he was right, maybe he was drunk, and this was just a deep cut, and this all just seemed so much worse because he was wasted—judging from the waft of alcohol on his breath, he might have even started that bottle he'd just finished tonight.

I needed to get a better look.

And I would break that promise if and when it came to it.

His trust wasn't as important as his life.

Propping him up against my side, his arm draped over my

shoulder like a shawl, I helped him through the entryway. We would only draw attention, maybe even the cops. And I had no idea what happened tonight, what led to these injuries, or whether Levi might be involved in a less-than-legal career path —as I was beginning to suspect.

There was no use standing out in the hall, I needed to check his wounds, see what we were working with here.

Surprisingly, he didn't protest, and he moved better than I would've anticipated given the state of him. When I started toward the couch, he redirected us toward my room. My phone was there anyway, so that was probably the better option.

Easing him onto my bed as gently as possible, I stared at the impossible amount of blood coating my hands.

This was no small wound, definitely not a trick of the hallway light or his intoxicated stumbling making this look worse than it was. It was worse than worse.

"Mars," he said again, grinning as he lingered on the name. Like this was just a regular day in the park and he wasn't bleeding out in the middle of my bedroom. "Mars—"

"Levi, stop saying my name and talk to me." I grabbed a clean shirt and pressed it to his stomach, holding more pressure there. Within seconds, it was coated in red, as if the cotton was draining the blood from him, drinking him dry.

"You mean I can't call you Mars anymore?" His features scrunched into a pout, like I'd stolen his favorite toy. "That didn't last very long."

"No, I mean—you can call me Mars."

"Good." He shot me a smug look. "I like the taste of it."

"Right now, you can call me whatever the hell you want."

"No," he said with a sad smile, "I don't think I can. Mars is a good second option. Definitely better than Rick."

"But right now," I continued, ignoring his rambling and the way his dark eyelashes perfectly framed the wildness in his eyes, "I need you—"

He pressed his finger to my lips. "You can stop the sentence there, you know."

"To tell me what the hell happened," I finished. "Levi, please—just tell me what to do, how to help you."

"Do you know how to sew, Mars?"

"Sew?" I asked, the word more a croak than anything intelligible.

He lifted the wrinkled bag at his side. "I brought supplies."

"Supplies," I echoed.

He rifled through the bag, tossing a cheap sewing kit, some rubbing alcohol, and a few packages of bandages on the bed next to him. Then he brought out a second, unopened bottle of whiskey and opened it.

"I think maybe getting wasted isn't the priority right now."

"Trust me, it is." He took a long drink, as if it was nothing more than an ice-cold bottle of water on a hot day. "I metabolize alcohol quickly."

"Exactly how much have you had?" I asked as he took another very generous sip.

"Not enough. But it helps with the pain."

"You know what else would help with the pain?"

"No hospitals," he said again. "Can you sew?"

I glanced down at the package of needles and thread. "Not well."

"Not well will do just fine for my purposes." He shot me a look that was maybe supposed to be comforting and assuring, but it lost all verity when it ended in a sharp wince. "Where's your bathroom, I need to get the wound cleaned up. Then we can begin."

My stomach dipped at the thought, but I showed him to the bathroom anyway and helped him sit at the ledge of the tub without another word of protest.

When I tried to lift his shirt up over his head, he groaned.

I dropped the fabric back down, terrified of hurting him more.

"It's out of the socket," he whispered, face scrunched in pain. "How'd I miss that?" His eyes shifted to mine. "Can you grab me that bottle, Mars?"

I nodded, then rushed to grab it.

When I got back, he was attempting to cut his shirt down the middle, while also trying to balance his weight on the ledge of the tub.

He was failing at both.

"Let me." I set the booze on the counter and took the scissors, trying to be as clinical as possible as I cut the material away, whispering a panicked "Sorry," when I had to slide it over his—now that I got a look at it—very-obviously dislocated shoulder.

Once he was no longer covered by fabric, I felt light-headed at the sight of him. His torso was a mottled canvas of bruises and blood—the worst stemming from the deep gouge in his stomach.

"It looks much worse than it is," he said, catching my look of horror, "trust me. I'll be fine."

"Levi, there's too much blood for this to be anywhere in the vicinity of fine. How the hell are you still standing? How did you even make it over here like this?"

He took another long pull from the bottle, until there was less than two-thirds of it left. If the blood loss didn't kill him, the alcohol poisoning was going to.

Maneuvering around me, he positioned himself next to the door frame, his fingers bracing against the wood, expression determined.

Then, in one swift movement, he pushed forward. A deep, agonized grunt echoed through the bathroom as he shifted his shoulder back into place.

My stomach clenched and I stood there, stunned and

breathless and hoping like hell I might wake up any moment to find this all a dream.

He kept his back to me, taking fast, shallow breaths through the pain, the muscles in his back contorting as he fought for control.

Though less disastrous looking than the front of him, there were still an impossible number of bruises and cuts on his back as well.

With as little pressure as possible, I set my fingers on his good shoulder, trying to offer comfort, even though I knew how futile the gesture was.

He shivered at my touch, then leaned into it a bit. After a moment, his breathing evened out and he turned to face me, most of the pain now washed from his expression. "Can you start the water? Not too cold, not too hot."

I did as he asked, because it was becoming abundantly clear that no matter how much I wanted him to come to the same realization I had—that this was a ridiculous project, he needed to see an *actual* doctor—he was going to do this, with or without my help.

He kicked off his pants but kept his boxers on as he stepped under the stream.

I averted my gaze—keeping it on his face to interpret his now stoic expression, or else on the floor of the tub, where the red-stained water slipped down the drain.

When I let myself catch a brief glance of his back again, I relaxed a little.

Maybe he was right. With most of the blood washed away, I could almost convince myself he wasn't an inch from death.

But then he turned around again, facing me, and I saw that the gash in his stomach was somehow worse than I thought, blood so dark it looked black still bubbling out from his skin.

He grabbed the rubbing alcohol I'd been unconsciously holding onto, my grip denting the plastic bottle. With hands somehow steadier than mine right now, he poured it liberally over the worst of his wounds.

I blinked back a fresh wave of tears and reached for some towels, then went back into my room to find the largest pair of sweatpants I had.

Handing them to him, I turned around, busying myself with grabbing his things and cleaning up as he put them on, as if modesty mattered at a time like this.

"All good," he said, his voice laced with the barest trace of amusement. "You can look now."

I added the boxers to the pile of his things when I noticed them on the ground, then glanced up. The sweats were at least a foot too short for him, but they were better than the soaked, bloody, and torn options he otherwise had. So, for now, they'd have to do.

He grabbed another towel from the shelf behind me, and the bottle of whiskey, then led us back to my room.

Eyes glassy, cheeks flushed with the heat of a buzz, he draped the clean, dry towel over my bed. After another healthy swig of booze, he tossed me the sewing kit, then collapsed back onto my bed, his head falling on the pillow.

I stared at the package, my fingers trembling.

This was just regular run-of-the-mill thread. The kind you mended stuffed animals or old clothes with. Not human flesh.

"Levi, I—"

"You just need to close it as best as you can. I'll pull the thread out in the morning when my people can take a better look at it. But I really think I just need to give my body a chance to heal while I sleep. Speaking of—" He glanced up at me, looking sheepish. "Sorry, I should have asked. Is it okay if I crash here? I can take the couch if you and your roommates are cool with it."

"Yes, and you're not taking the couch. But that's beside the point. This wound is how-are-you-still-alive serious, not sleep-it-off serious. I can't just sew you up like one of those bears in the mall."

"Trust me, you can. And it won't be that bad," he added, his face stretching into a loopy smile, "and if it is, I'm drunk enough now that I'll probably forget the pain by tomorrow."

Blackout or not, I had no doubt that he'd be intimately familiar with pain tomorrow. But sensing I was getting nowhere, I simply nodded, wondering, briefly, who exactly his 'people' were and if they were used to him showing up looking like Frankenstein's monster, then spent the next five minutes furiously washing and sanitizing my hands until they were raw.

When I got back, he had a satisfied smirk on his face as he scanned my room.

I kneeled next to the mattress, trying to get a better angle on the wound. It was still bleeding profusely. He had bandages pressed to his stomach and they were already soaked through.

"You know—" He leaned back against my pillow, eyes glassy and amused. "It smells like you in here."

"Well, I do live here." Under different circumstances, I might be concerned about that observation, wondering what I smelled like and whether it was a good thing.

With fumbling fingers, I opened the sewing kit, then took a slow, deep breath, trying to calm my nerves. The last thing he needed was me shaking while I tried poking holes through wounded flesh.

With the needle threaded, I lifted the bandages to study the wound. It was bad, but it did seem to be a *bit* less dire than I'd remembered it being when I first got a look in the bathroom.

I glanced at the clock next to my bed and froze, the needle hovering an inch above his skin.

It was a few minutes past midnight.

Realization of what that meant left my lungs forgetting how to work.

"It's my birthday—" I said, my voice flat.

"I know." He shifted to look at the clock, his eyes sparkling with the exact opposite energy that I felt. "That's one of the reasons I was in the area tonight. Happy Birthday, Mars."

"I can't do this." I shook my head and sat back on my heels. "We need to get you to the hospital." He didn't get it. I didn't mention the day because I wanted to celebrate it. The people I loved died on my birthday, and now Levi was lying here, pale as a ghost, with a serious gut wound. "You can't—Levi, you can't—"

"Just breathe." He grabbed my hand, squeezing it softly. "I won't die, Mars. Not today. I promise you that. You can kill me if I break it." His mouth twitched at the joke, but when I didn't react, his humor dried up. "It's okay, I get it, I shouldn't have asked this of you. I wasn't thinking. Didn't put it together—what this might mean for you, today of all days. Here, I can just —" He grabbed the needle, and shoved it through his skin, wincing as he sloppily tried sewing himself back together.

My mouth went dry at the absurd horror of the situation.

If I was bad at sewing, he was downright atrocious.

"Stop." I took the needle from him, and the bottle, so that I could coat my mouth with a small sip of whiskey. Not enough to impair me of course, but enough to get the taste in my mouth, to center my nervous system on something sharp and biting so that I could focus on the task and not my own fear.

The first stitch was the worst. My thoughts were attuned to every twitch of his body, acutely aware that it was my hand causing each inflection of pain. I had no fucking clue what I was doing, and I was absolutely terrified that I might make things worse.

But then, I created a mental wall around my emotions— something I was more than used to doing, but had grown sloppy about whenever he was around. This was going to happen, one way or another, and so the best I could do for him was numb my own terror and give it my best shot.

After cutting the third stitch, it got easier—both of us growing accustomed to what to expect. I closed the largest of the wounds as well as I could, then started properly sterilizing the other, smaller ones when I was done. One of them, though much better than the abdomen, also needed a stitch or two, so I got to work on that.

I was vaguely aware of Levi's eyes on me, but I didn't let myself look up, wouldn't let myself get distracted by whatever flash of pain I saw reflected there. Not until I was done.

His head dipped forward, studying my work. "Not bad, Mars. You're pretty good at this. Thank you."

"You're welcome." I went to the hall closet, returning with a scarf.

Sensing my intent, he leaned forward, and I wrapped his arm and shoulder in the thin material until it formed a makeshift sling. Not amazing, but it would hopefully keep the joint still while he got some rest.

Only after I washed my hands, cleaning up the final traces of his blood beneath my nails and the bathroom sink, did I finally let myself take a full breath.

When I returned, I set a glass of water within his reach, then kept my back to him as I wordlessly climbed out of my blood-soaked clothes and changed into a baggy shirt and pair of sweats.

Trying not to touch him or jostle the bed too much, I crawled over him to the other side of the mattress. I pulled my hair from the tight messy bun I'd had it in while I worked, then fell back against my other pillow, letting the weight of the evening sink from my bones.

Levi grabbed the slim hairband I'd temporarily set on my stomach and started stretching it around his fingers, the silence thick between us.

"I owe you a truth," he said, voice hoarse, "from that day on the bus."

"Don't worry about it," I said, trying to fight my way back inside my body, to calm the raging panic that still quivered in my bones.

"But I am worried about it. I don't like having debts. Ask me a question and I'll answer it. If I can."

"Fine," I said, my voice trembling. "What the hell happened to you tonight?"

He shook his head. "Not that. Ask me something easier."

I searched for an easier truth, but all the truths that I wanted from him were messy and hard. And right now, what I wanted, even more than the truth, was for him to rest, to get better, to survive. So, I went with the most frivolous thing I could think of. "Was Sora right?"

"About what?"

"The dog park?" I grinned, then sniffed back another threat of tears. "Favorite place in Seattle?"

"No." He shook his head.

"No?" When I turned to him, his face was so close to mine, our noses just an inch or two from brushing.

"This." His eyes found mine, the wild storm of grays more subdued now as exhaustion seeped into them. "This is my favorite place in Seattle."

He shifted slightly, then closed his eyes, settling in for sleep.

I turned off the light, and blew out my candle, easing back into the silence.

Then he added in a low, exhausted mumble, "Nowhere else even comes close."

It was hours before I finally let myself fall asleep. Instead, I stayed up until the sun greeted me, not moving, barely even breathing.

I watched him, my heart stopping each time his chest deflated with breath, as if that might be the last time.

My thoughts spiraled, and I found myself counting to three, tapping my fingers silently, wincing as my nails pressed into the fleshy pads of my thumbs over and over again in search of some ever-elusive valve to dissipate the fear—my brain conjuring images and possibilities of his death, what might happen to him, how it was all, somehow, my fault.

Diet friendship or not, it had been a futile pursuit. He'd found a way in. Obliterating my defenses, while giving me the illusion that I had control, that my armor could withstand him.

And now he would die, just like everyone else, and all I could do was sit here and watch, breathing in the same air until, inevitably, his body chose to stop. I'd wake up to find that I'd slept next to a corpse.

So, I fought off that reality, fought off sleep.

Obsessively, my eyes tracked his wounds.

At first, when I noticed some of them shrinking, healing, I thought it was a trick of the shadow, a product of my exhaustion. But when the hours passed and some cuts disappeared entirely—and even the worst of them, the one in his stomach, looking more like a week's old wound than something fresh and weeping as it had been just before he'd closed his eyes—I could no longer logic away the truth.

For so many months, I'd been focused on trying to understand what Levi did for work, where he went when he wasn't here, how he spent his time.

Who was this strange boy that had chiseled his way into my life?

Now, the ever-present alarm blaring sharp and loud in my head shifted the question from who, to what.

Only when the early rays of light illuminated him next to me, when I saw some of the color return to his skin, his breathing even and steady, did I fully let myself believe that he was alive, that whatever he'd experienced last night wouldn't kill him.

I set my hand on the warm skin of his uninjured shoulder,

soaking in the feel of his aliveness, and let sleep finally take me under.

I'd intended to only doze for a few minutes, but when I woke up, I found myself alone, my room empty of all signs that Levi had been here at all. The only tell was the soft scent of him on my sheets and a small box on the pillow where his head had been.

It was black, the cardboard crumpled in the corners and flattened on one side—a casualty of whatever brought Levi, bloody and broken, to my doorstep.

I opened it to find a thin, silver ring with small shifting beads—simple and elegant.

Underneath was a folded note:

Sorry about last night, I shouldn't have put you through that.

This is no family heirloom of course, but I saw it and thought of you.

The guy I bought it from called it a fidget ring—supposedly they help with restlessness and anxiety. Probably should have given it to you right when I showed up, now that I think about it. Sounds like a gimmick, but also maybe worth a shot?

Either way, I liked the look of it and thought you might, too.

Happy Birthday, Mars.

—Hot, Mysterious Savior (though I guess technically you're the savior now)

P.S. Lost my phone, but I'll be in touch when I can. Take care in the meantime.

I slid the ring on and ran my finger over the beads as my door burst open.

My head shot up, expecting to find Levi in the doorway, but it was Sora instead.

"Happy Anniversary Extraordinaire," she yelled, her giant smile melting into concern as she stepped into my room. "Mars, you okay?"

The first tears slipped down my cheek without my notice.

My chest was tight, and I choked back a sob, a useless attempt to even out my breathing, to swallow back whatever wave was threatening to drown me.

But then Sora wrapped her arms around me, holding me close to her, so tight I almost couldn't pull in a full breath of air —until I had no choice but to let the weight of the night pour out of me.

25

MAREENA

PRESENT DAY

Claude's car was one of those that didn't require an actual metal key for the ignition. There was a large button next to the wheel, but no fob in sight. After checking the glove compartment, the small little compartment under the rearview mirror, and under the seat, I was quickly losing confidence that Claude had been cavalier enough to leave it here for easy swiping.

"Well—" Kieran sighed from the backseat. "This was a good, not at all batshit idea and all, but I think we're going to need a Plan B. Preferably one with a little more rationality fueling it, if you don't mind?"

There was a lone water bottle in the cupholder. It sat tilted at an awkward angle, like there was something beneath it, keeping it from sitting flush against the bottom.

I held my breath, with one eye closed, and picked it up.

The fob. I lifted the small piece of plastic with a triumphant cheer.

"Um, Agony?" Kieran scooched forward, extending his arm between me and Thorne. I followed his finger to its point—the front of the bar, about twenty feet away. Claude stepped out with the bouncer, the two of them locked in what appeared to be a friendly, business conversation—any anger I'd induced in the vampire, already seemed like a distant memory. Until he looked up. Claude's eyes landed on mine, his expression moving swiftly through shock, then straight to rage. "Assuming you want to keep living, we need to leave. Now."

My stomach clenched as I started the ignition. The gentle rumble of the engine jolted the car to life.

Right. What came next?

Thorne grunted beside me, clearly amused by the situation as Claude started marching toward us.

The vampire was surprisingly collected and in no evident rush, which worked in our favor. He didn't think I was actually going to go through with it.

Then again, maybe I wasn't. When I tried tugging the stick into reverse, it didn't budge.

"Hit the brakes, shift to reverse, then step on the gas. Now," Kieran screamed in my ear.

For once, I did as he demanded, no questions asked. The car shot backward with surprising speed as I pressed the pedal to the floor. There was a loud crunching noise as the back bumper ran into what I could only hope was an abandoned fire hydrant, before I managed to hit the beaks again.

Claude's restrained anger cracked into something fiercer, his neck and cheeks flushing as he assessed the damage to his car.

Kieran's hands gripped the back of my seat. He was clearly trying to shake it, though his hold on this world was tenuous, and the cushion hardly even budged under the pressure. "Do the same thing but shift to drive. Go!"

"Fuck, fuck, fuck," I muttered. Just as Claude reached for Thorne's door, the car went tearing forward down the street. I kept my foot on the pedal, grateful for once that this wasn't the Before.

We were the only ones on the road, which made it easy to speed through, and my odds of accidentally killing someone were very low. My turns were, putting it gently, quite rough. Each one was accompanied by a loud, squealing soundtrack, as the rubber fought for purchase against the pavement.

Claude chased after us for a few blocks, his vampiric speed fast enough to get him within reaching distance of the back door a few times, but not quite enough to outpace his car's full throttle. And so long as I didn't slow down, there wasn't much of a chance for him to grab hold of anything with enough purchase to hang on long term. When he finally gave up, I glanced in the rearview mirror. His perfectly pressed shirt was wrinkled and untucked, his impeccably combed hair now falling listlessly over his eyes. And there, clear as day in the anger pulsing from his face, was the explicit promise of my death at his hands—to be carried out the very moment he found me.

That would be tomorrow's problem.

It took me a little while to get the hang of easing on and off the pedals, but once Claude was no longer chasing us, I grew comfortable enough to slow down a bit. Turns were a lot easier to handle when they weren't taken at full speed.

By the time we made it back to my neighborhood, I'd only hit two curbs, which I considered a reasonable success for a first-time driver. Of course, we did lose the passenger side mirror to a rogue sign I didn't spot quickly enough, but I figured that at the end of the day, it didn't really matter. Claude was going to murder me, whether I returned his car perfectly intact or not.

Ideally, I'd find and get the stuff with Sora sorted before he came calling.

When I parked the SUV outside of Frank's—poorly, judging by Thorne's condescending smirk—the brief flare of hope I'd allowed myself deflated. The diner was still dark and locked. It was past midnight though, so I wasn't sure what I'd been expecting. Even if Sora had made it back tonight, she wouldn't still be serving downstairs.

Thorne stayed by the car while Kieran and I ran upstairs. The apartment was just as I'd left it before, no sign that Sora had been by in my absence at all. Swallowing my disappointment, I went into my room to change. There wasn't time to wallow or worry more than I already had. The more leads that dried up, the more convinced I became that something was very, very wrong. Whatever Sora was caught up in, something told me that I was better off facing it in something a little more stealth than a short dress.

"Mareena?" Kieran asked, startling me with the use of my actual name. His back was turned to me as I buttoned up my jeans and threw on a dark T-shirt. "What exactly is the plan here?"

"What do you mean? Claude said he saw Sora at House of Wrath's compound today. So, we go there and either find her or someone who can point us in the right direction." I walked past him, into the kitchen. The food I'd left for Menace was gone, which meant he'd been back for his dinner already and was probably already camped out for the night. I tossed a flashlight, old map, and whatever else looked like it might be useful into my bag, making a mental note to grab a knife from the diner before I left.

When I turned to head back down the stairs, Kieran's arm reached forward, stopping me. "I don't like this." He shook his head. "This is dangerous and reckless and you're going to get yourself killed."

I shot him a look. "Good thing I have a guardian angel then, isn't it?"

"What are the odds that she's even there?" He turned away from me, then scrubbed his hands over his face, tugging at his hair with frustration. He winced, then dropped the ringed hand back to his side. Then he let out a deep breath before facing me again, his eyes imploring as they met mine. "Even if that Claude bloke was right and telling you the truth—which, I'm sorry, is a giant fecking leap in the first place—do you have any idea what it means if she's actually mixed up with the Seven Sons? Or the odds that if they do have her, she's still alive?"

My jaw clenched as I met his stare, the gravity of his words sinking in my chest like an anchor. "And what would you have me do? Just stay here and continue playing Operation Joy with you? Pretend that my best friend isn't in trouble?"

"Yes," he begged. "At least for tonight. I'll convince Thorne to leave in the morning, and we can figure out a plan tomorrow. When we're thinking straight. For fuck's sake, Agony, you've already broken into a demon club and carjacked a vehicle from a vampire—how much more luck do you think you have before you wind up dead?"

"Like I said, I'm out of leads and I'm not going to just sit on my thumbs hoping the problem mysteriously goes away by morning." I sidestepped him, then took the stairs two at a time. "Besides," I called back without turning around, "some of the people in the compounds are reasonable. If I show them the photo and explain Rex's ridiculous ritual scavenger hunt, they might know how to help."

"And tell me, Agony, what the hell's going to stop them from killing you the moment you step foot on their territory?" Kieran asked, hot on my heels.

When we reached the door, I locked up.

"I don't know." I gestured behind me, where Thorne was still brooding in the front seat. "I'll offer them Claude's car as a bargaining chip or something. I'll figure it out when the time comes, okay?"

Kieran was still arguing with me when I got back into the car, buckled myself in, and started it up.

"She's my family, Kieran." I unbuckled myself and spun

around, staring at him until the last of his protests fizzled into silence. "Okay? I don't care how ridiculous you think this plan is. It's happening. You can either continue haunting me or leave, but there is no more finding my joy or whatever it is you think your job with me is exactly, until Sora is safe and back home. Period."

Kieran's jaw muscles ticked, his eyes broadcasting his seething anger, but he didn't say anything more.

I felt Thorne's stare drilling into the side of my face when I turned back around and buckled up again, but I kept my focus on the road. Tossing the old map I'd grabbed into the back, I caught Kieran's eyes in the rearview mirror. "If you want to help, we're headed toward West Seattle. From what I've heard, that's where Wrath's homebase is."

It wasn't the greatest truce, but it was all I could offer him right now—some small semblance of control. For a moment, I didn't think he'd take the olive branch, but then he unfolded and dropped his gaze from me to the map.

As the crow flies, West Seattle was only a couple of miles from our apartment, but it always took a decent, winding trip to make it there on land.

The drive was bumpy and stilted at first, but I slowly grew more confident behind the wheel. By the time I pulled onto I-5, with the windows down and the summer breeze rushing through my hair, I couldn't help but enjoy the feeling of it. We drove by parts of the city I rarely got to visit anymore. And it had been so long since I'd been in a car that I'd forgotten how much fun it could be, how alive I felt when the wind cut against my skin.

Kieran spent most of the drive quietly stewing, but he broke his silence every now and then to whisper instructions and driving tips whenever his worry outweighed his rage.

Thorne, meanwhile, was significantly less tense than he'd been all night. The wind whipped through his hair, making him seem more human and alive than he was. At one point, I could've sworn that I'd even caught what might have passed as a crooked smile on his lips from the corner of my eye, but it disappeared as soon as I turned to get a better look.

After an hour of driving in circles and stopping two drunk strangers to point me to the right neighborhood, we were finally there.

I parked Claude's SUV a block away in a random driveway, making sure to lock up and pocket the key fob. Kieran and Thorne followed as we made our way toward what had been a community college many years ago. The once-welcoming campus was now almost completely fenced in, the tops of the fence accessorized with curling barbed wire. Signs warning against trespassing were plastered every few feet.

I'd never actually been inside one of the compounds before, and I wasn't exactly sure how to go about gaining entrance. But of all the Sons to pick a fight with, Wrath was certainly one of the worst. For a fraction of a second, I considered my options. Did I just climb the fence and hope that, once I was on the other side and showed enough people the picture, they might point me toward Sora?

Of course, that option also required that if Sora was, in fact, really here, she'd come of her own volition. I didn't actually think that she was working with the compound or working with their fighting circuit. I'd been serious when I told Claude that he'd been given bad information. Apart from the fact that Sora had no way of getting to this part of the city with any semblance of regularity, the tenets Wrath stood for were as divorced from her personality and values as it was possible to get.

But it *was* possible that she was here, that Claude really did see her today, that she'd gotten pulled into a dangerous situation while trying to collect everything she needed for Rex's necromancy ritual. If she legitimately thought it was possible to communicate with Rina, there were very few limits to the risks she might take.

Because there were also very few limits to the risks that I would take for Sora.

And if things turned south, which it sounded like they had, it was also possible that any connections she'd made along the way might turn on her.

"What's the plan here, Agony?" Kieran's gaze traced the fence along the road, stopping at a small post set up for security watch. Wrath had made enough enemies through the years, that I was sort of shocked to find the area otherwise undefended. "You don't really think she's here, do you?"

"I don't think Claude is the type of guy to tell a bald-faced lie," I said. "And we don't have any other leads."

The area was unusually silent, the kind of silence that didn't feel natural. It was still the way that a vampire was still, the illusion of safety just before the bubble popped . . . along with the nearest vein.

When I turned back toward Kieran, his eyes were round with fear. He pulled me toward him, and rolled us down to the ground, just as an arrow shot through Thorne, exactly where I'd been standing just a second ago. Thorne looked just as surprised as I felt, his face twisting with confusion briefly, before settling back on its factory setting: anger.

Okay, apparently Wrath was well guarded, they were just also good at discretion—and clearly went with a shoot first, ask questions later approach to guarding their perimeter.

Kieran tugged me back to my feet with surprising strength for a dead guy who only had limited corporality. "Run!"

For the second time tonight, and a new record, I didn't challenge Kieran's order. Instead, I took off at a blistering pace, my boots pounding a steady drum that kept pace with my heart rate, as I wound through the neighborhood, not stopping until an angry stitch shot through my chest and my lungs screamed for a break.

Kieran, not appearing winded at all, threaded his hand through mine, then pulled me behind what looked like a mostly vacant apartment building.

The street was dark, nothing but the soft glow of the moon highlighting the generally drab scenery around us. If people were living in the area, they'd likely be asleep.

"Thanks." I hunched over, trying to catch my breath. "That was close. Good, you know—" I waved my hand in his general direction. "Guardian-angeling and what not."

When I looked up, expecting to catch Kieran's familiar smirk, I found his face a blank mask instead. His attention was locked on Thorne, the two of them tense and coiled like predators just before a strike.

"What the fuck were you thinking?" Thorne shoved Kieran, his face contorting in disbelief. "Never mind." He shook his head. "You're very clearly not thinking at all." He started to walk away, then, after a few paces turned back, one hand buried in his hair as the other reached out in front of him. "That was it, Kieran. That was the bloody moment. You just had to stand there and let her fucking die. Better yet, she's right there—" He flung his extended arm in my direction, an exasperated look in his eyes. "Just shove your hand into her chest and end it now. You've done it a hundred times before. What the hell is it about this girl that you suddenly can't complete one simple job?"

"Kieran." My mouth went dry, and my stomach dropped as I watched the two of them square off. My lungs refused to let me take a full breath, like my whole body knew before I did where this was heading. I licked my lips and tried again. "What is he talking about?"

Kieran opened his mouth, searching for an excuse that

wouldn't come. He saw the realization crystalize on my face as he took a step toward me. "Agony—"

And for once, I felt the full force of that nickname, like a dagger buried deep in my back.

The silence was broken by a dark, ragged chuckle. It lingered in the air between us for a moment, before I realized it was my own.

"You're not a guardian angel, are you?" The question sounded ridiculous to my ears as I asked it. "No—" I shook my head, the truth suffocating me with every passing second. "There's no such thing as guardian angels." I fell back against the apartment building, letting it hold up the weight my legs no longer seemed willing to. My breaths came out loud and harsh as I studied the two of them. "Of course not. I'm just an absolute idiot."

I tilted my chin toward Thorne, his frustration with Kieran making so much sense now. "You're like him, right?" What had he called it? "A reaper?" My voice didn't even sound like my own anymore. It was hollow and tinny as it echoed inside of my head. "You're not here to protect my life." When I finally brought myself to look up, Kieran wouldn't meet my eyes. "You're here to end it."

26

MAREENA

PRESENT DAY

It was a strange feeling, knowing that after all this time, Death was going to win.

Of course, I always knew that was how my story would end eventually. It was how everyone's story ended. But there was something about the incontrovertible promise of it, the *nowness*, the confirmation that I was going to die soon—probably already should have died, from the sound of it—that had my head spinning like a top before finally fizzling into a steady, sobering clarity.

Kieran was in front of me, saying something. His lips were moving, but all that I could hear was the rush of my own blood through my veins.

I was going to die. And I had two reapers haunting me to prove it.

"No," I said. Not yet. Not until I helped Sora. If Death was going to take me, he would have to wait until I finished what I started. I wasn't giving up until I was certain she was safe. I owed her that much.

Fueled by the kind of raw conviction I suppose only came with the acceptance of one last hoorah, I shoved away from the wall and started walking back in the direction I'd come running from.

Fingers gripped my wrist, but I tugged my arm away, flinching at Kieran's touch. "No. You don't get to touch me."

"Agony—"

"And you don't get to call me that ridiculous name." I spun around and faced him. "For fuck's sake, Kieran, a few hours ago your head was buried between my legs. Last night, you slept in my bed—" I winced, then pressed the heel of my hand into my chest, as if that might somehow rub away the ache that bloomed there. "And this whole time you were lying to me. Is that what this was? A quick fuck while you were casually just waiting for me to die? Do you have any idea how irredeemably fucked up that is?"

"Jesus, mate." Thorne winced. "That's low, even for you."

I shot Thorne a glare, but he only held up his hands in surrender. My jaw was clenched so tightly that I was certain I was going to crack a tooth. Not that it mattered. Dentistry was the least of my bodily concerns at the moment.

"Mareena," Kieran started again, his eyes flashing with emotion that I had no interest in dissecting. When I ignored him, continuing my path back toward House of Wrath, I heard him rush to follow me. "You have to understand, I've been doing this forever."

I snorted. "Is that supposed to make me feel better? Do your other charges thank you for their pity fucks?"

"No." He let out a low, frustrated sigh. "That's not what I'm saying. I've never had a charge who could see me before—let alone one who remembered my face. We aren't built for this world. We're not meant to have any kind of foothold or tether to the living. And then I saw you, and you not only saw me, but recognized me, and I—I fecking panicked, okay? It seemed way kinder to let you think that I was here to protect you."

Ignoring him, I picked up my pace, trying to focus on the sound of my steps on the pavement and not his words.

"It seemed kinder," he continued, "to help you spend whatever time you had left doing the things that you love—the things that make you feel alive. To help you enjoy your life—revel in it. Isn't that better than looking around every corner, waiting for whatever the fates have planned? Spending the rest of your life wasted in a panic?"

"Bloody hell, just put her out of her misery," Thorne muttered behind us. "It'll take two seconds, just reach through her chest and end it. I don't understand why you're still carrying on about this, we have places to be."

Fucking hell, this guy was a dick. I rounded on him, my sudden stop so unexpected that he nearly walked right through me. He wasn't like Kieran, didn't feel solid in the same way. The few times he'd drawn close to me, I didn't even feel him. But however much I hated Thorne, I didn't want to waste any of the time I had left on him. It was pointless.

Infuriating as he was, he didn't matter.

Instead, I turned my ire where it had been truly earned—toward Kieran.

"No," I snapped. "It isn't better. If I'd known that this was it—that I was *dying*—I wouldn't have chosen to spend whatever time I had left with you—a guy I fucked once in a dark alley. I would've spent it with the people who actually matter to me." Kieran's face was sapped of all emotion, his eyes hard and unyielding as if I'd just slapped him. "With Sora. And Frank. And Jo and Aidan. The people who've given me a purpose—my family. Not gallivanting around Seattle with a virtual stranger while he butts his nose into my life making snarky judgments about it."

When he didn't respond, his stare vacant and unyielding, I started walking again.

"Wait." He reached for my shoulder again, but when I shot

him another glare, he pulled it back. "You're not seriously going back there?"

The fuck did it look like? "Of course I am."

"Mareena. Just—" His eyes narrowed, and this time he ignored my death stare, grabbed both of my shoulders and turned me toward him. "You literally just learned that you've been slated for death. You could die at any second." I shoved his hands off me and kept walking. He let out a frustrated groan. "And your response to that information is to charge head-first, back to the people who just tried to drive an arrow through your chest?"

"Yep," I said, letting my anger burn so hot that it ebbed the tendril of fear the truth of him had revealed.

He stepped in front of me, his expression dark, angry. I realized then, under the full force of it, how ridiculously naive I had been to think that the man in front of me foretold anything but death. "No." He shook his head. "I won't allow it."

I snorted. "You can't stop me."

This was the mortal realm; he wasn't of this world. Yes, he could touch me, but he didn't have the same stronghold here that I did. And the flicker of frustration in his expression confirmed the truth—I was right.

"Honestly . . ." Thorne's condescending voice cut through our battle of wills. He'd given us a wide berth for a minute or two but, like Kieran, he didn't seem capable of leaving me alone altogether. "The girl runs into danger with all of the grace and intent of an elephant in an operating room. It's a miracle that you've managed to keep her alive for as long as you have. Just let her get on with it and we'll find you a nice dead girl to fuck when we get home."

Kieran rounded on his friend. Then, in one fluid movement, buried his fist into his nose.

I didn't know much about the physics of the dead, but it seemed like a pretty good strike.

Thorne's head knocked back, and he nearly fell over from the force of it. When he steadied himself and looked up, blood streamed from his nose. I expected him to shout or swear, but he only grinned, his expression feral and bloodthirsty as red seeped between his teeth. Then, he charged forward, and the two reapers tangled together in a whirlwind of fists and grunts.

I left them to it and continued on my way back toward House of Wrath.

But when I turned the final corner, just next to where I'd left Claude's car, I found myself surrounded.

A dozen figures, all masked and dressed in black—wielding weapons, from guns to long knives, to the bow and arrow that had nearly taken me out earlier—formed a cage around me.

Fuck. Apparently, the time between learning that I was going to die and actually dying was going to be a very small gap.

"Where is he?" a deep voice asked to my right.

"Um," I said, raising my hands up as someone came forward and started patting me down for weapons. "Who?"

"Claude," the voice barked, "the vampire. You arrived in his vehicle, did you not? Where is he?"

Kieran and Thorne made their way over to me, both looking tousled and bloody and angrier at me for ditching them than they seemed to be at each other.

"He's not here." I licked my lips, hating the tremble in my voice as someone shoved what was undoubtedly a gun between my shoulder blades. Though when I considered the other options, I supposed that a gunshot to the heart would be much quicker than most. "I stole his car."

"You seriously expect us to believe"—the masked man behind me let out a dark laugh—"that *you* stole the vamp's car?"

"Easy, Agony," Kieran said, "don't make any sudden movements, don't do anything that's going to get you killed. Just do what they ask." His voice was low, raspy, and the way his gaze shifted over the group of Wrath's followers, assessing each of them, his shoulders tense and jawline tight, it seemed like he was more terrified of our predicament than I was.

Which didn't make any sense. They couldn't touch him. He was already dead.

"You don't need to believe it," I said, flinching when the guy behind me shoved the gun deeper into my back, "but it's true. He said my friend was here and I didn't have any other way to make the trip tonight. So, when he was preoccupied, I took his car. I swear, I'm just looking for my friend. I don't mean any trouble."

"What are you?" Someone else in the circle asked the question this time—a woman, maybe, from the sound of it. "A vampire? Or some other demon?"

"Suppose we could find out the slow way," someone else said, their tone taunting. "See how far her body can be pushed before it finally breaks."

"Human," I said, my voice cracking on the word. "I'm just a human."

There was a chorus of laughter, then the first voice said, "We can't afford more issues with Claude. Just kill her. But don't waste a bullet. Then, when the moody prick inevitably shows up to fetch his car, we can offer her body as proof we're not working with her, that we don't want any more trouble."

For a moment, my mind went blank at the simple directive. *Kill her.*

He'd spoken the demand with the same arbitrary conviction my customers often used when choosing between breakfast options—like, in the grand scheme of things, it hardly mattered. My life came down to a decision less meaningful than over easy or sunny side up.

Someone, Kieran, I think, yelled a deep, menacing, "No."

His voice was loud and desperate as it pierced through the strange calm, though no one else appeared able to hear him.

Another figure walked toward me, a large blade in his hand as the guy at my back locked my arms behind me, holding me still.

When the reality of the situation sank in, I tried to shake loose from my captor, to fight, but he was much stronger than I was.

Keiran stepped between me and the person approaching. When he tried to punch them, his fist simply passed through the guy's face. When he tried again, this time going for the knife the guy held instead of the guy himself, nothing happened. He didn't have a strong enough foothold.

It was a ridiculous thought to have in that moment, but I couldn't help but think that Thorne had a point. If Kieran's only job was to hasten my death, he most definitely wouldn't be earning employee of the month any time soon.

When I caught sight of Thorne, standing just outside the circle of Wrath recruits, he watched on with only a vague interest, though his eyes were locked on mine, the emotion in them unreadable.

"I'll make it quick," the man with the knife said as he reached me. And when he lifted the blade to my neck, I stopped fighting, closing my eyes only when the metal pricked against the sensitive skin of my collar bone.

"Wait!" a woman called, from somewhere beyond the circle. "Hold the order, I know her." The knife's cool metal stayed where it was, though the pressure lessened slightly. "I mean it, Jack. Drop the blade. Now."

My pulse thrummed an impossible rhythm against my neck, as I opened one eye, then the second.

"Bloody hell," Thorne grumbled, "this girl's got nine lives."

Jack stepped back, and I sank against the guy still holding me, my knees weak with relief.

No one spoke as a figure climbed down from a roof across the street, a gun strapped to their back, the circle of recruits parting to let them in.

They were short, dressed head-to-toe in black, like the rest of them.

And when they pulled off their mask, the breath emptied from my lungs.

The same dark eyes, button nose, and face I saw every day.

"So Claude was right. Sora is with Wrath?" Kieran asked, his mouth bent in surprise as he studied her. "She got a haircut."

Her dark hair was shorn off in a pixie cut, and there was a scar through her lip that I'd never seen before.

And then, for the second time in twenty minutes, my entire world turned upside down.

"Rina?" I stared at her, unblinking, half-convinced that if I closed my eyes for even a fraction of a second, I'd open them to find this all a dream. "You're alive?"

"Hey, Mareena," she said, her lips curving into a harder version of her twin's smile, "good to see you, too."

27

MAREENA

APPROXIMATELY SEVEN YEARS AGO, NINE
MONTHS BEFORE THE UNDOING

The sun was gone, the final low rays of orange and pink that cast a faint glow over the water disappearing from sight. I floated, my foot dangling in the water over my board, trying to get the energy to get up and leave.

There was an unusual chill as the few remaining water droplets from my swim cooled against my skin. Shivering, I briefly debated the merits of tipping back into the water, stealing one last lap through the bay before fall truly started to settle in.

I knew it was a bad idea. Swimming alone out here, once it was dark, was asking for trouble. It was only too easy to slip beneath the surface, and let the quiet stillness take over—a small reprieve from the strange metallic air I'd been suffocating on for months.

Before I could think too much about it, I shoved my board onto the dock, piled my dry bag and oar on top of it, and then kicked off, plunging into the dark depths, savoring the sharp chill of the water like it was a rich, luxurious dessert.

With slow, smooth strokes, I swam into the middle of the

bay. It was rare having the whole area entirely to myself like this. The quiet isolation, marred only by the handful of lights on in the surrounding houseboats made it feel like the entire lake belonged to me. Like I belonged to it.

As I shifted onto my back, staring at the gray-streaked sky above, the murky edges of the moon faded and brightened, as if a light switch had been flipped behind it.

This was, perhaps, the first moment of peace I'd felt all summer.

Things had been strange in the city. Intense.

There'd been countless disappearances, strange accidents, and odd stories on the news that hardly seemed explainable. Not to mention that the weather had been wildly unpredictable, even more than climate scientists could explain. In one day, we'd encountered all four seasons—ice storm to blazing-dry heat—unprecedented shifts in the temperature.

But even stranger than the unexplained events was the steady presence of something darker. Something suffocating.

Death.

I couldn't put it into words, but I felt him growing closer, like a phantom slowly shedding its translucence, becoming solid.

Sometimes, I swore I could almost taste the traces of him in the air.

Oddly, it wasn't an altogether threatening presence like I might expect—though I wouldn't call it particularly inviting either. It was something cold and sharp, asserting his existence in the few moments I almost let myself forget he was there.

Even Sora, who'd spent our entire friendship declaring that there were no such things as curses or omens, seemed to sense that something was changing, shifting in the world—like we were on the precipice of something big, something the world could never come back from.

She didn't speak of it often, only in the quiet moments of

the night, when we were alone, coming home from a night out into the soft safety of our apartment.

I wasn't sure whether to be relieved or not by this—that I wasn't alone in this awareness. Other people didn't really speak about it openly, usually only in the dark recesses of a bar where the steady buzz of booze gave them the courage to whisper about the strangeness, the sense of immanence in the air. But even when people didn't discuss it, couldn't put a name to it, I felt their lingering fear, their uncertainty clawing at me with every tight smile and averted gaze.

It was like the entire city was positioned on a cliff, and one small breath might send it plunging over into something new, something we could only imagine. We didn't know what it was, what it might mean, but I knew we all felt it, on some level—a bubble waiting to burst on the next, deep inhale.

Mostly, I tried to ignore it. But here, with the steady waves rolling over me, I let myself linger in the heaviness for a moment, to take a breath and let the fear pour out of me, somewhere I could leave it behind for the next few months.

I let myself sink below the surface, watching the gentle light of the moon ricochet above me as the world stilled to a quiet.

It would be so easy to stay here, to just float away and fill my lungs, until the edges where my body ended, and the lake began, started to blur and overlap—an inevitable end I was simply rushing along.

Maybe Levi had been right. There was no fighting fate.

I closed my eyes beneath the water, my finger tracing the ring, as flashes of Sora pierced through the fog. It wasn't fair to her—to leave her alone with this, another sister to grieve, not after everything she'd been through.

Slowly, I swam back to the dock, savoring each breath as it carved through my lungs.

When I pulled myself up, the biting wind sank into my bones.

Fuck. I hadn't brought a towel with me. I wasn't planning on a night swim and had counted on the heat of the sun to dry my skin from my earlier plunge.

It wasn't until after I slid my shorts over my wet bikini bottoms and tugged my tank top over my head, resigned to being cold and miserable until I made it back home, that I noticed the lurking presence behind me.

Sliding my apartment keys between my fingers, a makeshift weapon familiar to every woman, I spun around, my jaw aching with how hard I clenched it.

"Hey, Mars."

Levi.

He stood there, an unreadable expression on his face, dressed head-to-toe in black, looking as mysterious as he always did—like a shadow made solid.

My breath caught, and it felt as if I was drowning, as if I'd never reemerged from the lake at all.

"You're alive," I said, not bothering to fight the quiver in my voice.

"I am." Something flashed in his eyes, there and then gone, before his careful mask was back. "How've you been?"

For several seconds I couldn't speak—couldn't move, couldn't breathe.

And then I snapped.

"How have I been?" I popped the seal on my paddleboard so it could start deflating. Then, with rigid restraint, grabbed my oar to start disassembling the pieces. "How've I fucking been?" I tossed the metal back onto the dock, abandoning the pursuit where I started it, and walked up to him. "Fifteen months." I jabbed my finger into his chest, keeping my sightline there, because I couldn't stand to meet his eyes. Couldn't bear what I might find there. "It's been fifteen fucking months of no word."

"I—"

"You showed up on my doorstep a breath away from death, disappeared in the morning, and I haven't heard from you since. Not a"—I bent down, folding my board to hurry up the process, my back to him—"'Hey Mareena, I'm doing fine by the way, hope you're okay.'" My fingers trembled as I stuffed the board back into its bag, not bothering to take the usual care to dry it off or make sure everything fit inside properly with the pump. "Not even a damn phone call."

I threw the bag back on the dock, abandoning the useless endeavor.

"Mars," he said, and I felt him close the distance between us, though he was careful not to touch me. "Mars, look at me—"

"You don't get to call me that," I snapped, finally meeting his stare.

He flinched at whatever he saw reflected in mine.

Good.

"You want to know why I hate when anyone but Sora calls me that? Because nicknames are for people who fucking stick around. She's stuck around, that's why she's the one exception I've made. You . . ." My voice cracked. He wasn't going to get to see my cry over him. "You fucking let me think you were dead for over a year, Levi. I thought . . ." I swallowed back the knot in my throat. "I thought you were dead. I thought you were dead because of me. That I, my curse, killed you. Because I—and all this time—"

I hunched over, burying my head in my hands as I tried to calm down, to maintain some shred of composure, though I knew it was futile at this point.

Something curled around me, enveloping me in warmth and the soft smell of spicy citrus.

I felt him sit down on the dock next to me, though he was smart enough to keep some distance between us.

For a moment, I considered tossing his stupid hoodie back in his face.

But I was cold, and as angry as I was, I couldn't deny that there was something comforting about being cocooned in its warmth right now, like he was handing over a piece of my armor I'd long abandoned in his presence.

So, instead, I shoved my arm through the holes and pulled the cotton down over my knees.

"I broke a lot of rules that night," he said, cracking through the thick silence. "I shouldn't have come to you in that condition, shouldn't have done that to you." He let out a frustrated sigh. "I should have never inserted myself into your life in the first place, but I did."

His words cut like a knife through my chest, burning as they slid through my veins.

That was what I'd wanted, right? No more friendships, no more . . . whatever the hell this had been.

I'd spent over a year wishing that I'd been stronger, that I had pushed him away and ignored his attempts at friendship, diet and regular alike. That if I'd followed my own damn rules, he might still be alive.

So why did hearing that he shared that same regret twist and strangle so much?

I watched him from the corner of my eyes, not ready to look at him properly, not trusting what my brain might conjure up with the full view of him.

The last fifteen months had been filled with nightmares in which he had a starring role—of his death, of that night—but somehow the worst were the dreams that weren't nightmares, the ones that imagined possibilities of what our lives might have looked like if I wasn't haunted by this curse. If he didn't have the life or job that he did. If we'd been permitted the space to enter into an easy, simple friendship—maybe even something more. Of what it might have looked like to be loved by someone other than Sora.

Waking up from those dreams, to the absence of him, to his presumed death, was like losing everyone I'd lost all over again.

Seeing him now, I realized how off my dreams had been—a pale imitation of the man next to me. My brain didn't have the capacity to create the exact storm of his eyes, or the way his expression shifted so slightly when he was battling some inner demon he didn't want me to see.

His gaze lingered on the water ahead of us, and I realized that this Levi was different from the one I knew before. He'd changed in the year since I'd last seen him.

There was a hardness in his features, a darkness that clouded him. An edge that I'd seen echoes of that first day at Frank's diner, then later, in the bar with Ace, but never so clearly as now.

He was colder, looked more weathered—as if he'd experienced a lifetime of days in the time we'd been apart. But he also seemed lost, the loneliness he always carried now evident in every line of his face, each angle of his body. Like he was half in this world and half out of it. Unknown to me. Even more a stranger than he'd been the day we met.

But when I glanced down at his wrist, giving up altogether now on the pretense that I wasn't just straight up studying him, I saw a thin black band.

A hairband.

The one I'd had in my hair that night, the one he'd taken from me to fidget with while he settled in for sleep.

He still had it, and he wore it, and I wasn't sure why exactly, but that realization had my chest squeezing in on itself, like it might collapse.

As if sensing the object of my focus, he shifted to cover it—but I had his hoodie, so his arms remained bare, the band in plain sight.

"It was selfish of me," he said, "forcing my way into your life like I did. Pretending like our worlds could mix. After—after that night, I thought the best thing I could do for you was stay away." He took a breath, and when he released it, he added, "And so I did."

He pressed his palms into the dock and leaned back, the muscular lines of his arms thicker, more filled out, like he'd spent the last year growing into himself, growing stronger.

Meanwhile I was curled inside of his hoodie, tensed up in a ball like a feral little gremlin. "Then why are you here now?"

A muscle worked in his jaw as he fought to work out an answer.

"And how the fuck did you find me here anyway?" This was my spot, yeah, but I realistically only made it here once, maybe twice a week—and it was late enough in the season, and colder than it usually was this time of year, that most people had already long abandoned their summer hobbies on the water.

He turned, shifting toward me, the movement stiff and then rushed, like he was losing a battle with himself, the same one I'd already lost, until I felt his eyes rove over my face. They swept over every inch, cataloging me with an intensity that made me flush, and I wondered, briefly, how much I'd changed in his eyes, since he'd last seen me. "Stopped at Frank's," he said finally, "then your apartment. Sora was there, she said you might be here." He winced. "She . . . wasn't happy with me either."

"What happened to you that night, Levi?" I asked, the questions refusing my attempt to suffocate them a moment longer. "How did you survive that? I spent weeks studying those wounds—thinking about how much blood there was. No one should have survived that." I tried to ignore the way he looked at me, his eyes half hunger, half desperation. "And why are you here now?"

He dropped his gaze, his lips curling into a sad shadow of

the smirk I remembered, no dimple in sight. I fought the urge to press my thumb to the corner of his mouth and stretch until I found it. "Truth for truth?"

"No." I curled my hands into fists inside the hoodie. He hadn't earned any more of my truths, not after this year, not after everything I'd been through. "I don't want to play any more of your games. I want answers. I—I deserve answers."

When he didn't speak, I knew I wouldn't get any. With a frustrated groan, I stood up and started collecting my things together. I didn't need to sit through this, didn't want any more half-truths. That was all he ever offered—fractures of himself, sharp as shards and just as painful.

I didn't know anything about him, about his family, about his job, about where he lived or how he spent his time.

The only truth that mattered now was that I didn't know him at all, and I never would.

Why did I care? Why had I spent so many sleepless nights worried sick to my stomach about him? When all this time, he'd been alive and well, and just chose to let me simmer with concern and, eventually, grief for fifteen fucking months?

I was done.

No more caring about Levi—

Hell, I didn't even know his last name. How ridiculous was that? To have spent so much of my time thinking about someone whose name I didn't even know. No more.

After a brief battle with my paddle board bag, I gave up on it, wrapping the thin material around the board, holding the awkward bundle to my chest, as I bent down to collect the dry bag and oar.

"Mareena." He grabbed my shoulder, the shock of his touch enough to spill the precariously piled mess in my arms at my feet. "Please, talk to me." He let out a humorless chuckle. "Fuck, just look at me, even. Anything. Just. . .don't leave. Not yet."

Rage, hot and angry boiled in my blood as I stared at the useless equipment spread over the dock.

A lot of that rage was directed toward Levi, but there was a not-small part, some might even say a decent majority, that was directed squarely at myself.

For caring, for letting him chisel his way in, for not insisting over a year ago that we end things before he had a chance to matter—to mean something to me.

Because the most frustrating fucking part was that I always knew how this was going to end. That I'd end up hurt. I just hadn't expected it to be in this way.

I'd been so naive I didn't even consider it, didn't think to see it coming. That he would leave because he chose to, not because he died. Not because of the curse, but because he didn't want to stay.

Something about that broke something deep inside of me and I hated myself for admitting it, even just to myself. Hated myself for giving a fuck about Levi, because there was no putting an end to it. Even as angry as I was, I couldn't deny that I *did* care about Levi No Last Name. It didn't matter how much I wished I didn't.

I knew better, and I fucking let myself care anyway.

My vision blurred as I fought to keep the film of tears from becoming a full-blown breakdown. The last thing I wanted was for him to know how much he affected me; how much he'd gotten under my skin—burrowing under there until it felt more like it belonged to him than it did me.

He rubbed his hands up and down my arms and the friction of the contact sparked down my spine, all the way into the soles of my feet. "Mareena."

With a deep, steady breath, I calmed the storm churning through me, blinking back any trace of emotion. It was a skill I'd mastered years ago, and I'd never been so glad for it as I was now.

I turned around, finding only a foot of distance between us, the reality of his here-ness, his alive-ness impossible to ignore or deny.

"I'm sorry," he said, and because I *did* know him—fractured as the shards were—I also knew that he meant it. Deeply and intimately and in that annoyingly sincere way that only Levi seemed able to convey. "The very last thing I meant to do was hurt you. It might seem like a lie, but it's not. I stayed away to protect you. I didn't even think about the possibility that you might assume I was dead."

"Well—" My chin quivered, but I bit my lip before I did anything ridiculous like cry. "I'm glad that you're not, I guess."

When I let myself glance up, let myself meet his eyes again, my head felt light and dizzy at the depth of his stare—at the unreadable turmoil that I found there.

At the way he looked at me, like it hadn't been fifteen months but fifteen years—like he was mapping out every inch of my face, recommitting it to memory. Like I wasn't real, but he was trying to convince himself that I was.

I knew that look, that desperation, because I found myself staring at him the same way.

And then warm, sheer relief shot through my chest at the realization that he was here—a gnarled knot in my stomach, one I realized only now had existed since the morning I found him gone, finally loosened. He was, all things considered, okay. He was alive.

Except here I was caring again, and I didn't know what to do with that feeling, the impossibility of it, so I just tangled it right back up with hot, righteous rage.

I shook my head. "You know, you can't just do that. You can't just look at me like that and say that you're sorry and exp—"

But whatever else I was about to say was instantly lost, devoured by the press of his lips against mine.

His kiss was hungry and hot and demanding, and when he

pulled me close to him, one hand pressing against my lower back, the other twined through my hair, I sank into it, into him.

I wrapped my arms around his neck, my fingers digging in at the base of his skull, holding him closer, closer, closer—and when my tongue finally traced the seam of his mouth to meet his, a deep, possessive groan vibrated against me.

He tasted like bourbon and dark chocolate, and I couldn't remember a single kiss that had ever completely unraveled me like this—none that had even come close.

When he pulled back, eyes closed, he pressed his forehead against mine, and I realized that my cheeks were wet.

I didn't recall crying, but there they were—tears. Over a boy.

"I'm sorry. I just—" With gentle, almost reverent hands, he cupped my face. His eyes were still closed, and there was a soft, sad smile on his lips. Lips that I'd just kissed. Lips that I desperately wanted to kiss again, as angry as I was at the rest of him. "I needed to do that. Just once."

"You're leaving again." I froze, my heartbeat thudding in my ears. "The curse? Is that what you're worried about? We can go back to the old rules. Diet—"

He shook his head, his eyes snapping open as they landed on mine. "No. I told you before that I wasn't afraid of death. If given the choice, I'd choose you over a long life any day of the week."

"But you're leaving," I repeated, my body suddenly numb with the loss as I watched the truth unfold in his stormy stare. "And you're not coming back. You're leaving for good this time, aren't you?"

A muscle worked in his jaw, then an imperceptible nod as I pulled away from his touch.

"Then why did you come back at all?" I asked. My voice cracked, but this time I didn't bother trying to suffocate the pain. "Why did you spend so much time and energy trying to convince me to be your friend? To make me—" I sucked in a ragged breath. "To just leave all over again."

"I shouldn't have," he said. "But you have to understand, before you—before you, I was lost. I didn't give a fuck about anything. I was perfectly content to just watch the world crumble around me. And then I met you. . .and suddenly I found myself wanting to do everything that I could to save it." He took a slow, deep breath as his eyes searched mine. "I just— I needed to see you one more time, to remember what this was all for."

"What are you talking about? What *what* was all for? Levi, why—" And then, because I knew in my gut that I wouldn't get the chance again, I asked the question that had been plaguing my thoughts for more than a year. "What are you?"

Instead of an answer I knew he would never give, he pressed a kiss to my forehead, his lips lingering on my skin for a few breathless moments, before he pulled back far enough to whisper. "Yours. Please take care of yourself, Mareena."

Then, he left.

And, as usual, he kept his word. I never saw him again.

28

MAREENA

PRESENT DAY

It would have been less shocking if I found myself staring at a talking unicorn than my best friend's dead twin. Who, unlike my two reaper stalkers, was clearly not dead at all.

"How?" I asked.

Rina shot a glare at someone behind me. "Let her go. I said I'll vouch for her."

The feeling returned to my arms as the guy I'd all but forgotten about released them with a sudden shove.

Kieran caught me before I fell, his chest vibrating with a low growl.

I regained my footing, then asked, "How are you alive?"

"Rina, you can't just bring in outsiders," one of the Wrath guards said, their tone laced with frustration.

Everyone, Rina included, seemed deeply uninterested in helping me make sense of the current situation.

She took a deep breath, then scanned the masked figures still surrounding us. Several of them were whispering, though I couldn't make any of their words out clearly. "Is there a room available?" she asked. "In one of the neighboring buildings, maybe? I won't bring her inside the fence line."

One of the masked guards, a few inches shorter than me, stepped forward. "Danvers won't be happy about—"

"Danvers is asleep," Rina shot back, her jaw tight. "So unless you want to wake him or one of the others up, you'll respond to my command. I hold rank here. And," she continued, brow arched, "seeing as how you're intimately aware of how Danvers tends to respond to non-emergent disturbances, I suggest you follow my lead and stop challenging me. Just this once."

"But the girl could be from Lust or—" someone else in the cluster started, but their words dissolved when Rina shifted her glare on them.

"She's certainly a lot more terrifying than your roommate," Kieran said. His face was an unreadable mask, his posture rigid, though he kept shooting glances at the people circling us, like he expected one of them to attack at any moment—whether Rina sanctioned it or not.

Wrath was known for being rash, for killing first and asking questions later, so his concern wasn't exactly unwarranted.

"She's not part of the Seven Sons." Rina's focus darted to me briefly, the corner of her lips twitching as she considered her next words. "And she's not one of the magic-touched either. She's just a girl. She works in a diner in Wallingford, for crying out loud. I can assure you, this woman is harmless."

The breath collapsed in my lungs, and I ran my hand over my chest, half-expecting that the man behind me had run his blade through it after all.

Not only was Rina alive, but she was also apparently aware of the fact that Sora and I were, too. She knew where to find us and she'd...chosen not to? Why?

My vision blurred, and I felt a cool pressure against my arm.

I flinched at the touch, finding Kieran next to me, his brows furrowed with concern.

"Don't touch me," I whispered.

Rina glanced at me, then took a step back, as if she was the one I'd admonished. And, honestly, maybe she should have been.

Sora and I had spent more than a decade mourning her, and she'd been alive this whole time? Climbing her way up in House of Wrath, of all places?

I licked my lips, then buried the hurt as I stepped closer to her. "Sora—"

The masked minions all inched forward as well, like they expected me to attack.

"Easy, Agony," Kieran said, keeping close despite my protestations.

Rina raised her hands, calling them off, her attention locked on me now. "What about her?"

"Is she here?" I asked. The casual disinterest in her voice was gutting. "That's why I came. She's missing and when the trail led to Claude, and I showed him a picture, he pointed me here." Realization settled like a stone in my gut. "He thought the girl in the picture was you."

Of course. Sora would never have joined Wrath, would never have kept this secret life from me.

Rina's eyes widened, her brows softening in surprise, but the momentary concern was gone in a flash—back in its place, was a hardened mask.

Then, she turned away from me, clustering with a few of the other members of her house, their words whispered and hurried, impossible for me to decipher.

The man behind me grabbed my arms again, linking them behind my back, as if expecting me to try and run now that their cluster had dispersed. As if I stood a chance against a dozen armed guards.

As if I could just walk away, knowing what I knew now.

Rina was alive. And, more than that, she'd been living nearby.

I watched her, clocking her militant posture, the lean lines of muscle running over her body. Small scars freckled her face, her hands, the visible patches of skin on her arms. She still looked like Sora of course, but the differences between them were so much starker now than they'd ever been growing up.

Gone was the bubbly personality of my first real friend.

There was a hardness encasing her now, edges where Sora was soft.

"People just can't stop saving you, can they?" a voice whispered in my ear.

I flinched, then found Thorne standing by my side, his expression trapped somewhere between frustration and reluctant curiosity.

"At this rate," he continued, arching his brow at Kieran, "I'm starting to suspect we'll see the death of your guardian angel before we see yours."

Tension lined Keiran's face as the two men squared off in a silent conversation.

"What do you mean?" I asked, keeping my voice all but silent. "He's already dead."

Thorne's gaze dipped to Kieran's hand, which was now hidden behind his back.

Before he answered, Rina was back in front of me. With agile fingers, she tied my hands together with a zip tie and grabbed my upper arm with a grip tight enough to bruise. Then, not so much as even meeting my stare, she tugged me away from my captor and started ushering me down the street.

"Rina—"

"Not here," she whispered, her voice cold, her lips barely moving.

"Rina, not so fast," someone from the group yelled, and she froze. "The keys?"

The tension in her shoulders eased slightly as she tightened her grip. "Where did you put the vampire's keys?"

"In my front pocket," I responded, though her fingers deftly located the fob before I'd even finished speaking.

She tossed the keys back, then pushed me forward, both of us locked in heavy silence until she ushered me into a small house.

Only when she closed the door behind me, Kieran and Thorne materializing through the wall, did she ease up. She fished a switchblade from her pocket, and I flinched when the knife sprang open a few inches from my face.

"Relax." She rolled her eyes, then moved behind me, the zip tie cuffs breaking free with a soft snap.

Rubbing my wrists, I looked around. We were in a small house, standing in a kitchen that looked like it hadn't seen visitors in months. A thin layer of dust coated everything, the scent of must inescapable.

Rina jutted her chin toward the dark green table in the corner, one that looked like it had been rescued years ago at a vintage shop, the hardware relatively new and polished. "Sit down."

But I waited until she sat in the opposite chair, her dark eyes somehow both familiar and not as they tracked me.

"Where's my sister?" she asked, her voice hard, curving strangely over the word sister, like she hadn't used it in years. "Why did Claude point you here?"

"I don't know." I shook my head. "We've tracked—"

"Who's we?"

Fuck, that's right. She couldn't see the two reapers currently studying her—one with an expression of absolute distrust, the other with abject boredom.

"Me," I corrected. "I mean, I reached out to her friend at

the market—a guy named Rex. He told her about some ritual that he'd heard about, one that could bring back the dead." I shot her a look, letting the meaning of those words sink in. "That led me to a vampire at a club, who led me to Claude's bar."

"Why would she be at a vampire bar?" she asked, looking for all intents unaffected by the suggestion that her sister was trying to commune with her dead self.

"So, it wasn't you?" I sank back into the chair, trying to piece it all together. "At least that gives us some information." Sora was definitely seen last night at Claude's. "She needed to exchange blood with a vampire, it was part of the ritual."

She grunted. "And he assumed that it was me there last night?"

I nodded. "He pointed me to House of Wrath." I studied her, trying to fill the gaps between the Rina in front of me and the Rina I knew. "Said you were high up in the fighting rings. That he kicked you out of the bar."

"That explains why he flew in here today, lobbing accusations and threats. Fuck." She sighed, then leaned her elbows on her thighs, head bowed. "I didn't want her sucked into this shit, that's why I never—"

"What happened?" I asked. "How long have you been in Seattle? Why didn't you find us—" I let out a humorless chuckle. "Well, never mind, you clearly knew where we were. You just chose to let us believe you were dead. All this time. Do you have any idea what we've been through? What Sora's been through—"

Her head shot up, her eyes beaming into me with anger. "Do you have any idea what *I've* been through?"

I met her stare. "Obviously not, but that's because I've spent the last decade mourning you."

Though Rina looked a lot stronger, tougher than I remembered her, for the first time I noticed the dark rings beneath her eyes, the fact that every single one of her fingernails was bitten down to the skin, so far that it looked painful.

"Rina—" I let some of the anger, the hurt, bleed away. "What happened to you that night? He—" I bit my lip as the memory of that night lurked in my periphery, fighting to keep everything that came attached with it at bay. "He said you were gone. I—" I could feel the warmth of her blood as I tried to stem the flow, as if she was lying there before me now, an inch away from death. "There was so much blood, we were so certain."

But the truth of it unfolded before me. It was Blake who'd confirmed that she was dead. And while she certainly looked as if she was, had Sora and I actually checked for a pulse? Or had we been so terrified, so fucking filled with grief, that we believed that monster at his word?

"It was bad." Her eyes were hard, and it felt more like she was looking through me than at. "Doctors were apparently shocked. I should've been dead, but I wasn't. Cheryl took that as her little miracle, her second chance."

Cheryl and Joe—our foster parents.

"You stayed." It felt like I'd been gutted. "With them? All this time?"

"Recovery was a long process. My memory of that night wasn't great. Cheryl and Joe told me that you and Sora tried to run. That you died in a car accident. They did what they do." She shrugged, her expression void of emotion. "They fixed things, made it okay. Promised to protect me, assured me your deaths, Blake's death, weren't my fault. Then Joe won his election. And Cheryl—she turned all her focus on me. I was her second chance. After her son . . ."

"Are they"—I wet my lips—"are they still here? Part of Wrath?"

Rina snorted. "Fuck no. They used their son's death, and my miraculous recovery, to usher in their religious awakening.

They opened a giant mega church in Oregon, started carting me around. I think she legitimately believed I was a sign from God, a true miracle—the girl who should've been dead but wasn't. A chance to atone for her failures with Blake. And, for a while, I bought into it, too. The attention. The illusion of family." Her eyes cut to me, but only briefly, like she couldn't bear to look at me for too long. "That kind of belonging can be addictive when you've been starved of it your whole life."

"What changed?" I asked, after a drawn silence.

"For years, I didn't think of Sora, or you. I tried to let that part of my life die, like I'd assumed you both had. That it was God's will or whatever. There wasn't any trace of you on social media, the news, anywhere. I assumed that was because Joe had wiped everything after your deaths, to protect me. But then, after The Undoing, things took a turn." She traced the edge of her switchblade along the table, lost to her thoughts for a few moments. "All of their faith from before"—she glanced back up at me—"when there was suddenly confirmation of demons and the supernatural—when it started to become clear that they might have lived amongst them in the Before, they started to see my little miracle in a different light."

"They turned on you," I said, my voice soft.

She nodded, the corner of her mouth curving into a dark smile. "Thought I was the devil. That I was to blame for ushering in the Apocalypse, that I was the reason they weren't raptured into the beyond. Joe came after me first." She shook her head, her expression dark. "And I just lost it. Killed him. Then her. Then I took out a few of the members of their congregation who'd witnessed my rage, who tried to finish what Joe and Cheryl started. I escaped and lived on my own for a while, just fighting day-to-day, trying to survive." She shrugged. "And then one day, I met a guy. Danvers. He brought me into a group that didn't shy away from the rage that I harbored. From my aggression. That didn't try to make me into something that I wasn't. I found a home here, with the House of Wrath."

"How long have you known about me, about Sora?" I asked.

She looked up at me, holding my stare for once. "A few years."

It felt like she'd punched me. "Why didn't you ever . . ."

"The girl you knew, the girl my sister would have wanted me to be—she was gone." She closed her knife and leaned closer. "And I didn't want to become that girl again either. Seemed better to let her stay dead. For you two to go on living your cozy little communal life, none the wiser. I looked in. You were doing well for yourselves. I didn't want to ruin it."

My jaw ached from clenching it, from forcing myself to swallow down anger that she'd taken that choice from us all. Now wasn't the time. Maybe when we found Sora, we could have that conversation.

Assuming I was still alive long enough to be present for it, of course.

I glanced at the two reapers hovering next to us, their presence now a cloying reminder that Death was close.

"Do you know where Sora might be?" Finding Sora was the only thing that mattered right now. "Will you help me find her?"

Rina studied me, silent and unreadable, for what felt like forever. Then finally, she nodded. "Tell me everything you learned from Claude. And that guy . . . Rex, did you call him?"

Relief shot through me.

Burying the baggage of our past, I combed through our visit to the market, then to the bar—Rex, Lav, Manny, Claude, every detail that I could remember.

And then, the second time through rehashing it all, when my memory snagged on Manny, my words died away.

He'd been the last to see her. The one to escort her out, according to Claude.

The realization settled in my chest, a cloak of fear.

"He mentioned something." I glanced up at Rina. "There's a bounty on you, right?"

Her lips pursed into a thin line.

"House of Lust?"

She nodded.

That calcified it.

Manny, who'd bought everyone's drinks tonight, an uncharacteristic occurrence, judging by the bartender's reaction.

Manny, who was upset that his sister was getting involved with the Seven Sons.

Who'd handed over one sister, thinking that she was the other.

"What if one of the vampires called in that bounty?" I said, my body vibrating with the sudden certainty of it. "Is it possible they took her, thinking she was you?"

Rina cursed, then stabbed her knife into the edge of the table.

Her fingers shook—with rage, with fear, maybe both.

"Stay here," she said, then shot me a look when I started to argue. "I mean it, Mareena. Do you want my help?"

I nodded.

"Then do not leave this property. I need to get in touch with Danvers to see what resources he'll let me take. This war's been brewing between Wrath and Lust for a while now, and Danvers is hungry for blood. If I can frame it properly—as a reason to escalate things—then we might stand a chance with Wrath's backing. Otherwise, we don't have any shot at getting her out alive." Her eyes were wide, pleading, and I thought, for a moment, that I saw a flicker of the old Rina in their depths. "I'll come back for you. I promise. If all goes well, we'll head out at dawn."

29

MAREENA

PRESENT DAY

I should have been sleeping. Nothing was going to change between when Rina left and when she got back, but sleep was proving impossible.

The strange vacancy of the small house made me squirm. There were two bedrooms, one of which was clearly decorated for a small child. Something about seeing the abandoned toys, the impossibly tiny clothes still hanging in the closet, the race car starter bed, filled me with a thousand questions about what had happened to the people who lived here before? What could make them pick up and leave, without what appeared to be most of their things? Was the small child who lived here simply gone?

I knew the nature of the House of Wrath, knew how ruthless, how bloodthirsty they could be. Had they forced this family to leave behind the only home they knew? Or worse—had they killed them, simply because of the house's proximity to their stronghold?

Thinking that Rina belonged to their ranks made my head spin. I didn't blame her, of course, for murdering Cheryl and Joe. Not if they attacked her. And she was right, as much as

Sora and I had been through over the years, I had no idea what kind of suffering Rina experienced in our absence.

She was alone in that suffering. Sora and I at least always had each other.

But Wrath was . . . ruthless.

As much as I didn't recognize my old friend inside of this new iteration of her, I made a solemn vow to myself not to judge her too harshly. We all had to make decisions, allegiances in this new world. Ones that, in the past, might have seemed impossible to the versions of ourselves we used to be.

I trusted that she would help. Was it possible that Wrath's followers would use Sora's possible imprisonment as justification to start the war that had been brewing between them and Lust? Probably. But if it would lead to Sora's safety, I didn't care.

Maybe that made me just as ruthless as the rest of Wrath.

Right now, Sora was all that I could bring myself to focus on.

Because if I let my thoughts wander anywhere else, they turned only to the suffocating reality that I was, quite literally this time, being followed by Death. As haunting as Death's presence always was, it had never made me feel personally victimized. I had never been the one Death was after, not directly. Tangentially, yes, but it was strange now, realizing that my life was the one at stake.

And an awful, sinking part of me thought that it might be right, justified even. I'd brought death to so many people's doors, it seemed only fair that it be my turn now.

But faced with the very real probability that I would be running toward my own demise in a few hours, I couldn't help but feel a piercing fear. There'd been many nights over the years, when I laid awake in bed, reflecting on my death. Nights when I almost wanted it, thought that it might make the world better. Nights where my own grief ached so sharply, that death seemed like the only way to release my body from the pain.

Those nights had always haunted me after, the guilt of those thoughts crawling over my skin and sinking into my pores like a poison.

Now, faced with the inevitable reality, I couldn't help but linger on a different guilt. Assuming we could rescue Sora, I'd be finding her, just to lose her forever. And Menace—what would become of him? He could survive on his own, sure, and I knew that Sora would take care of him, but realizing that I wouldn't be there, that they'd have to reshape their lives without me, that I'd be putting the people I loved in the same position Amto Amani and so many others had put me—it was harrowing. Suffocating, enough to bring me to my knees.

But it also helped, in some small way, to know that when I was gone, Sora wouldn't be alone. Her sister was alive. Here. And she still cared about her enough to abandon her project of alienating us long enough to rescue her. Maybe they could shape something new in the future, a different relationship than the one they had growing up, certainly, but something just as strong, just as tender. Sora wasn't the sort to let Rina go, no matter what shit she was involved in now. And no one was strong enough to resist Sora's affection. She had a way of grabbing hold of someone and forcing them to see their worth, their importance. They'd be okay again, one day.

"You should be sleeping." Kieran's voice pierced the quiet.

I was lying on the couch, because I couldn't bring myself to rest on the bed—not without ruminating on the lives of those who'd abandoned it. My eyes were closed, but I supposed I shouldn't be surprised that Keiran could tell I was awake.

When I abandoned the ruse, I glanced toward the voice, spotting him leaning against the doorway, half-covered in shadow. Thorne didn't appear to be in the living room, but I had no doubt that he hadn't gone far.

The sight of Kieran there, studying me like a zoo animal, only amplified the uncomfortable tension whirling in my stomach, choking my breath. I latched on to all the suffocating fear and confusion, lassoed it and morphed into something else: rage.

"Don't you mean I should be dying?" I shot back, feeling almost satisfied at his flinch. "What use is sleep when we both know I don't have much time left."

"Agony." He stepped forward, stopping when I shot up into a seated position, pinning him with my glare. "You can't seriously consider going after Sora. You will die; don't you get that?" His hand flexed, and though I couldn't see it beyond where his sleeve opened at his wrist, I knew that the dark veins had only wound themselves higher. "This isn't something to fuck with. Why are you running toward danger when you know it will only lead to one fate. Just stay here." He shook his head, his jaw hard. "Better yet, go home. Lock yourself in your apartment. *Stay safe.*" Then, in a soft whisper that seemed more directed to himself than to me, he added, "I don't want you to die."

"No." I stood up, my arms shaking with rage. I couldn't even bring myself to meet his stare. "You don't get to tell me how to live what remains of my life. You don't get a say. You don't get anything from me. I don't want to talk to you. I don't want to see you. I don't want you around."

Before he had a chance to respond, I turned to the front door, slamming it behind me as I stepped outside. I couldn't go far. Rina told me to stay on this property, and if I wanted a chance to go after Wrath with her and the other recruits, I knew I had to obey that order. I also knew that Kieran couldn't stay far from me, as much as I wanted him to. And that I was taking my anger out on him, even the bits of it he hadn't earned.

But at least out here, I didn't see him. At least out here, I had the illusion of freedom from the thing he represented.

The air was cool, crisp, and the darkest edges of the sky

were slowly turning into a grayish haze. The sun would be up in maybe thirty or forty minutes, which meant that Rina would be back; that we'd be leaving soon.

I dropped down on the front stoop, the rough cement uncomfortable and cold against my hands.

As it always did, my thumb found my ring, twisting the small beads over and over—a soothing balm. For the first time in a long time, I let my thoughts drift to Levi. It felt safer now, to linger on those memories, now that I knew there wasn't much of a future before me. No reason to pretend I might one day find someone else, might one day have the semblance of that kind of connection.

Not that I would have ever let myself fall for someone like that again. He'd been the closest anyone had gotten—the only one in a decade, other than Sora, to chisel their way into my chest and carve out a home.

But he'd left. That home abandoned and forgotten, just like the one at my back.

It was an odd, indescribable feeling, living through what might be my last night. Everything felt so much sharper than usual, but also more separate from me. Like I was already gone, observing the world from outside of it.

I buried my head between my legs, fighting to suck in even breaths. It was only then, when my cheeks pressed up against my forearms, that I realized they were wet.

I was crying. The realization only made the tears fall faster.

"So, you're actually going to do this," a deep, snarky voice asked. "Drag out your death, waste what could be your last moments charging into what will almost certainly bring about your demise? Just ask him to end it now. If you do, he might."

Swallowing back a sob, I jolted my head up.

Thorne.

His expression, usually stiff with a mixture of anger and boredom, twitched briefly, as his stare catalogued me.

Great, I'd ditched one reaper, just to be bothered by another.

With trembling fingers, I wiped away my tears. "It's not a waste. I'm not leaving this world until I know that my friend is safe. She's my family." I shot him a defiant glare. "There's no other way I'd rather go out."

For a long moment, he considered me, his dark stare unreadable, save for the slight tension in his mouth that looked almost like a grudging respect. He sat down beside me, careful to put as much space between us as possible.

"You don't have to stick around, you know." It was so painfully obvious that Thorne despised every second that he had to spend in this realm. He wasn't drawn to it the way that Kieran seemed to be. "Kieran will be here . . . to suck out my soul or whatever. You don't have to monitor him."

"It's not souls that we're after," he said. His voice was quiet, but still somehow seemed lethal. "I don't even know if such a thing exists. We collect shadow magic. Before The Undoing, that meant we usually only pulled from the supernatural. There were some exceptions, special cases, of course—to appease the fates. Now, we're also tasked with the shards of it that have lodged themselves in humans, too." He was silent, so preternaturally still that there could be no mistaking him for a human. "Unfortunately, I can't leave until Kieran returns. And Kieran can't leave until you are dead. That means I'm stuck here, until either you die of natural causes, or he kills you. Seeing how you seem to skirt death at an impossible rate, and his general stubbornness, I suspect you'll be stuck with me for a while."

"Why don't you just do it?" I asked, though it was probably a bad idea to lodge the option in his brain. "Kill me, I mean. If you want me dead so badly, if you want Kieran back to his regular programming, why haven't you just handled it yourself?"

"I would." He shot me a look out of the corner of his eyes. "But I can't."

"Why not?"

"Reapers are sent to siphon shadow magic from one charge at a time. Usually, we aren't called to them until just moments before they die. On the rare occasion when they're still alive"—he turned to me, his stare making the skin on my cheek prickle with awareness—"the reaper on the other side of that tether can simply reach in"—he shifted his ringed hand between us, but stopped just before his fingers could touch me—"and take their life."

"But you're a reaper, too."

"I am, yes." Something passed over his expression. "But if a reaper steals the life of someone they aren't tethered to, something is stolen from them in return. The fates demand balance."

I narrowed my eyes. "What will they take?"

"The memories that it's taken me years of my death to collect, and all of the power that I have stored." Something flared in his eyes when they locked onto mine. Emotions that I couldn't pass, but that I hadn't seen in their depths until now. "We don't all waste our strength on a single night of frivolity in the mortal world."

"So, if you killed me, you'd forget who you were?" I nudged my head toward the house, where I knew Kieran was probably brooding. "But if he kills me, he goes on as normal—onto the next charge?"

"More or less."

"Why?"

"Because taking a life that we aren't asked to signals a connection we aren't supposed to have. It would be interpreted as feeling too strongly about something in this world: be it rage, nostalgia, or something else. Our memories are used to keep us in line."

"Oh."

It was the only thing I could think of saying in response.

Thorne nodded, his usual mask replacing the brief shadow of something else I'd seen in his expression. "So you see—" His lips curved into a dark smile that had the hair on the back of my neck standing on edge. "Personally, I'd love to kill you and put an end to this ridiculous production. End it—and you—here and now. But you're not worth losing everything I've worked for. So instead, here I am, stuck with babysitting duty until Kieran gets his shit together or you die."

"Does he do this often?" I asked, fighting the urge to inch away from Thorne after hearing how badly he wanted my death. "Draw it out, I mean."

"No." Thorne let out a dark chuckle. "He's as power hungry as the rest of us. It's unusual, to say the least, for him to drain the measly power stores he has left after wasting them on a night in this world. And unwise as hell, considering what he must return to."

A soft breeze blew my hair between us, and Thorne clocked the movement with vague, fleeting interest.

"What do you mean?" I asked. "What does he have to return to?"

"Our world is a dark one. Power reigns there, more obviously than it does here." He shifted his gaze back to the street, and I knew, just like I knew when Kieran was skirting a topic, that he wouldn't be adding more detail to that statement.

After a few breaths of silence, Thorne stood, as if to leave. And the possibility of him following through gave me the courage to voice what I couldn't until now. "Will I end up there? In your world? Like one of you?"

"There are many stipulations that need to be met to become a reaper." He stopped his retreat, staring down at me. "Only supernatural creatures end up as one of us." His nostrils flared slightly. "You are touched by the magic, yes, but you are decidedly human. Even if you weren't, even if you met the other requirements of our kind, which I don't think you do, the newest recruits to our . . . vocation have already been culled months ago. Another cohort won't be called for at least a year." He shook his head, then added, "So no, you will never exist in our world, never be one of us. You are one of the lucky ones. You will just go. . .on, I suppose."

When his eyes met mine, the depth of those words sank in. It was strange to think of myself as lucky, when I knew that I was about to die. But something about the way that his voice dipped when he spoke of his world made it clear that he meant it.

"Thank you."

There was something oddly calming about Thorne's presence, despite the constant anger boiling just under his surface, despite knowing that he wanted me dead sooner than later. In fact, maybe it was the latter point that I found comforting altogether. Unlike with Kieran, there was no question where things stood between us. The divisions were clear, the hatred and disgust unquestionable. There was no gray area.

In a lifetime of feeling caught between worlds, there was something oddly soothing about the easy binary of his starkness. A simplicity in his dislike of me, his desire for my death, that quieted the constant tumult of the last few days.

He walked by me, as if to go back into the house, but then paused just before reaching the wall. "I understand your anger toward Kieran, but you might consider going easier on him."

I narrowed my eyes. "He lied to me. For days."

"He did." He arched his brow. "But he's sacrificed a lot to try and give you more time—drawing things out for as long as he has, in the hope that the fates might change their mind before it's too late."

"Does that happen?"

He shook his head. "Not often, no. Though I suppose it's not impossible. The fates can be fickle." He studied me for a moment, as if deciding something, before finally saying, "Do you know why he calls you Agony?"

"Yes." I snorted. "Because he knows that I hate it."

The corner of his lips twitched, not quite a frown, but the shadow of one. "Perhaps. But I suspect there's more to it than that. Kieran spends his death chasing dopamine, fleeting pleasures. I've known him for years, but I've never once seen him attached to something in the way that he is to you. Your death will, I think, be quite agonizing for him. Even more, perhaps, than your extended life has been."

I licked my lips. "What do you mean?"

"You've seen his arm?" Thorne raised his own ringed hand. "It's painful for us—to not siphon the power we've been fated to collect. The longer we wait, the more painful it becomes. He cannot get power or any of his strength back, until he siphons from you." He tilted his head to the side, almost cat-like as his gaze swept over me. "Kieran is no stranger to pain. Like most of us, he's learned to build up a tolerance to it. But letting you live as long as you have . . . not many would be able to stomach that kind of pain. It's the longest I've ever seen a reaper last. If he waits more than another day or two, I suspect it might even kill him."

And then, with that, he stepped through the wall and back into the house, leaving me alone with my thoughts that were somehow more conflicted than they'd been before he'd found me, as the edges of the sun started to crawl over the horizon.

30

MAREENA

PRESENT DAY

The trip to House of Lust was an uneventful one. Danvers had given the okay to send four cars—one of them Claude's—and, in addition to me and Rina, ten other Wrath recruits were coming along to rescue Sora. Of course, the rescue mission was really only a priority for me and Rina. The others mostly seemed excited by the unexpected, hastened opportunity to escalate the conflict with one of their biggest rivals. As long as the mission resulted in Sora's safety, I decided it was best to ignore the dubious intentions of the others. The stakes were too high, and there was every possibility that I was running out of time.

Of course, Kieran and Thorne hadn't exactly given me much information to go on. I was either going to die tonight or I wasn't—same two options that everyone faced. And though I tried not to let myself linger on the possibility for too long, I couldn't help but let the smallest trace of hope leak into my system at the possibility that maybe Kieran was right—maybe the fates would change their mind.

Death and I had been moving through this intricate dance

for as long as I could remember, maybe this was just the next level.

The mysterious Danvers, who, from my understanding, was not one of the ten recruits in our current arsenal, had spent the few hours leading up to dawn conducting an elaborate plan with Rina. It included leaving Claude's SUV just outside of House of Lust's entrance, with the added hope that when the vampire finally came to retrieve it, any connection the vehicle had to traipsing through Wrath territory would be severed.

I'd raised concerns about showing up at daybreak, but Rina assured me that House of Lust lived a more nocturnal lifestyle, and most of the compound would be turning in just before we arrived, spent from the evenings more exhausting activities. In this sense, their lifestyle worked heavily in our favor.

As did the fact that Danvers had provided a pretty comprehensive floor plan of their compound, which included his best guess of where they might be keeping Sora. The location he marked was in one of the compound's older, lesser used buildings—close to the perimeter, and in what seemed to be an abandoned animal shelter.

The thought they might be keeping Sora cramped in a dog cage made my stomach turn, but that was infinitely preferable to how Wrath often dealt with their prisoners—death and dismemberment.

Rina filled me in on the plan on the drive over, and it honestly seemed . . . achievable. Which was strangely terrifying. But if it went as she and the others hoped, we'd be back in the cars, Sora in tow, in under thirty minutes.

Most of the recruits would create a diversion by sending some sort of message to Lust.

I didn't much care about the details on that end—their ridiculous turf wars and contrived ideological battles were of no interest to me. If they were going to use this as an opportunity to escalate things, I knew there was very little I could realistically do about it. Best choice for me was to ask as few questions as possible where that part of the plan was concerned, and hope that nobody got hurt, on either end of the situation. There'd been enough talk of death tonight for my taste.

While that was going on, two of the recruits would go with me, where we'd use their distraction to find Sora and get out as quickly as possible. Of course, unbeknownst to them, we'd also be shadowed by two broody reapers. Both of whom had spent the entire twenty-minute drive in sullen silence, crowded awkwardly in the back seat, Thorne sitting half through Rina, half beside her.

When we left the cars and made it to the split point, Rina turned to me, grabbing my arm.

"This is where we leave you," she said.

"What?" I asked, fighting to keep my surprise contained to a whisper. "You're not coming with me? You're going with them?"

Sora was her twin, for fuck's sake. Why the hell would she trust two randos with her safe retrieval? Especially when the members of Wrath were not known for their discretion or compassion.

Her face contorted with indecision before she shook her head. "I think it's best to save the reunion with my sister until after we're done here. Don't want the . . . shock of it all to add an extra layer of unknown to how this all might unfold. There are too many contingencies already." She nodded to two dark figures at my back. They'd both been packed into our car on the way over, but neither had uttered a word the entire trip. "Ben and Jason will go with you. If things go bad and you run into anyone on your way in, they'll take care of them. I don't want you or my sister to get involved in a fight. The boys are trained for this shit." She gave my arm a gentle squeeze, before adding, "It's better this way. Just get in, get out, and don't get distracted by the chaos we'll be causing on our end of the compound, okay?"

I nodded, biting back my disappointment that I'd have to rely on two strangers to help me find and break Sora out safely.

After a moment of hesitation, she handed me the switch-blade she'd been fidgeting with earlier. "You know how to use one of these?"

"Stabby end into flesh."

With a wry grin, her eyes cut to mine, a flash of the old her peeking through again. "Be careful, Mareena." Then the corner of her lips dipped, small lines of tension forming around all of the things still unspoken between us. "Get her out, okay? She's there because of me, and if something happens to her, I . . ." She shook her head, her teeth tugging on her bottom lip. "I won't forgive myself."

Sensing that no words could ease her fear, I only nodded once before we parted ways.

Ben and Jason were silent as we started on the route Rina and the others had laid out for us. It was perhaps unadvisable, but I kept closer to my reapers than the human boys, feeling oddly safer with them nearby . . . even though they were technically here for my death.

Maybe, after all these years, I was simply more comfortable with Death. My entire life was measured through the moments that he pierced into my world. I hated him, but the devil you know, I supposed. Ben and Jason were strangers.

Lust's compound was fenced in, but it wasn't as heavily guarded as Wrath's. Danvers's information pointed to a weak point in the perimeter, and when the shouts of conflict echoed from the opposite end—no doubt part of the recruits' ruse—we climbed and made it over the fence with relative ease.

Thorne and Kieran, of course, simply walked through the brick wall.

The politics of the Seven Sons never made much sense to

me, but it was strange to think that House of Lust was the strongest rival of the militant group I'd spent the last few hours with. Everything I'd learned about this compound had been centered around hedonism and freedom—a less intentional or safe version of Incendiary in some ways. Hard to see how their strength could match up to a house like Wrath. Or why Wrath would even be interested in picking a fight with them of all the Sons.

Then again, maybe a perceived lack of security was its own power move; the illusion of confidence did wonders sometimes.

Our path to the building where they kept their prisoners was quick and vacant. Rina was right—other than the distraction playing out on the other side of the compound, the entire place seemed to be mostly asleep, and the building where Sora was likely being kept was isolated far from the rest of the buildings on their grounds, which meant that we didn't run into anyone on our hike toward it.

When we reached the main door, it was locked. Ben, or maybe Jason, I honestly wasn't sure who was who—got to work picking it, but after a few seconds, Kieran shot them a tired look and passed through the door.

There was a soft click, and the door swung open.

It was Kieran's doing, of course, but one of the boys congratulated the other on a new personal record, by roughly punching his shoulder.

We made our way through the corridor, eyes peeled for the staircase from Danvers's notes.

Strangely, navigating our way through the building in the dark was the most difficult part so far. We didn't want to use a solar flashlight on the off chance that it would draw attention to our presence. When I tripped over a worn area of carpet, Kieran caught me before I fell on my ass. Wordlessly, he grabbed my hand, guiding me through the labyrinth with comparative ease, leaving Ben and Jason to scramble after us in a hushed rush. Apparently, reapers could see in the dark, no problem.

Clinging to him, I did my best to ignore the fact that I still felt safe with him. He wasn't my guardian, but he still felt like it. Which meant that, once again, my brain wasn't on my side. The bitch was allergic to logic and reason.

But as angry as I was about, well, everything, I couldn't shake Thorne's words.

This situation we were in—none of it was Kieran's fault. And, if I was honest with myself, most of the anger I'd been taking out on him was probably just my way of edging out the blazing fear that had been clawing at my lungs since the second reaper's arrival. Hell, since Sora's disappearance. Kieran was an easy punching bag through which to filter it all.

"I don't like this," he whispered, even though Thorne and I were the only ones who could hear him. "This is too easy."

I didn't respond, because unlike the reapers, my voice could actually be heard, but I held onto the hope that maybe this would actually turn out okay—end well, even. It had been a long ass night. The last twelve hours truly felt like twelve years. Maybe we'd earned easy at this point.

We'd get Sora, we'd all survive to see her reunite with her twin, and we'd go from there. Wilder things had happened. Tonight, alone.

"On the plus side," Thorne said, shooting an annoyed look at the two recruits we'd been saddled with for help, "demons don't particularly like fraternizing with the Seven Sons. If these dimwits were the best the girl's friends could spare, I assume we won't be contending with any particularly impressive sheep here either."

"This is it," I said, squeezing Kieran's hand to get him to stop.

We were in the basement, and a single lightbulb illuminated the otherwise vacant hallway. We stood outside of a giant room, the walls surrounding it made up of giant windows. And inside the windowed room was a winding labyrinth of cages where they used to keep animals up for adoption in the Before.

There, in the far corner, was a small, curled up lump.

"Sora!" My chest lightened at the sight of her. She looked like she was sleeping, cowered in a cage with only a bucket and water bowl for company, the door latched with a padlock.

When I tried to open the main entrance into the room, the knob wouldn't budge.

Ben and Jason got to work on their lock picking, but I nodded to Kieran when they started bickering over who was better at it. From here, I could see a ring of keys hanging inside the room, on the opposite wall.

Kieran turned to me, brow arched in disgust at Jenson's antics, then nodded. "I'll get her out."

A moment after he disappeared through the other side, a loud bang pierced the silence. Almost like a door had been swung open too harshly and crashed into the adjacent wall, the crash echoing through the empty floor.

"Hey, what are you doing down here?" a loud voice barked.

My neck pinched when I jolted it to the side. Three guys were running down the far end of the hall, all carrying blades of various sizes.

"Fuck." I nudged the two Wrath recruits, and they sprang to life at the sight of them, both taking off in their direction, lock-picking instantly abandoned. Clearly more amped for the chance to break some bones.

The hall itself was long, which meant that we had a good thirty seconds for Kieran to unlock the door and let me in, assuming Jenson could handle their primary job.

I glanced at Kieran.

He held up the keys, a crooked grin twisting his lips, but that grin melted into a look of horror as he made his way back toward the door and saw the commotion.

When I spun around to follow his stare, I found Ben and Jason trading blows with only two of the armed men. The third guy was gone.

Until a fraction of a second later when he, quite literally, rematerialized next to me. He took advantage of my shock, knocking Rina's switchblade across the floor before I even had a chance to open it, the clang of its echo on the linoleum floor, an ominous addition to the soundtrack down the hall.

The guy was magic-touched. And with a damn powerful ability. I didn't even know teleportation was actually possible.

Fuck, fuck, fuck.

This was very much not in the plan.

From the corner of my eye, I saw Kieran rushing toward me, his eyes wide with panic, but just as I raised my fists hoping to defend myself against the man's very large blade, my attention snagged on Thorne.

He stood just behind the man, his eyes darting between me and Kieran. He muttered a quiet, almost begrudging, "Bloody hell," then, with a frustrated groan, he shoved his ringed-hand through the magic-touched man's chest, just as the blade cut deep into my right forearm.

The man dropped to the ground, as if stunned, his knife pulling back from my flesh before clattering on top of him.

With trembling fingers, I quickly swiped up both his and Rina's knives, but one look at the wide vacancy in the man's eyes, made it abundantly clear that he wouldn't be using either of them against me any time soon.

He was dead.

How was he dead?

And when I turned to look behind him, I saw that Thorne had collapsed to the ground as well.

My stomach clenched. Was he dead, too?

I side-stepped the corpse, then folded to the ground, trying to find the reaper's pulse, but I wasn't sure if he'd even had one to begin with. As I shook his shoulders, and tapped his cheeks, trying to rouse him, I did my best to ignore the sharp pain in my arm and the deep splatters of blood I was trickling all over his pale face.

When I glanced up, I found Kieran hovering above me, his eyes sparkling with an emotion I couldn't decipher, the lines of his face simmering with tension.

He crouched, his eyes quickly cataloging the blood on my arm, then every inch of my body, his eyes frantic and mouth pinched into a tight line.

"Agony, are you okay?" he asked, a low growl riding his tone.

"I'm fine, but—"

"Thorne will be okay," he muttered, though it sounded almost like he was trying to convince himself of that as much as he was me. His stare darted briefly to the reaper, before finding me again to continue his assessment. "He's not dead. I mean, he is, but no more dead than he was two minutes ago. It's just . . . he fecking killed the human. I can't believe it."

My thoughts flickered to my conversation with Thorne only a few hours ago, and I turned to Kieran, trying not to panic. "Doesn't that mean . . ."

Down the hall, it appeared that Benson had finally incapacitated the other two guys, though it wasn't clear if they were dead or just unconscious, as they made their way over to me.

"Yeah." Kieran nodded. "It does." He cursed, then let out a frustrated sigh. "When Thorne wakes up, his memories—from both his life and his afterlife—will all be gone."

31

MAREENA

PRESENT DAY

"Why?" I shook my head, crawling away crab-style from Thorne and the corpse. My body was shaking, and it felt like if I stood up too quickly, I'd only come tumbling back down to the floor, though I wasn't sure if that was due to the blood loss or because I was on the verge of a panic attack. "Why did he do that? Why would—" I took a deep breath and tried to regulate my body's response, focusing on the flare of pain in my arm, letting it ground me. I looked up, searching Kieran's face. "I don't understand?"

"If there's one thing I've learned about Thorne, it's that there's no getting to the bottom of his decisions unless he wants you to." Kieran picked up the reaper's unconscious body and tossed it over his shoulder, then he grabbed my hand, helping me back to my feet as much as his foothold in this world would allow. "Let's get your friend and get the feck out of here before we run into any more issues, yeah?"

I nodded, then ran my tongue over my lips to bring moisture back to my mouth. "Okay. You got the keys, right?"

"Who's she talking to?" Benson One muttered to Benson Two. They'd made their way back during the chaos, looking a little rumpled but uninjured for the most part—and judging by the light in their eyes and the subtle curves to their mouths, they'd actually enjoyed that unexpected interruption to the rescue mission.

Fucking Wrath recruits.

"Don't know," Benson Two said, "but it looks like she took the third one on her own." They both shot me an impressed look. "Not bad, Rina's friend." Apparently they hadn't bothered memorizing my name either. "Maybe you should consider pledging to our house. Might fit in better than you think."

They spoke about House of Wrath as if it were a fucking frat house. And, honestly, if they were true representatives of the larger whole, it probably was.

Swallowing my frustration, I ignored them and opened the door that Kieran had unlocked.

Sora shifted awake as we spilled into the room, and I felt some of the tension ease in my chest. She was okay, she was alive. This room must've been sound-proofed because the chaotic battle in the hall clearly hadn't woken her.

"Mars?" she asked, her eyes wide with shock that then quickly bled into panic. "What are you doing here?" Her gaze dipped to my arm. "Oh my god, are you okay? What happened? How did you find me?"

I grabbed the ring of keys hanging on a coat hook and started the tedious process of figuring out which one actually opened her cage.

"I'm okay, it's okay," I said, convincing myself as much as her, as I moved from the third key to the fourth. "We're going to get you out of here and then we can answer questions. Are you okay? Did they hurt you?"

A cursory glance showed that she had a few bruises and cuts, and judging from the way that she seemed to be favoring her right side, I had a feeling that leg was injured. Hopefully nothing worse than a light sprain.

"Yeah." She sniffed; her expression stiff. "I'm okay." Okay was relative of course, and I could tell from the way her voice wavered and the tears clinging to her dark lashes that okay definitely did not mean good. She offered a small, tight smile. "Nothing we haven't been through before."

Also not the most comforting words. At the hands of Blake, we'd been through quite a lot, which meant there was a pretty exhausting range of shit they could have put her through in the last twenty-four hours.

I shoved the possibilities from my thoughts.

"We'll—" My words broke off at the sound of a click as the lock tipped open. I sighed with relief and swung her crate open. Placing her left arm around my shoulders, I had her lean as much of her weight on me as she could, guiding her out. "Let's get out of here. Sound good?"

She grunted. "You have no fucking idea how good."

The hall was silent, and Sora's eyes widened at the sight of three bodies scattered on the floor. I gave her arm a gentle squeeze, and we stepped over them, wordlessly retracing our steps back to the entrance.

But when we reached the base of the staircase, two men came bolting down the last few steps, expressions twisted in first surprise, then rage.

"Go," Benson said, a devious grin twisting the corners of his lips. "We'll take care of them and meet you back at the rendezvous."

The men looked downright giddy at the promise of another fight.

Well, they weren't going to get one from me.

Sora and I side-stepped their grunts and shoves as the four men locked in a battle of limbs and blows.

"I think I'm good," Sora whispered, pulling her arm back and quickening her pace up the stairs. She leaned heavily against the arm rail for support but made decent time up to the main floor. "Leg was really stiff, but moving it is helping I think."

Alarms greeted us when we emerged into the fresh air, and while the echo of fighting surrounded the compound, we had a pretty clear path back. I sent a silent thank you to whoever organized this particular layout, deciding to keep their captives away from most of the House's chaos. From here, we just had to hope that once we made it back over the fence, the Wrath recruits could restrain some of their bloodlust and stick to the mission. The faster we got out of here, the better. And that wouldn't happen if they decided to start a full-fledged territory war right now.

Getting over the fence proved to be a bit of a struggle. I did my best to boost Sora up to the ledge as much as possible, and though I could see the pain lining her face as she hopped down over the other side, she didn't make a sound or protest.

Out of fear of drawing attention to ourselves, we didn't speak again until we were almost a full block away from the compound, just a few minutes' walk from the rendezvous where we would meet Rina and the others.

"Thank you," Sora whispered finally. "I seriously don't know how you found me, but I'm profoundly fucking glad that you did." The corner of her lips twisted into a small grin. "Your guardian angel give you a tip or something?"

I grunted. "Turns out he's actually a reaper."

Her eyes widened. "As in . . . grim?"

I nodded, shooting Kieran a look from the corner of my eye.

"What? Is he here?" She craned her neck, like she was trying to find him, her gaze hitting everywhere except to my other side, where Kieran walked silently with Thorne lobbed over his shoulder.

I nodded again.

"Mars—" She shoved my uninjured arm, some of the playful energy I was used to seeping back into her features now that we were almost home free. "You seriously mean to tell me that you're being stalked by a literal grim reaper and you decided it was a good idea to break into one of the compounds on a rescue mission? Have you lost your mind? Do you have a death wish?"

"You didn't leave me much of a choice," I grumbled. "Sometimes, when it comes to the people we love, we make reckless decisions. Like"—I shot her a knowing look—"trusting a smarmy asshole from the market about some ridiculous necromancy ritual."

She winced, and her entire face scrunched with the expression. "Fair point." Then, after a few seconds of silence, she smirked. "You know what this means, right?"

"Hm?"

"Now you really *are* being haunted by death." She let out a bemused laugh. "Can't believe you were right in the end. The curse lives."

"Me . . . right?" I grinned. "I do like the sound of that, though I would absolutely prefer if it were about something a little less depressing."

"Hey!" a loud voice barked behind us.

The ease of the last few minutes deflated instantly when we turned toward the voice.

Kieran cursed next to me, adjusting his hold of the unconscious reaper.

There was a woman jogging after us, maybe in her early thirties. She wore a purple silky pajama set, and her blonde hair was crumpled on one side like she'd just been pulled from bed.

Definitely not a member of our rescue party.

"Agony," Kieran warned, fear riding his voice as he shifted in front of me.

I followed his gaze, and my stomach dropped. Dangling in her right hand was a gun. And when I slowly tugged my focus up, I saw that her eyes were laced with tears and a flaring hatred.

"You need to run," Kieran said, his voice quiet but firm.

Sora froze next to me, her hands held up in surrender. "Look, we don't want any trouble. We're not part of this fight. We just want to go home."

She was too injured to run, and I didn't trust that this woman wouldn't shoot us the instant we tried.

"Mareena," Kieran begged again, his body fully in front of me now, even though we both knew that wouldn't do anything.

A few people rounded the corner about two hundred feet away, and I recognized the masked, all-black uniform of the Wrath recruits—Jenson among them. When they spotted us, they took off running in our direction.

"Bit late for that, don't you think?" The woman sneered; her focus locked on Sora. She raised the gun, until it pointed at her head. "I told them to just kill you. Don't know why they insisted on fucking playing around. Children, all of them."

"Please, you have to listen to us," Sora started, but she flinched when the woman's grip tightened. "Whatever you think I did, I didn't—"

"I don't *think* you did anything," the woman yelled, spit flying from her lips. "I was fucking there last year. I watched you kill my sister." Her nostrils flared. "And didn't see a damn ounce of remorse or regret on your face when you did it either."

"Agony, please run," Kieran demanded. "Now. You need to get out of here—please."

But I didn't. And I couldn't.

I knew with a rigid certainty that the woman was going to pull the trigger only a half of a second before she did, but it was enough time for me to shove Sora to the side.

"No!" Kieran yelled, his voice piercing through the crashing cry of the gunshot.

When Sora fell to the ground, she looked up, then echoed his scream.

I pressed my hand to my chest and pulled away a palm covered in blood. And as my knees collapsed to the pavement, the only thing that went through my head was how silly it was.

That tonight alone, I'd survived reapers, a demon club, a vampire bar, and two compounds.

That this was a world filled with monsters and magic—but it was a human-made bullet and a woman's festering grief that finally delivered Death's invitation.

32

KIERAN

PRESENT

I dropped Thorne at my feet and sank to my knees next to her. My hands were numb but trembling as they pushed her hair back from her face.

Her eyes were wide, searching, but unseeing.

She coughed and a dark spray of blood colored her lips before dribbling down her chin.

A wet, slightly darker circle formed in her black shirt, the design spreading wider with every second as blood poured out of her.

I lifted her head, trying to cushion it, but my grip on this world was so tenuous that I had to settle for simply the illusion of comfort.

"No, come on," I whispered, "hang on Agony. You're okay. You're going to be okay."

But this wasn't the world of the Before. The kind of infrastructure that humans used to have—hospitals, doctors, well-stocked emergency rooms. Those were the things of the past. Even if I could find someone to help her, the chances that they'd be able to fix something this catastrophic were close to zero.

Her friend, Sora, was kneeling next to me, her body trembling as tears rained down on her roommate. She pressed her hands to the chest wound as if trying to stem the blood flow, but of course to no effect.

I could taste her death on the wind.

This—this was not how this was supposed to go. We rescued the girl; we got out, for feck's sake.

For this to happen now—it was just too cruel.

I tried to swallow, but it was like a brick was lodged in my throat.

Not for the first time with this girl, I found myself at an unfamiliar impasse. Never had I found myself so desperate to save someone, when every molecule in my body was designed to do just the opposite. I didn't know what to do with that incompetence. How to combat it. How to fix her—to keep her here. If not with me, at least with this world.

"Mars," Sora cried, her hands wrapped around her friend's shoulders, face tucked into her neck as she rocked back and forth. Her sobs echoed through the street, giving voice to the mirrored trenches in my chest.

No.

The pain in my gut carved sharper when my eyes sought hers again. Why did they suddenly look empty?

I tried to pull her to me, to press my face to her hair, to see that look of disdain she was so fond of tossing at me at every turn. But when I attempted to hold her, my hands fell through.

I was cut off from her.

My body tensed as a familiar surge of power sank into my fingers, burrowing deep into my veins, as my hand fell into her.

"No. No, no, no, no." My voice cracked as I realized what was happening. What this meant. I fought to pull my hand back, to disconnect from her power source. I didn't want it. I only wanted her.

But it was impossible. She wouldn't let go. And, as much as

I resented it, I felt her power bloom inside of me and take root. It was as bright and invigorating and intoxicating as she was— almost suffocating in its brilliance.

My vision blurred as the girl who'd turned my entire world inside out disappeared before my eyes. What did a world without her even look like? I was so profoundly uninterested in finding out.

The roommate's sobs were agonizing—both loud and deep as she clung to the empty shell of the first person I'd given a fuck about in decades. Maybe ever.

I realized then that the pain I'd been fighting for days had bled away—gone entirely now that I'd finally completed my duties.

No. Not gone entirely. Replaced. A different pain, one that made it impossible to breathe or see straight. One that burrowed deep in my lungs until it gripped at my rib cage.

I fell back from them both, my head spinning as I stood, my body drunk with a power I didn't want.

My chest tightened, and I wanted nothing but for this awful, indescribable feeling to disappear. To go back to the man I was a few weeks ago—aimless, bored, forever fighting to find whatever small surge of pleasure I could steal for myself.

The useless fecking Wrath members surrounded us now, silently watching the scene as the girl grieved for her friend.

Most of them seemed restless, ambivalent to the situation, their eyes still bright with the adrenaline from their fight. They didn't care, didn't understand what was really happening, didn't know what their world had just lost. Fecking hell, what I wouldn't give to trade all of their lives for hers.

The only one who appeared affected at all was Sora's twin. She stood, frozen on the sidelines, eyes brimming with tears as she watched Sora mourn the girl who'd been a sister to her for years.

And then I saw her—the one woman responsible for the

unfamiliar pain coursing through my body. She was detained by three guards, the gun nowhere in sight, her lips trembling, whether with regret at what she'd done or fear for what might come, I wasn't sure. Knowing the people of this world, probably the latter.

Why hadn't they killed her yet? Why the fuck were they just standing there? Watching on, letting her live?

I moved toward her, my body coiled.

I could be the one to do it. I could be the one to steal her life and, with it, erase the pain currently suffocating me. I'd join Thorne in his blissful state—back at the beginning. Before all of this—

"What happened?" a soft, trembling voice asked.

I froze, my body latching on to the familiar, electric cadence of it.

Slowly, I turned, until I found myself facing its owner, my chest tightening and then relaxing on a harsh breath at the sight of her.

Her eyes were searching, her dark brows furrowed with concern as she studied the scene.

She looked just as she had before the bullet stole her last breath, just as beautiful, just as defiant . . . save for the all-too-familiar set of rings now settled at the base of her knuckles.

"Oh," I whispered, the small shred of hope that had flooded my veins at the sight of her now hardening into regret. "How?"

She was human, I was sure of it. Could smell it on her from the first moment I encountered her. There was a surge of power from The Undoing, sure, but even magic-touched humans couldn't become reapers.

Besides, the next cohort of reapers had all already been culled. There shouldn't have been another one for at least another year or two. And when reapers were culled, they never spawned in this realm—they always reemerged in the Between, through Lethe. I'd have to find a way to transport her there before anyone noticed. Maybe Rafi could help?

Slowly, she turned around, studying the body at her feet, her face seeping of all emotion until it settled into an unreadable mask.

Several of the Wrath recruits were tearing Sora's grip from Mareena's body, as the girl screamed and fought to stay where she was.

Her sister was nowhere in sight now, nor was the woman who shot the gun.

"We have to go," a deep voice argued.

"I'm not leaving her," Sora shouted, spit flying from her mouth as she fought against them like a rabid animal. She was surprisingly strong for such a small thing. "I'm not leaving her!"

Strong and ferocious as she was, she couldn't fight off two towering men, especially not in her current state. They pulled her away, her limbs kicking and flailing, as they carried her toward their brigade of cars.

Until it was just me and Agony left in the clearing, her body still at her feet, just as Thorne's was at mine.

"What happened?" She turned to me, finding her voice again, her eyes widening when they fell on the set of rings at the base of her fingers. Those same eyes shifted up, wild and full of fear as they met mine.

"Fuck." I pressed my tooth into my bottom lip as I studied her, hardly believing it myself. "I'm so sorry, Agony."

I should have been excited by the prospect. The old me would have been thrilled. The object of his obsession wasn't gone forever. A new toy to play with in a world that was always so dark.

But all I felt was a barrage of fear and anger and resentment —because a normal death would have been kinder, freer than the world she would now have to embark on. My kind were ruthless. Parasitic shells. The world's darkest desires warped and contorted with unabated greed. Our world would break her—strip away everything that lit her up, that made her so goddamn magnetic—until all that was left was a relentless hunger and merciless struggle to survive.

And I'd have a front row seat to the entire process. Would have to watch, nothing more than a bystander, as the girl who'd made me feel alive for the first time maybe ever was sapped of everything that made her who she was.

33

MAREENA
PRESENT

"Kieran?" I asked, my voice strangely hollow as I pointed to the all too familiar body at my feet. My fingers felt heavy, weighted by the new, odd metal caging them. "Am I . . . am I what I think I am?"

His face shifted in surprise, and for a moment he didn't say anything. Just stared, as if he saw me and yet didn't.

I took a step toward him, frustrated by his sudden silence. "You literally never shut up. Now is not the time to start. In case you couldn't tell"—I gestured at my dead body on the ground —"I'm kind of freaking out here, and could really use that snarky voice of yours to clarify that I am not, in fact, what these"—I shoved my ringed hand forward—"suggest that I am. Thorne said it was impossible. That when I died, I'd go into the beyond or—whatever. I don't know, he very stubbornly refused to get into specifics. But suffice to say, he was very fucking clear that I would not become one of you." I glared at him, then took another step closer when he continued his silence. "Speak. Say something. Anything. Please. I'm literally begging you. Tell me I'm wrong—"

But he only closed the distance between us and tugged me

to him in an embrace that was both warm and comforting. One of his hands wrapped around my waist, holding me close, the other laced its way into my hair, tugging my face against his chest.

He felt . . . strangely warm. And it wasn't until confronted with the surprising solidity and intensity of his body against mine that I realized how different he'd felt before. How, though corporeal to me, he'd been like a shadow of the man I'd encountered that first night at Incendiary.

After a moment of resistance, I fell into his embrace, molding to him like clay. Tears formed along my waterline as the truth of it all crashed into me like a freight train, but for just a few seconds, I let his presence comfort the swell of over-whelm clawing against my brain.

Sora was gone. I didn't even get to say goodbye.

And Menace? What would become of him?

Or Frank?

The absolute deluge of grief threatening to suffocate me if I looked at it for another moment became too difficult to linger on, so I took a deep breath of Kieran, letting the familiar mint and morning dew settle around me, grounding me. I wasn't alone.

Apparently, the dead could in fact breathe, which was an oddly comforting realization. A small piece of this life I could take into the next.

He hadn't released his hold or moved even a single muscle since pulling me into his embrace, but I tilted my head back, straining to get a look at him.

His eyes were laced with a film of liquid, and wild with shock, the sharp lines of his features rigid and tense.

"Kieran? Are you okay?"

He made a deep sound in the back of his throat, then pressed his nose to my neck, as if he, too, needed to ground himself in scent to prove that I was here.

"You remember me?" he asked, his words muffled against my skin, cracking with emotion at the surface. "Do you—" He cleared his throat. "Do you have all of your memories?"

"I—" Right. Reapers were supposed to wake up detached from their former lives. I searched my thoughts, cataloging what I did and did not remember, but it proved a futile, useless pursuit. I wouldn't remember what I couldn't remember, and while I wasn't certain that I held onto every single detail of my life, I certainly remembered all of the important ones. The ones I'd carried with me up until my death, at least. "Yes, I—I think I do."

He let me pull back from his hug a few inches, compromising by cupping my face in his hands as his eyes searched mine.

Kieran wasn't an easy person to maintain eye contact with. Besides the fact that his eyes were just obscenely beautiful, there was always the threat that he'd see too much. More than I could see, even. And after safely locking away all the pain and panic I wasn't ready to deal with right now, I didn't want anything else tugged to the surface.

"Okay." He nodded, as if convincing himself of something. "This is going to be difficult, but we'll figure out how to get you through the trials. How to keep you safe. Whole." His thumb stroked my cheek, the gesture oddly adept at calming the simmering fear in my gut. "You can't tell anyone that you can remember your life, okay? That will spell instant death for you. The permanent kind."

I nodded, finding words difficult with his stare and hands and all the rest of him surrounding me in all the intensity I'd been protected from the last few days.

"I mean it, Agony." His eyes hardened, his grasp on me gentle, though every muscle in his body seemed coiled tight. "Not a word to anyone. It will be the end of you. Promise me."

"I . . . " I licked my lips, my stomach dipping as his gaze fell to my mouth. "I promise."

A low, pained groan pierced the tension.

We both turned to Thorne, who was just starting to rouse.

"Not even Thorne," Kieran said, as if answering the question before it could even fully form in my thoughts. "Not until I decide if we can trust him. He won't be himself. And I'm going to have to figure out what all of this means. How best to protect you."

"What do you mean?"

"He'll be familiar with himself," Kieran whispered, his lips pressed close to my ear, "his tastes, his skills, the way of living in our world, but he won't retain any memories of the people, relationships, or various things that have happened in his life. Either in the mortal realm or the Between. It might be a bit disorienting for a bit. But his memories will come back; faster than they do for most new reapers. Don't let on that you've met his former self."

Thorne's eyes sprang open, their dark depths holding me in their stare for an uncomfortably long time. I felt almost like a rabbit meeting a lion, the way he slowly uncoiled his body and stood—not once blinking or breaking his stare.

"So," he said, arching his brow. I took a deep breath when he finally severed the intense eye contact long enough to stretch and scan our surroundings. "I take it I've refreshed, then? Bloody hell, that's disorienting." There was something lighter in his tone than I was used to, playful almost, and when his eyes found me again, the corner of his lips curved into a soft hook. "Please tell me that you're part of my pack, beautiful?"

I opened my mouth to respond but had apparently been struck momentarily incapable of words.

"No?" Was all that I managed, the word more a squeak than anything used to convey meaning.

The rakish grin on his face deepened. "Do you want to be?"

"Leave her be, Thorne," Kieran growled, "she's newly awakened."

"Well, then in that case, there's still a chance." Thorne scanned me from head to toe, as if reassessing this new information, his expression almost a challenge. Then his focus darted to Kieran, his body tensing. "And who are you?"

"Unfortunately," he muttered, more to himself than the other reaper, "I am part of your pack."

"No offense, mate"—Thorne's expression curled in distaste—"but I would definitely prefer her."

I turned to Keiran. "Pack?"

He took a deep breath and sighed. "I'll explain the ways of our world later. First, we need to get you back there and I need to get shit settled with Rafi."

"Rafi?" I asked again, ignoring the dip of fear in my stomach at the prospect of leaving this world.

"Never mind him either," Kieran said. "Just don't forget what we discussed, okay?"

I nodded, side-eyeing Thorne who'd moved significantly closer to me.

"Just saying," he said, tossing another feral-looking smirk at me, "she smells like she could be mine."

"Thorne," Kieran groaned. "Enough. Let's go." Then, with his ringed hand, he made a gesture in the air, revealing a door that hadn't been there before. When it opened, it was as if he'd created a tear between worlds all on his own.

There was the oddly quiet street we stood in, the sun sparkling down on the splatters of blood that belonged to . . . well, me, but beyond the doorway, there was also an untarnished view into the world I'd occasionally caught glimpses of since The Undoing.

Only it was more solid and real than it had ever been before, no longer the dark, willowy phantom-image of a ghostly world projected onto my own.

Thorne stepped through first, then Kieran gave my hand a squeeze of encouragement, before following suit.

For a moment, I almost considered staying here, though I didn't know how long I could actually linger. Stepping forward meant shifting into a new world, leaving everything I knew behind.

But then Kieran turned around and offered me a soft smile, his eyes encouraging. Well, maybe not everything.

I stepped through, and the door slammed behind me.

We were in what appeared to be an entryway. There was a chill in the air, though I thought I heard the familiar crackle of a fire in the room ahead.

I clung to Kieran's back, like a shadow as I adjusted to the strangeness of this place.

When he paused outside a doorway, a soft light emanating from the room, I nearly ran into him.

"You're finally back," a deep voice said, an ember of familiarity curling in my stomach. "The hell took so long? Rafi's ready to kill you both at this point."

"Who are you?" Thorne asked, the muscles in his back tightening.

The owner of the deep voice groaned, the sound low and grumbling. "Fucking hell, Thorne's wiped? This is seriously the last thing we need right now. Kieran, what the fuck happened out there?"

"There were"—Kieran glanced back at me, then took a step to the side, nudging me into the room—"a few complications."

My breath caught at the familiar figure in front of me. He was dressed head-to-toe in black, as always, his dark hair curling slightly into a pair of gray eyes that made me dizzy with relief to see again.

Levi.

His mouth pressed into a firm line when I shifted closer, but he otherwise didn't move or react at all.

He was . . . dead?

For how long?

Tears clouded my vision as I ran to him, wrapping my arms around his middle.

"No fair," I heard Thorne mutter behind me. "I definitely didn't get that greeting."

Levi stiffened at the contact, but otherwise kept still, his arms pressed down at his sides. For a moment, I thought I felt his face bend toward me, the barest pressure of his hands moving to meet my waist, but then Kieran clapped my shoulders and pulled me back.

"Sorry, Levi," he said, his eyes meeting mine briefly, wide with warning, "new recruit. You know how disorienting it can be. Can you please go find Rafi? We need to talk."

Kieran pulled me to his side, his arm wrapping around me as if preemptively protecting me from whatever was about to come next.

When Levi's focus shifted to where Kieran's hand met my waist, he instantly dropped it, before carving a few inches of distance between us.

Levi didn't move at first. His expression was almost blank. Though there was a flicker of something in his eyes—anger, maybe—when they took me in again, before shifting back to Kieran. A muscle in his jaw pulsed, some silent challenge playing between the two of them as my heart raced loud and angry in my chest.

He was here. He was alive.

Well, sort of.

"And might as well take Thorne with you, too," Kieran said, his tone clipped. "I'll need to speak with Rafi privately."

In a hurried and desperate attempt to catalogue all the differences between this Levi and the one I knew, my attention immediately landed on the dark rings adorning his fingers.

Like Thorne and Kieran, he had quite a few tattoos now, though not nearly as many as they did.

But then my stare caught on his wrist, and I had to swallow back a gasp.

A small, black band circled it.

My hairband.

As if sensing my stare, he inched his sleeve down, until the band was covered, then left the room without another word, not even sparing me another glance.

Thorne—who'd been watching the scene unfold with a kind of calculating focus, as if combing for bits of information —turned one last, lingering stare on me, before following on Levi's heels.

"Levi's only been dead for two years," Kieran whispered, when we were finally alone, his voice gentle. "If you knew him in the mortal realm, he won't remember you. Not for years. You can't do that again, Agony—don't draw attention to yourself. Whatever he was to you, you have to sever it. He's not the boy you once knew. Erase him in your mind altogether if you can. For his sake and yours."

I nodded; my throat tight.

"And—" He ran his hand through his hair, the movement frustrated and tense, then pinched the bridge of his nose as if resisting the next part. "Same goes for me."

My head shot up, searching his face. "What do you—"

"Blank slate. If you're going to survive the trials—" He exhaled, his tumultuous gaze burning into me. "And this place, I'm going to need to stay away from you as much as possible. And you're going to have to pretend like we didn't meet until you crossed into the Between."

I nodded, fighting desperately to hold on to the final strand of composure I had left. All I wanted to do was hole up in a room and cry. Ideally with Sora and Menace. "Okay."

"You've got a world of explaining to do, Kieran," an unfamiliar voice barked into the room.

I turned around, searching for the voice's owner, and that final strand of composure snapped.

Standing in the doorway was the man who'd haunted my dreams for more than a decade. The man who'd ripped my aunt from me with an unflinching callousness.

His bright amber eyes were wild with barely constrained rage as he stepped into the room.

And when that fiery gaze fell on me, I knew that the time had finally come.

I was staring into the eyes of Death himself.

Find out what happens next in Game of Styx and Stones, the second book in Mareena's story.

Want to read Mareena and Kieran's first steamy night at Incendiary from his perspective? Grab a bonus chapter and character art when you **join my newsletter here:**

WANT TO LEARN MORE ABOUT THE WORLD BEFORE THE UNDOING?

Check out **The Protector Guild**—a completed series that tells the story leading up to the events in Veil of Death and Shadow. You'll encounter some familiar faces and meet Levi's older brother 😉.

Welcome to The Protector Guild:

Rule Number One: Guild above everything.

Rule Number Two: Hunt or be hunted.

Rule Number Three: Stay away from the demons locked in the basement.

In the shadows of the human world, a secret society of demon hunters fights to keep humanity from the supernatural forces that threaten to tear it apart.

But for Max Bentley, a rookie hunter struggling to find her place amongst her kind, the biggest threat might just be the four brooding, enigmatic members of the most elite team of hunters - all of whom seem to have taken a special, antagonistic interest in her.

She quickly discovers that their past is as dark and complicated as her own. As she is drawn deeper into the mysterious world of demon hunting, she finds herself torn between her duty to her people and her growing attraction to her team.

It's more than her heart on the line, it's the very fabric of our world.

Tropes you can expect:

- Why Choose
- Slow burn Angst
- Forbidden Romance
- Enemies to Lovers
- Forced Proximity
- Found Family
- Major Character Growth

THANK YOU SO MUCH FOR JOINING ME ON THIS JOURNEY WITH MAREENA!

Indie authors owe so much to our readers. I cannot put into words how much I appreciate the time you've spent with these characters and this story that's existed in my head for years. If you loved this book, I would be so grateful if you left a review.

We rely on readers' word of mouth to help us get these stories out into the world. Thank you, thank you, thank you!

ACKNOWLEDGMENTS

This book would not exist without the love and support of so many people.

To my family, friends, and dog—thank you for helping me carve out the space and time to craft this world. Your constant support keeps me going. Thank you.

To my editors, Jennifer and Zee, this book is so much better thanks to your thoughtful eyes and skills.

To my cover designer, Michelle, at Damoro Design—thank you for another beautiful set of covers. I don't know how you nail the vision every single time, but I'm so incredibly grateful that you do.

To Seattle, thank you for being my home for most of my adult life. This book serves, in part, as a love letter to you.

To my readers and the bookish communities that have offered a home to my stories—thank you. Your encouragement, shares, and kind words mean more than I could ever say.

And finally, to you. Thank you for taking a chance on this book (and me!). I know how valuable your time is (and how many amazing books there are to choose from). I'm so appreciative that you've chosen to spend some of it lingering in this world with me. I hope you'll be back for more!